Great Novels from SIGNET

GENTLEMEN OF ADVENTURE

ERNEST K. GANN

A SIGNET BOOK

NEW AMERICAN LIBRARY

NAL BOOKS ARE AVAILABLE AT QUANTITY DISCOUNTS
WHEN USED TO PROMOTE PRODUCTS OR SERVICES.
FOR INFORMATION PLEASE WRITE TO PREMIUM MARKETING DIVISION,
NEW AMERICAN LIBRARY, 1633 BROADWAY,
NEW YORK, NEW YORK 10019.

Copyright © 1983 by Ernest K. Gann

SIGNET TRADEMARK REG. U.S. PAT. OFF. AND FOREIGN COUNTRIES
REGISTERED TRADEMARK—MARCA REGISTRADA
HECHO EN CHICAGO, U.S.A.

SIGNET, SIGNET CLASSIC, MENTOR, PLUME, MERIDIAN AND NAL BOOKS
are published by New American Library,
1633 Broadway, New York, New York 10019

First Signet Printing, November, 1984

1 2 3 4 5 6 7 8 9

PRINTED IN THE UNITED STATES OF AMERICA

AUTHOR'S NOTE

This story covers more than half a century during which much of aviation history was created. While I have tried to maintain absolute accuracy in portraying people against time and place, this is a work of fiction and there are a few occasions when I have been obliged to rearrange minor facts to meet dramatic demands.

It has been my privilege to meet and to know the majority of the aviation "greats" who appear in this story. I do believe I have portrayed them in a true light. If professional historians disagree with certain technical details then I beg their tolerance. A few mistakes are inevitable in a book of this scope. The subject is so vast and total accuracy in a fictional history so stifling I can only apologize for not including at least a sidelong glance at every aspect of aviation. That would be impossible to accomplish in a hundred volumes.

Like the historic figures involved, I have flown most of the aircraft in the story. Thus it has been easier to take fact and make it fiction.

The men and women of aviation in this story will never die. Their past is our future.

—Ernest K. Gann
September 1983

Paris

JULY 1916

It was a Sunday in the Bois de Boulogne and the fine weather which had arrived so late in July had flushed out the Parisians and the wild bouillabaisse of nationalities now temporarily inhabiting the capital. Larks tittered in the trees and there were so many people on the side paths around the lakes there was hardly room for the lovers to maneuver much less enjoy any sort of privacy. From Neuilly all the way to Saint-Cloud there was not a hope of being alone, a condition which Lily Cranwell wished otherwise. It was not so much that Lily preferred being alone, rather the opposite was generally true—but these were not general times and she longed for solitude until she could restore at least some clarity in her reasoning. For the first time in her young life she found herself perplexed and she wondered if that recognition was not criss-crossed with hazard.

She strolled slowly along the gravel path ignoring the not so subtle visual and verbal approaches of the countless soldiers who seemed to be in equal numbers to the civilian holiday makers. A few were drunk, but not so many as she had expected since Paris had become a rest camp for troops fresh from battle. They shouted at her or at any female who walked alone and some made rude gestures which she knew were suggestive of fornication. She also knew she would not be troubled unless she invited trouble; it was the way of the French who preferred to think of themselves as lovers rather than rapists. As if to shake her confidence she did encounter a challenge by two young aviators who stepped across her path and blocked her way for a moment. They said they had just come from near Verdun and had been killing Bosche and should have some reward which they could remember—a long matinee nap with a girl who looked exactly like herself. Although their diction suggested they were sober

7

and they stood before her steadily enough with their arms
akimbo she saw that their eyes were glazed and their nos-
trils dilated and she wondered if they had been sniffing
cocaine like so many aviators who came to Paris with the
intention of forgetting everything they had done or seen at
the front.

"I'm sorry," she said in English, "I don't understand
you. I don't speak French."

She saw a look of disappointment drift slowly across their
faces and if it were not for the Croix de Guerres which
dangled from their uniforms she would have told them to get
the hell out of her way. "I'm an American," she said solemnly lest the slightest smile be interpreted as an invitation.

"Ah? Americaine?"

The effect was magical. The two young aviators bowed
almost simultaneously and while they were still bent she
slipped between them. She half ran to a middle-aged couple
who were promenading with their children and hoping to
appear as one of the family, fell in beside them.

As soon as she saw that the aviators were not intending
pursuit she turned away and crossed the grass to an adjacent
path. Alone again she tried to recapture the usual logic of her
thinking which the encounter with the aviators had sent gallop-
ing through the Bois like a runaway horse. All sorts of
random oddments rattled through what she liked to identify as
her "System." There was the silly rumor that Joffre had
really been killed in the Battle of the Marne but they had dug
up an old soldier from the Quartermaster Corps who looked
like him and he was now doing the job. . . . Clemenceau,
and the reports of mutinies among the French troops. . . .
Poincaré, was he going to save France? Was anyone going to
save France? . . . . and then as usual these trying days, there
was Toby Bryant. Dear God what a glorious chunk of humanity!
Mother would approve if she were alive because she always
loved the illogical. But Daddy? Would Daddy, the paragon of
stuffed shirts, approve of her marrying any man who was
only a sergeant? An American in the French Army? What
would be the exact size of Daddy's conniption fit? A coronary?
Or would he just hurl some lightning bolts from his exalted
security in the Embassy at London and thunder, "Now listen
my dear, you are all I have left in this world. You have been
educated in everything from high calculus to Greek mythol-

ogy and you are fluent in four languages. You have been brought up as a lady in the long tradition of the Cranwells and your present position at the Embassy in Paris at so young an age is due to your linguistic brilliance which I will make bold to remind you was acquired at my expense. You are also employed there because of the several thousand influential relatives and political acquaintances I've known over the years who have been soft enough in the head to foster such an unusual career for a young female. Now would you give all this up, surrender the ideal career you have nurtured since early childhood just to spend the rest of your life with some unknown man from Lincoln, *Nebraska?* Is that a state or is it still Indian territory? Does anyone know Degas in Lincoln? Or Flaubert? Or Nietzsche, Spengler, Rabelais, Ravel, Cadmus, Manet. . . . not to mention Aeschylus? Would you forsake the chance that some day you might become America's first woman ambassador, to dwell amid the Nebraskan prairies with a man who never finished college? A man who doesn't have the faintest idea what he's going to do once the war is over?''

Daddy's shirt would stiffen and so would his upper lip as he inquired icily, ''Who has ever been his employer except the French Army?''

''Poof!'' Daddy would say. ''Freud is needed here. I should send you to a sanitarium in Switzerland until your sanity can be unscrambled.''

Lily stopped at the stand of a mobile peddler and bought a *beignet de pomme*. She munched on it as she walked on, savoring the sticky sweet icing and wondering where the sugar had come from since rationing was supposed to be so strict. Her thoughts meandered then into questioning why Parisian fashion leaned so toward voluminous skirts and high boots when the price of cloth and leather was twice what it was a year ago. So silly, and yet the world followed as if the fashion houses of Paris were far more necessary to preserve than the grim-faced soldiers who arrived only hours from the trenches with death still in their eyes.

She strolled more aimlessly now, thinking of her father whose lifetime had been spent in the Foreign Service as had his father's. As career diplomats they did the work, the daily bureaucratic chores which were the raison d'etre of all embassies. The ambassadors, mostly political appointees who could afford to take the post, also took the glory and such as it was, the professionals hardly cared.

Thank heaven for sweet fathers, though they might be a bit obtuse at times, she thought. He had understood or at least pretended to understand her ambitions and had proven his faith by wangling a job for her in Paris rather than directly under his eye in London. And now was she going to tell him that it had all been for naught because she was going to marry her flying prince from the hinterlands?

A nasty blow you would give to the progress of womanhood, she thought. You would be behaving exactly as all the male pig-heads in the world proclaimed any woman would; given every opportunity and advantage and then chucking the whole thing for some sallow young man and a house with a white fence around it. And babies, God forbid!

For shame, Lily Cranwell. For shame and be damned except that Toby was far from sallow and he didn't have a house of any kind to offer.

Maybe he thinks I have money, she thought, knowing in her heart that the notion was nonsense. And then who knew for certain what kind of a world would come out of this war? A German world? They had claimed to have captured thirty-eight thousand prisoners at Verdun and had even offered to publish their names. That was a lot of Frenchmen and the war was far from over. Supposing Toby failed to survive the war—how would widow's weeds look on a seventeen-year-old?

She remembered a statistic she had read in one of the Embassy reports. Out of one hundred ninety-two students at the Teachers' Training College who had been commissioned as Second Lieutenants in the Infantry, one hundred ten had been killed. Well, thank heaven Toby was not in the infantry, but then how did the percentages go in the Air Service?

She banished such thinking and concentrated on the cobalt blue of the sky overhead, (a passionate blue if there were such a thing), and the way the tree leaves appeared so black when viewed against it. The colors of July in France, she decided, were incomparable to any place she had ever been which had, thanks to Daddy's profession, included Greece, Italy, Spain, and even a brief spell in Morocco. What were the colors of July in Nebraska, she whispered to herself. Prairie brown?

Lily was perhaps too thin for her height. She was not a tall

girl yet she gave the impression of height because of her very
erect carriage. She held her head high when she walked, a
shade of the self-conscious at times, although her flowing
movement was pleasing to watch and she never displayed the
ultra-feminine saunter employed by some women who thought
to attract attention via the sinuous twisting of their bottoms.

Once, at Easter time, she had been taken for a walk down
Fifth Avenue in New York. She was a little girl then and after
watching the fashion parade she said, "Some women walk
like alligators." She resolved then and there to walk like she
was going somewhere.

Lily Cranwell's walk was a direct revelation of the basic
directness in herself. She had never had to fight for recognition or attention; both came to her automatically as a result of
her precocity, and she accepted her due with inherent
graciousness. Even when she was a little girl she had been a
study in contrasts. The tomboy was there along with her
rather knobby knees, but the female was also as present in the
curvatures of her legs, which were as harmonious in form as
the rest of her body. She was an instinctive mistress of the
rare art of movement; to watch her doing anything was an
almost sensuous action to behold and the fact that she was
totally unaware of her special attribute made it all the more
attractive. The head she held so proudly was asked to compliment the rest of her without embellishment, a typical reflection of her confidence and sense of independence. Defying
current fashion she kept her dark brown hair very short and
disdained all the powders and rouges employed by her con-
temporaries and many of their mothers. She herself said she
would be damned if she would "gild the lily," and apologized instantly for so gauche a pun. In fact her brunette
coloring, the relatively dark skin, the nearly black eyebrows
and the deep red of her lips would have resisted any cosmetic
tinkering. Except when she had just awakened there was
always a lovely blush of color in her cheeks. At all times her
natural eyelashes framed a pair of warm brown eyes alert and
glittering with intelligence.

Lily was fully aware that her provocative mind was a
handicap in a world where women were supposed to limit
their thinking to the kitchen and when necessary the raising of
children. Older women found much to disapprove about her
over-bold behavior and the younger ones admired her when

they could overcome their nervousness in her presence. Most men were secretly afraid of her.

As a consequence she was sometimes lonely and dissatisfied with herself although such slippages from station were rare and soon passed away.

She saw "their" tree in the distance, a great old elm which had served them as a rendezvous much preferred over the noisy cafés. Her plan was to sit under their tree and think about Toby without his presence to give her that giddy feeling. She would add and subtract in a logical fashion.

She would say to herself in every language at her command that she was too young and he was too young. She would say that heritage was everything and physical attraction nothing. She would say that people are ruled by their hearts instead of their brains which is why the world is in such a frightful mess.

And under the elm she would recite the names of Reginald, Gaspard, Harry, Eugene, Boris, and Antonio, each of whom had at one time proposed marriage.

Why had she so easily erased their names from her thoughts while Toby's seemed chiseled in stone?

CALIFORNIA

JULY 1955

CHAPTER
1

Beyond the window he could see that it was a lovely June day. One of those sparkling segments of time quite common to the coastline in summer. There might be a deck of low stratus, he knew, extending from the shore westward and its monotonous expanse might be relieved by a few husky cumulus. Then the deep and strangely ominous blue of the Pacific would become visible beneath the cloud bases and the sunlight bounding off their fat faces would dazzle the eyes. And far aloft, strewn like palomino manes across the sky, there would be fifty-mile-long wisps of cirrus clouds.

He knew it would be that way because he had seen it so many times. There was a Pacific sky which was somehow feminine and there was an Atlantic sky which was much more masculine for reasons that were difficult to analyze. Like the lines of thunderstorms along the West African coast and the haze which always seemed to suffocate India, some things just were.

He ran his fingers through his spiky gray hair and frowned at the hump his foot made in the bed sheet. What was he waiting for? There had to be some way out of this, a way that even a man with barely a gram of self-respect remaining could manage. Not through the window; that would be messy. Then why not right out through the door like a gentleman? "Humpty dump . . . One . . . two . . . three . . . four . . . to the right . . . March!" Into the lovely June day.

Who was this stranger who had allowed himself to be confined by other strangers? They had swiped most of his clothes, draped him in a silly open-at-the-back gown, and dumped him in a bed with more controls than many of the early airplanes. He was supposed to lie here while more strangers stuck needles in his carcass and said, "Now . . . now . . . this will ease things a bit."

15

They could not understand how the fires in his gut were boiling him. Only Christ knew, but his captors had not stuffed a hot iron down his throat.

Question. Does a man lie here quietly like a good little Blue Cross customer or find a way out?

He raised his arm to look at his watch. Noon. A good time. Half the nurses would be down in the cafeteria eating yoghurt and cottage cheese on lettuce for their figures. The others, if there were any around at all, would be busy or unbelieving. And that last was important. It must not register on their sense of orderliness that a man in his condition could contrive a resurrection, if not in the manner of Jesus and certainly lacking his style, at least a departure suitable to the occasion.

Let one minute pass before it struck the nurses that all was not as it should be and it would be too late. The fire exit was almost directly across from the door to the room, say ten or fifteen steps no matter how awkward.

Now was the time. If ever.

He pushed himself up on his elbows and groaned with the effort. The movement roused the pain which was telegraphed with every bodily action and it repeated itself with such ferocity that it vibrated right down from his intestines and slid shrieking through his testicles.

It was beyond belief that anything could hurt so much. Punishment for past misdeeds?

He eased himself to the edge of the bed with great care, panting like an exhausted animal with every movement, sucking at the room's sterile air and cursing his weakness. He reached for his artificial leg that stood against the wall and with the quick dexterity of long practice, strapped it to the stump of his left leg. He pushed himself erect and stood for a moment leaning against the agony which had become the overriding reality of his world. Almost. There were a few loose ends to be tidied up.

He opened the drawer of the night table and took out his wallet. He smiled at it mischievously and tossed it back in the drawer. Then he took off his wristwatch and dropped it on the wallet. He reached further back in the drawer and brought out a small checkbook with a pen clipped to the cover. Clutching it firmly he shuffled to the mirror, paused long enough for a glance and turned away. This must be Halloween. The face in the mirror was not his. It was the mask of some frowsy, cavern-eyed stranger dressed in a white gown. The thin line of moustache, trademark of all early aviators, was still visible, but it was untrimmed and blended too easily into the mealy flake-white of his face.

No, the man in the mirror was not Kiffin Draper. That man's eyes were furtive and worried. He might be trying to qualify as the ghost of Kiffin Draper, but more likely he was an impostor, some character born in the little paper cups full of sedatives the nurses brought to the room. He was a person trying to tag along on this important occasion and, ho-ho, once away from the mirror he ceased to exist. Like so. Adieu!

He smiled in secret amusement. The real Kiffin Draper was alive and not so well, thank you.

He made his way across the ten thousand miles of floor to the closet. By the time he arrived he was convinced that he was finding new strength in all his parts—by God, he was going to make it yet.

He opened the door and pulled his trench coat off the hanger. He placed the checkbook in the pocket and wriggled into the coat. He reached around the corner of the closet and in the semidarkness found the handle of a violin case. He brought it out then reached to the shelf above the hangers. He was grateful now that he had always been a tall man for it was a long reach. He pushed away a spare pillow and clutched at the bottle of Glenfiddich Scotch whiskey Lily had brought to him. Bless her conspirator's heart. She must have sensed how useful it might be.

He closed the door with one bare foot, tucked the bottle under his arm, and paused for breath. Lightning bolts of pain daggered through him and for an instant he wondered if he could continue.

Yet he was pleased to see that his fingers were not trembling when he unscrewed the bottle cap and took a long draught of the Glenfiddich. The burning sensation as the liquid slipped down his throat and a momentary sense of relative well-being made him think of Toby and Lily and of how glad he was that they had each other. He opened the door cautiously and peeked down the hall. The nurses' desks were unoccupied.

He took the best brace he could manage and moved through the door. He crossed the hall and propelled his body against the brass fire-door bar with all the force he could muster. As the violin case bounced along the door it made a clattering sound which he regretted. It was a shame to disturb sick people.

The door closed behind him. Well done, Kiffin. It was only half a flight down the stairwell to the outside world. And hospitals were so accommodating about sharing needed information. The floor plan displayed on the inside of his room door showed there was a walkway outside this exit which led directly to the ambulance entry. A hundred paces and there it was, all white and glistening chromium.

He made a brief reconnaissance of the ambulance and saw that it was empty. Of course. It was noon hour and people were not supposed to have accidents or die during the lunch break.

After depositing the bottle and violin case inside he slipped into the driver's seat. The key was in the ignition and why not? Who would steal an ambulance right out from under its mother?

Toby Bryant was an out-sized man in every proportion. His leonine head rested on a strong neck emerging from massive shoulders. His hands were broad and heavy fingered and in spite of his nearly sixty years his physique still gave the impression of enormous power. The years had brought some fleshiness to his face and now glasses often obscured the intense blue of his eyes, but the formidable jaw was still there, unencumbered by extra chins. His voice was perhaps one key to the present man for lately it had taken on a deeper and graver tone as if to mark its owner indelibly as a man to be depended upon. And it was so that ever since his youth Toby Bryant III had been regarded with a mixture of appreciation and envy—how could one so young be graced with so much common sense?

Those who knew Toby Bryant only casually were inclined to think of him as an unenfranchised prince, a categorizing that would have amazed and bewildered him. Like the vast majority of those long engaged in his profession he was bound to the code of self-deprecation. A career pilot deliberately credited pure luck with a good landing—never his skill.

Those who knew Toby best—Lily his wife, and Kiffin Draper—were aware of his imperfections and they forgave them all except his occasional lapses into tedium. It was said that if a space ship landed right in front of Toby Bryant's blue eyes and huge men even larger than Bryant himself emerged he would have said, "Very interesting. Anything we can do for you?"

Bryant's overall sense of total calm and command of any situation had served him well during the forty years of his long and distinguished flying career. His faults were regarded by those close to him as humanizing scars on their public demi-god. They knew he was essentially a shy man obliged to push himself toward people when he would have secretly preferred running away. He believed unequivocally in God, country and duty, and no one, not even his wife Lily could induce him to question that triumverate. As Lily once said about her husband, "When Toby dies God will shave and declare a holiday in Heaven and the United States of America will be directing traffic."

People who were in trouble gravitated immediately to Toby Bryant. Those who were looking for trouble struck up an acquaintance with Kiffin Draper.

The pair were sometimes referred to as an unholy mixture and it could even be said that the two men were in love with each other, although that possibility would never have entered their thoughts. Probably it was true as is so often the case when men have been both terrified and triumphant together. A bond is formed which is stronger than blood.

Bryant's outward reserve was sometimes enlivened by flashes of searing temper. He knew it was always lurking nearby and on most occasions he managed to stifle it while he reconsidered what had caused his self-control to stampede. This noon when he had come to the hospital and found Kiffin gone from his room he marched on the area where the nurses and orderlies were gathered at the end of the hall and totally forgot his normal objection to profanity.

"What the hell goes on in this so-called hospital? Where the hell were all of you when he got out—down having another coffee break? Can patients who are supposed to be in intensive care just get up and walk out any time they damn well please? And where the hell are all the doctors and interns and all the rest of you piss-ants who are supposed to tend to the sick?"

The nurses found reasons to be needed elsewhere immediately. Bryant fumed as he listened to the head nurse relate how every effort was being made to find Mr. Draper and how it was that with the shortage of nursing help these days it was impossible to keep a constant eye on every patient—

"Where are you looking for him? Tell me exactly."

"That is not my responsibility. I suggest you check with the front office. They are coordinating things there."

Bryant found that he was having trouble seeing the traffic ahead. He wiped at his eyes and drove so slowly the cars behind him hooted with impatience. But he did not hear them; it was so easy to visualize that barn again. . . . easy to slip back to the outskirts of Lincoln, Nebraska, where so many good airmen had originated.

That would be 1905. You were ten and Kiffin was eleven. It was not the minor age difference, but his nature that made him the original Tom Sawyer. The Wright brothers had made their flight two years before, and Kiffin knew about it as he knew about so many things normal kids never heard or cared about. He did some long thinking and plotting and came up with the idea that flying was easy. If the Wrights could do it, why not you?

Specifically, *you*. Kiffin appointed himself Director of Flight. The High Cock-o-lorum, he called himself. He made most of the wing using the longest bamboo fishing poles he could afford to buy. They formed a main spar and the ribs were rusty bicycle spokes he found somewhere. He conned his mother out of one of her old petticoats and the two of you glued the fabric over the ribs to form a wing surface. The spokes would not hold a bend well, so the camber of the wing was uneven. Still, the whole assembly did resemble a bird's wing.

The barn was located in what had once been the countryside and had since become the fringes of Lincoln. It was a favorite spot for all sorts of secret activities and sooner or later all the neighborhood kids went there to play doctornurse or just masturbate. There had once been a house to go with the barn, but it had burned down and no one but kids ever went near the place. Always wary of parental reaction Kiffin knew his aerial experiment might not be applauded. Every kid in the neighborhood was sworn to secrecy when he finally decided the roof of the barn would be just right for a launch pad.

Never let it be said that Kiffin was selfish. When the big day came and all was in readiness he hitched up his knickers and said, "Toby, I was going to make the first flight myself, but that wouldn't be fair. You don't weigh as much as I do so you get to go first."

It was surprising how Kiffin understood one of the basics of aerodynamics even then. Not to mention survival.

The top of the barn was about thirty feet in the air—looking down it seemed like the highest mountain in the world.

Kiffin helped you slip through the aperture in the center of the wing and made sure it rested on your shoulders. There were two rope straps on the under side of the contraption which you could grasp with your arms fully extended.

There was a pile of old hay in what had once been the barnyard and Kiffin recommended you steer for it. Steer? One of the several things Kiffin had neglected in his bird copying was some kind of tail feathers.

A whole gang of kids were watching, including a couple of girls. Turning chicken was out of the question.

Kiffin asked if you were scared and you said, "Hell no!" Using the word hell proved just how tough you were.

He raised his hand and counted, "One. . . . two. . . . three . . . GO!"

And off you went on the shortest flight of your career.

The damages were considerable—a broken right arm, left wrist, and numerous scratches and bruises. Your parents and his parents did not speak for months.

Kiffin pleaded total innocence. According to him you two had built the wing just for fun and trying to actually fly it was your idea. What's more, he claimed the wing would have flown perfectly if it hadn't had such a dumb pilot.

That was Kiffin, even in the earliest times.

As he drove away from the sea Toby found himself glancing ever more often at the sky, which looked exactly like the kind of sky that had been so blue and influential during that special afternoon ten years later. Yes, it would have been 1915. Was that really such a long time ago, or was it only yesterday?

It was Nebraska against Iowa, the big game of the season. Kiffin's number was seven and yours was nine—one hell of a winning combine until that afternoon. There wasn't much padding then, just the old leather helmets and the game was pretty much straight rough-and-tumble with one charge after another through the opposing line. You played right end and Kiffin, true to form, held the quarterback slot. He had become a minor hero because Nebraska hadn't lost a game all season. Kiffin had the nerve to even try a forward pass now and then. The officials didn't care for such shenanigans, it smacked of trickery to avoid the rules; but there was nothing in the rules against it. And Kiffin always passed to you.

It was still unbelievable and much funnier now than it was then. Iowa had made two touchdowns for a score of twelve and Nebraska had only one. It was late in the fourth quarter and something had to be done to save the day. Kiffin called for a pass. The ball was snapped and you ran your guts out toward a clear field. It was beautiful. There was not an Iowa player around. You turned at just the right moment expecting to see the ball spiraling into your extended hands. But the ball was still in Kiffin's hand. There he was, back where you had come from, all poised for the throw. An army of Iowans were charging down on him and he was not even looking in your direction. He was like a statue, looking up at the sky as a tiny airplane passed directly over the field. The whole horrible scene took no more than three or four seconds until a triumphant Iowan grabbed the ball out of Kiffin's paralyzed hand and ran for a third touchdown. The airplane kept right on going, and it took with it Nebraska's chance for a victory.

And Kiffin's reputation.

Nebraskans took their football seriously, and while Kiffin was not tarred and feathered he did achieve instant disgrace. At the time he didn't seem to care. He had been mesmerized by the first real airplane either one of you had ever seen. As far as Kiffin was concerned, life began at that moment. He was stunned, a zombie, and some of it rubbed off on you.

After the game Kiffin learned that the airplane had landed at the site of the Nebraska State Fair and nothing would do but he must have a closer look at it. When he passed the coach and the rest of the team on his way out of the locker room the silence was awful. And outside the same fans who usually cheered Kiffin looked right through both of you. Any friend of Kiffin's was also a hyena.

The airplane was a Curtiss Pusher, and it was flown by

Glenn Martin. He looked like a high school teacher, but Kiffin thought he must be God in a black leather outfit. He had his name painted in bold black letters on the top of the upper wing and the bottom of the lower wing. The fabric was so fine you could see what was left of the pale October sun right through the wings.

Kiffin turned his special million-dollar smile on Glenn Martin and said his airplane was the most beautiful thing he had ever seen. And it was obvious he meant what he said. But his approach seemed to leave Martin cold. He wore glasses which seemed strange for a genuine dare-devil aviator and there was no warmth in his manner at all. You thought he was sort of fishy-eyed, but now after forty years it seemed more likely that he was just shy.

Maybe it was because Kiffin started following him around like a puppy dog that he finally introduced both of you to a woman who had driven up in a Buick. She was a little bit of a thing while Martin was as tall as Kiffin and as rangy. He said she was his mother and after about thirty seconds it became very obvious who was in charge of things. The little lady said that if you two were so interested in flying machines you might as well learn something by helping them disassemble this one. The flight over the football game had been the last of Martin's midwestern tour, and now he was going to put his machine on the train for California, where he could fly in winter.

Mother Martin gave all the orders. She was a pistol—a born slave driver. "Here you," she kept saying, "do this—do that—hold this—carry that." She could have coached the Nebraska team.

Kiffin, who thought big even then, had the nerve to ask Martin where he could buy a machine just like the one you were taking to pieces. About this time Mother Martin had both of you hoisting the eight-cylinder Curtiss engine off its mounts and carrying the thing to a crate she had brought in the back of the Buick. The thing weighed more than a pair of Iowa tackles and you wondered (silently of course) what the Martins would have done if two football players hadn't arrived on the scene.

Martin told Kiffin that he had built the machine himself.

"With no little help from his mother," Mrs. Martin

squawked. She had a skin like faded burlap and eyes that glittered like little diamonds.

"Oh, she did indeed," Martin added approvingly.

No wonder you were both confused. Kiffin was the son of a lumber merchant and held his own mother in great affection, but it was not the same as this strange relation. The same applied in your own family. Because your dad was the traffic manager for the telephone company you didn't see too much of him when the Nebraska weather was bad, which was much of the time. Sleet storms in winter and thunderstorms in summer were always knocking wires down somewhere. Your mom was a sweetheart even if she was a militant suffragette, but you both told your parents only what you thought they ought to know and no more. Martin treated his mother like a girlfriend.

Toby smiled wryly at a single nimbus cloud which had developed directly above him. How could a couple of innocent football players from Lincoln, Nebraska, understand that the famous Glenn Martin who defied death every time he flew—was in love with his mother? And how about later on when Martin became the biggest aircraft manufacturer in the world and employed people like Donald Douglas and Larry Bell who was nuts about helicopters; it was still difficult to comprehend what Ma Martin was doing behind the throne.

That evening when the airplane was ready for shipping, Kiffin asked Martin if he would teach him to fly. He said he would go to California or do anything to learn.

Mother Martin cut in before he had a chance to answer. She said, "Glenn is too busy. You should go to the Curtiss school at Hammondsport, New York. And you'd better get back there before the snow does all the flying."

Mrs. Martin gave you the creeps.

Whatever she did to Kiffin was different. Maybe she inspired him, because he vowed to leave in the morning, and damned if he didn't. The University of Nebraska never saw him again, and for months afterward it was your job to explain to the curious, which included several females, what had happened to Kiffin Draper. His family went into a sort of semi-mourning for weeks after his departure and the general reaction was that he was certainly going to kill himself. And for a time you were of the same opinion.

But then, unlike now, friends were easier to come by.

Curtiss Pusher. 1913 era.

When Kiffin Draper arrived in Hammondsport on a shimmering October afternoon he spent the balance of the day moving about almost on the tips of his toes as if he might somehow profane such sacred ground with the vibrations of his tread. This was wine country in the full bloom of fall harvest and the foliage everywhere smacked the eyes with flamboyant oranges, magentas, and ochers. Kiffin, who normally would have joined in enthusiasm for such colorful surroundings, now ignored them. For here was the home of the Curtiss Aeroplane Company and somewhere nearby he knew the master himself must be found.

He knew exactly what he wanted to accomplish. By applying all the charm he possessed he had finally managed to crack the cast iron reserve of Mother Martin and had left her with a head full of stunning figures. He would show his father who was always chattering about settling down to a job in the lumber yard and someday taking over—"It's a nice family business, son, which I've worked very hard to build. All you have to do is learn it from the bottom up and with any luck plus the growth I know will take place in Nebraska, you should do very well for the rest of your life. . . ."

If he didn't die of boredom, Kiffin now reminded himself. Here was the chance to show his father what real money was like and it didn't take twenty years before it was in hand. As if anyone really cared about the money. The real fascination of this flying thing was the danger.

Now Kiffin smiled at the self-portrait he had so recently made up. In it he would be not quite twenty years old and already world famous. Being a football hero was all very dandy, but striding about as an aviator was far more extraordinary. Swarms of young women would admire his feats of daring. It was only necessary to lease an airplane

from Mr. Curtiss and do exhibitions around the country like
Glenn Martin. Mrs. Martin had explained that for the first
year he would be paid *only* twenty-five percent of the exhibition fees, but then as he became more famous it could go up
to fifty percent and the Curtiss Company would take the rest.
The real experts, according to Mrs. Martin, could make as
much as one thousand dollars a day and a few of them even
five thousand a day. Could any lumber yard in the world top
that?

Of course he would have to learn to fly first.

Kiffin encountered the first hitch in his plans when he
checked into the Hammondsport Hotel. A single room with
breakfast was six dollars a night. Transportation and other
expenses (a haircut in Buffalo was fifty cents for the love of
Mike!) had wrecked what he chose to call his budget. When
he left Lincoln he took what little money he had and borrowed fifty dollars from Toby Bryant, who squirreled the
stuff away and would always come through whether he had it
or not. Now he had only nine dollars left.

He inquired for a cheaper place to stay and was directed to
"Lulu Mott's place" where he was offered the last room in
the house at three dollars a night. At Lulu Mott's, even
before he had time to make a pilgrimage to the factory or the
shores of Lake Keuka, where he hoped to see the Curtiss
aeroboats flying, he learned things were humming in Hammondsport. He was told that it was a boom town now "because
of the war, you understand." There were no places left to
live in Hammondsport what with the influx of outside workers and everything was "at sixes and sevens."

The other rooms at Lulu Mott's were occupied by young
men who seemed to be about his age and to his surprise most
of them were foreigners. He spoke briefly to a genuine
Englishman and was struck nearly dumb himself listening to
his strange way of speaking English. And there was a young
Frenchman—Artois, he said his name was—who only smiled
uncomprehendingly when Kiffin tried what little he could
remember of his one semester of high school French. And
then, just as he left Lulu Mott's to find the factory, he
collided with a very slight young man who bowed immediately from the waist and said "pardon" several times. When
it was not even his fault, Kiffin thought. And he was a
genuine Oriental of some kind, slant eyes and all. Kiffin was

impressed. Imagine living in the same boardinghouse with so many real foreigners! For sure, things like this would never happen in Nebraska.

When Kiffin finally made his way toward the Curtiss factory he moved as if in a dream, because the town of Hammondsport was exploding with energy. People dressed differently than they did in Nebraska, the streets were busy, there were far more automobiles than horse-drawn vehicles and there were so many pretty girls he found it hard to avoid staring.

At the factory entrance he paused long enough to make sure his bow tie was straight and his hat brim level. This was far more exciting than any football game; this was what real life was like away from a dumb university.

He checked his hands and fingers for cleanliness, tugged at his vest until it was perfectly smooth. His pants were rumpled from sleeping in them for the past three nights on the train, but he had buttoned a fresh collar on his shirt before he left the boardinghouse and he could only hope no one would notice the pants.

A young woman greeted him just inside the entrance doorway. She sat behind a long table and smiled when she saw Kiffin.

"*You*," he said, removing his hat, "just happen to be the best thing I've seen all day." He sighed and added, "I've come a long way, but the view right now is worth it."

Her reaction was not quite what he expected. A nice Nebraska girl would have laughed out loud, maybe even blushed a little or said something like, "Oh you're full of hogwash," or "flattery will get you everywhere, sir," or anything sassy like that to prove they were on their toes. If they wanted to prove how intelligent they were they might even launch into a little speech about you and the sinking of the *Lusitania*—certainly they would say *something*, but this woman just sat there watching him like he had dropped in from Mars. He found her lack of response unnerving.

"My name is Kiffin Draper, and I came all the way from Nebraska," he said. There was still no response, although he thought he saw a new hint of warmth in her brown eyes. "You know, *Nebraska*? It's a long way from New York State." Were those eyes laughing at him? "You know the Germans admitted they attacked a ship called the *Nebraskan*

. . . that was last July, that is, well about the same time as the *Lusitania*. . . . ?'' How did he ever get on this? He wished now that he had thought to polish his shoes and maybe have his damn pants pressed before he came here.

The woman's stubborn silence made him increasingly nervous. Maybe she was another foreigner and didn't even speak English. He had heard that people back east were not very friendly—that is, compared to Nebraskans, anyway— but this woman was not exactly hostile, she just sat there smiling.

He could not seem to avoid the note of pleading in his voice when he said, "I came here to see Mr. Curtiss. I'm a friend of the famous aviator Glenn Martin." The last of course was somewhat of an exaggeration, but at least he had met Martin and that should mean something.

"Mr. Curtiss is not in Hammondsport," the young woman said crisply. "He's in Buffalo starting a new factory. If you're looking for employment come back and ask to see Mr. Pomfret in the morning. He does the local hiring."

"That's not exactly what I have in mind. I'm a customer and I'm thinking about buying a Curtiss aeroplane."

There was a significant pause and he thought by God that at last he had her attention. He decided her smile had become just a shade more receptive.

"Then you're an aviator?"

"Well, you might say so, but I thought a little refresher in your flight school might polish off some of the rough edges . . . . . if you understand me, miss?"

"I think I do. Then the man for you to see is Becky Havens over at the school." She handed him a printed folder. He glanced at the cover—A SCHOOL FOR PRACTICAL FLYING AND PRACTICAL AEROPLANE OPERATION. He opened the folder gingerly and looked inside. He tried to conceal the sudden despair in his eyes:

The Curtiss Aeroplane Company is pleased to offer a two week course in flying. Length of course two weeks depending on weather conditions. Guarantee minimum six lessons. Deposit of five hundred dollars required to cover breakage and damage. If applicant desires to purchase a Curtiss aeroplane the five hundred dollars deposit will be applied to the final purchase price.

Kiffin cleared his throat and placed the folder carefully in his coat pocket. He saw that the young woman was watching him skeptically, although those eyes, he thought, while not unfriendly now were certainly saying that she doubted him. "What's your name?" he asked quietly.

"Bessie."

"Well, Bessie, I might as well get this over with. I'm not an aviator. . . . yet."

"I didn't think you were."

He saw that her smile became suddenly warmer. "How could you tell I've never flown?"

"I don't know. I meet a lot of the real ones passing through here. There's something . . ." She paused and made no attempt to finish her sentence. She shrugged her shoulders as if an explanation was unnecessary.

"I want you to know I really have met Glenn Martin in the flesh. It's on account of him that I'm here."

"You picked the right place. We have the best flying school in the world."

"Unfortunately. . . . I. . . ."

"You don't have have that much money."

"How did you guess?"

"Because we have about ten young men a day come here with the same idea. And they're always broke."

Kiffin allowed his shoulders to sag. There was no use fighting or pretending any longer; this woman was different from any he had ever met before. She was not very beautiful; her mouth was too large, she was on the plump side, but her eyes made up for all her defects. They seemed to be constantly challenging him, offering an invitation to join her in some secret amusement. "Bessie," he said, "it's almost five o'clock and I'm not completely broke. How about my taking you someplace for supper?"

"You have your share of gall, Mr. Draper."

"Something tells me I'm going to need it."

Bessie Stringfellow was not the first of Kiffin's conquests. Not that he ever considered exploiting Bessie; he was of all things and in all ways much too forthright to bother with dribbling schemes through his busy mind. Instead it was Bessie who did the plotting; utterly lost within twenty-four hours to his simple charm she would have done almost anything short of setting fire to the Curtiss factory if he had asked. She was a minister's daughter from Albany and had decamped for the west when the religious restrictions of her family threatened to overwhelm her. She had ventured only as far as Buffalo when she saw an ad for a secretary-receptionist in the *Courier* and applied by letter to a Mr. Glenn Curtiss. Now she had been with the company for three years and was known as "the professional virgin" by those local young men who had attempted to establish close relations with such a convenient and apparently vulnerable female. They underestimated her. Bessie was quite as unique as her situation; there were very few young women in America who could afford to live alone in any sort of dwelling, let alone a small house overlooking the lake at Hammondsport. What no one in the town knew was that the house had been bought and furnished by a German vintner named Sebastian Kupper who hoped to immigrate and establish a vineyard in such a productive area. The transaction was arranged by one Konrad Muller, a German emigré who had preceded the unfortunate Kupper, and no one realized better than Muller that he faced an ever more threatening problem. Because of personal commitments Kupper was unable to leave the Rhineland in 1913 as he had planned, and when the Kaiser went to war later his class was called back to military service. He had not been heard of or from since, and antipathy toward anything even faintly related to Germans or Germany was spreading rapidly throughout the United States. Even second and third generation American families with German or Germanic sounding names pronounced them softly and in some areas found it expedient to modify or actually change their name. As the war in Europe escalated Muller saw the resentment was increasing with alarming rapidity. The slightest Teutonic accent became suspect and shopowners presumed by name to have even faint connections with the Fatherland were losing customers. By the end of 1914 schoolchildren with Germanic names were tormented as the offspring of spies and saboteurs and were often called "Heinies" or "Fritzes" or "Huns" regardless of what their true names might be. It was inevitable that physical violence should erupt and vandalism should follow.

Muller reasoned that a house standing alone and thought to be owned by an absent German was asking for trouble and when by chance he met a young lady with a name like

Stringfellow who was honestly employed he offered her the house rent free.

Bessie Stringfellow not only took Kiffin to her particularly voluptuous bosom, but concerned herself in furthering his chosen career. She had ten years more of life than her new star boarder (they settled for "boarder" as his official role although he paid no rent), and the difference in their ages troubled her somewhat, but their energies during the day were so absorbing, and in bed at night so exhausting, that she lived in a sort of serene cocoon. Whereas previously she had been prone to a certain nervousness and occasional intermezzos of depression, now not even the ominous reports of the European war could disturb her new and mellow composure.

On his part Kiffin was blossoming under Bessie's subtle guidance, and all of his willingness and desire to please soon won others to his cause. After the end of his first week as Bessie's guest he was able to carry his share of the grocery bill and take her to dinner at the Hammondsport Hotel once a week.

Less than twelve hours after Bessie Stringfellow discovered a primary essence of life and while still floating high in her own very private balloon she went directly to Mr. Pomfret and described to him in glowing terms the young man who had come seeking employment three days previously. (She lengthened the time span by forty-eight hours thinking it unseemly and possibly disadvantageous for her prodigy if her enthusiasm became evident too soon after his arrival in Hammondsport.)

"Does he have any skills?" Mr. Pomfret wanted to know.

Normally Bessie would have anticipated such an obvious question and have a ready answer, but she had been so distracted by Kiffin's formidable love-making and her own ecstatic reactions she felt as if she were drowning in a sea of all-consuming satisfaction. A true virgin she had been, but she had experienced none of the ugly or painful results which she had been told would accompany the loss of her hitherto precious chastity. Instead those same warm oceans of passion just kept rolling through her body until finally a singularly large and active wave would crash through. "Here comes another typhoon," she would happily whisper into Kiffin's ear . . .

"He knows Glenn Martin," she said, avoiding Mr. Pomfret's

original question, "and he has a lot of muscle . . . he is very strong."

"Good. We need a clean-up man down at the floats." Mr. Pomfret smiled. He was anxious to please Bessie; it was said she had the ear of Glenn Curtiss himself, and one never knew about casting bread upon waters.

After working hours and between sessions of hyperactive love-making, "the Stringfellow girl," as Kiffin was fond of addressing her, enlightened him on many matters aeronautical, some known to other Curtiss employees and some not. The actual name of the firm was the Herring-Curtiss Company because a Mr. Herring, who Bessie described as a strange man and not the sort she thought Curtiss should be in business with, was involved in financing the company. How he had wormed his way into such a position she could not explain, particularly since much of Curtiss' financing had been provided by Mrs. Alexander Graham Bell, whose husband invented the telephone and who thought the world of Curtiss, a simple and kind man who had drifted into the flying game after establishing himself as a motorcycle racer and manufacturer of motorcycle engines. Now at age thirty-seven he was a full-scale industrialist, with the growing pains of his airplane company, not the least of which was a suit by the Wright brothers, who claimed that he was infringing on their patent. Although Curtiss did his best to mollify the Wrights he had little success, and the threat of an injunction that would close down his factory was still very real.

Curtiss, Bessie explained with a vehemence born of total loyalty, was being persecuted by the stubborn Wrights. On Saturday afternoon when the music in her heart had been sufficiently muted for her to think of something other than the power in Kiffin's loins, she confessed that Curtiss really needed a keeper. Certainly he had proven himself the premier pilot in the world during the early days when there was only the Wrights, Blériot, and perhaps Santos-Dumont as competition; he had won acclaim in France and elsewhere in the world, yet he was essentially an engine man, most content when he was pottering about with the latest version of his engines and experimenting with new mechanical ideas.

Now with orders from Great Britain for fifteen flying boats and potential orders for the new trainer to be built in a separate factory, Curtiss seemed overwhelmed by the complexity and size of his organization. "Thank God for Doctor Bell," Bessie said. "He's come to the rescue so many times. His wife puts up the money, but he puts up the brains."

She explained then that one of the major advantages of Curtiss airplanes over the Wright versions was the employment of "ailerons." The Wrights managed to attain a degree of lateral stability in their machines by warping the wings, the pilot moving a shoulder yoke and causing enough change in the angle of incidence of either wing to bring about a turn. No one liked the method, and Dr. Bell had suggested that the use of "little wings" near the tips or between the wings would create better control over keeping the wings level and turning the aircraft as desired. Casey Baldwin and Tom Selfridge, both pilots for Curtiss, flew some tests with ailerons, found it worked, and now the Wrights were more displeased than ever. "They say they're going to put Mister Glenn out of business, but I think they're too late now," Bessie said.

While she was not quite sure what was happening to her Bessie still retained enough emotional equilibrium to recognize that she commanded an extraordinary situation and one which would probably not endure very long. She held in vassal a young man who caught her every word as long as it was even vaguely applicable to aeronautics and unconsciously she began preying on that fixation with the same devotion she gave to toying with his privates. Although she had picked up considerable aeronautical lore vicariously she foresaw that once their mutual feasting on each other was satisfied she might lose Kiffin's interest unless she could offer more professional stimulus.

No intellectual thief hungry for knowledge could have acquired so much so fast. She ransacked the files for information on Dr. Alexander Graham Bell's "Aerial Experiment Association," of which Curtiss was a vital participant. She brought home to the house on the hill little personal facts about Curtiss himself—his devotion to his family, the scar across his chin acquired while experimenting with a propeller on an ice boat, or how he always wore a little metal propeller device on his cap as a good luck charm. One evening after the offices closed she took Kiffin back to Curtiss' private sanctum and showed him a few of the countless trophies their boss had acquired: The Gordon-Bennett Trophy won at Rheims, France, and among many others the Doubleday Trophy donated by some book publisher to encourage aviators. "It was made by Tiffany's if you can imagine. The *real* Tiffany's right in New York City!"

Bessie was unsure whether the collage of fact, gossip, and rumor she lavished on Kiffin every night was intended to inspire him toward a greater future or simply divert him from becoming discouraged with his present employment as a company handyman. Or to hold him to her. The thought of his quitting and leaving Hammondsport was becoming sheer torture, and she became almost frantic in her anxiety to keep him happy. She knew that washing down the flying boats was a cold and dreary job and cleaning the tenacious moss off the floats was hardly a challenge to a young man of his education and abilities, but what to do? Once she had ventured to ask if his father might not stake him to flying lessons. After all, he had enough money to send his son to a university.

For the first time in their brief romance she saw Kiffin's face cloud over and his voice took on a new tension when he said, "Let's leave my father out of this. He would say I made my bed and will have to lie in it . . . and he'd be right. I don't know yet how I'm going to do it, but I'm going to fly. I'm not going to do it to prove anything to my father, or my mother, or even you, but I'll manage somehow . . . . and on my own."

Kiffin was also expected to serve as the plant janitor, cleaning up wood chips and discarded metal parts after the day's work and even cleaning toilets. All of this he did with good spirit. After two weeks Bessie was convinced that such an arrangement could not last for long and to perpetuate just a little longer the bedroom delights she approached Beckwith Havens, who was in charge of the company's flying school. Although she knew Havens well, the purpose of her mission was a delicate one and she sidled into it uneasily.

She chose an hour of a rainy day when she knew Havens would not be too busy and she began by asking if he had ever wanted to help someone toward better things. When she received an affirmative reply she ventured further. "You know Kiffin. He wants desperately to learn to fly. It's an obsession with him—"

"Yeah I know, all right. How could I miss since he's always hammering away at me? I got him wiping down the machines every day and I promised some day I'll give him a flight. Nice guy.''

"But he can't learn to fly from just one flight—"

"For sure he can't." Beckwith was a dedicated realist and not one to squander words or money.

"How much would it cost for him to learn?"

"The school fee is five hundred dollars. . . . but that's minimum in my estimation. I told Glenn the students ought to have more than six lessons, but hell he practically taught himself to fly and so did most of his exhibition pilots, so he can't see how a body needs any more."

"But Kiffin's an employee. Shouldn't he get some kind of a rate?"

"Nope. Not unless Mister Glenn authorized it. We got a lot of foreigners here now and I'm just up to my ears—"

"Couldn't you just kind of after official hours give him some instruction? A few minutes at a time, maybe? He's very bright and eager to learn."

"Commendable. But I'm just an instructor here now. You'd have to talk to Mr. Glenn himself."

Which was exactly what Bessie did not want to do. She met Haven's eyes and saw that he knew or at least thought he knew, and dismissing caution she swung boldly into the breach. "Supposing you could find a half hour a day, maybe three or four times a week to make a test flight and you just happened to invite Kiffin to go along with you. How much would *that* cost?"

Havens kept silent while he allowed himself the pleasure of surveying the more interesting curvatures of Bessie's frame. Finally he smiled knowingly and said, "You're really sweet on the guy, aren't you?"

Bessie did not reply, since it was obviously unnecessary.

"Tell you what," Havens continued, "you tell your friend to show up around here about four every day. Most days I'll be all through flying by then, but some days I won't and if he just happens to be in the way, like I would run over him with an aeroplane, then I might just as well scoop him up and take him along."

"And the cost?"

"Seeing as how you'll be paying . . . how about ten dollars a time?"

"Just don't let him know . . . . that's all I ask."

*   *   *

Now in the autumn of 1915, which coincided with the delayed explosion of springtime in Bessie Stringfellow's life, even her boundless energies were being taxed to the limit. Although she longed to lie abed with the first male body she had ever touched she propelled herself to the bathroom every morning at six and by seven had served up a hearty breakfast for her contented lodger. It was apparent to her now that something quite unexpected had resulted from what she had this long pretended was a mere friendship—she advised herself that the bonuses of carnal discovery were a divine right of ministers' daughters who always had to wait longer for such realities—she knew she was in love. She had read about it and heard others speak of being in love, always with only one eye or half an ear; the lack of passionate release was easier to accept if she believed it did not really exist other than in the imaginations of the committed, or the weak and utterly lonely. Since none of those conditions had ever prevailed in her life, shrugging off the notion of emotional entanglement had always been easy, but now here it was staring her right in the face through the bright gray eyes of a young man who moved like a landed prince, though he had no money and laughed at hardship and discomfort as if he had never known anything else. She saw that men were drawn to him and liked him, which someone had once told her was the ultimate test for a prospective mate, and she was painfully aware that the few females employed by the Curtiss company sparkled shamelessly when he was even within hailing range.

When Bessie counted her own shortcomings she had the grace to let their number exceed her qualities. Yet the comparison was discouraging. Kiffin was nineteen, "going on twenty," she remembered every time she tried to hasten his aging, and she was barely on the near side of thirty. She had bowling-pin legs. She had a high school and secretarial school education and a family that could read the Bible and nothing else. The omens, she thought, were not promising for a lifetime union.

Yet there he sat at the breakfast table, his ruddy face announcing his booming good health, his alert eyes so full of curiosity and amusement, his manner so mature and controlled, yet exuding a marvelous animal strength and agility. She reached out whenever she dared and ran her fingers through his thick dark hair and listened enraptured while he told her about his former life.

". . . . Toby, now, you'd like Toby. He's about my size, but heavier. He eats too much and he's going to fat as soon as training is over which would be about now. I'll tell you one thing; there was never a person you could trust more. Toby doesn't know the meaning of quitting. We were playing Minnesota last year and the score was ridiculous, thirty to nothing in the last quarter and in their favor. But Toby was playing like a madman. . . ."

"You miss him, don't you?" she said, wondering if a wish-you-were-here postcard would be appropriate.

"Sure. Ever since we were little kids Toby and I have been closer than brothers. I can hardly remember a day when we didn't see each other. We settled everything together. . . . talked things over, understand? I sure wish he *was* here."

"Why isn't he? How come you took off alone?"

"Because I'm impatient. Toby has to think everything over about ten times before he decides what he's going to do. I tell him he's got moss on his brain and he says the moss keeps his brain cool. If I told him to get the lead out the building is on fire he would say wait a minute, let's see if we can find a fire extinguisher. If you're a stranger in town and ask Toby for the way to the nearest drugstore he'll take you by the arm and lead you there no matter how far away it is. The guy is a born Boy Scout."

"Were you a Boy Scout?"

"Yes. Both of us were in the same troop, but I got into trouble."

"What kind of trouble?"

"At summer camp. I stole an automobile. It was only for a few hours and I wound up in a ditch because it was night and I'd never driven one before. That's why I appreciate what Becky is doing for me. If he didn't sneak me in for instruction I might steal one of the machines because I just couldn't stand on the side looking at them any longer. . . . and I might kill myself."

"We certainly wouldn't want that to happen," Bessie said with her full sincerity. Strangely, the fact that Kiffin might be killed like so many others she had known during her tenure at Curtiss had never entered her head. Even now the specter of his possible demise came as an almost tangible shock.

"I wonder," she said, marveling at her own generosity, "if you should go up to Buffalo and try to do some flying in one of the new J Ns."

"That's a tractor airplane. I better stick with a pusher where I don't have anything in front of me and can see what's going on. Becky says the pilot loses his feel with all that engine and fuselage in front of him."

"I talked to Mister Thomas and he says the J N is what the British want and will buy as many as we can build. I think it's cute calling them 'Jennies.' " And Mr. Thomas should know, she thought, since he was an Englishman himself, hired as an engineer from the Sopwith Company.

Perhaps Kiffin would have eventually gone to Buffalo to fly the new Curtiss trainers, or perhaps if he had dallied in Hammondsport all through the winter Bessie's idyll would have survived longer. She could uncover no rational explanation why two people should collide so abruptly and remain locked together so joyously. Why hadn't this happened to her before? The juxtaposition of the planets or whatever it was that had brought them together was as good an explanation as any, but planets changed position. The only question now was, how soon?

Although he had never soloed, Kiffin managed to acquire several hours of actual air time in the Curtiss flying boats before the lake froze over, and by February he was acting as an assistant instructor on the pushers. Becky Havens was delighted with the arrangement, because even on the good days flying a pusher in February was a painful experience. Pilot and student sat directly exposed to the full force of the slip-stream and twenty minutes at a time was all that most of them could tolerate. Bundled up like mummies, eyes watering despite leather face masks and goggles, every limb and appendage purple with cold, most students surrendered and took the train to the Curtiss School near San Diego.

Without Kiffin to serve in his place Becky Havens would have been left to teach those students tough enough to remain. As it was he contrived to remain in a heated hangar most of the winter. There, hovering close to the pot-bellied stove, he was pleased to offer in some detail how Kiffin had come to him wanting to fly and how he could not refuse such eagerness and what a natural pilot he had soon proved himself to be. He was so successful in keeping Bessie's secret to himself that it was not long before he began to believe in his own magnanimity.

A few students, mostly foreign, remained in Hammondsport taking their chances on the weather and the cold. There were two Russians, several Frenchmen, and a single Belgian, Raoul de la Chevalrie who was rumored to be a very wealthy young man. He had been desolated by the German invasion of his country and had personally financed his American flight instruction in the hope of someday finding revenge. He spoke fluent English and was very popular among his fellow students who lived at Lulu Mott's. He had done very badly in his flying lesson one gray afternoon and would certainly have destroyed the pusher and possibly the pilot if Kiffin had not been quick to take over the controls. Sensing that his melancholy might have something to do with his dismal performance as an aviator, Kiffin invited him to dine at the house on the hill.

Bessie was delighted and provided a double brace of roasted duck for the occasion. Enjoying himself immensely in his new role as chieftain in his new castle, Kiflin regaled the Belgian with the story of how he had lost a football game for his team because of a passing airplane. And Chevalrie laughed heartily, although he had not the vaguest notion what an American football game was like.

It was not until the last duck leg had been gnawed clean and the second bottle of the local Pleasant Valley wine was half gone before it came to Bessie that this little dinner party might have unwelcome consequences for her future.

As the wine and food warmed Raoul he began to talk of the war in Europe. While most Americans were aware that some kind of conflict had been going on, only a very few were directly affected and none had suffered the slightest deprivation because of it. Raoul was an intense young man with a talent for description and somehow his accent seemed to give unusual authority to his words. Looking at Kiffin over the rim of his wine glass he said, "You belong in France. That is where the flying action is and every day there are new developments. Here it is very comfortable, but of *course!*" He shrugged his shoulders and spread his hands palms up. "You go your merry way and all is well. The world is coming to pieces and you Americans only stand watching.

This is not real life here . . . . this is a dream and I cannot blame you. But also I must tell you, it is not living.''

"At the moment there's not much I can do about it," Kiffin said.

"Ah, but there *is*, dear Kiffin. You would be very valuable in France now. There is a great shortage of instructor pilots. So many students are killed because it is the blind leading the blind. If instead of coming here I should take my instruction in France, then maybe I be killed before I have the chance at the Huns. And that would not be nice, no?''

"I can't just walk up to the French army and say here I am, Kiffin Draper. I can't even remember my high school French.''

Raoul smiled tolerantly. "That is obvious. But it is no matter. You can say no and yes, bad and good. That is enough to begin and in a few weeks you will speak like a magpie.''

"How would I go about it? It must cost a lot of money to go to France, money I don't have.''

But of desire, Bessie thought, you have a huge over-abundance. She needed no further signals to tell her that Kiffin was already on his way. It was as if a gauze had fallen over his eyes; they lost their sparkle and instead sought something far away. Fear sent the blood pounding through her ears so that she barely heard Raoul saying, "I think money will be no big problem. Give me a week. I will see what can be done.''

That night there was no squeaking of the springs from the great brass bed which on every other night since mid-October had accommodated the hungers of two very healthy people. "I've got to do a lot of thinking," Kiffin said to the darkness. "Raoul is right. This is not real life.''

He lay flat, the coverlet pulled up to his chin, his hands still beside him. Bessie was trying desperately to bring peace to her racing thoughts, and desires, uncertain whether she should reach out for him or let him be in the hope that by morning he would forget what Raoul had said.

Later in the week Bessie had cause to brood about the influence of planets on the meeting of individuals and their subsequent influence upon each other. Some mysterious force had brought Kiffin to her a scant four months previously and now that same power had whisked him away. She *tried* to be grateful for the time they had spent together; memories of his kisses and caresses, she thought, should last her for a long time. But they would not be enough, because to the early physical fires had been added far stronger emotions. She had definitely discovered, or thought she had, that true love actually did exist, and it would be impossible to repay Kiffin for that revelation, or to substitute for it.

Raoul de la Chevalrie had written to a friend in New York, a Frenchman whose patriotism was as strong as his own. If Kiffin would report to him at number twelve Wall Street, any weekday before noon, transportation for him to France would be arranged.

"Voila," Chevalrie said as he handed Kiffin a letter. "When do you leave?"

Bessie took two days off from work and accompanied Kiffin to Buffalo, where he could catch a New York train. At the new Curtiss factory she also arranged special permission for them to watch the construction of the new "Jennies." Glenn Curtiss himself heard of their visit and joined them at the production line. He was an easy-going man with a dark moustache and a rather solemn air. After confessing that he missed living in Hammondsport and that he was relying on Bessie to keep things humming there, he expressed his regrets that Kiffin was leaving his employ. "You've come up very fast," he said, "and we have so many airplane orders we're going to need a lot of pilots. Maybe you're missing an opportunity, because I'm about convinced we'll be in the war too before very long."

Kiffin said that he would have liked to stay and probably the French would toss him out and he would be back with his tail between his legs, but he couldn't turn back now. "I can't really explain why, Mister Curtiss, but I just have to go."

That night they stood in the station waiting for the train to come through from Chicago. They stood on the platform for a long time, huddled in each other's arms, oblivious to the train crews and other passengers. It was bitterly cold and the vapor of their breath rose in little geysers above them.

"I love you . . . . oh, I love you so," Bessie said over and over again. "I'll never be the same. I promised myself that I won't cry when your train leaves . . . but I probably will."

"When I have an address I'll send it to you . . . Please write."

"I will, I *will*. Every night. Without you, what else would I do in Hammondsport?" After a long debate with herself Bessie had decided against telling Kiffin what she would really be doing with her evenings in Hammondsport. For one thing she would certainly be preparing for the baby she now knew she was carrying. She would tell him in good time—if ever. The last thing in the world she wanted was Kiffin returning for any other reason except herself.

She watched him until he vanished ghostlike in the clouds of steam coming from the locomotive, and then she turned away. She found to her surprise that for the moment at least she was not woefully unhappy, and she indulged an impulse to stop for coffee and a large chunk of apple pie in the station. She was ravenously hungry and she was certain she knew why, and smiling over the pie she decided that maybe she had more than enough reward for having given so little.

Somehow Kiffin never got around to sending Bessie his forwarding address, and somehow Bessie never got around to writing the towering prose she had once visualized. Instead she was soon preoccupied with a Norman Hardwick, a supplier of varnish and other chemicals to the Curtiss Company. Even with the richest stuffing of her imagination he was no Kiffin, but he was not going to be called off to the war, either of his own volition or his now officially pugnacious government. A slight heart murmur excused him completely from the new draft, and he announced that if Bessie would share his future he would not be too inquisitive about her past.

CHAPTER
2

One month to the day after Kiffin was swallowed in a cloud of steam at Buffalo another train bucked and swayed and rattled through the lavender of a French country evening. The train was jammed with people and the locomotive seemed to protest such an unbearable load by spasmodic screechings.

Many of the passengers on the train were civilians, although the drabness of their appearance was relieved by a sprinkling of naval uniforms from several nations. The train was bound from Bordeaux to Paris and carried a number of important passengers who were relieved to have crossed the Atlantic on the *S.S. Mongolia* without being torpedoed. The train also carried a wide-eyed Toby Bryant in a third class compartment where only his bulk saved him from being buried alive beneath the bodies of French sailors and fiercely determined little French women wrapped in black shawls and violently asserting their rights to a seat. Toby could remember some football scrimmages which were mild in comparison with his present experience. For a while he considered climbing out the window and riding on the roof, but it was bitterly cold and in a reverse of his usual consideration for the comfort of others he had by now suffered long enough to fight for his own elbow room. When he saw that the French respected his new attitude and heard them blame the war for their mutual misery he felt better about his fellow man and watched the countryside slide past the window. The fields were fallow, but they had recently been tilled and he wondered, "What war?" Over and over his companions had complained, *"L'guerre, M'sieu. . . . L'guerre. . . ."* and from the phrase book he had been studying aboard ship he at least knew what that meant. But outside there was no sign of anything except bucolic peace. As the towns and villages and hamlets of western France were left behind in a blur he saw nothing to disturb that peace. It was a little like Nebraska in late winter, he thought, but there was no snow and the fields were much smaller.

As darkness enshrouded the landscape Toby decided to read Kiffin's letter one more time before the light was completely gone.

". . . I will find out when the *Mongolia* is supposed to arrive in Bordeaux and I will meet the boat train that comes from there. Don't bother looking for me, I'll look for you. Probably the train will come in to the Gare du Nord, but because there's a war on over here it may go into one of the other stations. Or it may be stopped outside of Paris and you'll have to walk. It's happened. *Don't worry*. If I don't show up in thirty minutes take a taxi to Doctor Edmund Gros at thirty-two Avenue Bois de Boulogne. I'll meet you there so just wait. I hope you brought some francs with you, but don't worry about that either. The taxi driver will take American dollars, it should be about two dollars fare.

"If I don't meet you it'll be because I've been transferred or I'm dead. In that case just ask to see Dr. Gros, tell him what you want to do, and he'll take it from there.

"Hurry up before you miss any more!"

The letters Kiffin had written from Hammondsport had been so interesting they'd made Toby's attention wander during lectures at the university. And when Kiffin wrote that he was going to France his concentration became near-impossible to control. With things going the way they were who gave a damn about Zoology I, English II, and Applied Chemistry?

Almost as if another person was involved, Toby had found himself reading more and more about the war in Europe until the original Toby Bryant seemed to have been replaced. He found some reassurance in noticing that he was not the only student possessed by a new and apparently all-powerful urge to get out of Nebraska and join *something*. . . . almost anything as long as it involved putting on a uniform.

When Kiffin had sent his first letter after his arrival in France Toby knew his student days were numbered. With his usual enthusiasm Kiffin had written " . . . This is the greatest event in the history of the world! The French are terrific people and they say they really appreciate my coming. As if I could personally win the war for them. Ho! Ho! While my flying so far has been very confined I'm told that will change soon and I will be given a chance to fly at the front. So, better get the lead out!''

Now bouncing along in the last of the twilight Toby found it difficult to understand how he could have been so gullible that he would cash in the savings account he had accumulated after years of doing afterschool and summer jobs; all just to buy transportation to Europe—all because of the tempting words of a man he knew was as reliable as a Rumanian gypsy. Not entirely fair, he now told himself. Kiffin was a great fellow to have at hand in an emergency; it was just that his enthusiasms were subject to almost instant change, along with his energies that went with them. When mixing with Kiffin it was a good idea to stay quick on your feet.

With a final screech from its whistle the train pulled into a railway station and once again only Toby's size kept him from being knocked off his feet as his traveling companions made for the door. When he stepped down to the platform he was stunned by the instant recognition that here at last was the war. A hospital train was unloading on the opposite side of the platform, and the collection of humanity emerging nearly unnerved him. The troops were all French and must have come directly from the front. Their uniforms were still caked with mud and blood; those who could walk were bent, and those who were carried lay very still in their litters. Toby could not look away from their empty eyes—they were so unseeing, so resentful if they expressed any emotion at all.

Now everywhere about him the war was suddenly a reality instead of the abstract commotion which as far as Nebraskans were concerned could have been happening on another planet. The scene on the platform became dreamlike as he searched over the heads of the people surrounding him for some sign of Kiffin.

A crowd of French poilus moved noisily across the end of the platform saying farewells to a mixture of women, old and young. Most of the poilus looked like they were drunk. The trainmen kept yelling, *"En voiture! En voiture!"* and a new squadron of black lace ladies jostled him roughly. Almost simultaneously he was seized from behind in a fierce bear hug. Whirling around to defend himself he saw his attacker was a French corporal.

"Tiens, Toby! *Comment ça va, mon vieux!"*

Toby saw it was Kiffin who grabbed him by the ears and was trying to kiss him on both cheeks. He shoved him away vigorously. "What the hell are you trying to do? You turned into some kind of a fairy?"

"I give you a warm welcome to the war, *mon vieux*."

"You're crazy," Toby yelled, repulsing a second attack. "What the hell's got into you? You have me mixed up with one of your girl friends."

Laughing, bubbling with pure joy, Kiffin said, "But, *m'sieu!*, we're in France. If we're going to fight for France then we must do things the French way. I'm very damned glad to see you, Toby."

"Just say so and that's enough. I'm not sure I want to be mixed up in this. I'm not mad at anybody."

Kiffin picked up Toby's suitcase and ushered him along the platform. Toby grumbled that he was lucky not to have received a knuckle sandwich with that kissing stuff, that he'd been recognized just in time. He surveyed Kiffin in his kepi and dark blue uniform and said that he looked pretty fancy for a Nebraska boy.

"Don't worry. You'll look the same by tomorrow, although you won't make corporal right away."

Kiffin hailed an ancient taxi and explained that it was probably one of those that had saved the day for Paris by making a desperate last minute transfer of troops to the Marne. Then as if anxious not to be questioned too closely he rushed through their immediate plans at such a pace Toby gave up trying to follow him.

"All we do is see Doctor Gros. He's the American who clears the way for American volunteers. Then you enlist in the Foreign Legion and after a little while you're transferred to the Air Service."

"How long is a little while? From what I've read about the French Foreign Legion it's very hard on the back."

"I'm in it. That's why this uniform. We all are. Not to worry, it's a technicality. If you're in the Legion you only have to swear you'll obey the orders of the Legion. You don't have to swear loyalty to France or anything like that so you don't lose your citizenship. Not to worry, my friend."

Toby searched his memory for any time Kiffin had said "not to worry." Damned foreign sounding. "How about losing my life?" he asked.

"That's the chance you take."

"I don't want to die for France, the Legion, or anybody else."

"No problem. Besides, you were born to be hung and I'll do my best to be assigned as your flight instructor. If anyone asks if you've flown an airplane just say 'of course' or something like that."

"That really could hang me. Have you seen any Germans yet?"

"Not yet. I'm still instructing at Buc."

"Frenchmen?"

"Of course."

"You speak this mumbo jumbo well enough to do that?"

"Enough. When people are scared they listen very carefully no matter what language you're using."

The house on the Avenue Bois de Boulogne, and particularly the clublike waiting room, was well known to an odd mixture of young Americans who needed advice and assistance, as well as to many young Frenchmen who sometimes needed medical attention not easily available through their over-taxed military services or even the Red Cross. On this early evening the waiting room was bustling with newly graduated students from the flying schools at Buc, Avord, and Pau. There were also two young men who wanted to transfer from the volunteer American Ambulance Service to French fighting units. And there were three veteran aviators who had recently been flying at the front.

Toby and Kiffin had to outwait them all.

At last, when Toby had become so hungry he was not sure he could stand without reeling, he was admitted to Dr. Gros' office. He proved to be a somewhat pompous man who seemed determined to confirm his reputation for giving very short interviews. He eyed Toby curiously and allowed a slight smile to cross his mouth. "You are a big fellow. As a foot soldier you might have some trouble hiding from the Bosche. How much do you weigh?"

"Two hundred."

Dr. Gros tucked the ends of his stethoscope in his ears and shoved the diaphragm hard against Toby's chest. He seemed disinterested in what he might be hearing.

"You have flown an airplane?"

"Naturally."

"You like sports?"

"I played a little football."

"So your friend told me. You are aware that the United States is still neutral in this conflict? You are fully aware of that?"

"Yes. But everyone says we won't—"

"Why do you want to fly for France?"

"I don't really know. My friend Kiffin—"

"Very good." Dr. Gros plucked the stethoscope from his ears, moved quickly to his desk and handed Toby a sheaf of papers. "Take these papers to the Bureau de Recrutment at the Invalides in the morning. They are already signed. One of the papers is your physical examination report."

"Is that all there is to it?"

"You look healthy to me. *Bon chance.*"

"That means good luck, right?"

"Clever lad. On your way now."

Toby was awakened the next morning by a rough shaking. He opened his eyes wide enough to see Kiffin standing over him fully dressed, even to his kepi. "Rouse out, slob, it's your big morning."

Toby eyed the window of the tiny room and after a moment remembered they were in the cheapest hotel they could find. He couldn't recall the name of it.

"It's still dark." He closed his eyes and fell back on the cot. At least there were two cots. The thought of sleeping with another person was unique to Toby. It had never crossed his mind until they had so much trouble finding shelter. Paris was jammed with soldiers and refugees from all over Europe. Every room everywhere was armed, and troops lucky enough to be in the city for *"trois jours de permission"* were obliged to sleep on floors.

"I have a hangover," Toby groaned. They had spent hours in a Montparnasse café called Le Dome (at least he could remember that), and he was also now reminded that they had consumed three liters of wine. No one drank in Nebraska except Catholics at communion, Toby had protested, but Kiffin had kept on pouring while he explained that the water in France wasn't fit for human consumption. "Look around you," he said, "do you see anyone drinking water?"

Toby also barely recalled chewing on an inadequate sausage and a barber pole of bread which tasted like nothing like the Nebraska variety.

He said softly, "I'm going to die."

Kiffin yanked the pouf off his cot. "This is reveille. The French get up early and go to bed late. God only knows when they sleep."

Toby rose slowly and padded around the room in his long underwear, trying to get his bearings. "Where the hell's my suitcase?"

"Under your bunk." Kiffin smiled shyly. "You insisted on hiding it there so the women wouldn't steal everything you had."

"What women?"

"The ones we were with last night. I liked yours better than mine . . . especially the way she sang 'Roses of Picardy.' "

"Bull. I don't remember any women."

"How could you forget Yvette? You promised to marry her. You should have seen yourself . . . the old French boulevardier."

"When are you going to give up lying? How is *your* head?"

"Splendid. It's a beautiful morning." Kiffin went to the window and looked down at the street. A heavy rain was bouncing off the cobbles. "It's a bit damp. Your mother would want you to wear your rubbers. On second thought, don't. The French army will furnish you with a good pair of boots. You get them well soaked right through, don't take them off for three days and they may fit."

Toby was at the wash bowl sloshing water on his face. He sputtered a great deal and his response was somewhat garbled. "I don't think. . . . maybe I better. . . . what's the next ship back to Nebraska?"

"They don't run boats to Nebraska. How can you be homesick? You just got here."

"Something tells me this is not going to be a Saturday afternoon matinee. I think I'll change my mind."

Changing Toby's mind might have been easy for him, but changing Kiffin's was a different matter. Barely two hours after Toby had eventually found his razor and shaved the stubble on his face in the hotel's chill water he became Second Class Private Toby Bryant in La Legion Etrangére. He was nineteen years old.

Like Kiffin, Toby had sworn allegiance to the Legion along with a mixed bag of whites, blacks, and Orientals, all of whom were bound for infantry units. No one asked him if he could fly. It made little difference since he would not have understood the question. No one then available in the vast echoing hall at the Invalides spoke a word of English. Until they handed him a heavy blue great coat, baggy red trousers, a sash to go around his waist, and a pair of heavy brodequins for his feet Toby was not sure whether he had committed himself to anything, although Kiffin now assured him he was a *soldat de deuxième classe*.

Kiffin made a slow circle around Toby, judging him as he might a fashion model. Once he reached out and tugged gently at the back of his tunic. "Not a bad fit, considering. Now that you look presentable, we'll go out on the town."

"Oh God, not again. Don't you ever get hangovers?"

"Never."

And it was true, Toby remembered. Kiffin was one of those people whose chemistry denied them the remorse of hangovers.

"What you need is a stiff brandy," Kiffin said. "I know a small bistro—"

"Please . . . ." Toby closed his red-rimmed eyes.

"We'll have a snort, then go see the sights. . . . maybe take in a show. For men in uniform some are almost free."

"Please, I just want to find a place to lie down."

"With your charm and my looks and what's left of your money I'm sure that can be arranged."

"I'm almost broke."

"Just think, when you get your pilot license you'll be made a corporal. And after thirty hours over the front the French will be paying you fifteen dollars a month."

Christ XI.

There were several times during the next two weeks when Toby could have throttled Kiffin—if he could have found him. He was a very disillusioned man with all of his gloomy fears confirmed. Three other young Americans had joined the Legion for the same purposes and were also becoming extremely restless. There was Ken Littauer and Charles Dolan, both from the Midwest, and Bill Wellman, a handsome and feisty Bostonian. It was Wellman who asked Toby, "Where the hell is this friend of yours Kiffin . . . the guy who said he could do so much? Does he get a bounty for every addled head he sucks into this outfit?"

Once they had reported for duty at Buc, where a battalion of Legionnaires were quartered, they began to understand that they were at the absolute bottom of the French military manure pile. The food which the French called "monkey" was scant and terrible, and the raw, red pinard which was issued in lieu of water was worse. Their fellow Legionnaires were an assortment of thugs, criminal hard-cases, and cunning Algerians. The Americans soon discovered that all of them were thieves, constantly stealing from each other and then re-stealing to regain their few bits of personal property. As the noble ideals of the Americans soured rapidly they began to realize that they had joined the Legion with the wide-eyed innocence of children. Their new comrades were utterly devoted to their own survival, and to maintain that status they were quite as willing to kill each other as in the future they might a German. They knew no loyalty except to the Legion, recognized no authority except the military caste system which Toby found to be personified behind the sergeant stripes of one Armond Delacroix, a Corsican with a monumental hatred for new recruits, particularly those who were not of Corsican, or at least of French, extraction. He spent the majority of his day berating Toby, Littauer, Dolan, and Wellman as American pigs directly related to even lower varieties of animal life. He commented at the top of his lungs on the role of their mothers in society, the shape of their noses, their eyes, the color of their balls, their habit of fellatio, their devious reasons for seeking the protection of the Legion and the certainty of their betraying it, their uselessness inherited from their incestuous sodomizing fathers, and the loathsome diseases carried by their sisters and any other females they had ever known.

Fortunately these diatribes were delivered in Corsican-French and were not understood by any of the Americans. They did, however, gather the impression that their voluntary service to France was anything but valued except for the task at hand, which was the digging of an enormous drainage ditch parallel to the perimeter of the aerodrome. Their only view of aeroplanes either flying or squatting in the apparently universal mud was from afar.

What the Americans did not know was that Kiffin Draper had escaped a similar ordeal. He could and did bargain with the French because he already knew how to fly.

In a desperate attempt to maintain their senses the Americans gathered for talk whenever they could lay down their picks and shovels. Like all recent exiles they spoke mostly of home and their own folly in leaving it. Littauer speculated on his literary ambitions, and Wellman regaled them with tales of those Boston misadventures which had made it advisable for him to leave home and disappear as far over the horizon as he could manage. "Do you really think your friend Kiffin can do anything about our situation?" Wellman asked. "He's only a corporal."

"I don't know."

"Does he even know our ass is in his hands? The way it looks to me this outfit could be sent off to the front any minute."

Littauer said that he was becoming increasingly nervous with the passing of every day, and they all agreed that the infantry, regardless of their identity, usually ended their marching in a trench.

Now, in their peculiar isolation, actual battle seemed a rapidly approaching threat. The Americans had volunteered to fight, but if they had to die they wanted it to be in their own style, and the bloody struggle at Verdun where other units of the Legion were experiencing shocking losses was exactly what they had hoped to avoid. Rumors multiplied with every hour until their departure for Verdun seemed likely within a few days. Fort Douaumont was said to have been lost after a frightening toll of the defenders. General Pétain had been fired and his command taken by General Nivelle.

As tales of the tragic events at Verdun finally filtered

through to Buc, Sergeant Delacroix seemed all the more determined that his charges would become fighting infantrymen. In addition to their ditch-digging he required all formation drills to be done at the double. He instituted long route marches starting at all hours of the day and night—"to make you like steel," he yelled. As a result his company moved as if drugged, and in their exhaustion they discussed open mutiny, which at least would bring a merciful end to all of them.

The consensus in the ranks was that Sergeant Delacroix could not wait to get to Verdun, where he would undoubtedly add to the medals on his chest if he survived. The little group of Americans became ever more resentful; they were by now convinced that they had been tricked and that the French had no intention of transferring them to the Air Service.

Wellman, particularly incensed, was not a man to take any offense lightly. "I almost hope they do send us to Verdun," he growled. "The first sonofabitch I'm going to shoot will be Delacroix."

At last Kiffin did appear one morning, trailing in the company of a young lieutenant who spoke only French. Serving as an interpreter, Kiffin identified the four Americans for whom they had brought transfer papers. Sergeant Delacroix scrutinized the papers as if he suspected some hidden trickery and finally scratched his signature with a grubby hand. He sent the Americans off with a fervently expressed wish that they would all kill themselves for the glory of France, turned his back, and marched away.

The four Americans were escorted through the mud to the other side of the aerodrome where to their profound relief they began a new kind of life.

Pilot training at Buc was founded on the old Blériot system which led to frequent moments of comic relief and occasional tragic consequences. The French aero-philosophy was unique. Had Toby been a Frenchman he would have been sent straightaway to the trenches because that was where they believed the strong belonged. Those of weaker physique, as already proved at the front by the indomitable Guynemeyer, were best off in the Air Service.

Now with Kiffin standing at a distance and critiquing, Toby soon found himself "driving" a "Penguin." It was an aptly named contraption with such short wings it could not actually leave the ground, but its little three-cylinder engine did enable it to race up and down the field at high speed. After only a few minutes Toby discovered, as had all others who had tried to make a "Penguin" behave, that the problem was keeping it going in a straight line. Once up to speed it became extremely unstable and most neophytes found themselves engaged in a sort of high speed aeronautical rodeo.

On his first day at piloting a Penguin Toby terminated his third run across the aerodrome by diving into the very ditch he had helped dig for Sergeant Delacroix. Damage to the machine was superficial but the ditch was full of muddy water which had already passed through the vicinity of Buc's latrines. Toby's almost perpetual good nature was strained. Also stained.

When at last Toby was able to race the Penguin from one end of the enormous flat field to the other end without colliding with another student in an identical machine or otherwise humiliating himself, Kiffin announced that he could graduate to Rouleurs. It was a tremendous advance and Toby was grateful that he was the only American of the four who had been assigned to an English speaking instructor. The others had not fared nearly as well, except for Dolan, who was pronounced a natural by Leonid Strasky, a Polish instructor in the French Air Service. Both Wellman and Littauer had badly damaged their Penguins and were considered difficult students.

Toby asked Kiffin how it was that out of some ten instructors at Buc he had arranged to tutor his old friend from Nebraska.

Kiffin smiled in the way of a connoisseur who had just tasted a noble wine.

"Our esteemed commanding officer is a religious man and a good family man," he said solemnly. "Unfortunately, he's also one of the better patrons of Madame Georgette's."

"Who's Madame Georgette?"

"She runs the second best whorehouse in Paris. I happened to drop in there to improve my French the night before your ship arrived. Lo and behold, who should I encounter—?"

"You mean . . .?"

"None other." Kiffin shrugged his shoulders and spread his hands wide. *"Voila . . ."*

The Rouleur was a real flying machine, although of very

limited performance. Like the Penguin it was a monoplane assembly of bamboo, various woods, wire, and stretched linen. It was powered by a twenty horsepower Anzani engine which was able to hoist it off the ground to heights of ten or twelve feet. The action was called a Decollet.

The pilot of a Rouleur sat on a small wicker seat with half his body projecting above the wing itself. As some protection against the slipstream and the considerable likelihood of a crash, he was provided with a long leather coat, goggles, and a leather helmet reinforced with steel rods which presumably would prevent severe brain concussion.

The Rouleur was a recalcitrant machine with a decidedly maverick ancestry and most students soon learned to respect its unpredictable ways. Unless the pilot was very much on the alert it could complete a "cheval de Bois" or ground loop almost before the student knew what had happened. Toby's attention was distracted just long enough one afternoon for his Rouleur to get away from him. On landing, it caught the tip of the left wing, broke it backward and stood on its nose. The action left Toby hanging ignominiously at a ninety-degree angle to the ground.

Kiffin came running to the wreckage and seeing Toby was unhurt added to his embarrassment. "*You,*" he shouted, "are in the wrong Air Service! The Kaiser sends his congratulations along with an Iron Cross."

Toby looked down at him in disgust. "What the hell do they expect for ten dollars a month?"

The Blériot training plane was not very much different from the one in which the famous French aeronaut had flown the English Channel in 1909. It was powered by a fifty horsepower Gnome Rotary engine. There were no ailerons so turns were made by a coordinated use of the rudder and warping the wings.

Toby could barely squeeze his bulk into the little cockpit and he projected so far above the wing and fuselage that he seemed to be straddling the machine. His fellow students said it looked like he had caught something in his foot. All of the accoutrements of the Legion had been disposed of since he had been transferred to the Air Service and had become an *élevé*. Now, like Kiffin, he wore blue-gray breeches and leather puttees, a tunic with huge side pockets, and a light gray scarf. A wide leather belt was secured around his middle by a brass buckle.

After his capricious adventure with the Rouleur Toby found the Blériot relatively easy to fly—which was exactly the goal the French had hoped for when they designed the program. He began with very short hops around the aerodrome, all under Kiffin's watchful eyes. He rarely exceeded a height of thirty meters, a measurement he still translated mentally as about 100 feet. After three days of circuits without disaster Kiffin told him he must climb to 2800 feet, then spiral down and land within a 200-foot circle which had been outlined in the center of the field. Next he was to climb back up to the same altitude and make a dive at the field until the wheels of the Blériot almost touched the ground, then climb away again. The maneuver was called a *piqué* and although Toby swore it was the quickest way for a man to freeze solid he did admit that for the first time he knew a tremendous exhilaration. Kiffin was obliged to warn him repeatedly about the steepness of his *piqués* . . . "The Blériot is not a fighter. Wait until we get to Nieuports before you try tearing the wings off. Just keep on the way you're doing and I'll be stuck with sending your effects back to Nebraska."

Toby did modify his *piqués* because he was anxious to catch up with Kiffin, who had at last been assigned to Nieuport training at a nearby aerodrome. Yet before Toby could be breveted as even a Blériot pilot he was required to maintain an altitude of at least 6800 feet for one hour, which on chill mornings with a clammy mist hanging in the valleys proved to be more of a test of the pilot's resistance to physical torture than a demonstration of his aeronautical skill. Swaddled in everything he owned or could borrow Toby made a successful ascent and descent and was so stiff with cold when the ordeal was over he could barely climb out of the Blériot.

Finally Toby was required to make two *lignes droites* and two triangles, which consisted of a flight from Buc to Chateauroux and back, then to Issodun and return to Charost, then Charost, Florent, Bonnges, and return. The first flyable day of an unusually wretched late April Toby flew and navigated to Chateauroux and back without difficulty. Three days passed until he was able to go aloft again into very dubious weather. Still, it was the first of May—a time when the weather was *supposed* to be improving whether it was or not.

They were flying at the front, the commandant declared, and being shot at as well, so why should his students be babied? He further excused himself from accusations of over-optimism by reminding his staff that the actual fighting front was devouring available pilots at an alarming rate and replacements were needed.

Toby took off bound for Florent just after scheduled sunrise, a spectacle which remained invisible from the ground. He flew an easterly course, hoping to find a higher ceiling in that direction. He soon began to regret his decision. The cloud level kept him barely above the hedgerows for the first twenty minutes. Then unscheduled and unwelcome things began to happen—one by one, a little at a time yet accumulating with ever-increasing rapidity.

The cloud ceiling sank lower rather than lifting. Now what little horizon had been visible had disappeared and was replaced by chunky coffin-gray clouds punching down into the valleys and treetops, and dark smudgings of rain squalls were developing in every direction. Looking down at a village Toby saw a tri-color whipping in a strong wind and noted that he was drifting sideways almost as fast as he was progressing ahead. It was a new experience for him and he knew he must reckon with the wind in his navigation.

The wind brought another problem. It made for turbulent air, and the frail Blériot became difficult to control. Toby considered landing it in one of the open fields, but the vision of Kiffin's disapproval and the certainty of his finding an Iron Cross somewhere and presenting it if he so much as scratched the Blériot made him carry on. Another ten minutes passed and still there was no sign of Florent. Or had he passed it? The timing was about right and it should be right here . . . somewhere.

He looked back over his shoulder. There was no retreat. The cloud level was right on top of the trees. Ahead? Slightly better, but far from reassuring. Kiffin, why the hell did you ever get me into this?

At last a town. It appeared to be jammed with French troops on the march behind a long horse-drawn wagon train that stretched from one end of the town to the other. As Toby circled the town he contemplated *piquéing* and yelling for help from one of the officers he saw on horseback. For a moment he rehearsed the phrase in his special brand of

French. "What's the name of this town." If he could identify it maybe he could match it up with something else and find Florent. And by God if he ever got there he would stay there for the rest of this day. Maybe forever.

He ran his gloved finger along the map strapped to his knee trying to identify the road through the town, but in the few brief glances he could allow himself he could find nothing that corresponded with what he was observing.

He continued to circle until he was reminded that diving on any troops, regardless of nationality, was not recommended. At Buc it was said that *all* troops were nervous about airplanes diving on them and at least one man in the horde would certainly take it on himself to bring down a fat pigeon.

Suddenly Toby was flying in rain and almost immediately his goggles became nearly opaque. He wiped at them frantically and still his visibility did not improve. Vapor covered the inside of the glasses. Almost blind, he pushed the goggles up on his helmet and exposed his eyes to the painful stinging of the rain. He held his gloved hand across his eyes trying to see through a narrow separation of his fingers.

Where the hell was the town? In seconds it had vanished. Where were the troops? There was a railroad bridge and a stream below his left wing. He circled, trying to identify a mix of railroad and stream on the sopping wet map. Still nothing matched. By his watch he had now been aloft almost two hours. His fuel was not going to last all morning.

Hallelujah! Here was the town again . . . or at least some town. Where were the troops? He thought it must be a different town . . . the main road circled around this town rather than cutting right through it. And there were no troops.

Turn left? Turn right? Why this queasy feeling in his bowels?

He ducked down as far as he could, trying to find the new town on the map that he was ready to swear must have been drawn for a different country.

It was while he had his head down that he felt a sharp jolt followed by a wild shuddering throughout the Blériot. He looked up to see his left wing bent back almost twenty degrees with what looked like the cross of a church spire projecting from it.

The Blériot skewed to the left at the instant Toby's brain could accept that he had actually collided with a church.

There it was just off to his left, the top of the spire sheared off. Like a bad dream.

The amount of time between the actual collision and the fluttering descent at a steep angle toward the town square seemed endless. He wrestled with the controls, tried to move the rudder bar. Nothing that was being done had any effect on the broken Blériot which twisted downward with the engine still running and apparently trying to roll over on its back.

He reached for the small valve that cut off the fuel. There was eons of time and while the wet cobbles of the square and the fountain in the middle were moving upward at such a languid pace, he knew a strange sense of relief. Dying was not so fearsome after all. Adieu, as Kiffin would say. So much time . . . oh, so much time. What should have taken fifteen seconds was apparently taking thirty minutes, more . . .

He closed his eyes just before the left wing hit the fountain. He heard a rasping sound, then a series of hard screechings as wood splintered and tore itself apart. While he was still marveling at how remarkably slow everything was happening he was thrown violently against the side of the cockpit. Even then he had time to reflect that the blow to his shoulders and ribs was no worse than a football block.

And then suddenly he was lying on his side with his face on the wet cobbles and the rest of his body hidden beneath a crazy pile of wood and fabric. Soon there was no other sound except the rain drumming on the stretched linen and on the cobbles, and now what seemed several hours after he had hit the church spire he returned to his body and grunted and said aloud, "Aw . . . shit . . .!" allowing his voice to linger long on the last word.

He lay perfectly still. After a moment he wondered if he had the nerve to inquire what damage the hidden part of his body might have suffered. He was reasonably certain that he felt no pain and yet considering the circumstances that was, of course, impossible. He looked about for blood and found none and realized that the cobble which supported his left cheek was unpleasantly cold. Perhaps he was not feeling anything from the waist down because his legs were paralyzed? As visions of wheelchair life floated through his mental confusion he tried to wiggle his toes and found them obedient. Could he dare hope for the impossible?

As he gingerly raised one arm he heard a sharp clacking of wooden shoes approaching and wondered if he had somehow landed in Holland. But then he remembered that the French peasants also wore wooden clogs, and now the owners of the footwear were yelling at each other . . . in French. Welcome, he thought. I'm very damn tired . . ."

He tried moving the other arm, found it normal. He flexed his fingers, saw them do as they were told to do. Maybe, he thought, he was not quite dead after all.

His limited vista from cobble level was soon solid with clogs, hobnailed shoes, boots and ordinary house slippers. The rain speckled down on his face and trickled from his nose down into the darkness below his chin. He knew people were tearing at the wreckage. From within the roughly formed cave of the wreckage it sounded like his rescuers were having a terrible argument and there were moments when there was no activity at all. Were they afraid they might be too hasty and injure the lower half of his body? Or could they see it from outside and were commenting on the gore?

Gradually, piece by piece, the townspeople uncovered him, then stood in the rain looking down at him, gesticulating and asking questions he could not understand. When he was free he carefully moved one leg and then the other. He muttered a brief thanks to God and pushed himself up on his elbows. The crowd cheered.

He placed his hands behind him and pushed the upper half of his body to the vertical and immediately was seized from both sides and hauled to his feet. Two bronzed elderly men with huge moustaches held him erect for a moment, then allowed him to stand unaided. *"Formidable,"* they said.

Toby's reception in the small town of St. Boniface was as unexpected as his arrival. He accepted several handshakes and a few embraces from the ever-growing crowd now gathered around the broken fountain. It had featured a concrete representation of some long forgotten saint who had now been decapitated, and two young women were trying to fit the head back in place when a man with one arm and a short fence of medals across his chest pushed his way through the crowd. He was short, stocky, and his remaining hand was large enough to accommodate both a brimming glass of brandy and the handle of an umbrella. He handed the glass to Toby, held the umbrella over his head and commanded him to drink. Toby gathered he was the mayor, and when the conflagration from the terrible brandy left his throat he tried to convey to him that his squadron at Buc should be notified of his whereabouts.

Toby was not encouraged by the strange response. The mayor became extremely voluble, punching with the umbrella handle at the area of his coat where his arm should have been, gesticulating at the church where the spire should have been, and at the statue where the head should have been. Toby gathered that he was not happy.

Indeed, it soon became evident that the townspeople were of similar mind, an attitude that became increasingly hostile when they discovered the severe limitations of his French. For the life of him Toby could not remember how to say he was sorry for the damage he had done. He saw more scowls than smiles, nor was the atmosphere lightened by the fact that the whole assembly of people were clothed almost entirely in black. Their common expression of belligerence made him wonder if the dream he had seemed to enter the instant he knew he was going to die was on-going. They moved about in the rain, glum figures in black, muttering dourly about the possible curse that had come their way.

At last a priest arrived, an ancient man whose dank cassock made him smell even in the cleansing rain. He was nearly toothless, which made his halting English all the more difficult to understand, but Toby did learn that there were no gendarmes in the town, due to the war, or he would have undoubtedly been thrown in the local jail. It seemed the townspeople did not believe he was an American as he claimed— and therefore he must be a German spy.

"But my uniform and the markings on the plane are French—"

"*La guerre, monsieur*. People are crazy. The mayor knows you are *Americaine* because he has been at the Marne and has heard of such things, but the people do not believe a man would come so far to die."

"Neither do I," Toby said. "This isn't something I do every day," he added, and was at once disappointed that he had not drawn even a hint of a smile from the priest.

Now the crowd was tearing at the wreckage, pulling off bits of fractured wood and torn canvas as souvenirs. Toby asked the priest to telephone his escadrille and was astounded at his reply. First, the priest explained, some agreement must be reached to pay for the damage to the church and the fountain. Certainly they could not be left as they were, monsieur? Was it not obvious, monsieur, that the holy cross itself had been forcibly removed and therefore the hand of Satan must be involved? In fact, monsieur, it was only because of the broad-mindedness of the townsfolk and their patience not to say their magnificent tolerance, that they did not seem to hold him personally responsible for the work of the Devil. *Voila.* Some reparations were certainly in order, and it would be advisable if monsieur would make immediate compensation for both steeple and fountain in which event he might see a remarkable change in the demeanor of the citizens.

Three hours later, held hostage in the town's blacksmithy, Toby was still trying to convince the mayor and a group of his more curious supporters that he was not in a position to dictate settlement terms for the French Air Service. He could not be sure if the continued lack of understanding was due solely to the priest's translations or simply the greed of his captors.

At least it was an easy arrest. They had given him cheese and bread and more wine than he needed on top of his brandy. He was developing a certain affection for his hosts and even admiration when he realized that their ire was not directed at him personally; indeed several had come forward and anxiously expressed their regard for Americans in general and inquired if they were all of such formidable physical dimensions. The more wine he accepted the more clearly he understood that the target of their resentment was the French government, which had denied them before and would again unless they took resolute action.

By noon, at which hour one lieutenant and Corporal Kiffin Draper arrived, Toby staggered toward them with open arms and welcomed them to meet the best damned group of people in the world . . .

"You're drunk," Kiffin said, retreating from his embrace.

"You're under arrest," the lieutenant added.

"Bullshit," Toby said grabbing the lieutenant by the ears. "Come on, have a drink. We're celebrating being alive."

The priest, who had been dutifully translating every remark, was feeling extraordinarily mellow himself by this time and once the mayor and his friends understood the exchange they cheered with gusto.

The lieutenant was a short man with a thin waxed moustache, a uniform that was too big for him and a confusion about the purpose of his mission. He was an officer from the Personnel Registration Bureau, a euphemism for that special department of the French Air Service charged with recording the physical ailments of the troops and in the event of their deaths from whatever cause making arrangements for the disposition of their remains. The report which had come through to Buc had been fuzzy in detail, specifying only that a flying machine had crashed at St. Boniface and the pilot was "probably deceased." The commandant had sent Kiffin along out of personal interest in his welfare. If his student had crashed because of some oversight in Kiffin's instruction, then as first on the scene he would have an opportunity to place the blame on something else.

The mayor, the priest, and those members of the community still sober enough to understand that the new military arrivals were powerless to offer them retribution were at first chagrined and finally fatalistic. After the application of more wine to their injured feelings, they agreed to Toby's release in exchange for what was left of the Blériot. It was the consensus that the engine itself must have some value . . .

Just before dark of what had been a very long day the three were given a boisterous send-off in the lieutenant's truck. He insisted on driving even though Kiffin protested that he was in a non-operational status. The lieutenant ordered silence. It was his truck and he was going to do the steering. Kiffin could shift the gears if it pleased him. There followed an argument about the proper direction to turn for Buc, which resulted in some twelve different finger-pointings by their teary-eyed hosts.

As they careened through the town square and passed the wreckage of the Blériot, Toby gave it a little salute and laying his head on Kiffin's shoulder, went quickly to sleep.

There were rumors to the effect that the reason Toby and Kiffin were both transferred to Le Plessis-Belleville soon after the events at St. Boniface was that the commandant of the training center at Buc would have tried anything short of treason to get rid of them. Somehow, perhaps for reasons that will never be known, he persuaded his counterpart at Le Plessis-Belleville that he should admit two outstanding Americans somewhat prematurely to training in the Nieuports of his command.

And so on the seventh of May, 1916, Private Toby Bryant and Corporal Kiffin Draper said farewell to their envious comrades at Buc and proceeded via train to their new assignment. They were overjoyed, and Kiffin, who had the advantage of a few hours in a Nieuport, spent much of the journey coaching Toby on their special characteristics. They also spoke of the rumors coming out of Verdun and wondered if the battle would be over before they could get into it. And they spoke of their own country, wondering if it would ever join in the war—and what would happen then? Would they be transferred out of the French Service?

Kiffin, who now spoke at least a simplistic and badly garbled French, was adamant about staying where he was.

"In fact I might live here after the war," he said.

Toby was far from as enthusiastic. He could barely make his basic needs known in French and was having trouble with the food. While Kiffin reveled in every opportunity to try new French dishes or drinks, Toby said he was just a meat and potatoes boy and would give a month's pay for ten ears of Nebraska corn.

At Le Plessis-Belleville they stayed at the Hotel Bonne Recontre, a scruffy little inn inhabited by voracious mice and snarling countrywomen without a gram of mercy or illusion remaining in their souls. Since there were no official mess facilities they ate mainly at the "Café des Avions" or at the Hotel Metro, where a buxom Jeannette was a very available waitress. Here were also gathered such pilots as Norman Prince, Bill Thaw, and Bert Hall, who were trying to form something they had hoped to call the *Escadrille Americaine*. They were having trouble obtaining official clearance for the name. German diplomats still in Washington protested that Americans flying for France represented a gross violation of neutrality. To save face for the United States the French promptly assimilated the unit as simply N124, the *"N"* signifying "Nieuport."

Kiffin and Toby were not ready for assignment to an operational unit. They began their schooling in "flat winged" Nieuports which were unsuitable at the front because of their poor climbing ability. The later model Nieuports had cambered wings and were able to give a much better account of themselves. Even so, both Toby and Kiffin began to improve their *glissades,* their *sur l'ailes, vrilles,* and *spiral verticales.* The French weather had turned benign, they lived their task day and night and made such rapid improvement that after two weeks they were sent off to the combat flying school at Pau.

"Sometimes," Kiffin said as they boarded yet another crowded train, "I feel like we're just tourists, and sometimes I wonder if they're just hurrying us up because so many are falling down." They were thinking of Verdun which had become an ogre in everyone's lives, but they were young and had never seen viscous mixtures of brains, intestines, and bones blotching their view, and so could still be certain that such things could not happen to them.

The flying course at Pau was also given in Nieuports and included more advanced aerobatics and some training in combat tactics given by pilots fresh from the front. Suddenly now, more of the reality of their new lives faced them. They realized that the peculiar euphoria of flight which had thus far so enraptured them was now about to become a hard business of kill or be killed. The instructors were glum men given to speaking in curt sentences, as if they were being imposed upon by the questionings of handicapped children. Kiffin and Toby found it was difficult to tell whether they were happy to be away from actual combat or resentful because they had been ordered back to relative safety. Their advice was simple if, as they often hinted, the execution was difficult.

"Sometimes it's a beautiful day over the front . . . beautiful clouds, beautiful sun, smooth air. Life is very wonderful. Do not be deceived. You are really in a dark alley and you are surrounded by thugs who can leap out at you in seconds. Do not develop the fancy that you are the world's greatest pilot. Those who have wear a cross on their nose. You must get the jump on the Bosche before he realizes you're there. Otherwise your chances of being murdered are at best . . . fifty-fifty."

Once their instructional duties were accomplished for the day the instructors withdrew to form little groups by themselves and did not seem to welcome outsiders.

An exception was the fabled Didier Masson, an American instructor with a French heritage. He was an older man who had been flying continuously since 1909 and had, as late as 1913, been Chief of the Air Service in the army of Mexico's General Obregon. "I was the entire Air Force of the nation," he joked, "and my aeroplane was the only one."

No one knew Didier Masson's actual age—in fact he was thought of as ageless. He had joined the French more than a year earlier and had served at the front flying Caudrons with Squadron 18. Later, after taking pursuit training, he flew with N68, a Nieuport squadron. He took an immediate liking to Toby and Kiffin and said that he would take them under his wing . . . "Do not be discouraged by all you hear. The Bosche is a good fighter. . . . true. But I have seen too many of our boys begin a sortie with the idea they might not be coming back. When that happens, he usually proves himself correct. Remember, the Bosche is scared too. You have to be just a little less scared."

Masson proved to be such an inspiration that within two weeks both Toby and Kiffin were notified they were being sent back to Le Plessis-Belleville for disposition to the *Groupe des Divisions d' Entrainement*.

"They really are in a hurry," Kiffin said as Masson congratulated them. Assignment to the *Groupe* meant an almost immediate reassignment to a squadron at the front, and meanwhile they would have a chance to fly some actual service machines. Masson, a dedicated gourmet and a magician at promoting feasts from scraps, arranged a farewell party at the Hotel Tinco. It was not only a sumptuous banquet far exceeding the prevailing governmental rations, but fine champagne flowed until dawn. Throughout, the indomitable Masson maintained his aplomb. During one of the many toasts he announced "This is not really my party. I'm merely the *chef de popote*. The money which created this miracle amid the gastronomical gloom of our times was furnished by a man whose generosity toward all American volunteers has often made the difference between life on one franc twenty five per day and enjoying life as long as we have it. Let's raise our glasses to William K. Vanderbilt of Paris and New York!"

Among the Americans who raised their glasses was Raoul Lufbery, who was already an ace, and Bill Thaw, a hearty man who had brought along his pet lion cubs Whiskey and Soda for the occasion.

CHAPTER
3

The return to Le Plessis-Belleville was a bitter disappointment to both Kiffin and Toby, if only because they were reminded so abruptly that they were only a pair of numbers subject to the appetite of a vast French military machine that once begun chewing could not be satisfied. Although they had vowed to stay together throughout their service, even Kiffin's persuasive pleas failed to halt the jaws of bureaucracy responsible for their destinies.

Kiffin was assigned to Escadrille N3 and dispatched almost immediately to a place called Marson not far from Verdun. To avoid being separated, Kiffin threatened to desert unless his orders were changed. Only Toby kept him from open mutiny, which under the weight of his own disappointment was all the more difficult. Whether his crash in the Blériot and his somewhat mediocre record during training had any effect on his assignment was impossible to discover; but instead of being sent off to a *chasse* squadron Toby was ordered to remain at Le Plessis-Belleville until such time as he had received sufficient instruction in Caudrons to qualify him for breveting to a Franco-Belgian squadron, C74.

It was not until he had been with Escadrille N3 for more than a week and had made his first uneventful sortie into the sky above the German positions near Verdun that Kiffin Draper took time to evaluate why he had been called to the front so quickly. Just before his arrival the skies over Verdun had been torn with almost constant encounters between the French and the Bosche. A single bad afternoon's flying with the Escadrille had resulted in the loss of four pilots and their aircraft. The Germans had finally flown away unharmed, and Captain Desmereaux, the commander of N3, a man who took every pilot in the Escadrille as his brother, was devastated.

While it was understood that he would eventually receive replacements, at the time of Desmereaux's demand for help the only available bodies included an American. There were just not four officially qualified pilots available at Le Plessis Belleville when his need became known. Had the requisition reached the supply source even a few days later Kiffin would undoubtedly have been sent off to Luxeuil, where he would have joined and flown with the likes of Norman Prince, Rockwell, Bert Hall, McConnell, Victor Chapman and Lufbery in N124.

Marson was one of the many airfields scattered within a thirty-mile area of Verdun, and the Escadrille had been operational during the full fury of the German attack. They were exhausted mentally and physically when Kiffin arrived along with three French pilot replacements sent straight up from Pau. The veterans greeted them with such enthusiasm as they could manage, given their expectation that the replacements were not likely to last very long. Desmereaux himself took them on their first sortie and saw to it that they stayed away from the dangerous areas. "We'll just have a look around this first time," he said, "to get you used to understanding that the Bosche are waiting for you and will not come to you. We have no choice but to go after them. So if you are so unfortunate as to be shot down behind their lines and survive your chances of getting back here are practically nil."

The various Escadrilles de Chasse in the vicinity of Verdun worked in relays, with one Escadrille always over the lines. A field wireless was supposed to report the presence of German airplanes, but by the time the information circulated through the command post and was given to the pilots before take-off the German formations had moved. And so it was almost always an eye-to-eye discovery, with the Germans in command of the situation.

Kiffin's Nieuport, which he promptly dubbed "Bessie" in honor of his hostess at Hammondsport, was one of the oldest in the escadrille. It had taken a beating at the hands of its original pilot, one Fresnay, a man of whom it was said, "He will never learn to fly." Even so Fresnay was extraordinarily courageous and defied the Germans at every opportunity. He overdid things one April morning by swooping down on a flock of the new *Albatros*. He got himself another victory (his ninth), but also a bad wound in his hip. He barely made it back to Marson and had to be carried from the Nieuport. Evidence of his copious bleeding still stained the fabric and seat, and the wings and fuselage were peppered with patches over the bullet holes Fresnay had acquired on his many sorties.

Like the others, Kiffin's inheritance was a model 11 Nieuport powered with an eighty horsepower Le Rhone rotary engine. It was supposed to be able to climb to 15,000 feet, but his comrades warned him he would be lucky to make 13,000 with a full tank of fuel and enough ammunition to give a decent account of himself. The Nieuport's armament was a single Lewis gun mounted on top of the upper wing and firing over the propeller arc. The gun was fed by a drum holding ninety-seven rounds, all of which could be fired in five seconds, providing there were no jams. This particular gun was old and worn from so many rounds passing through the barrel. Its reliability was chancy and there were no available replacements. Very shortly, the armament people were insisting, all the Lewis guns would be replaced by a new type with an interrupter gun that could fire through the propeller arc as the Germans had been doing for some time. Also, reloading during combat was a clumsy and dangerous process. While still trying to escape or pursue the enemy a pilot had to raise himself in the cockpit and pull down the gun on its arced track until it was vertical. Then, fighting against the slip-stream, he had to fit the drum over the spindle and return the gun to its position. Some said that more pilots had been killed trying to reload their Lewis guns than at any other moment in battle.

On his first day over the lines, flying in formation off Desmereaux's wing, Kiffin repeated his leader's action by firing four shots to make sure his gun was working properly. He longed for a true target, but the sky was empty as the Nieuports climbed and slid between the bulbous clouds of May like so many fingerlings in a gigantic aquarium.

The escadrille stayed aloft for an hour and a half before Desmereaux led them home. When they had landed he called the neophytes to join him over coffee in the heavy tarpaulin tent which served as their mess. There was a bemused smile on his face when he regarded the four young men who had seated themselves on the opposite side of the table. Kiffin saw him wipe at his eyes and thought that although Desmereaux was about his own age he was already an old man—he moved so slowly, his eyes seemed as exhausted as his body, and his speech was so halting that Kiffin had no trouble understanding his French. *"Alors,"* he said, "you have now been over the lines. What did you see?"

There was silence for a moment, then La Frenier, who had just turned eighteen and was almost pathetically eager to prove himself, said, "I saw some flak . . . way down—"

"What color was it?"

"Black."

"And what did that tell you?"

La Frenier shrugged his shoulders.

"What do they teach you at Pau these days? Only to be the dashing aviator and fly the machine? And how to tie your scarf?" Desmereaux's voice like his eyes was exhausted, but somehow he continued to avoid bitterness. It seemed there was nothing in the world he had not seen and nothing would surprise him. "You should know that if the flak is black and is exploding in little groups the chances are it is German, which means that there are no Bosche in that area. It means that they were firing at one or more of our planes engaged in artillery spotting. Our flak is usually white and we put up a lot of it at the same time. If you see it, look for the Bosche."

Desmereaux turned to Ponnard, a handsome Alsatian. "And you, Ponnard. What did you see?"

Ponnard displayed his glistening white teeth in a smile that said he thought the questioning rather silly. "A lot of clouds, and my own breath . . . my God, it was cold."

"This is spring . . . therefore it is warm. If you last until next winter you will know what it is to be cold. Pinchot . . . ?"

Pinchot was a dour young man who was still brooding about the landing he had made in his Nieuport. He had neglected to flare, and the wheels of his Nieuport had met the ground at such speed and angle he was instantly propelled aloft again and had sat frozen at the controls some fifty feet in the air. Only then did the Nieuport quit flying and, as if in shame, lowered its nose and ricocheted twice more off the earth before it fractured its propeller. The empennage then slammed down and broke the wooden tail skid, thereby balancing the damage. Pinchot's rigger had joined with Pinchot's mechanic in contributing to his natural gloom by calling him a gorilla brain who should immediately be emasculated. It had not been a good morning for Pinchot, and now his melancholy eyes proclaimed an inner remorse even greater than what he otherwise exhibited. It was obvious now that he was obliged to make some response to his flight leader's question. "I saw," he said, "four Bosche very close to the ground. They were flying south along the trench line and I thought you would give the signal to go after them. They were camouflaged in a brown and green diamond pattern . . ."

"Aha!" Desmereaux said. "Were the rest of you blind? Did Pinchot alone have eyes for the enemy to be where you might least expect him to be?"

Desmereaux favored Pinchot with one of his conditional, weary smiles, and for a moment the youth who was nearly incapable of smiling thought it was not such a bad morning after all.

But his leader was not through with him. "Did you see anything else of interest?"

Pinchot shook his head. And then Kiffin offered in his labored French that he had seen several airplanes to the north, but they had been so far away he couldn't be sure if they were French, German, or English.

"Congratulations," Desmereaux said. "You at least had your eyes open. They were Bosche and they were waiting for us to jump into their trap. So it would have been if we had gone down for the bait. They looked far away to you, eh, Monsieur Draper? Your future is limited if you fail to realize they can be upon you very quickly. We do not deal with normal perspective when we are aloft. Distance becomes flexible. The visual relations you have all known since childhood must now be revised or most certainly you will die somewhere in this sector. What escapes the careless eye aloft, those empty-looking regions where you perceive only a bald sky, is an illusion you can no longer afford. Somewhere in your vicinity there is a man who wants to kill you. Be sure of it . . . You may fly sortie after sortie and nothing will be seen, nor will anything happen. When it is not so cold you will be lulled by the beauty of your surroundings, but pretty clouds and an azure sky do not make dying any easier than it is for the poilu in his trench. *Alors*. Keep your head on a swivel and your eyes on ball bearings. Never nurse an *idée fixe* for more than seconds. The lack of oxygen at our operational altitudes will incline your mind to sleep, but you must fight against it. Be the hunter, not the hunted. The life of a pilot de chasse is dependent on three things, of which, strangely, flying ability is not the most important. First . . . alertness. What is my situation in relation to the Bosche? Can I be surprised? Second, planning. You will be amazed how your ability to think clearly will evaporate when you spy the first line of tracers in your vicinity. When fear takes over you are left with animal intelligence, and it is not enough alone to get you out of trouble. If you are surprised just don't sit there and wait to die. *Never* leave your leader, who at least is supposed to have a plan. Have a secondary plan if he is knocked out. If you leave the flock and go off on your own, you are doing exactly what the Bosche wants. His whole staff will be on you like buzzards and you are starting your own funeral . . ."

Desmereaux lit a Caporal, sucked the pungent smoke deep into his lungs and sent a cloud of blue to press itself against the glaucous green of the tarpaulin. He coughed a brief melody, then smiled upon his listeners.

"Finally there is the chance for attack, which of course is what you are up there for. The Air Service is not paying you such a magnificent salary simply to go joy-riding . . ."

Desmereaux waited for the expected, obligatory reaction to his humor, and got it. And hopefully, he thought, he had injected enough fear into their innocent minds that they would be incapable of a more optimistic sound.

" . . . You are here to kill Germans, as many as possible. If you can successfully accomplish that assignment several times without major damage to yourself or your machine, our grateful government will reward you with medals and a pension. You will not achieve same unless you recognize that the Bosche are better-gunned and are flying faster and better machines than you are and that they know it. Your salvation is to hold your fire until you have a sure thing. Reloading in actual combat is an exercise in futility so you must get in much closer than your senses tell you is advisable. When it looks certain that you are going to collide, when you can see the fur around his goggles, then fire. It will only take a few rounds. With a great deal of luck you may have a chance at another Bosche. Do not be ashamed or even worried if you

re terrified up there. So is your antagonist. We all are. This
s not a nice experience.''

Desmereaux stood up and rubbed at his strawberry eyes.
Ie paused for a moment, wondering if there was anything
nportant he had forgotten today, or was everything he had
aid unimportant? Some, or perhaps even all of his listeners,
vere going to be killed very shortly and each one would die
ccording to rules that had not yet been made. Time and
vents would mix to spare one individual while condemning
ne other, and all the talking he might do was ultimately of no
onsequence. Who was to predict that a faulty motor next
veek would cause the cancellation of a sortie by Ponnard or
.a Frenier, and so spare their lives, or an errant shift of
unlight glistening on a propeller arc at four thousand meters
night mean the end of a Pinchot or a Draper? As long as their
leaths were not attributable to his neglect, well . . . Desmereaux
ould hope for no more. He had deliberately armored himself
gainst overconcern for his pilots; that way led to lunacy,
vhich he had seen and knew to be worse than callousness.
And was it not so that they were all volunteers . . .?

As he passed Kiffin he said softly, "Thank you for coming
o the party," but his French was so colloquial, his only
esponse was a look of bewilderment.

Kiffin did not think it at all extraordinary that he managed
o score five victories and win a Croix de Guerre within five
weeks of his arrival at Marson. As with everything else, he
applied himself to the business of combat with all his enor-
nous energy. He said that he simply did as Desmereaux had
old him and after each sortie tried to review the things he had
lone wrong. He realized very soon that while he got a certain
ieady exhilaration from the hunt itself, he found no satisfac-
ion in the result. His eyes nearly always told him that his
quarry could not possibly survive, but his mind kept wishing
hat he would. After his sixth victory, a lumbering "Roland
C'' two-seater with its pilots overly absorbed in some kind of
a reconnaissance mission, he was haunted for days afterward
by visions of the two helmeted heads rolling crazily as his
bullets tore through their bodies and felt an almost irresistible
need to know who they were. He made several attempts to
find out where they had crashed, but even though his victory
was confirmed by ground troops, it seemed the "Roland"

had either crashed behind the German lines or had been so consumed by fire there had been nothing left to recognize.

When Ponnard and La Frenier were both killed on the same morning sortie Kiffin learned for the first time that they had enjoyed less than his own twenty years, and he allowed himself to wonder, momentarily, how much longer he would survive. As if the loss of Ponnard and La Frenier were not enough, the clumsy Pinchot had gotten lost on a clear day, run out of fuel and made a disastrous landing in a turnip field. His Nieuport was destroyed and his back was broken so he would never walk normally again. Desmereaux had also been wounded in the leg and sent off to hospital with the hint that he would probably lose his limb.

Yet all of these calamities couldn't diminish Kiffin's appetite for combat flying. It was as if the more hazards and uncertainty, the more he was drawn to it. He raised his thumb to the crewmen who held the Nieuport's wing tips while he adjusted the engine's needle valve to achieve maximum revolutions. When they let go their grip, the little Nieuport charged forward no more than sixty meters before it leaped off the ground, and at once Kiffin Draper knew a powerful sense of exhaltation. The terror about which Desmereaux had so frequently reminded his neophytes never came to him. Instead, the chance that he *might* not survive only seemed to add to each sortie. From the instant Kiffin left the ground he knew the danger that was surrounding him, and while his pulse rate quickened so did his spirits soar right along with his Nieuport. His euphoria persisted throughout the sortie and until his feet touched earth again. Only if there had been actual combat did he take time to analyze what had happened and consider his personal reactions. *During* the mission he got so busy concentrating on a target he forgot everything else and his exhilaration gave way to an unswerving calculation.

Still, after-the-fact suspicions about himself began to come, one by one, and by his sixth victory he discovered that he could not drive a new doubt away in spite of his secret admission that it might be a signal of increasing weakness.

When one rainy afternoon Wellman dropped by N3, Kiffin was overjoyed to see another American. Since the weather made flying out of the question they stayed in the mess drinking a Bordeaux that Wellman described as "horse piss" and relaying their woes with their French masters.

"Tell me we're not murderers," Kiffin said to the feisty Bostonian, who had demonstrated great courage in combat but had somehow managed only one victory.

"You guys who have all the luck are always the first to complain," he said.

"You're avoiding me," Kiffin slurred.

"We have a license to hunt. General Nivelle says so."

"And who's he but a fat Frenchman?"

"It's Joffre who's fat, not Nivelle. He says you kill Germans, you kill Germans, and that's that."

"What if he said kill Eskimos? Do we take our Nieuports to the Arctic Circle and blaze away?"

"That's silly and you're drunk. The Eskimos have never done anything to him—"

"The Germans have never done anything to me either. Least of all the ones I killed."

"Know what's wrong with you, Kiffin? You're a godamned masochist because you do things you don't believe in. Why don't you put in for two days in Paris and get yourself screwed. Don't worry, this war's going to last forever, you won't miss a damn thing."

Kiffin did not apply for leave, although Pressmen, the new Escadrille Commander, would quickly have granted it. Long before joining the Air Service he had been a regular officer serving with the Legion and he had known those few strange men who simultaneously were inclined to become afflicted with guilt and wild determination. It was his belief that they soon brought about their own destruction. Pressmen was torn between ordering Kiffin to take a leave and his reluctance to manage without him—he had been appointed to the rank of adjutant and was a veteran of nearly six weeks over the front. N3, Pressmen thought, needed him badly—at least for now.

As if rising to that need Kiffin became ever more dedicated. If Pressmen was concerned about the deep circles under the American's eyes and his tendency to fall asleep at mess, he had no complaint about his aerial energies, which set a stunning example for every new pilot in the Escadrille. Something happened to Kiffin even before he actually began a sortie. He had lost so much weight his stilted walk seemed like a mechanical doll's, an impression that was reinforced when he was bundled to the chin in his teddy bear suit. He smoked incessantly and had developed the French habit of

holding the cigarette between his lips as he talked, causing it
to waggle up and down like a conductor's baton. Lately he
had developed an occasional tremor in his right hand, and
Pressmen noticed that whenever the quivering began he was
quick to conceal it with his other hand. He repeatedly declined offers of the leave Pressmen thought he needed, and
when threatened with grounding unless he went along, he
promised to leave right after his next victory. Pressmen could
not decide if he was crazy or just bloodthirsty; there was such
undeniable power in the gaunt young man, Pressmen found it
even inspired him.

That Kiffin was considered by even his most tolerant comrades as extremely eccentric was well-established, but now
his actions on the ground as well as some of the theories he
expounded confirmed their opinion that the Yankee who had
come so far to fight by their side was quite mad. He was
constantly trying to improve the flying qualities of his Nieuport,
which was by far the oldest and most abused in the Escadrille.
Now fabric patches covering the entries and exists of German
bullets speckled the wings and fuselage like a pox, and the
Gnome rotary engine had gone far past the customary six
hours between overhauls, throwing so much oil Kiffin's face
was always smudged a deep sepia when he landed. Everyone
in the Escadrille from the lowest mechanic to Pressmen himself urged Kiffin to accept a new Nieuport; he refused. His
Nieuport, his "Bessie," he explained when he felt like explaining anything, had saved his life several times; it had an
esprit of its own and he could not desert it just because of a
few surface blemishes. What his advisors failed to understand
was how the little Nieuport had become a target for Kiffin's
always ready affections. He chose a machine because there
were no women, and if there had been both available he
would have simply and easily doubled his output of ardor. In
spite of his fierce determination to take other lives and repeatedly risk his own, his true inamorata was, of course, life
itself. "Without at least some risk every day," he once said,
"we drop our guard and take the arrival of evening as
automatic. That in itself is a very big risk."

Kiffin said some other things which contributed to his
reputation. He took considerable chaff from his messmates
because he claimed the skies would one day be crowded with
airplanes. The French dismissed such theorizing with a shrug

of their shoulders. Their first business was to stay alive here at Marson, living and let living with the Bosche as much as possible. Next the daily efforts of the *chef de popote* had to be carefully monitored lest some delicacy such as a brace of geese be overdone or the sauce for the snails brought back by a pilot on leave in Normandy be too tart. They countered Kiffin's imaginary flights into the future by suggesting that perhaps a few crazy Americans might make an occasional flight but in no way would any sensible French man or woman be persuaded to put on helmets, scarves, boots, and teddy bear suits simply to freeze their asses off between Paris and Toulouse. They also noted that if Kiffin did not eat more he would soon be mistaken for one of the cadavers they saw occasionally during low-level missions over the lines.

It was on just such an assignment that Kiffin's voluntary exposure to risk overpowered his high quotient of skill. Pressmen suddenly and inexplicably resolved to make a name for his Escadrille by borrowing a tactic from the Germans. He divided his forces in two, one to fly high and the other to fly at treetop level—a curious instruction, he wryly agreed, since there were almost no trees still standing along the front itself. Pressmen was hopeful of two possible results—both of which were bound to be noticed and commended by his superiors. A low level flight of five Nieuports would penetrate behind the German trench lines and if unopposed continue to the German aerodromes and give them a thorough strafing. He visualized the loss of Bosche machines as considerable, and with Kiffin leading the low-level pack felt there was a good chance all his own fighters would return.

The alternative was not as attractive, but still offered a reasonable chance for a few victories. If the low-level flight was discovered in time for the Bosche to rally and take to the air, then the high fliers would swoop down on the melee with the combined advantage of altitude and surprise.

Pressmen did not allow himself to think what might happen if the Bosche were already in the air and waiting, because then his split forces would be heavily outnumbered.

Later, Pressmen had the courage to reflect on the limited success of his plan. The high level Nieuports simply made a flight deep into enemy territory and returned without firing a shot except for the necessary clearing of their guns. The low level Nieuports got through to one aerodrome, which unfortunately did not have many aircraft on the ground—two Albatros, an ancient Pfalz, a Fokker DIII which looked like it had already been damaged in a landing. All these were destroyed, but it was not a very profitable venture, considering the men and materiel committed.

The worst debit in Pressmen's opinion was the loss of the American, and not from an enemy bullet. Soon after his flight had passed over the German lines, those who were following his lead saw his speed fall off until they nearly overran him. Then they saw him wave them onward. They saw his propeller stop, which could only mean that his rotary engine had for some reason frozen and with so little altitude for maneuver he was obliged to attempt an immediate landing. Sussotte, who was the last in line and therefore had more time to watch the event than the others, reported that the American was apparently trying to land in what had once been a farmer's field, but it had now been so abused by artillery and military vehicles there was not a smooth place visible on it. Sussotte said that as he watched the Nieuport it disappeared behind the ruins of the original farmhouse and did not reappear. He was very dubious about the American's chances for survival.

"So do such flamboyant warriors so often die," Pressmen thought. Too often it seemed they fell not on a lance or even a sword or other weapon of war. The best, the most courageous were kicked in the head by a horse, run over by a camion, or stabbed by a whore. What had seemed a charmed life came to an end via influenza or in some other fashion the dullest of individuals would have disdained.

As he ordered Kiffin's effects sent to the only address he had provided, the American Embassy, Pressmen thought it a pity that his personal Don Quixote had perished because of the very attitude which had made him so, temporarily, famous. His stubborn refusal to allow a new engine in his beloved "Bessie" had brought about a finality as unreversible as the bullet of an enemy.

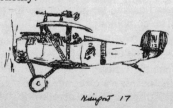

Nieuport 17

Fifty kilometers north of Marsan, flying above a different front, Toby Bryant eased his powerful frame out of his wooden bunk and regarded each new day with increasing distaste. For this war was not at all as he had supposed it, much less as Kiffin suggested it might be. His escadrille was quartered in a building that had formerly been a shoe factory situated for reasons no one could determine on a large open field. As a result a passable aerodrome was available and shelter against all elements except the cold. Toby could not decide whether it was colder inside the unheated stone factory or outside, where the wind swept down from the North Sea and made a mockery of spring. There was nothing inviting or even interesting to meet the eye anywhere Toby looked. He rarely saw the sun; the persistent flat gray overcast extended across the flat terrain until the two met at a vanishing point that appeared to vary with the temperature and time of day. If there had been any church steeples to break the monotonous horizon they were long ago knocked down by the artillery belonging to one side or the other; even a man standing at some distance stood out like a building.

Everywhere the ground had been covered with patches of dirty looking snow, which was gradually replaced by endless mud near the front. Along with his comrades flying in Caudrons, Toby wore all the clothes he could find and was so bundled up he could barely waddle out to his aircraft.

The Caudrons of the Escadrille were "GIVs," designed, it was said, by an idiot child the Kaiser had spawned on a holiday in Bohemia. It was powered by two Le Rhone rotary engines placed on each side of the "bathtub" which held the pilot and an observer whose duties were multifold. He was expected to navigate the Caudron to the proper area for reconnaissance, photographing, or spotting for artillery. He was expected to assist in the defense of his frail craft by operating a Lewis gun mounted on a ring in the rear of the bathtub. Unfortunately his forward field of fire was limited by the two engines flanking the nacelle and to the rear by the Caudron's tail. The combination rendered him nearly useless in any serious attack. During artillery spotting the observer strapped a wireless telegraph key to his leg and sent Morse signals for "long" or "short," "left" or "right," which were passed on by mobile ground units directly to gun aimers. It was almost impossible for the observer to keep track of any heavy firing while at the same time keeping an eye out for enemy fighters. And the pilot had only a single fixed Lewis gun that demanded he bully the whole ponderous aircraft into position before he could hope to hit anything. The German fighters considered the Caudrons as sitting ducks, and even their ground troops, presented with a target that was flying at low altitude and at only seventy miles an hour, usually let go with everything they had. And since the Caudrons were obliged to operate between their own artillery and the targets, they were sometimes knocked out of the sky by their own guns.

Flying Caudrons was a thankless, grim, and extremely dangerous job, which Toby endured stoically. He herded the reluctant Caudron back and forth above the ochre devastation of the front, knowing it was simply a question of time before some sort of nasty collision with something bound his way would occur, and he tried to prepare himself for it without giving way to excessive brooding. In the escadrille he was thought of as so much the essence of sangfroid that others tried to imitate his Buddha-like composure. Toby was solid.

Toby's massive head and body seemed incongruous projecting from the Caudron's bathtub, an ill match emphasized by the presence of Gaston Fremont, his observer, a young man rejected by the infantry because of his diminutive stature. The infantry failed to measure either his penis or his heart, Toby often said, or they would have discovered he was obviously descended from a Nebraska bull.

Fremont affected a thin moustache that did little to enhance his smallish face but did give him a certain dapper air which contrasted nicely with his pilot's evident tranquility. When Toby had inadvertently left a copy of an old American newspaper in the mess and a browsing pilot had discovered a cartoon series, they were known thereafter as "Mutt and Jeff." After only a few flights they became devoted friends, and it was Fremont who tried to sustain Toby for much of the afternoon when he learned that Kiffin was reported "missing in action and presumed dead."

Fremont had been assigned to Toby because he read and spoke English as well as German and Dutch. The son of a French industrialist and a Dutch mother, he was in his second year at the Sorbonne when his class was called to the colors. He had looked forward to a career in international finance and his head was always full of numbers . . . "But not his heart," Toby said to whoever would listen.

They sat together now on a bench with their backs against the damp granite stones of the shoe factory, and Toby stared into the flat distance as if he might find relief there. He wiped a fist at his big nose from time to time and said over and over that he just could not believe Kiffin was dead. His face, already more rutted and crinkled than was normal for his age, took on the look of a forsaken hound as he talked about how Kiffin, so full of life, "rambunctious, everyone always said, and by God that he was. Always into trouble and dragging me after him." Toby blew his nose into one of the red bandana handkerchiefs he had brought from Nebraska. When he regained his composure he said to Fremont, "Why don't we get drunk?"

"It is not recommended," Fremont said softly. "When you lose one close to you wine is the worst medicine to apply to the wound. It inflames the hurt and does nothing to heal. It's better to talk of him until he lives again in your mind as a new and separate being. Then you can think of him all you want with less pain, you will find him a comfortable individual to live with . . ."

"Gaston," Toby said, searching the evening horizon for anything worth his attention, "you should have been a preacher."

"I have lost two older brothers to this war."

Toby shook his big head and said he was sorry and apologized for his behavior. "Hell, they're not even sure he's dead."

"Keep watching the lists. The Germans are not so terrible about reporting . . . sometimes."

"He had so much *balls*," Toby said after another blow into his handkerchief. "He had a way with men, and with women . . . you wouldn't believe . . ."

Soon after his posting to the Caudron escadrille Toby realized that the reluctance of the German pilots to venture deep into any Allied territory further reduced his chances for long survival. The strategy allowed them to concentrate their aerial forces just behind the trench lines, and the air above them was Toby's beat.

It was on a chill June morning while on a photo mission over Lassigny that Toby's Caudron took a hit from his own

artillery. The projectile removed most of the Caudron's right
wing and pieces of the empennage. Since Toby's altitude at
the instant of impact was only one hundred meters the Caudron
had barely time to disintegrate before falling into what was
surely one of the last patches of forest still standing on the
Western Front.

The trees sufficiently broke the Caudron's fall to spare
Toby more serious injury, and it was little Fremont who
pulled him groaning from the debris with a broken arm, a
dislocated shoulder and what later proved to be several fractured ribs. The same trees which had eased their final descent
concealed them from discovery until night fell, but when it
was dark enough to entertain a reasonable hope they might
find their way back to their own lines a new complication
arose—somehow in the crash Toby's right boot had been torn
away, exposing his foot. Fremont wrapped it in his scarf
against the cold, but the foot went numb and nothing they
could do seemed to restore the circulation.

They pulled the compass out of the Caudron and hoping
the impact had not made it too inaccurate, followed it to the
west. After only a short distance Toby said his whole right
leg had become so numb he couldn't go any further. "You
keep on going," he told Fremont. "I'll see you after the
war."

Fremont said, *"Merde,"* then studied the hulk beside him
who blotted out the stars. His breath rose in a cloud. "You
have to keep going. A flea can't carry an elephant."

"Then you'll have to be my crutch," Toby said, placing
his forearm on Fremont's shoulder.

It was a long, painful walk, and they were obliged to stop
repeatedly to rewrap the scarf around Toby's foot. And each
time they argued in hoarse whispers about the insanity of
their attempt . . . at their present rate how could they find
their own lines before dawn . . . "Go while the going's
good," Toby said. "Beat it, you can make it easy—"

"No, they would shoot me if they knew I left you here."

"No one will know, tell them I died."

"Let's try for another hundred meters."

"Think of your family—"

"I am thinking of myself . . . I am the man who must live
with me for what I hope will be a long time."

"It may not be if you don't get the *hell* out of here . . ."

As they started off once again, with Toby leaning heavily on Fremont's neck and shoulder, he said, "I'm damned if I don't smell soup."

"So do I, German soup."

"How do you know?"

"The cabbage. If they are eating that's good. The Bosche will not let anything interfere with his eating."

"You could say that for the French."

"There is a difference. We are civilized."

They turned away from the odor of cooking and followed a gully that ran conveniently toward the west. They trudged on in silence except for occasional grunts as they slipped in the mud or Toby's body took a twist that felt like a sabre across his ribs.

Finally they came to more open land, but the going became even more difficult with the increasing number of shell craters, most of which were at least half full of water. Each time a star shell illuminated the landscape they slid down into the freezing water and waited in quiet misery until they thought it safe to move on the surface again. Just as the sky behind them lightened a chill rain started to fall, and they tried to convince themselves that somehow they had passed through or around the German lines without being discovered.

At five-thirty on the morning of June 3, 1916, they were intercepted by a patrol of the Seventh regiment of the line and were nearly shot before a now very voluble Fremont could explain their presence. Despite his eloquence, the four members of the patrol were still extremely suspicious once they heard Toby's inadequate French. Fremont goaded them with a long series of insults directed toward, among other things, their lack of intelligence as they were escorted at bayonet point to a dugout where a Captain Doubet eventually confirmed that they were, indeed, from Escadrille C4. At noon they separated, Toby bound for the hospital and Fremont back to the escadrille. One week later the little man was wounded when an Albatros slipped down out of the sun and made a contemptuous pass at his Caudron, letting loose a burst from its Spandaus that put three bullets through the same shoulder that had served as Toby's crutch.

CHAPTER
4

Toby was sent first to an army hospital some fifty miles to the south of Paris, where a medical staff officer was horrified to learn that because he could stand erect the American had received no treatment for any of his injuries during the entire time he was en route. The officer confessed that he could not diagnose why Toby's leg went numb and certainly there was nothing to be done about it here. "Maybe it's a nerve being pressed by your spine. Such a repair is beyond me." The shoulder was another matter; it would heal itself in time, he supposed, and likewise with the ribs. Since they were not splintered, a good taping would hold them in place until they would heal themselves. He brightened when he said that Toby like so many Americans was formidable and eventually the most severe pain would go away.

So while feeling somewhat the worse for his hospital experience, Toby was advised that the space his body occupied was needed for the more serious cases arriving every day from the front. As if in recompense he was signed over to a Rest Establishment at Trouville on the Riviera. It was a small and too long abused hotel operated by a Madame Lissonier, an ex-midwife who was said to be charging the French government an enormous sum for the daily keep of each patient. It was Toby's impression that Madame Lissonier's cupidity was not too different from her fellow citizens'. At nearby Deauville the bathing resorts were jammed with French people who behaved as if there had never been a war. Toby was bemused at the sight of the terraces extending from the cafés overflowing with people, and he watched for hours as battalions of girl cyclists whirred by in white dustcoats. Maybe it was the weather, he thought . . . at last the month of June had turned marvelously benign and the French seemed almost desperate about making the most of it.

Some slight recognition of the war was reflected in the music provided in the countless little bistros and in some cafés. The librettist Jean Bastia had written a so-called patriotic song which had a profound effect upon Toby for several weeks. Syphilis, a disease which had multiplied beyond reasonable calculation since the beginning of the war and was reported to have affected a large percentage of the French troops, was now a subject of open conversation. The Germans, it was also said, had developed a cure for such venereal disaster in a formula known as "606." Bastia had attempted to profit by the rumor while striking a patriotic note at the same time. The Parisian chanteuses and those on the Riviera gave their throaty best to his:

> Keep, O Bosches, your knavish tricks,
> Discoveries like six-o-six!
> We'd sooner have the dread V.D.
> Than vandals hailing from the Spree!

The song haunted Toby. He had first heard it on the most memorable evening when he learned that he had been promoted to sergeant, been awarded the Croix de Guerre, and as if to crown those events with the ultimate, lost his virginity. He had known for long that Kiffin had experienced and enjoyed his first intercourse when he was barely fifteen and he had never gotten tired of hearing the details of that conquest until it was superceded by a long series of liaisons about which Kiffin was curiously reticent. It was not the way of a gentleman, he'd said, to name your partner or describe particulars. Since Lincoln, Nebraska, was not exactly a recreation of Sodom or Gomorrah, Toby was never quite sure whether Kiffin's numerous and cooperative female friends were real or a product of his ever-active imagination.

As they passed into their late teens and entered the university, Kiffin was always promising to make "arrangements" for Toby, insisting that he should not be allowed out in the world in his virginal state. Yet something always interfered, and when Kiffin went away to Hammondsport and then to France, Toby remained as innocent as the day he'd acquired his first Boy Scout merit badge. Maybe if he'd been in a different place or if his sometimes overwhelming shyness hadn't stood in the way he might have been regarded as more available—

not be considered just a friendly giant, unapproachable and unattainable and most likely already the property of some female. Massive, ruggedly handsome men just didn't go wandering around loose and available, according to a self-perpetuating female legend of the time. Toby was isolated by the very fact that he was so desirable. All of which left him bewildered and frustrated; he hadn't the faintest notion of how to break down the iron wall between his public image and what he really was and was feeling. And in time, during those occasional bull sessions when copulation became the obsessive subject among his peers, Toby found it convenient to let them assume he was an old hand at such matters, dreading the day when some overly inquisitive acquaintance might ask him for details.

But this was France. And he was a warrior newly crowned. Her name was Denise and she worked as sort of a girl of all trades for Madame Lissonier. She did literally everything about the Rest Establishment, attending the questions of the twenty uniformed inhabitants when madame had withdrawn with her poodle to talk to him about money, the injustice of a war that had inflicted her hotel with so many unwanted guests, and the inadequacies of the payments she received for same. Denise did the shopping to supply the kitchen, saw to the weekly changing of linens, collected the mail for those residents too infirm to get about, and supervised the activities of the two peasant girls who came ten kilometers by train each day to cook, clean, and wash. It was a demanding job and as a consequence of madame's expectation that she be on it twenty-four hours a day Denise had her own room—a cubbyhole under the eaves with only a narrow cot and a washbasin on a tiny dresser. It was within the confines of such very limited space that Toby Bryant discovered rapture.

Ever since his arrival it had been Denise's special dedication to improve Toby's limited French vocabulary. There were no formal lessons and the instruction was never of any fixed duration, yet if they only met in passing Denise would pause long enough to smile and supply him with a new word or two, or a phrase, or even an occasional colloquialism from her native Lyon. After the first week the pauses became longer and Toby began making a conscious effort to improve his cockeyed grammar. But her obligations persisted in tearing Denise away from their quick exchanges and she suggested that after her long day was done he come to her cubbyhole for more concentrated instruction.

She was a petite young woman with large ripe olive eyes, ebony hair which she entwined in a bun at the back of her head, and skin offering both the soft coloring and sensual texture of travatine marble. She had a lovely and particularly beguiling voice although she was not a beautiful young woman. Her eyes were close together and her Gallic nose seemed out of proportion to the balance of her face. Her generous mouth was a definite attribute, and even without makeup her lips retained a luscious hue further enhanced when she smiled. She was due for weight problems in later life, but right now her curves were, as the boys liked to say, all in the right places, sufficient yet modest enough to give her an air of tempting nubility. Toby was not unaware of her attraction when he tapped on the door of her cubbyhole, although he certainly had not anticipated what met his eyes.

"Entrez, s'il vous plaît," Denise said as if she were welcoming an ambassador, and for a moment Toby had trouble finding his ability to move. In place of the severe cotton dress with white cuffs and tight fitting collar that she had always worn when about her duties, Denise was now in a kimono of such fine silk the gas lamp behind her clearly revealed every line of her body.

She took his big hand, drew him in, and closed the door. He watched her lock the door and stood staring at the door handle while she backed away and rose on her tiptoes.

She clasped her hands behind her back and said in English, "Kiss me, please."

Toby looked down at her breasts and saw them moving in harmony with her quick breathing and wondered what it would be like if he pressed his mouth into the inviting ravine between them.

He narrowed the distance between them with a single step.

"Please," she said again, but there was no plea in her tone, only an amused challenge.

Toby stood there. His carnal senses were uncoiling at a furious rate but there was a knot that threatened a hopeless tangle. What was wrong here? The sudden turbulence deep inside urged him toward her while his natural shyness chained him in place.

"I—" he said, swallowing hard and finding himself incapa-

ble of making further sound. No matter, because Denise
stretched out her arms and pulled him to her. He bent down
to meet her open lips, but suddenly she tipped her face away
and pushed him toward the cot.

"You are too tall," she whispered.

"I . . . can't lie on you on account of my ribs," he said
apologetically.

"*C'est d'accord.*"

She maneuvered him to a sitting position on the edge of the
cot, forced his legs apart with her own and squirmed between
them until they were locked together. Now standing in her
bare feet, her eyes were on a level with Toby's. She took his
head in her hands, tilted it gently and pressed her open mouth
to his lips. She rocked slowly and rhythmically back and
forth for a time, making mysterious little sounds deep in her
throat as she opened the kimono and pressed her breasts
against his face.

Suddenly Toby lost track of events, and the calm control
he'd presented to the world for all of his twenty-one years at
last was unshackled. Now without thinking he was fumbling
at her pubic triangle and she was opening his uniform pants.
He heard her saying things which were meaningless to him
because the French words came so swiftly between her little
cries and gasps. When she raised her legs and straddled him
he fell back against the wall and was amazed at how the
unfamiliar moist warmth about him now totally obliterated all
other sensations.

Instinctively he began to raise his hips to meet her undulating movements, but new pains shot down his leg and he
stopped. She began to hum softly and whispered for him to
be still—she would move for both of them. Never in his life,
Toby thought as if he was a spectator, had he known such
feeling. He realized suddenly that Denise smelled of perfume
and powder and a strange musk that half-blinded him although his eyes were open. He saw her sitting erect nearly at
arms' length, watched her breasts ascend and descent in
perfect resonance with her hips, but she was as out of focus,
unreal as she would have been in a dream.

Suddenly her tempo quickened. He felt her fingernails
digging into his neck, heard her give out a long, almost
shocking groan. She lurched and careened and pumped until
she was panting in fierce counterpoint to the squeaking cot.

And then an explosion for him like none he'd ever known before, and he heard nothing at all for several moments.

When he opened his eyes he saw her silhouetted against the gas lamp on the dresser, but there was enough reflected light to see her smiling. She was still mounted on him, her bare legs making an inverted *V* across his uniform pants, and now she reached out her fingers to touch his lips. *"Voila,"* she said simply. *"C'est bon?"*

"Yeah . . . *bon.*" He didn't know what else to say. It was so simple, and so wonderful . . . this event he'd heard about for so long.

"Tu est formidable, cherie. Merci."

"Merci," he answered, wondering if he should now feel like he was in love with Denise. What next? She was still twitching her hips occasionally, as though echoing her previous surging. He got confused when she leaned down and flicked her tongue along his lips. He wondered if he should do something special to please her. What? Since he was still taped almost to his armpits there seemed to be very little else he could do except lie still and wait for her to take charge once more. . . .

Later he had trouble trying to remember the sequence of events that filled the rest of the evening; certainly any lingering lust that might still be in him was gone. When she had finished with him, a situation made apparent by her repeated yawnings, he wished her a pleasant night and departed in a daze. Descending the stairs to his own small room he was grateful for the handrail. He touched at his hair wondering if his strength had been stolen like Sampson's. He wasn't complaining, just marveling.

It took him a very long time to take off his uniform; everything seemed to take him a very long time except falling into the brass bed, which he did with such abandon that he twisted both shoulder and ribs and yelped with pain. But instead of falling instantly to sleep he stared wide-eyed into the darkness . . . Bastia's song suddenly tolling through his thoughts. "My God . . . suppose she had V.D. . . . ." Visions of himself staggering about, eaten away by the dread disease zoomed across the brass bed and turned him so cold he hauled up the pouf despite the warmth of the night. Supposing . . . supposing he would some day arrive in Lincoln the returning war hero with his mother and father waving little pairs of French and American flags and the man who stepped—no, had to be *helped* off the train because of his blindness—had only half a nose, no teeth and giant swollen balls . . . !

Lying in the darkness, he thought of Denise, who now slept so dangerously near to him, and decided he'd abstain for the duration no matter what the temptation. That's what he thought . . .

It was 1916. For the moment at least it was plain that the French army did not know what to do with Sergeant Toby Bryant. He was released from Madame Lissioner's establishment early one sultry afternoon, and after a perfunctory and rather tepid embrace from Denise, departed for Paris. As ordered, he reported to Headquarters of the First Air Service Brigade for assignment. It was the tenth of what already promised to be a very hot July.

A doleful captain who seemed much more interested in the sea water temperature and the price of accommodation on the Riviera than in dispatching another body to fight the Germans asked Toby if he wanted to return to his Escadrille 3. Toby said no, if possible he'd like to be assigned to any other flying duty.

"Then we shall have to see what can be done," the captain said, as if the prospect of doing anything at all gave him great personal anguish. "Meanwhile here's a chit for your living allowance and you'll be quartered at Saint-Cloud. You'll have the barracks more or less to yourself since the occupying unit has been sent to Thiepval to back up the British. The slobs have run out of shells because their antiquated donkeys became lost somewhere between the supply base and the front. Dreadful people, the English, very set in their ways."

Thanks to Denise's patient tutoring, Toby found that he could understand most of what the captain had said, and he decided against trying any response except a salute and a hasty departure. He had no desire to return to actual fighting if only because French troops were said to be near or in actual mutiny in many places along the front and he saw no reason to expose himself while they were squabbling among themselves.

Toby likely would have made a different decision if he had better understood the dilatory ways of French military bureaucracy. The mice-ridden barracks were indeed nearly deserted except for the remnants of a Sudanese company that had been so badly mauled there were only eight survivors. The other occupants were thirty raw recruits for the Legion, commanded by none other than the abusive Sergeant Delacroix, who had thus far never been near the front. Since they were now of equal rank and Delacroix's evil little eyes had spotted the Croix de Guerre on Toby's chest from the twenty meters of their first encounter, they never approached any closer. They exchanged a glance of mutual recognition and dislike and went their ways, Toby at once to the American Embassy, where he thought there might be a long chance he would find some mail from home.

When he paused to look up at the Stars and Stripes flying over the embassy he was momentarily stunned by the beauty of his flag against the hot July sky. He thought that if he could somehow escape from France without being shot for desertion he would return immediately to Nebraska and never again be tempted to even think about going over the horizon to Tipperary. And he thought unhappily that now there was no one around to tempt him . . . With Kiffin gone life would never be the same for him. He had written to Kiffin's parents describing their last times together and expressing the hope that he would yet be reported as a prisoner of war. He had written the letter soon after his arrival at Madame Lissonier's, and now the sight of the flag set off a whole sequence of nostalgic images, including an all too vivid portrait of Kiffin's mother and father, who were almost as close to him as his own parents, reading his letter.

"I'm plain damn homesick," he thought. "I feel like a kid who went away to summer camp and everything didn't turn out like it should and now I want to take off for home. Some warrior. Real Croix de Guerre material . . ."

When the Marine guard saluted him as he passed through the embassy gate he felt better, deciding that his current life wasn't so bad after all. There was no quick explanation why the metal numerals on his uniform collar should be honored any more than the original cloth "3s," but he had noticed that even café proprietors, notorious for their indifference to anything but the cash box, actually deferred to him. Once they saw he was in the Air Service and a pilot he was treated like a general, and in a few instances a substantial amount had actually been subtracted from his bill.

He was surprised to find the embassy swarming with people, most of whom were speaking French. Just inside the entrance he saw a prominent sign chalked on a piece of plasterboard with an arrow pointing down the entrance hall: MILITARY MAIL. THIRD DOOR ON LEFT.

He knocked on the door, and hearing no sound of welcome or rejection, opened it enough to stick his head inside. A young woman glanced up from behind her desk and spoke to him in rapid French. "Are you sure you're in the right place monsieur? Perhaps you have confused us with another department? The French Liaison Office is down the hall . . . Lieutenant Baker."

Toby summoned all the training—linguistic, that is—Denise had given him, adding a seasoning of French grammar he invented on the spot and tried to say he wasn't interested in meeting a Lieutenant Baker and that he was an American looking for his mail and would mademoiselle be so kind—?

To his surprise she motioned him inside and addressed him in the sort of English he hadn't heard for a long long time. "An American you may be," she said, "but a linguist you are not. What's your name, Yank, and where are you from?"

He took off his kepi and brushed the sleeve of his uniform across his moist forehead in a gesture of vast relief. "My God, it's good to hear you speak," he said seriously. "Just beautiful . . . music to my ears. What's your name?"

"You've got it backward, soldier. I have to know yours, otherwise I can't even look for your mail."

"Toby Bryant.. . from Lincoln, Nebraska."

"That's away out west with the hostile Indians, right?" She swung around in her chair and started fingering through a metal filing case.

"Well . . . it's in *eastern* Nebraska. There're still a few Indians out on the reservation and here and there on the prairies but they're not exactly hostile."

"I think of Nebraska and I think of Apaches and General Custer's last stand."

"That was in Montana Territory and they were Sioux, not Apaches."

"Thanks for the education . . . I'm sorry to say, there's nothing under B for Bryant."

There was a moment's silence broken only by the whirring of the electric fan on top of the filing case. Toby caressed the brim of his kepi, suddenly feeling ill at ease. It was her eyes, he thought. They were inspecting him as if he was some just-discovered specimen in a laboratory, a new kind of two-legged animal with a pine tree sticking out of his forehead. "What are you looking at?" He smiled when he said it.

"You. I'm wondering what you're doing in the French army."

"So am I."

"A sergeant and you can hardly speak French?"

"In my job not much has been necessary."

"You're an aviator with a Croix de Guerre. You must be very brave—"

"To tell you the truth I've been scared out of my wits ever since I came over here."

"When was that?"

"Years ago. I'm not going to tell you any more of my secrets unless you tell me your name."

"Lily."

The eyes were changing now. They had become more sympathetic and her mouth was more relaxed.

"Where are you from, Lily?"

"Everywhere. I was born in Washington, D.C."

"I'll bet you wish you were back there."

"I do not."

"Hey, why are you so defensive on a great morning like this? Matter of fact it's almost noon. How about some lunch?"

"No." She hesitated a moment, then added, "But thank you."

"I don't know Paris; can you recommend some place nearby here?"

"Are you rich?"

"*No.*"

"I thought all the Americans who came over here to fly for France were rich."

"If I go out and come back in again and say I'm rich would you let me take you to lunch?"

"There's a little place called the Owl near the Quai d'Orsay, 11 Rue Cecile. You can have bean soup with onions, bread and a glass of decent wine for just under a franc—"

"I'd never find it alone."

"Then how do you find your way around the sky?"

"Whenever I get lost I just hold course and wait. If someone starts shooting at me I know I'm going in the wrong direction."

He caught a trace of a smile around the corner of her mouth—a mouth he thought extraordinarily expressive.

"Watch it, you might smile," he said. "Give me a chance, I may be the best laugh you'll have all day." He was amazed at his unaccustomed forwardness.

"Don't you know anyone in Paris?"

"I just got in last night. The only person I know in this whole city is a Corsican sergeant named Delacroix and I don't want to take him to lunch anywhere at any time. Ever."

"I gather you and the sergeant aren't the best of buddies."

"You could say that."

There were many people in her world who regarded Lily Cranwell as somewhat of a nuisance, and if she had more years on her or if she held more than a clerkship post she might have been labeled as downright dangerous. Her connections in the Foreign Service were all known—after all she was the daughter of a man who was most highly regarded in his profession, a man known from Peking to Budapest and from Rio to Sydney as a patrician with common sense.

The trouble was that Lily, whose breeding at least was never questioned, was inclined to rebellion, a tendency which did not sit well with the conservative bureaucrats of the United States Foreign Service, much less their fat-geese wives. She often made a provocative display of her cleavage which had a way of nearly deranging the younger attachés and their equivalents if only because, bachelors or no, not one of them could persuade her into even a date. She simply said that she did not believe in "in-house" social relations and thus her private life away from the embassy remained a relative enigma. When it pleased Lily she was inclined to light up a small cigar, thereby inspiring such comments as "She's a harridan . . ." "Mark you, she's heading for trouble, that girl," and from a relative few, "What a lovely package of trouble."

Lily sang well, but she was not encouraged by anyone at the embassy when she visited the French military hospitals peppered all through Paris. She sang what the wounded wanted to hear—the raunchy songs from the Parisian bistros and cafes, and her superiors at the embassy were afraid she might present such an unwholesome example of young American womanhood it would reflect not only upon the national image but even upon *them*, God forbid.

Lily Cranwell's self-created social insulation made her open-game for the busy tongues of the embassy community. News of her latest capriciousness traveled through the building like the wind, and it was even possible that because she knew she was a marked woman she felt obligated to provide a certain degree of whimsy at regular intervals. If Toby's impressive physical appearance alone was responsible for her accepting his luncheon invitation, then it would not have been beyond her to abandon him at the front entrance, but whether she knew it or not, some dormant chip of fire had been ignited within her that unmistakably warmed her whole being. When she was observed striding down the hall and out the entrance on the arm of an extraordinarily large and handsome French sergeant, the word passed quickly from unit to office until it finally spent itself at the door of the ambassador himself.

It was a voluble lunch with far more interest given to conversation than to the Owl's mediocre food. It was as if Lily was as hungry for male company as Toby was to hear the even, rolling sound of her English. He confessed that the French habit of speaking in short little phrases separated by significant pauses sounded too much like the speakers were preoccupied with listening to themselves rather than anyone else.

Because the day was so warm, they drank sparingly of the wine, but no stimulus was needed to ease their conversational exchanges. At first, during the time when they were each feeling their way toward the thoughts of a stranger, they spoke about the obvious local scene. They commented on a pronouncement pasted on a kiosk they had passed and bearing the stamp of approval of the military police. It stated in no uncertain terms that all men in military uniform were forbidden to read a newspaper. Lily pointed out that whoever inspired the notice was apparently unaware the war had been going on for almost two years.

She told about Poincaré's arrival at a hospital where she had gone for an aftenoon's singing. Before his arrival the official who dealt with ceremonial expeditions involving the president specified that he would have to leave his car at the bottom of the driveway. The entrance stairway was on the left of the drive and it would be unthinkable for a man of Poincaré's grandness to dismount from his vehicle except on the *right*.

"By such meticulous attention to detail," Lily said, "France will undoubtedly be saved."

Toby countered with Poincaré's last visit to the front. According to what he had heard, the president was becoming very unpopular with his own troops and his car had been shot at twice.

Gradually they then veered away from topics related to their immediate surroundings and slipped into the more personal.

"You are . . . how old?" she asked, surprised that she would have any interest after so short an acquaintance.

"Twenty-one." He laughed. "I'm legal. How about you?"

"I'm seventeen. What did you do before you came over here?"

"Play football."

"By yourself?"

"That would be tough. You'd never know it from my writing but I was at the university."

"Nebraska has a *university?*" She smiled when she said it.

"Classes are held in covered wagons and we circle them every night in case the Indians attack."

"You're a funny fellow. I like that."

"I told you I'd be your laugh for the day."

"Do you plan on going back to college after the war?"

"Maybe . . ." And to himself, first I've got to survive that long.

After the cheese she asked him how long his leave would be and he told her he hoped that he'd been "lost" and that as long as he avoided official attention it might be who knew how long before anyone got around to sending him off again.

"I should think you've done your part—"

"Not very well, I'm afraid. I doubt if I put much of a dent in the German armor. I guess I'm must not a natural hero . . . I had a buddy who was, though . . ."

And suddenly he was telling her about Kiffin, how he had been the first to fly and come to France . . . "He was the greatest guy you'd ever want to meet . . . full of life, always up to something . . . I bet if he was the one who came for his mail this morning and asked you to lunch you'd have said clear the tracks, let's go on the double . . ."

Because the light inside the Owl was subdued, Toby failed to notice the glaze that crept across Lily's dark eyes. Her father would have seen it, because her habit of drifting away on her own magic carpet during moments of even semi-bordeom had annoyed him for hears. He would say, "Lily, come back, earth calling . . ." and eventually she would shake her head, smile and at least pretend interest in whatever conversation she had just left. Toby carried on about Kiffin for several minutes before he realized that Lily's attention had drifted.

"Maybe you could help me," he said, switching the conversation. "If he was taken prisoner, wouldn't someone at the embassy know about it?"

"I doubt it. Not if he's not on the official list furnished by the Germans. The fact that he was in the French army complicates the problem."

"Maybe he's just not on any list yet, or the Germans mixed up his name with someone else's or . . . and I wouldn't put it past him, he wouldn't give his right name."

"I'll try. We have contacts in Sweden and in Switzerland who can sometimes find out things no one else can. I'll ask the supervisor in that department to get with it."

"If you do I'll love you forever." There he went again.

"Is there something special that makes you say things like that? I mean, have they got a Blarney Stone in Lincoln, Nebraska? . . ."

After lunch they went for a walk along the Quai des Tuilleries. They played a game. Who could spot the most number of things that denied the war? Toby counted six men fishing and seven watching them fish. Lily saw five fishermen and eight watching. Together they noted two lines consisting of some thirty-five people. Toby claimed them first and lost the point. The people were waiting to buy potatoes. Lily took the second line, which proved to be made up of people waiting to buy shares in a new issue of bonds by the Credit Foncier. They called the game a draw and seemed to take their laughter as naturally as they did the fact that they were now strolling along arm in arm.

An afternoon breeze brushed their smiles as they ambled back toward the embassy. Toby watched the sunlight slice through the trees and dapple Lily's face, and it occurred to him that he had never before seen such a beautiful face. Who else could he talk to like this? Had he ever talked to like this? She listened to almost everything he said as if it really was worth listening to, and it seemed that everything she had to say made wonderful sense. When they stopped in front of the embassy he took her hand, moist with the heat. "You do know you're a very special girl?"

"I know, sergeant, that you have filled me with enough malarkey to last for a very long time."

"When can I see you again?"

"A smart girl would say in about a week."

"Too long. They could send me back to the Escadrille at any minute."

"I thought you were lost—never mind . . . how about tonight? Early dinner."

"I guess I can almost wait that long."

"My flat is at Eleven Boulevard Raspail. Seventh floor. Do you think you could find it?"

"Bet on it."

"My, my. Your confidence in your navigational ability has certainly improved since noon." She squeezed his hand. "Six o'clock," she said, and left him.

Thus in the twenty-fourth month of the first great war, in a city soaked by water spouts of cupidity, anxiety, avarice, and bravado, did two young Americans begin to fall in love. Except for the mutually agonizing hours of separation their conversation went on nonstop; they discussed the ifs and whens should the United States get into the war, they enjoyed hours condemning the value of money in relation to happiness, and as if they were following some historic tribal ritual, informed each other of their close and even distant relatives.

Lily wrote to her father in London,

Daddy dear, I know you will not believe what has happened to me here. It is incredible, as much to me as it must be to you. You know that I have many peculiarities (HO! HO! and where do they come from?), but I have tried to be a good and loving daughter in the hopes of perhaps taking up some of the slack since mother has not been around. A part of that filial devotion backfired somehow and left me with such a strange disinterest in men I sometimes worried about myself. Biology told me that my interest should have been peaking the last two years—always leading toward the inevitable young chap who would call on you asking my hand in marriage.

I know now why I've been waiting, because only a week after meeting *him*, I'm in love. I can't understand it, but there it is. His name is Toby Bryant and he's from a place called Lincoln, which is in Nebraska. Or did you know? Anyway, lest I bore you with details, please be assured that he is a gentleman and comes from a nice family. And yes, I am as chaste as the day I was born but I must warn you that I can't promise how much longer that situation will prevail . . .

Although Lily's letter was not intended as either a torture message or a suspense story she desisted from any further personal description at that point. Instead she went on to describe the overflowing crowds at Maxim's and the refusal of the government to put a five percent tax on restaurant bills over five francs. She described her Sunday walk (omitting the fact that it was more of a promenade with Toby so close at her side), and she told of the gore-seeking crowd that had gathered around the smoking remains of a crashed Zeppelin airship which had fallen on Paris after being hit by a shell. She described how crowded the city was and how the consumption of fine and expensive wines was said to be already double that of 1915. Finally she assured her father that if "this affair becomes so serious we feel destined to spend the rest of our lives together then you must somehow exert enough diplomatic pressure to wangle a trip to Paris and give me away. Be sure I will give you forewarning of any nuptials. . . ."

It was not until the middle of August that Toby was reassigned to Escadrille C74, a new Caudron outfit organized to augment the bombing missions at the front. Allied planes had already dropped bombs on Mulheim, Fribourg, Kundern, Holzen, Mappach and Heitersheim and the thought that he might be involved in killing civilians troubled Toby very deeply. This was not why he had come to France.

Many Americans flying in the more glamorous Escadrille Chasse were now becoming celebrities and Toby had mixed reactions to what he saw of their lives. There was Lufbery, the maestro of course. And then Didier Masson and Paul Pavelka, Norman Prince, and Bert Hall. They all flew exciting and extremely nimble little Nieuports and usually their antagonists along with the danger they represented were visible.

Once Toby was back in the air again he was immediately reminded that although the one thing he loved about this job

was the actual flying, herding the clumsy Caudrons around
the sky was almost all hazard and little glory. One misty
afternoon near Bar-le-Duc his Caudron took a shell through
the right engine and since it refused to maintain altitude on
the other engine alone he was obliged to make another forced
landing—this time, at least, within his own lines. It was a
good landing considering the only available place was the
side of a steep hill. His observer was an excitable Gasconian
with a soprano voice. Wrestling with the control wheel and
rudder bar Toby managed to make the Caudron obey his need
for a long side-slip down to the face of the hill. Since there
was no wind to complicate the quick descent the maneuver
became quite beautiful to observe—something, Toby was told
later, like a blue heron alighting in a swamp. The instant the
Caudron came to a stop undamaged they heard loud applause;
yet no one was to be seen. They dismounted and looked
about. The applause ceased suddenly and they heard someone
call from the brim of the hill.

The Gasconian turned pale and screamed at Toby, ''He
says run for your lives!'' He started up the hill at a furious
pace and Toby, still experiencing more pain in his leg than he
dared to reveal, did his best to keep up with him. Once at the
brim they saw it was cut clean across by a trench line jammed
with poilus. Willing hands hauled them down and there was
much more embracing and congratulatory kissing from the
long unwashed and bearded poilus than Toby wanted. He
realized soon enough that they were nearly all half drunk and
were delighted to find something to celebrate. Even more zest
was added to the party when a German shell screeched down
out of the copper twilight sky and made a direct hit on the
otherwise undamaged Caudron. Looking down through an
observation slit in the trench Toby sought in vain for any sign
of the Caudron. Unless there were a few bits and pieces at the
bottom of the new shell hole, he thought, not a trace of his
machine remained.

Toby was correct in his assumption that when he returned
to C74 his inability to account for the total disappearance of
one Caudron was going to cause a bureaucratic dilemma and
a few raised eyebrows. He found also that life in the French
trenches made his own wooden barracks complete with bath
house look like some distant Nirvana and after only a single
night on the brim of the hill he was more understanding of the

nfantry's faltering morale. He learned that almost every regiment had at least a few mutineers and in some locations whole companies had sat down on their arms. Several so-called ringleaders had been shot. And winter, when trench life became nearly unendurable by the most determined of men, was already to be seen in the pale October sun.

Lily wrote to him frequently. She explained how Paris had not changed much in spirit, but that now lights had to be shaded by six in the evening. The fruit stalls, however, were permitted to light up with candles after that hour and presented a very charming picture. The boulevards were still jammed with people as were the restaurants. It was all because those not in uniform were receiving ever higher wages and had promptly developed a taste for luxury.

At the beginning of December Toby's Escadrille was alerted to the impending visitation of two very important visitors who proved to be Quentin Roosevelt in a United States Army uniform and the King of the Belgians. Toby noticed that although he was a supply officer Roosevelt wore a pair of wings above his breast pocket and he was not at all sure he approved. Roosevelt did go out of his way to congratulate Toby on volunteering so early and assured him it would only be a matter of time before America would be officially at war. Toby's comment was direct, flat and simple. "They better hurry up or there isn't going to be any war to come to."

He did not elaborate because his Escadrille commander who had thought to exhibit his only American to Roosevelt was jumpy enough about discontent among French troops, and he spoke only a smattering of English. Just enough, Toby thought, to misinterpret any further remarks on his part as an indication he might believe the Germans were winning. Unfortunately that assessment might have been very close to the truth.

After stewing in the barracks a week and standing by watching others take off on artillery spotting missions, or for bombing or reconnaissance, Toby came to the conclusion that inaction was worse than trying to survive in Caudrons. Drifting in limbo after the rest of the Escadrille had taken to the air Toby had only the Gasconian to talk with and the lilt of his soprano delivering a variety of French that was nearly incomprehensible left him bored beyond measure. How many

people, he wondered, understood that except for occasional
moments of abject terror and even fewer of triumph, war was
the most ennervating of human endeavors. He found himself
yawning with astonishing frequency and he slept often. There
were no Sergeant Delacroix here to tie the anger of one
afternoon to the next morning; everyone in the Escadrille was
almost overly considerate of each other. Kiffin now, he thought,
if he were here the unit would be dancing in a different style.

On the third of December he was told to make his way to
Buc and bring back a new Caudron. He was granted permission to stop off in Paris for two days and suddenly all pain
left his leg.

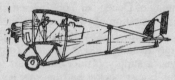

Caudron G. 3.

Since everyone in the Embassy was invited Lily attended a
showing of paintings by Duchamp, one of the new "Dadaist"
school which had the Parisian art sophisticates bristling with
controversy. She was urged to contemplate the deep significance of the paintings and after what she thought was a
reasonable attempt to do so announced that she had seen
enough. She could not decide whether they were "just awful
or is someone pulling our collective legs?"

A very light snow was falling, the first of the winter, and
she decided to walk back to her flat despite the considerable
distance from the gallery. She wanted to think about Toby in
the special privacy she enjoyed while walking, dozing, eating
and bathing. Although raised as a Methodist she now stopped
off frequently at Notre Dame to pray for Toby's safety; it was
so much easier to find a direct and visible line to God using
Catholic facilities, she thought. If she had known the protocol
she would have lighted a few candles in Toby's name and she
hoped a franc dropped in the collection box for each visit
would somehow justify the presence of a heathen amid the
perpetual parade of black cloth so common to French wives

nd mothers. At the Embassy she learned that the losses had
been appalling: 750,000 Frenchmen had been killed or died
of wounds and disease and almost half a million were prison-
rs of the Germans. Their families crowded the churches
presenting a sober contrast to the vivacious life-as-usual to be
seen along the boulevards.

She was, as usual, out of breath when she reached the
seventh floor on this evening. Her pounding heart came to a
near stop when she was seized from behind in a bear hug and
several frantic seconds passed before she discovered her as-
sailant was Toby. He hoisted her off the floor until he could
ook directly into her eyes. Then he turned until the hall
gaslight illuminated her face, and said, "Will you marry me?
ay yes or no."

"Yes."

"Good. I like prompt answers. When?"

"How about tomorrow morning? . . . . Oh, I forgot, my
father has to give me away. How long do you have?"

"Forty-eight hours, now less six."

"I feel an impulsive decision coming on. Father will just
have to understand."

He kissed her and set her down. Once inside the flat they
held each other in silence for a long time. Finally they began
to whisper of their love as if there were others nearby to hear
them and clinging to each other, moving imperceptively in
the darkness, they finally lowered themselves to her bed.
"Aren't you hungry?" she whispered. He said yes, that he
was for her and it was nearly an hour before they spoke
again.

Since Toby was in the military they were able to bypass the
official publishing of the banns and were married by a depu-
tized woman clerk of the Second Arrondissement at ten o'clock
on the next morning. She was a prune faced woman with
badly fitting dentures and had trouble pronouncing the names
of Lily Horton Cranwell and Toby Palmer Bryant.

CHAPTER
5

By the autumn of 1917 Sergeant Toby Bryant had been awarded a Palm and a Star to his Croix de Guerre, and had been made a Chevalier de l'Ordre de Leopold along with the Belgian Croix de Guerre. With the exception of two leaves and a brief spell of instructing at Pau, he had been flying at the front almost continuously since his marriage. He was immensely cheered when America declared war on the Germans in April 1917, but he was disappointed in the French reaction. When the image of President Woodrow Wilson was seen at the cinema he'd inspired only a disinterested silence among French viewers and reactions in the French press to the man were usually lukewarm.

Toby thought that he would be transferred to the American Air Service within weeks, but the summer passed and October came again before there was any existing force to accept him and the French were extremely coy about parting with his now much valued experience.

The trouble was, Toby realized, that he had too much experience and it seemed to him that by the law of averages his phenomenal luck could not continue. Sometimes because of bad weather or other circumstances a whole week would go by without his having been shot at, but every trip over the lines was a provocation to chance and as time went on he sensed that he was much less inclined to engage in any hazardous duty. Now except for Captain Pinsard, the Escadrille's commander, Toby had become the "old man" of the Escadrille, a legendary foreign giant to the new pilots and observers. Every observer in the Escadrille schemed to fly with Toby, partly because he was considered to be incredibly lucky and also because of his flying skill which had become nearly a sensuous joy to watch. If anyone could bring a crippled Caudron back from the front the genial Yankee could. Among themselves the new arrivals discussed his strength, his even temper in actual combat, and his open disapproval of unnecessary risk. When headquarters demanded a "fishing exercise" he voiced his opinion of the order in no uncertain terms, *"Fou . . . criminal . . . inutile"* He particularly objected to the use of the Escadrille as bait; the occasional ploy of sending Caudrons to an area where German batteries were suspected to be hidden and hoping to draw fire for later retaliation.

What Toby now called the "gypsy lunacy" of the military took charge of his daily existence. Although he continued with his artillery *réglage*—photographic and reconnaissance missions—he was transferred constantly. He was stationed at Luneville for a while then sent off to Manocourt near Nancy. Then he spent a month on the Lorraine Front followed by shorter periods at Villeseneux, Villiers, Saint-Georges, and Lormaison. Twice a week he wrote to Lily although the letters she wrote in response rarely caught up with him.

. . . . Now that we are in the mess I'm thinking of transferring to the American Air Service and so are most of the other Americans I've managed to talk with from time to time . . . Bill Dugan, Bob Soubrian, Bill Thaw, and Ken Littauer. For one thing we would be promoted to officers right away.

The French won't commission us as officers, I suppose because they're afraid they'll be starting a precedent. At this point I'm more than ready to fly a desk for a while, but apparently I have that age-old male demand on myself not to let my buddies down. In their way the French have accepted me and treat me as one of them in spite of the fact that I don't know what they're talking about most of the time. How I wish I had your talent for languages . . .

One of the few letters Toby received after Christmas had been written by Lily a month earlier.

. . . . I was near the Gare St. Lazare today just after a trainload of troops arrived. How I wished one of them had been you . . . They looked dirty and tired but seemed to be in very good spirits and were yelling at the buildings and the street, *Pantruche! . . . Pantruche!* (which, if you haven't heard it is a colloquialism for *Paris.*) It is very hard for us here to realize how close you are . . . . and yet living in such a different atmosphere. Sometimes I think I must be watching a play. Yesterday in the Parc Monceau I saw a captain. . . . I think he was in the cavalry . . . anyway he was wearing a sky-blue tunic and boots and spurs. He had a most defiant air about him and a craggy, arrogant face decorated with a magnificent moustache. He was pushing a baby carriage with one hand and he held a Baedeker in the other. As if that were not enough of a show the babies in the carriage were twins. . . .

. . . . Paris seems to be in a constant state of change. One day the Boulevards are crowded and everyone seems determined to play the fiddle while Rome burns. The next day all seems solemn and sad. At the cinema they cheer wildly for Teddy Roosevelt, possibly because his sons are already in the service. The French attitude toward Wilson has not changed and I think I know why. The man has the personality of a near-sighted beetle and I think he eats truffles for breakfast. Parisians still keep their *heure verte* and take their *aperitif* as if nothing at all was wrong in the world. . . .

. . . . Last week coming back from a hospital where my golden voice must have made at least some of the patients wish they were back in the trenches, I passed through the Luxembourg Gardens and watched the children playing for a while. They were pretending a battle, with some of them French and others Bosche. I noticed that everyone wanted to be the Bosche because their side had the most wounded and they were taken off to the hospital first. There, some little girls were attending them as nurses. I could only think that it would all be very quaint and charming if it were not for the fact that the real thing was transpiring only a few kilometers away and I had just left the hospital where the pathetic real victims were trying to make a new life for themselves. And it made me wonder if we ever wanted to have any children and watch the same thing happen all over again. . . .

Toby was extremely shy in his letters about his regard for his bride.

. . . . I guess I'm like John Alden or one of those other guys in books who can't find the right words to tell someone else how much they love them. I get the stutters when I try—or rather this pen does. I've told you about my mother and father and how distant they are with each other and maybe some of that reserve is my inheritance. My kid sister is the same way. She recognizes me as another member of the family and that's about all. So all my life I think I've been looking for someone like you, another human being who will not be too careful about their feelings and maybe help let some of mine out to fly. . . .

. . . Maybe we did marry in haste and now that I think about that at some distance I realize we hardly know each other. Maybe we would know each other better if there had been a chance for a long engagement, but maybe not. Because I think people don't start being themselves until *after* they make it official. The piece of paper doesn't mean much, but the ceremony does. Something happens when it's over and I want to assure you that even though I didn't understand half of what that old goat said, whatever I promised during our ceremony I intend to fulfill. . . .

. . . Right now my main concern is getting away from here in one piece and upright. I want to get back to the woman I love just like about two million other men do. Peace. It's a lovely sounding word and sometimes I wonder if we'll ever have a chance to say it the way it should be said. . . . Clemenceau and Wilson must be doing something to earn their keep, but if so reports of their efforts certainly don't reach any of us who are doing the fighting. You know much more than I do which doesn't have to be much. We are completely in the dark all the time about what is really going on and I suspect the ground troops have the same problem. It makes us all wonder if they are afraid to tell us what is really happening. I guess when this war is over I'll have to buy a book to find out what it's all about. My God, the Russians had a big revolution in November and we didn't know anything about it until December. Then we heard something about a peace conference at a place called Brest-Litovsk but nothing more. We heard they shot that woman Mata Hari way back in October! Is that true? If you know what's happening please put it in your next letter . . . .

Toby's last letter was signed, "your loving Sergeant" and contained a postscript scribbled on the back of a printed aircraft maintenance form.

. . . I can't put Kiffin out of my mind. Sometimes he seems so much alive and so near. One of the regrets of my life is that you never met him. It's almost impossible for me to believe that he is gone forever—he was so much a part of my life. Please be sure to keep your eye open for any name that might even sound like his in the P.O.W. listings or if you hear anything (even the bad) around the embassy, let me

know right away. It is a terrible thing not to know whether
Kiffin is just letting the world grow old or is he maybe still
trying to set it on fire . . . . somewhere.

Early in October Toby's high-voiced Gasconian observer
became one of the thousands of typhoid victims in the French
army and was taken away to hospital, where he eventually
recovered. He was replaced by Achille Michaud, a thin and
very fragile looking youth fresh out of Observer's School. He
had only been aloft a few times during his training and
confessed that he was frightened of airplanes. His huge and
dolorous brown eyes became fixed and unseeing when he was
introduced to the foreigner who would be his pilot, for by
now Toby's long exposure to his dangerous and thankless
environment was beginning to tell on him. He had lost some
weight which in moments of total inactivity somehow gave
the impression that he was carved in bronze. There was no
surplus flesh anywhere about his face and his eyes were as
hard as his jaw line. Only his smile, still tolerant and warm,
rescued him from presenting a majestic portrait in bitterness
and tough usage.

By the end of 1917, Toby had become the classic appari-
tion of the veteran who knew his business thoroughly, a man
for whom fear had become a daily burden to endure and
hazard to be accepted, as he stalked cautiously through the
high jungle he knew so well.

There had been some slight improvement in the weapons
now his to command. The ridiculously slow and nearly de-
fenseless Caudron GIIIs which he had flown originally had
been replaced by the GVI model powered by two LeRhone
engines. The original twin-tail boom fuselage had been replaced by a conventional fuselage and tail feathers. The
observer operated his camera and a ring-mounted Lewis gun
from the rear cockpit. The two engines eliminated the slight
gyroscopic effect created by the single rotary engine in the
old Caudrons. The pilot no longer had to consider that any
turn he made to the left would be sluggish while to the right
would be very fast. Yet among all aviators at the front those
who flew Caudrons were still regarded with open pity and a sort
of dismayed admiration for their dogged courage. No one had
ever been known to volunteer for service in Caudrons and those
who could escape to any other duty departed in great haste.

New pilots and observers arrived at the front were easily identified even from some distance. There was no shine as yet to the fabric of their uniforms nor had there been time to take on the physical mold of the man they protected. Their gloves were uncreased and their belts still stiff. Their puttees were unscarred and the brims of their kepis still shone.

By now his uniform and all of his accoutrements fit Toby as if he had been melted down and ladled into it. The fur around his flying helmet was greasy from vaporized engine oil and the natural sweat of his repeated anxieties. His goggles had been tarnished by the sun until the lenses had taken on almost the full color spectrum from chrome yellow to soft violet. Between his morning and evening patrols there was always a slight indentation below his cheek bones left by the pressure of the Caudron's slip-stream against his goggles. He rubbed at the areas automatically when he was on earth again, but the marks were sometimes an hour in vanishing.

Toby's heavy winter flying suit made him look all the more imposing and when the young Michaud reported to him for the first time he could only stutter his name.

"Can you hit anything with a Lewis gun?" was Toby's only question.

Michaud said he had fixed a machine gun in the school at Le Plessis Belleville and confessed he had not done very well.

"Let's hope you'll be inspired to great accuracy if someone starts shooting at you," Toby said in English.

Michaud said he did not understand.

Toby said in French, "You will."

November second offered the torn land below a blood red dawning, softened in the valleys and minor depressions by thick fog which covered much of the ugliness. Toby's Caudron was still shedding the morning dew from its wings as it climbed toward the line of trenches in the vicinity of Luneville. Ascending toward a base of broken cloud Toby was undecided whether to attempt a flight on top where navigation to his objective might be difficult, or staying below and becoming a target for an unknown number of guns. Fine days brought the chance of both hazards. There had been only a very few sorties from which Toby had returned without a new blemish on his Caudron.

This morning provided extra complications. He was leading a flight of three Caudrons and until they reached their different objectives all decisions were his alone. Now with winter withering what was left of the French terrain the Germans were reported to be withdrawing and consolidating their forces. The Front had been suspiciously quiet for a week and French army headquarters wanted photographs which would reveal any new construction or troop concentrations accomplished by the Germans. For the Caudrons that meant relatively deep penetration beyond the regular German lines and the consequent much greater danger of attack by German fighters. Toby wished that he had a more experienced observer . . . it would be young Michaud's duty to do the photographing and at the same time keep an eye out for an attack from the Caudron's rear.

There was always hope, Toby thought, if a man got knocked down over his own territory, but here . . .?

He fought off a sense of foreboding. Wasn't it just another morning? He had lived through them all and would continue after the same pattern. The unlucky were just the unlucky and he was not one of them. Hadn't he now survived hundreds of such dawns?

The Caudron's two LeRhone engines purred nicely, and Toby had them so exactly synchronized they sounded as one. Little rivulets of the night's moisture formed tiny streams and wriggled upward along the windscreen. The air was so marble smooth Toby found the Caudron would fly hands-off, a rare accomplishment for such an ungainly bird.

There was a gash of scarlet, a wound cut across the eastern horizon and Toby saw a glint of its reflection strike the nose of the Caudron. And he thought how soothing this flight would be, how grand might become his sense of pride and satisfaction if this was not a "sortie," but a flight for some sensible purpose and without the chance of dying before it was done.

Although men were dying every minute in the land below, they perished insignificantly and one by one. Toby was not sure why the thought depressed him so on this morning which was no different than so many other mornings. The dying, he thought, were not terminating their lives in any great battle eventually to be embroidered on regimental colors. They were dead because a small bit of real estate was in long dispute and had itself now become forever useless because of abuse by the dead and soon-to-be-dead.

He marveled at the change in his thinking since he had arrived in France. All the slogans and resounding words by the mighty were so much garbage now. He must survive this day and he must survive the day after. *Nothing* else mattered. He must not let his guard down for an instant; Michaud now, why had he agreed to take the youth along on this morning? It was always some little thing that got you in the end; some obscure and apparently innocent factor which combined with something also unforeseen, brought instant disaster.

He could prove it. DeLage, a veteran pilot returning from leave, had been bringing a precious case of Moroccan oranges to the squadron mess. He was anticipating the wild welcome he would receive when he was jumped by an ordinary Hannover whose pilot had become hopelessly lost and wandered far behind the French lines. *There* was the totally unexpected. Trying to escape the Hannover, the oranges broke loose during DeLage's frantic maneuvers. They jammed the Caudron's controls at just the wrong movement and DeLage's life span ended in seconds. The poilus who found him said his corpse smelled of fresh oranges. They ate those that had not been crushed.

It was that way up here, and Toby supposed it was that way below. The battles of the Marne, Verdun, the Somme were great affairs and the dead were part of history. And then there was this morning and all other mornings like it when a single bullet fired carelessly into the air just happened to kill a man. They would be non-historic men who were simply delivering oranges, or relieving themselves, or taking pictures of mud holes from two thousand meters.

Toby shook his head violently. There was another way to die—even more insidious and quite as certain. He had also seen it happen and now what had begun as superstition was recognized throughout the Escadrille as reliable fact, or for the more cynical, as reliable as any other influence at the Front. It was sometimes known as the *"idée fixe"*— that is if you took off on a sortie with the notion you might not return the chances were heavily against your actual return. Every aviator flew with the ghost of the *"idée fixe"* at his side and it was ever a deliberate contest of the will to keep it tamed.

Now from aloft the land appeared to be still sleeping with a blanket of fog pulled over its features. When the sun rose even its feeble warmth would slowly dissipate the blanket and by midday the crater-pocked moonscape would once again be revealed. The very first of the sun sparkled across Toby' goggles as he turned back to young Michaud and made a fis with his gloved hand. It was his prearranged signal that he would clear his own Lewis gun and then Michaud should do the same.

Toby reached forward and pulled the trigger. The Caudron shook as he held the trigger until ten rounds had gone. He noted with regret that only two tracer bullets had left the muzzle. There was a shortage of the flaming type and the armorers were sparing until the Escadrille's supply could be replenished. Toby did not like using incendiary bullets, bu he had finally decided that even if they missed their targe their fright effect was matchless. Certainly if they scared the Germans as badly as they did him, then they had to be considered a valuable tool of his trade.

He turned momentarily to watch Michaud, who had not as yet fired a shot. He saw him place one hand on the Lewis gun's magazine while the other rested on the hand grip. He leaned back and away from the gun as if it were a wild animal about to spring at his throat. "God, please don't le him shoot our tail off," Toby muttered.

He pointed at Michaud's hand on the magazine and shook his head vigorously. If the fool pressed the trigger he might lose a finger. Michaud obediently took his hand away, but was apparently still reluctant to squeeze the trigger. At least. Toby thought, the gun was aimed at the open space between the Caudron's lower right wing and the tail.

Toby made a closed fist again and watched in fascination as Michaud took a number of deep breaths and made a movement to suggest he was actually looking through the ring sight although his face was so far away from the gun he could not possibly have achieved any accuracy.

Toby became fascinated with his observer's continuing struggle. Please God don't let any fighters come our way this day! It suddenly occurred to him that these moments when Michaud seemed to have no control over his own instincts were typical of the lunacy of the whole war. Here was a youngster with his mind and body both half-frozen a mile above the planet upon which he had been born and reared. He should be preparing for school at this hour, perhaps his mother would be making his breakfast and kissing him on an ear as she put down his plate. Here was a schoolboy confronted with a large black metal instrument which he knew made a lot of noise and jumped violently when activated. Never mind that it might spare his life and perhaps take another. Toby thought that Michaud had not gone that far in his reasoning—in fact reason had fled from him as it must temporarily for any combat soldier lest he lose it permanently.

"Come on! Pull the goddamned trigger!" Toby shouted above the sound of the engines, although he knew Michaud would not hear him. He would not have heard him if he had been standing by a secluded pond with only wilderness surrounding him. Michaud was in his own tight world for these few moments, a special little hell reserved for the overly sensitive, for those born of caution. He was in the air service of his country for God only knew what combination of reasons: a relative had urged him toward it, someone had told him he would at least live in relative cleanliness, a girl thought he would be a hero and he was trying to oblige, or perhaps he just liked the uniform. As for glory he would have been hard put to explain what glory was, let alone offer it as a cause of his present inability to perform an extremely simple act.

Toby checked all around the sky and found it empty except for the two companion Caudrons who would soon break away on their own. For this mission they had all been promised the protection of a dozen Nieuports, but of course they were not in evidence. If all went as usual they never would arrive, there being always some tangle in communications which was rarely unsnarled until everyone was back on the ground. And yet, he thought, they might be very high above at this very moment, their blue-gray paint making them nearly invisible against the slate sky; if by some miracle all the logistics had fallen properly into place they should be looking down on the Caudrons waiting to pounce on any attacker.

They would not see Michaud fussing about his gun. They would not see into the young man and find the inner terror which thus far prevented him from doing anything right. They would not see a seventeen-year-old who was trying to grow a moustache and failing as he must fail at everything else in such a hostile environment. Everything, Toby decided, except an extra portion of courage. Without that he would most certainly not even be here.

As they passed over the area where Toby supposed the

German lines must be, he knew a gathering sense of doom. Once again he must take the "idée fixe" by the throat and choke it. Son of a bitch. This was going to be a rough morning. He could smell it.

More minutes passed and still Michaud had not tested his gun. Was he going to take all morning to pull the trigger? He was not looking at the sky as he should have been; he was staring at the floor of his cockpit, presumably his boots held more interest than an early warning of death's approach.

Toby rose in his seat until his head was buffeted by the Caudron's slip-stream. He turned half around and swung his fist at Michaud's shoulder. *"Feu,"* he yelled. *"Allez."*

The blow knocked Michaud off balance and trying to recover he pulled instinctively at the gun handle. The Lewis responded with a long series of explosions and sent empty shell cases leaping into the slip-stream. Michaud looked appalled at what he had done and Toby resolved almost instantly that if they were attacked he would do his utmost to wrestle the awkward Caudron around until he could bring his own gun to bear on an enemy.

The area around Luneville held a cluster of German fighter fields, and although Toby had never seen one of the remnants of the dead Richtofen's yellow-nosed Jasta it was reported to be still in the vicinity commanded now by a Oberleutnant Goering. Those were the fancy boys, the "Kanones," as the Germans called them, and it was Toby's fervent wish they would never come close to his poor Caudron.

The three Caudrons came to the edge of the cloud deck which had formed a huge spatula poised between the low hills beyond Luneville. One of the other Caudrons turned right and the other left as planned. Now they would begin looking for something to photograph while Michaud photographed whatever lay straight ahead.

It was a senseless risk, Toby thought. The mission should have been scratched until there was something besides the top of a fog layer to photograph. He saw a church spire projecting upward through the fog and he thought that at least no fighters would be rising to meet them. On the ground the Bosche would not be able to see more than a few meters.

Toby circled over the outskirts of a factory town which emerged from the lip of the fog. He noted several crumbled factory buildings and a few streets—all deserted. He glanced back at Michaud who was at least doing what he was sent out to do. Take a lot of pictures, Toby instructed silently, the staff are never happier than when they have more pictures than they need. If only the so-called Intelligence officers would show a little more intelligence and realize that good men had died to take a photo that was sometimes swept away with a single gesture. One life, one sortie. Smile, earth. We want you to look pretty this morning. Watch the birdie now.

Why had he been so apprehensive on this glorious morning? Maybe because it had all been so easy? Michaud signalled that he had taken all the photos he could and the kid actually smiled. The sun, now quite mellow, splashed a lovely hue across his childish face, causing his features to take on a firmness they did not really have and presenting him altogether as a young golden statue clad in leather. And for the first time Toby saw an enchantment in his smile, the kind of projected warmth he must reserve for his family or those close enough to know him well. His smile said his peculiar work was now honestly done and the furtive fear so reminiscent of a cornered animal had left his eyes. Now he knew comradeship with his pilot and in the assimilation process generated by their mutual loneliness he had passed through one of the most fundamental mutations of man. In these few moments Toby thought, Michaud had gone directly from childhood to maturity; his mother would never know him again as she had before, nor would his friends. Now the alchemy of the sun in a lonely and dangerous sky made a mockery of his ridiculous moustache, yet no one could deny that he had become a soldier at war. It was fitting, Toby decided, that the most vicious act he had so far performed was to accidently shoot a few bullets into the empty air.

In a way I love him, Toby thought. An hour ago he was a stranger, but now he is like a kid brother and what I feel for him is just as solid and inflexible as it would have been after a lifetime together. The few seconds it had taken to spark the feeling for this boy in a man's clothing were magic without reasonable explanation. The sensation was a million years old, an unfashionable sharing that arrived as a companion to mutual threat. As if there was some embarrassment attached, the emotion was almost never acknowledged.

Well enough, my new friend, we will turn for home now. Continue to smile if you will and cheer the sky. Duty and discomfort and all that bullshit for La Belle France is done now and we can think of other things. The fog is our friend because it padlocks the Bosche to the ground and one more morning in an empty sky is ours to enjoy together and alone. Breathe of it deeply, young Achille, you who have hardly four years less than I—suck it into your deepest parts because it is always possible you will never see another morning like it.

Toby turned the Caudron away from the sun and felt a hint of its warmth on the back of his neck. Impossible! Surely no winter sun could penetrate the layers of mufflers and leather which bundled him against the cold. Yet even if it was his imagination, who cared? This was the kind of sky a man should inhabit.

It had been the farthest Toby had ever ventured behind the German lines and for a time it seemed the Caudron's westward progress toward Marson and safety was nearly zero. A westerly wind? Looking down there was no way to tell since the fog covered everything.

The LeRhone engines drummed steadily, the sun climbed higher and still, like a single fish in a vast aquarium, they flew on alone. Why had he allowed himself so many dire premonitions? It was unhealthy, a sign the war was getting to his brain as it did to so many who had flown long at the Front. It was a weakness he must not allow to fester.

Here on this morning there was peace embracing thousands of sky kilometers; it was a time to appreciate the near sensuous pleasure of flying the Caudron in such smooth air, to feast on the blueness of the sky above, and finally for the first time on any combat sortie, to allow his attention to drift from the task of staying alive. There was Lily floating across his vision. Saucy Lily, rambunctious Lily, complete with mischievous smile. My *wife*, he thought in some astonishment. Now why should he want to tell former stranger Achille Michaud that this was no place for a married man, phrasing it just that way to impress of course, announcing to him and to all the world for that matter that he was now, at twenty-one, a family man? Hello there, Achille, when the day comes you meet the right one, don't hesitate. Out here the most important thing in the world besides plenty of ammunition is to know someone cares.

He looked down at a small hole in the overcast and thought

he saw the jig-jag of a trench. German or French? It was there and then it was gone, and there was no flak anywhere to identify its nationality.

Never mind. They had been gone nearly three hours since takeoff and the Caudron held fuel for four. With a little help from an east wind it would even be possible to make Paris! Lily would just be off to work at the embassy. . . . perhaps not quite so early. She might even still be in the bed where he belonged with her slight smooth body almost lost in his arms, her lips and tongue exploring his mouth in subtle arousing ways he had never dreamed about.

He jumped at the tapping on his shoulder. Jesus, Achille! Have a care for my nerves. I am old and flighty.

He turned to look accusingly at Achille for spoiling his reverie and changed his mind. They were still a long way from Marson and Achille was unhappy.

"Are we lost?" Michaud yelled.

"No!"

"Then where are we?"

"Over Claremont!"

"Merci!" Michaud flashed his almost feminine smile again and assurance returned to his eyes.

Toby was glad that he had lied. Claremont? Why had he chosen the name when there must be fifty Claremonts in all of France and none at all that he knew, or would ever see? The important thing was that Observer Michaud who had entrusted him with his life should believe he knew exactly where he was. Claremont? It was easy to pretend there really was a Claremont hidden somewhere in the void below.

It occurred to him that he actually was lost. The trenches were behind him—or were they? Yes, according to the time elapsed they should be some ten minutes back east, but then where was home? It would be ahead, of course, onward to the west, but the land about Marson which had been clear of fog when they left was now obscured. And in between there was a new layer of gray scud, tightly packed like a long ill-formed sausage.

Toby pushed the nose of the Caudron down slightly until it was in an easy descent, then moved the elevator trim tab until it almost flew itself. Now then, where was *where*, and for that matter, where were the hundreds of thousands of human beings known to be crawling about in the mud below trying to move something from A that belonged to B and had somehow become misdirected to H where it was not needed at all? Where, no matter how ugly, was anything recognizable?

The Caudron's brass altimeter indicated they were at one thousand meters, but Toby had found it to be highly unreliable and rarely paid any attention to it. On artillery sorties he seldom flew above two hundred meters and on photo sorties the rule was to climb as high as the Caudron would go. Yet now, sandwiched between two layers of cloud and with the sun gone, it might be comforting to know how high they were flying. There were hills around, and after such a gloriously successful morning it would be disgraceful to ram into a hill.

Toby's first flying lessons echoed through his mind as he watched the closure narrow between the two cloud layers ahead. *Never* under any circumstances enter cloud with the idea of staying there for more than a few seconds. Disorientation would be immediate and a fatal crash was sure to follow. *No* man could fly in cloud. Observe the birds, *monsieur*. They knew better. Advice from the veterans had always been consistent: land and wait for the clouds to clear.

Yet it was too late to land and he could hardly turn back to the welcoming arms of the Germans. How much fuel remaining? Another thirty minutes, give or take five. Anything at all below? Only the scud, greasy gray and rumpling endlessly to the horizons. Above? A flat deck of lighter gray—bland and featureless. There was at least a vague horizon ahead, but it was fast becoming less sharply defined.

Toby squirmed in his seat. Yes, he was still going west according to the large compass on the floor. It was a reasonably accurate compass but the information it now offered was somewhat superfluous. There was no need to go further west, there was a need to settle down to earth—just anywhere by now would be landing in the middle of the French Army.

He saw a dark place off to the left and thought it might mean a clear spot beneath the overcast. He turned and was disturbed to see the compass revolve in the opposite direction. What was wrong here?

He knew a sudden sense of giddiness. He must get hold of himself.

Kiffin once said he knew what he would do if he were ever caught in cloud. As for everything else that challenged him he had a solution.

"First I'll take off my goggles and hold them in my hand. Then with my other hand I'll take out my wang and piss in the goggles. If the liquid doesn't spill then I'll know I'm right side up."

When asked who would be flying the airplane if both his hands were so busy he responded with a smile. "That's the trick. If you leave the airplane alone it will probably keep its feet pointed at the ground."

Toby felt another tapping on his shoulder. Jesus, would the kid behind him please have faith? Sooner or later there would be a break in the cloud and he would find out where they were, which certainly could not be far from Marson.

He turned to chide Michaud the boy observer—he must be told to mind his own bloody business—

Just then as he turned he saw it. A biplane was coming almost straight down on them. Michaud made a half-hearted attempt to swing his Lewis gun around when the nose of the biplane glittered with twin white flashes. Seconds later Toby heard the quick hammering of its machine guns and he saw Michaud's head recoil as if it had been yanked by a spring.

Toby's reaction was instinctive and immediate. He rolled the Caudron over in a steep dive.

Then he became aware of something passing; a mottled green and purple biplane cut across his nose at tremendous speed, and climbed almost straight up. He lost sight of the biplane just as the Caudron's nose plunged into the lower cloud.

Jesus! How could he have been so sound asleep? A Bosche from out of nowhere . . .. probably lost himself or he would never have been alone. Nor so far to the west. It was not the German custom. And he must have been in a hurry. He had not waited around for a sure kill—a mistake because the Caudron was flying normally.

It was considered unpleasant to hide even momentarily in a cloud, but then flying at the front was a series of unpleasantries. Everyone who flew Caudrons tried it sooner or later if they were lucky enough at the crucial time to have a cloud handy. He would remain cringing here a few seconds more, then ease up into the clear to make sure the Bosche was gone. Caudrons were no match for fighters. Jesus, what a stupid way to finish off the morning . . .

He turned apologetically to glance at Michaud and a heavy

groan escaped him. For there was the pretty boy face looking straight at him—but half the face was gone. Where the rather aristocratic nose had been there was a fragment of white bone intertwined with vines of scarlet pulp. The mouth which had only minutes before offered Achille Michaud's somewhat girlish grin was now a huge toothless crevasse. A vanilla white jawbone dangled in the slip-stream banging and twisting against his blood-soaked muffler.

But the eyes.

Michaud still lived in those eyes which were splattered with blood yet quite as intelligent and expressive as ever. The eyes cried out to Toby. For an instant he held the insane notion that he could hear the eyes. They were screaming at him. They were yelling, *You . . .* You told me everything would be all right . . .

A month of seconds passed and still he could not look away from those accusing eyes.

He caught himself wordlessly saying to the eyes, It will be all right. I'll get you down . . . please don't worry—

Don't worry, to a man with no face?

Tell a man who should be dead, a child who was even now reaching out a bloody claw as if to tap your shoulder one last time . . . tell him all would be well because you had been shot at so many times and were still in perfect health? Please have a look. Tell the claw and the eyes there was a first time for everything?

About to vomit, Toby turned away from the eyes. He knew now that he must make an immediate choice and they were both poor ones. He could violate all he had been told and try to stay in the cloud, descending as slowly as the Caudron would fly and hoping for flat land when his wheels finally touched earth. Or he could climb back up until he found some forward visibility (it could not be more than a few meters), and take his time looking for a hole large enough to reveal the ground. That would be the safe way. But how long would he be searching for a hole and then spiraling down? Michaud's face was torn away, but his eyes said he was alive and he might at least continue to exist if the flow of his blood could be stopped. Someone had to help Achille Michaud immediately and there really was no choice. My job, Toby thought during the seconds it took him to make the decision, is to deliver what's left of this boy . . . this man . . .

He closed the throttles on the LeRhone engines and pushed the nose down. And at once there was only the thrumming sound of the Caudron's many flying wires, a basso effect at first and then a pitch Toby discovered he could adjust from high to low by pulling back on the control yoke or pushing forward.

He reminded himself that he needed iron discipline if he intended to remain in cloud. He must reject the usual messages of his senses. If he felt he was turning then he should resist a temptation to correct for the turn and if he somehow thought one wing was low he should dismiss the thought and try to find some comfort in remembering that the Caudron's inherent stability was the one quality it had. If he could restrain himself and simply keep the rudder bar straight across the fuselage and the control yoke at the wings level position and then, most important of all, keep enough speed to avoid a stall, there would be a fair chance the Caudron might hit on an even keel.

It could be done, it *must* be done. God would provide a beautiful flat field without a shell hole in it.

Toby found that keeping his speed in the descent was easy. Just once he had allowed the nose to ease up and the Caudron began to shake violently as it approached a stall. He shoved the nose down instantly, the crazy vibration ceased, the flying wires took up their eerie chorus again.

How long? Toby glanced at the brass altimeter. Five hundred meters. Say it was off a hundred meters? Then an eternity would pass before they hit something—Michaud's private eternity.

Wait. Not so private. For the first time it occurred to Toby that he was sitting on the arrival end of a projectile. The wood and canvas bathtub which formed a visibly reassuring barrier around him was as fragile as an eggshell. Achille, you may have company. I could be waiting for you.

The engines, still revolving slowly in the slip-stream, spasmodically backfired. Toby found their occasional popping distracting and debated cutting off the fuel entirely. He changed his mind. The engines might come in very handy if he was lucky enough to break out of the fog a few feet above the ground. Just a few feet, God, if you don't mind.

Soon it became much darker in the cloud, a hint, Toby knew, that the ground could not be far below.

He continued, gasping at the clammy shroud which now so

enveloped the Caudron he could barely see the wing tips. The altimeter read four hundred. At least it was working.

Four hundred meters . . . one hundred meters per minute . . . four minutes to a collision. But how to compensate for the inaccuracy of the instrument? It might be three minutes or even two. So soon, this strange twilight had come while still the glorious morning must not be far above.

Toby's bowels ached until for a moment he thought he might lose them. His mouth was dry, eyes burning with fatigue. He raised his goggles, wet now with the clouds' accumulated moisture. Little globules of water riveled down his face. He ran his tongue around his lips, tasted salt. Some moisture from the cloud perhaps, but mostly his own sweat. Sweat from a man who not so long ago, on a former morning of a former life, was quivering with the cold.

He swallowed hard to relieve the increasing pressure in his ears, and as if the difference triggered something basic inside him he was no longer afraid. Suddenly now with less than a minute at best, when he was certain something huge and immovable would come looming straight at him out of the fog, he became removed from the scene. The transformation was incredibly easy. He was riding along at one side of the Caudron's blunt nose, witnessing the unfortunate demise of a valued friend. It was uncanny, unexplainable, and altogether real. He sensed that he would not be hurt, but his condemned friend, good old Toby Bryant of Lincoln, Nebraska, would be. He was on his way to destruction in a far away land and there was absolutely nothing he could do about it. It was true then, the legend that so many soldiers had told—there is a moment between life and death when you leave your carcass and simply bear witness to its destruction. Those who had experienced the sensation talked about it in wonder. Some argued that it was nature's last protection, others never quite recovered from their sense of awe. But none who had come so close to death were willing to deny the experience no matter how sharply their story was ridiculed. They stuck by their conviction that something extraordinary had occurred, and now Toby knew why.

A single brick smokestack rushed at him out of the murk. It was a little below and to the left and it vanished as instantaneously as it had appeared. The ochre ruins of an industrial building appeared and disappeared, then directly below for but part of a second, a railroad locomotive. Its steam joined the fog and the vision was gone.

Toby could see beyond the Caudron's nose now, but only long enough for flashing images. A company of poilus scattered like blue seeds as the wheels slammed down on a road and the Caudron bounced back into the mist again. A line of parked camions swept by the left wingtip—all but the last in line. The last camion had a trailer of sorts that caught at the wing and swung the Caudron around until it slid sideways across an accumulation of rubble and with one final spasm of half-flight, crunched to a stop in a stone quarry.

Soldiers came running from everywhere.

CHAPTER
6

The stone quarry was nearly fifty kilometers west of the lines and ten minutes flying time beyond Marson. It was used as an ammunition and supply dump by the French Transport Corps and would have been an ideal locale for a crash landing if an unknown German's timing had been five or ten minutes later. The army maintained a first class dressing station within the shelter of the quarry itself, and the doctors on duty said that although Achille Michaud would have been disfigured for life and would never have uttered a word again, given a few more minutes they could have saved his life.

The photos taken from the Caudron were destroyed in the crash. Achille Michaud, age seventeen, was awarded the Croix de Guerre and promoted to corporal posthumously. His father, a prosperous merchant and a widower, accepted the honors in the name of his son, and two weeks later shot himself.

Sergeant Toby Bryant suffered no more than a broken nose and right foot and was fully conscious when the crowd of curious soldiers pulled him from the wreckage. Later he was grateful that all he saw of his observer was the bottom of his boots as they carried him away. He dreaded seeing those eyes again, although he did for many nights thereafter.

Toby was first sent to the hospital at Etamps for repairs and crutches, and on January sixth, on an afternoon of freezing rain, Lily met his train at the Gare St. Lazare. For minutes they said nothing, managing somehow to isolate themselves from the hubbub surrounding them. He held her in his arms and pressed his lips to hers and they stood swaying ever so slightly as if a soft breeze had set them in motion.

"Dear God, how I love you," she said at last.

"I'm grateful to the same guy for bringing me here," he said.

124

The cobbles outside the station glistened in the rain and they had a long wait for a taxi. No one, military or civilian, seemed to care that Toby was on crutches; they ran into the street and flagged the first available taxi and then were gone.

Lily was soon exasperated. When a fat burgher tried to elbow his way past them bound for an approaching taxi her reaction was instantaneous. With two quick gestures she closed her umbrella, reversed her grip on it and caught the burgher's ankle in the handle. He went sprawling headlong across the cobbles.

Toby was still laughing when she slammed the door behind her.

"We could have used you against Iowa," he said as she bounced down on the seat beside him. "Am I ever glad you're on our side!"

"I must leave this country soon," she said. "I'm becoming much too French."

The following weeks were a pleasant interlude. There was the memorable night they dined at Prunier's—a wedding present from Lily's father, who sent them enough British pounds to pay the bill. It was outrageous enough to convince them they had sinned shamefully against the rules of war.

The occasion of their dinner, which included those gastronomical delights of a wartime Paris and which most of the other patrons seemed to take in their stride, was of double significance. Toby's transfer to the United States Army Air Service had at last been officially approved. Because of his experience he was commissioned a first lieutenant, and this night was the first time he had worn his new brown uniform complete with wings, medals, and Sam Browne belt. He had been assigned to the 99th Aero Squadron as a combat flight instructor. Now rid of his crutches, he would soon take up his duties actively at Pau.

Prunier's fairly glittered with high ranking officers of every allied nation and an assortment of politicians, profiteers, and expensive whores not to be seen anywhere else except possibly Maxim's. Toby said he thought this place with its bowing waiters was a pretty fancy joint for a Nebraska boy, but as long as the food kept coming he had no intention of leaving. He also noted that nearly everyone in the restaurant, including the women, were smoking and he said that fact alone would convince many people in Lincoln that the devil himself was in charge.

Because Toby's French was so limited Lily appointed herself to the selection of their repast. "It's all on daddy," she laughed, "so let's do what he said and go the limit." She ordered a bottle of Dom Perignon *blanc de blanc* to precede the salmon fumé. It would be followed by a Supreme de Sole Cremaillere with a change of wine to a Pouilly Fuisse from the village of Solutré. Next they would have the Cotelettes d'Agneau Marigny and wash it down with a Hospices de Beaune 1910. Finally, she thought, there should be room for a pair of Meringue glacée and a final coffee. Even before the champagne arrived they estimated the cost to be more than Toby had been paid in his first half year as a soldier of France. He asked if it had always been like this while he had been away flying but there was so much laughter and noise all about them he missed Lily's reply. Unaccountably then his mind drifted, and for an agonizing moment he saw the face of Achille Michaud pasted like a mask on every man within his line of sight.

"You're sad, my love," she said, and he found his smile again.

"Oh . . . I was thinking of Kiffin," he said, "and how his wake might last for a hundred years. But never mind, I'm fine now. I'm with the most beautiful girl in the world in the finest restaurant in the world so how can I be unhappy?" A moment later he said to himself in wonder, "Is this real? Can I really be alive?"

There was a prolonged wait between the entreé and dessert out of respect, Lily explained, for the cultivated digestive patterns of Prunier's patrons. He saw then that she was looking at him with a strange light in her dark eyes.

"What are you staring at?" he asked, and noticed that he was having trouble focusing his own eyes. Was his good wife a little drunk?

"I'm counting my blessings," she said. "The world is full of young widows and I'm dining with the handsomest officer in Paris. Except for his nose."

She kissed her finger and pressed it gently against his still slightly discolored nose. It was now obvious that the rock quarry doctor had not been interested in cosmetic repairs.

"I must look like an unsuccessful prize fighter," he said.

"Wrong, my love. All wrong. That new nose gives you a certain air of distinction. It embellishes the face of a man who has done something . . . and will do a great deal more. It goes with the jaw and the eyes and the way you carry your head. I find it quite beautiful."

"You're pie-eyed," he said solemnly.

"I see us now," she went on, "ten years from now. We are settled down in New York or Boston. We have a house by the sea . . . an old fashioned dream house with mullioned windows. People will ask how it can be that a successful businessman has a busted proboscis like yours and you can be mysterious if you please or tell them how you were a genuine hero in the great war—"

"You're ruining my appetite for the dessert."

"You don't like the picture?"

"No. First, I don't want to live in a big city. They scare me. Second, I'm no businessman and never will be."

She pretended to pout. "This conversation strikes me as being between two people who have just met. You *are* willing to work for a living?"

"Sure. I'm sort of interested in airplanes. Who knows, I might even stay in the Air Service."

"Somehow I never pictured myself as a military wife. I grew up with so many in the embassies . . . . daddy's friends. It always seemed to me being nice to the colonel's wife was too important."

"Unless you're the colonel."

"Do you suppose you'll be tired of me then? After all, this is a wartime romance. Everyone warns against it."

"You can pretend I'm a different guy. I'm in a different uniform—"

"Shall I slap you now for that insulting thought or wait until later?"

"After the meringue, please."

"Can't we have our first fight and get it over with? Then we can settle down and live happily forever after."

"Not in a big city."

"Okay, we'll compromise on a middle-size city."

"I'll settle for a big town like Lincoln. I'm homesick."

"What in the world would I do all day in *Lincoln?* Play bridge?"

"I don't know. We'll probably have to compromise on a lot of things."

"I love you, Lincoln or no Lincoln."

The meringues arrived, and they wept a little because it tasted so good and because the wine had finally taken almost total command. Lily ordered a brandy to go with the meringue and their eyes were half-closed before they finished it. They mumbled and began to say things they forgot to finish and were alternately filled with delight and distress, as drunk on themselves, and their personal future as on the wine they had consumed. An English brigadier at the next table insisted on buying them another brandy, "to welcome my American comrade to the war," and it was during the consumption of that final glass that Lily laid her head against Toby's shoulder and closed her eyes. She was still more asleep than awake when amid the cheers of Prunier's staff and gourmets he picked her up, carried her out of the restaurant and deposited her gently in a taxi.

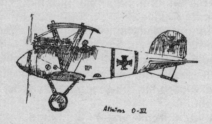

Albatros O-III

Forty miles away a hundred thousand men were living in knee-deep mud and doing their utmost to kill each other.

Like Toby, most of the Americans who had been flying for the French, including those who had flown in the now-famous Lafayette Escadrille, transferred to the American Air Service. James Norman Hall, who flew in the Lafayette and aspired to being a writer, was pleased when his personal insignia, a hat in a ring that had decorated his Nieuport, was adopted by the U.S. 94th Aero Squadron and would be flown into battle by such young Americans as ex-racing driver Eddie Rickenbacker and Reed Chambers. The Americans were being assigned the new Spads to fly, and everywhere among the airmen of all the allied nations a new atmosphere of optimism prevailed. The Germans were still vicious ntagonists, particularly when flying their new Fokker D–VIIs, ut the tide of war on the embattled ground was beginning to wing, and the more intelligent Germans knew it.

The fortunes of the opposing nations in the air was of elatively little concern to the majority of the generals, who till thought in the traditional style of tribal chieftans. Through he depth of the 1918 winter both sides were unavoidably ocked in an appalling waste of lives and materiel while ighting for a few yards of constantly pummeled mud. The asualties on both sides were victims of the inflexible theory hat only the foot soldier could establish and hold dominion ver whatever landscape was in dispute.

Few generals, much less their staffs, held airmen in much egard. They were inclined to employ airplanes in a strictly uxiliary role, as reapers of information, in essence no more han fast moving balloons. They had some cause for their eeling. Airplanes were next to useless at night and in bad veather, and for damage accomplished against the enemy as veighed against the cost and effort, there was little encourage-ment to be found. The use of aircraft as bombers proved to be a two-edged sword and was logistically disappointing. Since he first Zeppelins attacked London in 1915 the bombing of England had continued in one form or another and Paris itself ad been bombed by both airplanes and lighter-than-air-craft. The results seemed of questionable value, mostly to terrorize he citizens and weld them more tightly than ever to their own overnments. Accuracy on target was poor, the lumbering Gothas, the Royal Flying Corps's big Handley Pages, and the talian Capronis were expensive to build and maintain and vulnerable to both air and ground attack. The damage they lid to military targets was relatively negligible and was usu-lly repaired or replaced in a very short time.

Most disenchanting of all was the relatively few numbers of bodies actually engaged in air combat; the generals, Foch, Ludendorff, Haig, and now Pershing, dealt constantly with he fates of millions committed to the march. The much-oublicized exploits of a few proper heroes in the sky was nainly supportive of war bond sales. Many high ranking officers were openly critical of the airmen, labeling them spoiled adolescents whose curiously special status eroded norale among the regular troops. For every pilot, they said,

at least twenty sound men who would make good foot so
diers were required to keep him in the air.

The insatiable human body appetites of the vast armie
engaged from Palestine to Russia, through the Balkans and o
to the western front made the numerical proportion of thos
men who actually went aloft seem miniscule.

There were additional influences which made open acclai
for the Air Services still reserved. While the Central Powe
were reeling from their difficulties on all fronts, the revol
tion in Russia put an end to any effective resistance and th
Germans were thereby able to transfer large numbers of me
and materiel to the western front.

There were other signals interpreted by the Kaiser, Vo
Hindenberg and Ludendorff that there still might be time t
rescue the fate of the Central Powers. The blockade of Er
gland by their undersea boats was reasonably satisfying an
was now becoming manifest in the nourishment of the Er
glish people—a recent conscription of military-age males i
Britain found only three out of nine fit for active duty.

Time, however, was actually running out. In spite of th
afflictions suffered by English and European civilians th
arriving American troops who now came pouring into Franc
in ever increasing numbers fared so well that only an occa
sional lack of tobacco gave them cause for grumbling. Per
shing himself found time to cable Washington insisting tha
tobacco was indispensible as a daily ration and thousands o
tons should be shipped without delay. In contrast Nikola
Lenin, whose enormous influence in pulling the claws o
Czarist Russia and thus prolonging the dreary progress of th
war, forbade smoking in his vicinity.

Although the generals of both powers studied aerial photo
with more than passing interest, the newly commissione
First Lieutenant Toby Bryant decided an actual flight over th
front would prove more educational than any other means at
general's command. Knowing his recommendation would nc
go far unless he complied with the proper channels, he wrot
a letter to his commanding officer at Pau offering to take an
Allied general for a flight over those problem areas pertinen
to his command. The flight would be under very heavy escor
of the new Spads and there should be relatively little dange
to the general's person. Lieutenant Bryant never received
reply to his letter.

Perhaps if the origin of Toby Bryant's persuasion had been higher than that of a lieutenant at least one general might have been prewarned of the major offensive launched by Ludendorff on the 21st of March 1918. While the majority of American ground troops were still unloading their supplies to the tune of "K-K-K-Katy" and "Somebody Stole My Gal," the Germans began their drive with a bombardment of six thousand guns and a heavy attack of poison gas. The fog which prevailed in the area of St. Quentin for several days hampered the support of the Allied airmen, but Toby was convinced that an affirmative response to his letter would have made concealment of such a prodigious offensive impossible.

The Germans pushed back the British line for forty miles and soon took Ham, Paupame, Chauny, Noyon, Montdidier, and Toby's old base at Marson. It was the beginning of the German army's desperate attempt to salve their situation before sufficient American troops arrived to alter the balance of strength. Like some beast snarling in a final spasm of ferocity the Germans pressed on, stormed the ridge at Messines, and took Armentieres. The defending British were badly bloodied, with an opening in their lines large enough for Ludendorff to begin the third battle of the Aisne with some confidence.

While most generals preferred to deal with the traditional confusions and perplexities of war, they were also obliged to be foster parents to the rambunctious and unpredictable flying units which had a way of taking the war into their own hands. The frail relative had multiplied upon itself until it was now evident on every hand. There were now so many aircraft darting about the skies along the western front, that their noisy presence and unpredictable arrivals made them as difficult to ignore as hornets' nests. The Royal Flying Corps after three years of heroic sacrifices trying to fight and survive against the better-equipped Germans had been designated a separate service known as the Royal Air Force. The extraordinarily courageous English, Australians, South Africans and Canadians who made up the volunteer force were at last equipped with aircraft suitable to their courage and devotion. They were flying the S.E.5, the Sopwith Camel, and the new British de Havillands.

The spring of 1918 also brought a revival of *esprit* in the French Air Service. While many Nieuport squadrons were

still very active, the new Spads were gathering in ever greater
swarms, and their performance aloft caused the Germans to
treat them with extreme caution.

America's military minds lagged in acceptance of the
aircraft as a legitimate weapon of war and the men who flew
them as a separate breed of soldier. Toby Bryant and most
Americans who transferred from the air services of other
nations or those who had trained in England were actually
commissioned in the Signal Reserve Corps, United States
Army. They continued in such ambiguity even when attached
for actual fighting duty with such outfits as the 65th Royal
Air Force Squadron. Likewise Toby Bryant, who instructed
almost as many French as newly arrived Americans in the art
of "seeing the enemy before he sees you," was asked to
divide his loyalties. He lectured on survival at the front one
day in his funny, halting French, while the next day found
him among his own countrymen.

The big German spring offensive also prevented any hope
of frequent reunions with Lily; the need for more and more
airmen and Toby's bilingual ability on the one subject kept
him hard at the instructing business until summer. Then even
the long evenings were scheduled. He was rather surprised to
discover that he was not longing to join those who left his
care and went off to the front with his final admonition to
"keep your head on a swivel and never relax for an instant."
He knew that day by day the air war was heating up and even
the best of airmen had been killed. Guynemeyer died for
France in September of '17 and Werner Voss for Germany
the same month. Nineteen-eighteen promised to be even cru-
eler to the veterans. Manfred von Richtofen was killed in
April and Raoul Lufbery in May. Lieutenants Hobbs and
Van, Americans who had flown with the Lafayette Escadrille,
were both killed in action, a sorry day for Toby, who knew
them well. He began to question the sum of a man's luck;
was there a point of exhaustion or did it carry on to infinity?
And how much of his own had been spent?

By September when the British began their big drive
toward Cambrai, a short tour at the front convinced Toby that
what little appeal the air war had once held for him was pretty
much gone. Where he and Kiffin had been part of a unique
little group of self-styled warriors fencing aloft with an unknown number of equally individualistic enemies, now com-

parative armadas of aircraft cluttered the skies. During the previous year of 1917 the Germans had built nearly twenty thousand airplanes, so many that by 1918 the experience level of their pilots had fallen drastically. Yet even in the hands of their neophyte airmen the Fokker D–VII was considered a deadly fighter and the Albatros C–XII and the new Pfalz were almost as dangerous. The French, now in full production on the Spad XIII had turned out nearly twenty-five thousand airplanes by 1918 and more than ninety thousand engines. Despite that they would never fly American built airplanes at the front, new American squadrons were being formed every day and the total effect of men and materiel on those who had served as one of the handful of pioneers was strangely uninviting. Now, Toby thought, there was much more future in the air than flying war machines and his interest in their more peaceful uses became a new dedication for him. He began to gather as much aeronautical lore as he could manage and among other discoveries found that the Russians had built enormous four-engined bombers before the war had begun. These 1913 behemoths were known as the Ilya Mourometz and he wondered why they could not later be used in aerial commerce. Even the Italians were building the huge Caproni CA 30s before the war began. Toby was mesmerized by a photo he saw in a French magazine of the new Italian Macchi flying boat. He thought her graceful lines were a feast for the eye and he wrote a long letter to Lily describing the Macchi's virtues and his regret that his own country, where powered flight had first been successful, was now far behind the Europeans in all phases of aviation.

Lily's response was on the testy side:

> I look forward eagerly to our life together when this dreadful war is done with, but am I due for a shock in finding my husband is more in love with airplanes than with me? You write about airplanes as if they were some gorgeous blonde and I'm not sure whether that's unhealthy or just a quirk of your nature. Forgive me, love, I guess I'm just jealous, but I do wish you would devote just a little more space to our grand love affair and perhaps somewhat less to the glorious future of flying machines . . .

Midsummer brought the second battle of the Marne, and the dominance of Allied air superiority forecast the steady and final precipitous decline of the German ground armies.

Germany's allies fared no better. In June during the battle of the Piave, the Austrians lost a reported one hundred thousand men, and from then on the morale of the Austrian army was left in tatters. By September the Austrian government requested a peace conference with President Wilson, and in October they were joined by the Germans in pleading for an armistice. All of these appeals were rejected. After all, a sense of total victory was in the air. Everywhere in the Austro-Hungarian Empire there was confusion and the despair of revolution.

Ludendorff's exhausted troops managed to slow the Allied advances in the Argonne and at Ypres, but the futility of their brave effort was reflected in the dismay of the German flying men at their inability to hold their own in the sky. The foundering of the German war gargantua began almost simultaneously with the confusion, unrest, and finally revolution inside the fatherland itself. As early as October repeated pleas were made by the Central Powers for an armistice. To no avail. Subsequently, Ludendorff in a temporary recapture of his personal confidence, spoke of renewed attack in the spring of 1919, but he was no longer trusted by his own government and his threats were not taken seriously. There were already widespread mutinies in the Geman navy, and then the Kaiser abdicated.

At last, on the eighth of November 1918, a German armistice commission met with General Foch in his railway car at Compiégnee, and on the eleventh of that month hostilities came to a whimpering end.

Oberleutnant Hermann Goering, then in command of the *Richthofen Geschwader,* thumbed his nose at the armistice terms and eased his humiliation in the fact that his fighters had not been defeated in the air and were willing to go on fighting if so ordered. And he saw to it that when his aircraft were finally delivered to the French as agreed, they were damaged as much as possible. The red painted machines were to be handed over at Aschaffenburg, and he told his pilots, "If you make a terrible landing we will be proud of you." And he at once began to form the nucleus of a new luftwaffe.

As for Lieutenant Toby Bryant, who had anticipated an appropriate celebration with his wife in Paris, he was bitterly disappointed when he was assigned to the 141st Aero Squadron and sent off to the army of occupation headquarters at

Coblenz, Germany. His enthusiasm and dedication to aeronautics, duly noted by his superiors, had backfired on him. He was considered the ideal candidate to survey and evaluate what was left of the German aircraft, arrange for the shipping of those he thought worthy of further study in the United States, and oversee the disposal of the dregs. To assuage him and give him somewhat more authority in his new duties, he was promoted to captain. It was three long long months before he was able to return to Paris.

All through those three months the city of Paris became the central staging area for the unraveling of the gigantic war effort that had been structured by the Allies. The wounds of France itself healed slowly, and certain sections of the western front such as the territory about the Chemin des Dames and Verdun would never again be fit for any useful purpose. The blood and bones of countless young men had been mixed and pounded into the tortured earth, and huge shellholes overlapping rim to rim rendered the terrain as desolate as the surface of the moon. Refugees from throughout Europe were washed up on the beaches of Paris like so much flotsam, and their orderly disposition became a diplomatic problem for every continental identity.

Hundreds of thousands of military survivors, prisoners, the lame and the sick had now to be sent home; the Germans to what was left of their fatherland, the English to a land left scrungy by deprivation, the Americans and Canadians to lands which had been spared any ordeals but were far away and subject to many difficulties in transport. The sweetness of victory was soon lost to the hordes of young Americans who could only think of home and wait impatiently for the magic order that would send them home.

It was automatic that the American embassy in Paris was overwhelmed with the details involved in the transport of goods and men to their homeland, the Red Cross, the forthcoming peace conference, the creation of a League of Nations so dear to the heart of the American president Wilson, and his own pending arrival at Versailles.

As a consequence of these many demands and her multilingual ability Lily worked at the embassy almost all except her sleeping hours and was employed at many jobs normally handled by higher officials. One rainy evening of mixed rain and snow showers, after darkness had long enshrouded the

streets of Paris, she had been assisting in the passport division
when a gaunt young man approached her desk. He looked
like any one of the countless refugees she had seen in the last
month and she sighed because it had been a long day and she
thought his story would be one more pathetic version of all
the others she had heard. She wanted to go home to the
freezing little flat on the Boulevard Raspail, crawl into bed
for warmth, and write more of the letter she had begun to
Toby. Like all the rest, this young man smelled of his anxieties and displayed a sort of invincible belief that she, Lily
Bryant, could pass a miracle. Like all the others he needed a
shave, and his rumpled suit looked like he had slept in it for
weeks.

She realized quite suddenly, though, that this young man
was different . . . he was smiling and he carried a strangely
audacious air as well as a small duffel bag and a violin case.
A traveling musician? A gypsy perhaps, lured by those hopeful thoughts that brought all kinds of refugees to the American embassy? He had a confident go-to-hell look that she
found challenged her own sense of independence.

She addressed him in French. "What can I do for you,
monsieur?" she asked, wondering why his eyes seemed to
look right through her. She was astonished when he answered
her in English with an unmistakable American accent.

"I would like a passport."

"You're an American?"

"What else?"

"What happened to your passport? The one you must have
come here with . . . or did you come with the troops?"

"I came under my own steam."

"When?"

"Two years ago."

"My, my. Where have you been all this time?" Lily could
not explain even to herself why she was so compelled to ask
for such personal information. She was serving only as a
clerk and was certainly not authorized to issue passports. Yet
there was some instant magnetic influence emanating from
this young man, and she told herself she would be both a liar
and a hypocrite if she refused to admit it.

"My real name is Rip van Winkle . . . that is, it could
be . . ." He paused and smiled. "I've been unavoidably
detained," she vaguely heard him say, but she was not really

listening. She was looking into his eyes and reminding her inner self that she was not as free as she used to be.

"Did you lose your passport or was it stolen?" Suddenly she found herself wanting very much to help him, but she knew the honest thing to do was to tell him to come back in the morning when an authorized official might actually do something. And yet she was strangely reluctant to see the back of the man . . .

"I'm not sure what happened to my passport. I guess it's like a lot of other things in this life. You forget who you are for more than a few minutes and when you wake up you realize a lot of things you counted on as being in the right place aren't there any longer. After they lock you up for a couple of years and then let you go it's hard to get back in synch. Everything's changed. Everything's moved around or gone."

"You've been in jail?"

"Sort of . . ."

"May I ask where?" Here she was at six o'clock on a wretched, bone chilling night chitchatting with a criminal. Thank God for the marine guards. She shivered involuntarily and wondered if she was coming down with a cold.

"I've been in a place called Landshut."

The name meant nothing to her. "What did you do?" The *nerve* of myself! she thought. Who gave her the right to be so prying?

"I murdered several people . . . all legal, I assure you."

She swallowed and reached for her raincoat. She decided to be huffy. "It's past closing time," she said. "I suggest you come back in the morning . . . and perhaps present yourself more seriously."

"I'm very serious. And I have some papers to prove it. *Viola*."

He handed her a dirty, much-abused envelope. Overcome with curiosity she peeked inside and saw an identification card complete with a small photo. She glanced at him and saw only a vague resemblance to the face on the card which identified him as a member of the French Armed Forces, specifically La Legion Etrangere, the 183rd. Infantry Regiment. Then she saw the name and her heart stopped.

"*Kiffin. Kiffin* Draper." She threw herself at him, covering his face with kisses. He retreated in astonishment.

"Hey, lady . . . wow, things have changed. Just a damn minute. Shall I say we hardly know each other?"

"Oh, but we *do*. And lordy have I got a surprise for you. Come with me." She seized his arm and pushed him only half-protesting toward the door. Once in the street she hailed a cab and gave the address on the Boulevard Raspail.

"Don't say anything," she said, taking his hand. "Just don't say anything until we get there."

"Get where? If I'm being kidnapped you could at least tell me where we're going."

During the ride he kept the violin case on his knees and drummed his fingers on it.

"What are you doing with a violin?"

"I thought you told me not to say anything."

"Touché."

"I learned to play it in prison camp . . . not very well, but it kept me from going nuts."

The five flights to Lily's flat were hard on ex-prisoner of war Kiffin Draper. "I've lost a lot of steam," he apologized when they reached the top landing. "And I seem to be slow getting it back."

As she sought in her bag for her keys he leaned against the wall painting from his exertions. "There is something very fishy here. Why is anyone from the embassy being so nice to me? All I want is a passport."

"I thought you'd like to meet my husband," she said, opening the door.

"I'm not so sure about that."

She turned on the feeble electric light which hung from the ceiling and watched smiling as he made a wary entrance. He stood for a moment in the middle of the room still holding the violin case and the little duffel bag. His eyes surveyed the room, the small table beneath the skylight which extended almost to the floor and was now opaque with mushy snow, the two chairs, the packing crate which served as repository for books and magazines, the kerosene heater with its grill of brass hot water pipes, and the single gas burner and copper sink in the corner which served as a kitchen. Beyond an open doorway he saw the vague outlines of a brass bed.

It was so cold in the flat he could see the vapor of his breath.

"Welcome to our home," Lily said.

He looked at her carefully. "Who are you? You don't talk or even look like a real American."

"Put your things over there in the corner and stay a while. Have you eaten?"

"Not too recently."

"Good. I have some leftover stew from last night. It will warm you up a bit."

"I was wondering if you were an Eskimo." He put his violin case and duffel bag in the corner, placing them exactly as if he thought they might be needed in a hurry.

She knelt by the brass heater and lit the wick beneath the pipes. "This thing will not exactly produce unbearable heat, but it will take off the chill," she said. "There's no central heating in any of these old buildings but we do have a more important luxury. Would you like a hot bath?"

"Madame," he said in mock offense. "Are you hinting that my person might be on the gamey side?"

She moved quickly around the flat, lighting two gas burner lamps projecting from the wall. "As you see, we do have gas up here. I've only to light the thermal in the bathroom and you'll be cooking in no time."

"Aha," he said, cocking his head. "Now I know why you brought me here. You're a cannibal. I must warn you there's not much meat left on my bones."

She went in to the bedroom and returned almost immediately. She handed him a large framed photograph. "Meet my husband."

He glanced at the photo, caught his breath, then canted it toward the light for better illumination. "*You're* married to *Toby*? You really *are*? Oh for God's sake! Oh, for the love of Mike . . ." He muttered and seemed at a loss for words. "Well . . . well, I'll just plain be damned. Where is the old goat?"

"In Germany. He should be back next week. To stay forever, I hope."

He reached out and took her shoulders in his hands. His blue-gray eyes inspected her cautiously, as if he were seeking some known disfigurement or some reason to question the truth of what he had just learned. "You are one lucky gal," he said finally, "and it looks to me like Toby is a lucky man. Congratulations to both of you."

He kissed her on both cheeks and she said, "Thank you," and brushed away a tear. "Pardon. I cry easy."

"I assume you're happy?"

"Yes. I cry most when I'm happy. It's a family trait."

She took out a handkerchief and wiped at her nose. "I love him with all my heart and soul. He has become my life, my joy, and my pride."

"Good. I can go take a bath in peace now. With that kind of an attitude and unless old Toby has changed, you can't lose."

They ate the stew and sopped the bread she had bought that morning in the gravy, and they drank a half bottle of *vin ordinaire* before they had finished their toasts to Toby, their future, and Kiffin's plans for the next few months.

"This is January and you were released in November? Where have you been the last two months?"

"Here and there."

"I would think you'd come running toward the next ship home."

"There were some problems. When they first captured me I was well fed and a bit nasty. I gave them a name out of my imagination and a nonexistent serial number. I lived to regret being a wise guy."

"Because your friends couldn't find out if you were alive or dead? Toby was in mourning for weeks. That wasn't very thoughtful of you."

"We didn't know the Germans would actually publish P.O.W. lists. And at the time I rather enjoyed being a man named Jacques Poole. The trouble came after the Armistice. No one could prove who I was and they didn't know what to do with me. So the bureaucrats procrastinated."

"For two months?"

"One month. The rest of the time I've just been wandering, trying to pick up the pieces and find out who I really am."

"Who are you, then?"

"After all that time I'm not at all sure. Maybe that's why I need Toby. He's so damned dependable."

Kiffin told her he did not want to be tied down to anything for a spell. His long confinement at Landshut had taught him something about the true value of time . . . he wanted his health back first and then a chance to sort out his thoughts before he tried himself against the big bad world.

She questioned him endlessly about life in Lincoln, about Toby as a boy and a youth, about his family. Finally she pressed him to tell her how he thought she might fit in to a life on the prairie.

"You'll do fine. If you have any troubles just call on old Uncle Kiffin."

"Ever since Toby and I first met he's been telling me stories about Kiffin Draper. Sometimes I think I know you better than I do him."

"Sounds like he was a big bore on the subject."

"Toby is never a bore—" she hesitated—"except once in a great while when he starts on his love affair with airplanes."

"Better it be airplanes than a belly dancer. I suggest you start taking an interest in aviation. Then you can both talk about the same thing."

"You've been here two hours and you're already giving me advice on my marriage?"

"Excuse me. I can't help but feel part of the family. In fact I was about to ask you if you would mind my sleeping on the floor tonight. I'm sure it would be all right with Toby."

"How can you be so sure?"

"Look Lily. Be realistic. Toby and I have been friends almost since the day we were born. He's the one man in the world I can't live without. You don't give up your best friend just because he goes off and gets himself married."

"Can you play 'That Dear Old Gang of Mine' on your violin?"

"I'll practice so I can play it for Toby when he comes back."

They laughed and he held out a candle while she lit a small cigar.

"I can see right now, Kiffin, that you're in trouble."

He held up his hands in protest. "Oh no, not me. I never want to be near any trouble again. I've learned my lesson. But I don't see any harm in my sleeping over there on the floor. Of course I *could* go to a hotel if I could find one with an empty room at this time of night . . . or maybe you could send me off to the Red Cross. They might be able to help old Rip van Draper here—"

"You're breaking my heart."

"I don't want to be a bother. It's just that my French is

terrible and I don't know anyone in Paris, and forgive me, here I have a feeling that I've come home.''

"Knock it off, husband's long lost best friend. You can sleep on the floor."

"I'm grateful. By tomorrow I'll have everything straightened out."

Months later when Lily and Toby were bound for the United States aboard the former troopship *Manchuria,* she was to remember Kiffin's remark with a mixture of resentment and wistfulness. He would have everything straightened out on the morrow. Indeed.

They had all gone to London in the spring of '19, making the detour so Lily's father could meet his new son-in-law. In contrast to the uproarious celebration ignited by Toby's return from Germany, (a golden moment when Lily said she had a surprise for him and they were greeted at the door of the flat by Kiffin), the meeting between her father, Toby, and to her annoyance Kiffin, was so sedate and reserved she considered it potentially dangerous. For Kiffin had not quite got around to "straightening everything out" the next day or for many days thereafter.

That boisterous night on the Boulevard Raspail Lily had stood aside while Toby and Kiffin embraced and pounded on each other with wild enthusiasm.

"You're alive, you wonderful son of a bitch! You're alive! It's got to be Easter—a regular first-class resurrection!"

There followed a second round of punching and handshaking and mutual wonder at the miracle that had once more brought them together. They roared with laughter at "Kiffin's Corner," that place on the floor where he had made himself at home for more than a week. A box contained his new toilet articles and on top of the box was a candle and a book. "Home Sweet Home," Kiffin said, "and you're paying the rent."

That night Kiffin invited all those he had met in the neighborhood to join in commemorating their reunion. He included a pair of gendarmes who had been patroling the Boulevard Montparnasse, the flower vendor on the corner of the Boulevard Raspail, a sausage maker whose shop was across the street and a Russian count presently serving as a waiter at Le Dôme. Lily marveled at Kiffin's capacity with people; she had lived in the flat for two years and knew only the building's owner—Kiffin knew half the residents and told them to bring their friends. Congratulations and wine flowed in almost equal torrents and it was not until early morning that Lily had a chance to capture her husband alone for a moment. "Love, we haven't even seen each other for almost three months. Who needs all these people?"

"Oh you know how Kiffin is. Come one, come all. He's the original jolly good fellow."

"Yes, I do know how Kiffin is since he's been camped on my doorstep. But this is *our* flat, our little love nest if you want to put it that way. When are we going to have some privacy?"

"They'll go home soon. I'll start easing them out the door." Toby had never been a successful drinker; for such a big man his tolerance for alcohol in any form was remarkably low and now flushed of face and slightly unsteady on his feet, he resembled a genial bear. He took her face in his big hands and tilting it gently he pressed his mouth to hers. She reached for his groin and felt him grow.

"I can hardly wait," he whispered.

"What about Kiffin?" she asked. "Do you expect me to go into our bedroom and make love with Kiffin rummaging around six feet away?"

"We can't just throw him out in the street."

"Why not?"

"Because he's my old friend. I thought you understood—"

"I understand that I have a perfectly natural urge to make love with you but I don't think I'm capable of performing same in a *ménage à trois*—"

"Now . . . now, he won't bother us. He's had enough wine to make him sleep like a baby. Look at him—" Toby nodded at Kiffin who was leaning against the wall near the brass-piped heater. He was deep in an animated conversation with the middle-aged seamstress who lived on the second floor back. "Isn't he a pistol? He probably can't understand a word she's saying but he's making her feel like a queen."

"I wish she'd feel enough like a queen to take him back to her palace for the night. We just can't go on like this."

Toby took her in his arms again and held her tight. "He thinks the world of you," he said. "He told me so a while ago in no uncertain terms. Said I was the luckiest guy in the world to have you and I sure agree. I'll have a talk with him tomorrow and send him on his way."

Lily stumbled off to work at the embassy on the following gray morning and deliberately avoided returning to the flat until evening. She had decided it was best to leave her husband and Kiffin alone for as long as possible. Maybe they would have enough of the old boy club and get each other out of their systems. Maybe Kiffin would be thoughtful enough to have taken off.

As soon as she let herself into the flat she knew that her hopes were quicksand. There had not been the slightest alteration to "Kiffin's Corner" and the two were seated at the box table sipping at a bottle of Amer Picon one of the guests of the preceding night had left behind. At least, she thought, they were sober.

Kiffin got to his feet and held out his glass to her in salute. "Here's to Joan of Arc, who saved my life. Your ravishing beauty becomes more spectacular every hour."

"And you're full of beans," she said, going to Toby and kissing him.

She only half-listened while Kiffin was saying, "Tonight is my chance to show how much I appreciate what you've done for me . . . food and shelter, saved me from influenza, no doubt, showed me happiness when all I've seen for so long was misery. Today the French gave me full back pay. I'm taking you both to a little place called Chantillion for the best *ragôut* you've ever tasted and afterward to the Théatre du Gymnase. As a quiet antidote to last night perhaps you'll find it refreshing."

Lily slipped out of Toby's arms and said she would go change her dress. She slammed the bedroom door behind her and stood in the darkness for a moment. She was tempted to throw herself on the bed and have a good long cry or perhaps she should let her anger explode. Nix on such antidotes! The evening promised to be one that would not appeal to her.

She lit the gaslight over the wash basin and decided she absolutely would not go to a café and/or the theater with two men whose relationship was so powerful and hard-fixed she might as well be riding in the caboose. Goddamnit, this was her marriage and her man and Kiffin had no right to move in bag, baggage, and lousy violin playing and take over their lives.

She reconsidered. "Am I just a spoiled brat? Am I making a mountain out of something that isn't even worth thinking about . . . and will surely pass?" Another month, maybe less and they would be on their way home. Surely Kiffin would not still be trotting along like the family dog, dutiful, devoted, ever-faithful . . .

As she changed into her new dress with its outrageously short skirt her mood mellowed slightly. True enough she was being selfish. Here were two boyhood chums who had been through a great deal together. Now finding each other alive and well they were enjoying a mutual rediscovery and when it came right down to the basics it was just plain old-fashioned jealousy that was irritating the third wheel. For a time, for a little while, let it be, she thought. Eventually, when they were through refighting the war they would go about their business whatever it turned out to be and maybe see each other a few times a year and that would be just fine. A man could not confine himself to his woman exclusively; he needed masculine companionship in regular doses and all would be well. "Ah, the trials of a bride," she sighed as she swirled in front of the little mirror, "especially one who must be her own mentor."

Lily repeated to herself the essence of the same monologue many times during the following weeks. She was not altogether surprised nor even greatly distressed when Kiffin announced he would "go along" to London with them. He said he would like to meet the father of such a perfect woman and ask where he might find a duplicate for himself.

Toby was delighted Kiffin had decided to accompany them. "There are big things going on with the British. The RAF flew several of the ministers over here for the Versailles conference. And they're starting a London-Paris air service on a regular basis. Things are beginning to make sense and we've got to find out what's going on in the air."

Toby was unaware that even as they packed their meager belongings the first scheduled flight service in the world had already started—in, of all places, Germany. *Deutsche Luftreederei* gathered a small hodgepodge of ex-military aircraft and employed ex-combat pilots to fly the route between Berlin, Leipzig, and Weimar. At almost the same time Lignes Aeriennes Farman flew eleven passengers from Paris to London in a former bomber.

*   *   *

Lily's father was as tall as Toby although far from as heavy. His rather patrician air was greatly relieved by his refusal to take himself or the vicissitudes of the Foreign Service too seriously. He was quite storklike in his way, seeming to ponder the rest of mankind down the length of his noble nose and finding much to light a twinkle in his eyes. After a diplomatic period of careful and sensitive interrogation he allowed his approval of Toby to become apparent, but he admitted a certain perplexity as for the future. "Are you," he said to them all at breakfast, "a reincarnation of the Three Musketeers? All for one and one for all . . . that sort of thing?"

Kiffin seized the chance to respond. "No sir," he said. "I'll be out of their hair very soon. It's just that I've been so hungry for human companionship of the right kind. When you're locked up in close quarters with hundreds of strangers you'd be surprised how lonely you can get. You have a tremendous need to be with someone who knows you and your past. Besides I got Toby into the war and I feel responsible to see him well out of it."

Lily held her peace while she reviewed this new prospect. At what point would Kiffin decide her husband was well out of the war?

"Actually I'd like to stay over in England for a while," Kiffin continued. "I like it here and I like the British and they have a lot of things going."

Pray that you like them enough to stay for several years, Lily thought, and then was ashamed of herself for being so self-seeking. There was nothing wrong with Kiffin except that he was right here and underfoot so much of the time. There was a genuine sweetness in his nature, a puckish naughty boy demeanor that was somehow almost irresistible. Probably, she thought, he would risk his life defending either Toby or herself if the need ever arose and he was extremely careful to pay his share of whatever expense might be incurred. Yet as he had demonstrated so clearly in the Paris flat what was theirs was his to enjoy as well—as long as his presence did not require extra expense.

It was Lily's father who made arrangements with his British counterparts for Toby and Kiffin to have a look at what was being done in the air. Thus they saw the first flights of the new air mail service the RAF had started between Folkestone and the armies of occupation in the Rhineland. They stood watching in wonder as the R-33, a rigid airship built by Armstrong Whitworth, made her maiden flight, and they enjoyed an inspiring lunch at the Vickers plant with ex-Captain John Alcock and ex-Lieutenant Arthur Brown who were presently absorbed in shipping a converted Vickers Vimy bomber to St. Johns, Newfoundland. As soon as the weather improved, say June at the earliest, they intended to fly the big aircraft across the North Atlantic. Lord Northcliffe, publisher of the London *Times* and the *Daily Mail*, had offered prize money of ten thousand pounds for the first successful crossing.

Several times during that luncheon Toby thought he sensed a new restlessness in Kiffin. Riding back into London by train they sat in silence for a long time. Finally Kiffin said, "Know what? I think maybe we've got our heads in the sand. Maybe we should do something about all this—"

"All what?" Toby asked, knowing perfectly well what he was thinking.

"The air. I don't want to go back to school and you've got to start supporting your wife. A guy can be an ex-soldier for just so long and then you start being a pain in the ass."

"Strange," Toby said. "I was just thinking the same thing."

CHAPTER
7

It was a time of incubation, an interval of international gasping as if the world was recovering from near suffocation. Small, apparently innocuous events slipped past almost without notice, but they were harbingers of things to come. The weary and now dissolute Hermann Goering continued to work for a reestablishment of German military air might while other nations began to concentrate on commercial uses for the airplane. His yearning for power in the sky was shared by Ernst Udet and many other ex-German aces now condemned to obscure mediocrity and inaction.

Along with the recent capitulation of the Germans there came at first a deadness aloft, as if the sky itself was mourning the multitudes of young men who had been lost there. Then gradually, quite as if the proper amount of respect had been paid to their memory, man's urge to explore and utilize the upper dominions gathered strength. On the day before they departed for the United States, Lily's father showed Toby and Kiffin a confidential report that had come to the embassy covering the recent experiments of a certain Professor Goddard with rocket flights. He believed that such propulsion was the most practical way of attaining extremely high altitudes.

Although no American-built airplanes ever saw service at the front, the production of de Havilland 4s and "Jennies" became phenomenal during the closing months of the war. As a consequence the machines that were completed now roosted ignominiously in airports all across the land, unflown and decaying, a past reminder that there had actually been a war—somewhere.

Even so the America Toby and Kiffin returned to was different from the one they had left in what now seemed like another life. And Lily had been abroad so long she felt more a foreigner than a native and had little of the old in her memory to compare with the new.

As the hordes of "doughboys" returned and attempted in various ways to resume their former civilian lives, a great inconstancy prevailed in the United States which would soon create a new mood for most Americans and would so greatly transform their culture they would accept the "roaring twenties" as the natural order of things. Suddenly bootleggers were important and the violation of prohibition accomplished with new vivacity. National attention was directed toward such undemanding matters as the behavior of Bill Tildon on the tennis courts and Jack Dempsey's prowess in the ring. Of more interest to Toby and Kiffin was the crash of the Goodyear balloon into the Illinois Trust and Savings Bank at Chicago's LaSalle and Jackson streets. Twelve were killed and twenty-eight injured. That same July of 1919 which introduced Lily to the searing heat and withering hot winds of the Nebraska plains marked the start of a daily air mail service between Chicago and New York.

The trio devoured the newspapers, Toby and Kiffin reading the "Help Wanted" advertisements with little heart and Lily trying to establish some kind of rapport with the vastly different and curious culture in which she had been so abruptly deposited. "Sometimes," she said, "I feel like I've jumped out of an airplane in a parachute and landed on another planet."

Lily adjusted slowly and somewhat reluctantly. After the ceremonial reading of the newspaper one morning she was quick to point out that it was a Frenchman, Raymond Orteig, who was now offering a 25,000 dollar prize to the first aviator who succeeded in flying nonstop from New York to Paris or vice versa. He specified that the aviator must be a native of an "Allied" country, which eliminated anyone whose country might have opposed France in the late war.

"Why don't we win it?" Kiffin asked.

"For the simple reason that our financial condition is terrible and promises to be worse. It takes money to fly the Atlantic," Toby said. "And some lot of luck."

Lily said that she was pleased to see someone around their present establishment who viewed their finances realistically. Toby's mother had inherited a tiny bungalow on the outskirts of Lincoln and had let them have it rent free, but as Lily pointed out, "We have this awkward habit of eating and I'll be damned if I came all the way out here to live on corn pone and chitterlings."

Soon after their arrival she wrote to London.

> Heaven only knows when our friends will get around to writing you, so I'll be the first to thank you for your marvelous hospitality. We are now settled down in Lincoln. Ho, ho, father dear, that is the biggest lie I ever told you. I've never seen such a pair of fidgets in my life and I'm waiting patiently until we run completely out of money. *Then* maybe things will change. As it is, the *we* part is correct and I do mean this *ménage à trois* sticks together like cement. I find it hard to believe that Kiffin is still with us, but there he always is . . . very much alive and always thinking up some new scheme to make us rich overnight . . . it seems I married two men whether I like it or not. We live in a wee house, which is really quite nice but it's barely big enough for two. I can't even go to the bathroom or wait my turn without feeling I'm being watched by two pairs of eyes. Toby is wonderful as always . . . steady as Gibraltar and never a harsh word even when I wreck his eggs in the morning. Kiffin does a lot of the housework and I must say he keeps things tidy, but he just will *not* go away . . .

"Jenny"

Lily debated the wisdom of telling her father about the little scene between Kiffin and herself on the morning Toby had gone down to the lumber yard to apply for a job. If he had no luck there he had said he would try Herpelshiemer's, Lincoln's biggest department store. "Maybe I can sell ties." He laughed. She did not.

Left alone with Kiffin she invited him to pause in his repair of the kitchen drain and join her in a cup of coffee. She had begun as indirectly as she could so he wouldn't be too much on the defensive and stop listening. This time "Kiffin's Corner" was the attic—a loft conforming to the roof line and so cramped he was obliged to stoop at all times. "I don't see how you can live up there," she said. "The heat must be unbearable."

"Sometimes I feel a little slopeheaded, but it's not too bad. I've managed in worse."

"Have you ever thought about a little place of your own?"

He grinned. "You're trying to get rid of me again. Why should I go live alone?"

"Because Toby and I are what is called man and wife and we have a right to at least some privacy. There, I've said it."

Kiffin nodded his head. "Look," he said. "It's hard for me to make a separate entrance and exit to my attic unless I use the chimney. I understand and sympathize. If you guys want to have a little bounce in the hay that's fine. All you have to do is suggest I go for a walk or to the movies. I'll get the drift. Hear no evil, see no evil, speak no evil . . . that's your friend Kiffin. You can depend on it."

"But eventually—?"

"Eventually is a long time from now. I'm working on a deal right this minute that will net us enough to take on a bigger house . . . much bigger."

"That's what you're doing under the sink? Making a deal?"

"I'm thinking while I'm fixing. It's the best time for your imagination, which Napoleon said is what really rules the world. So Toby does get a job that will pay him a few dollars an hour. Where does he go from there? Who wants a gold watch twenty-five years from now? What I have in mind is much much bigger and much more exciting."

She censored the incident as she expanded the letter to her father.

. . . What does one do? Just about the time I'm ready to bash him over the head with something handy (and preferably heavy), he shows up with a dozen roses or some little bauble that throws me all out of kilter. (The roses are probably stolen). I could kill him . . . . and yet I suppose I love him in a way, if only because he's Toby's friend. Or is it because he's so cheerful in adversity? Like all dreamers he really believes that one of his schemes will work and next week we'll make a million dollars. . . .

It was the last of the twilight and usually during the long
Nebraska evenings they would hear the sound of Kiffin's
violin squawling down from the attic. Toby and Lily agreed
that usually it was not so loud as to be unbearable; they
were more concerned with his apparent lack of initiative
in making new acquaintances or even renewing those he
had known before the war. "He needs a woman," Lily
said as she listened to the wind purring through the screened
windows.

She wondered if she would ever learn to ignore the unceas-
ing winds of the Nebraska summer. They blew monotonously
out of the west, gathering strength across a thousand miles of
relatively uninhabited flatland. It was curious, she thought,
how the tones of Kiffin's violin sometimes mixed with the
sighing of the wind in such a way that his playing almost
seemed to gain quality.

Yet tonight there were no sounds from the attic, Kiffin
had not yet returned from what he said was an expedition.

"An expedition to where, do you suppose?" she asked
Toby. She knew it had not been the best of days for him.
A lineman's job at the telephone company he had been
counting on had fallen through and at Herpelshiemer's
they suggested he come back for another interview some
time before Christmas. It was now only late July. And
these days, she noticed, Toby spent a lot of his time
pacing up and down the living room, which was much
too small for his bulk. Now, as she watched him march
thoughtfully back and forth, a fragment from her peripatetic education floated across her memory. Tacitus said
something about even the most savage animals would
forget their natural courage if they were too long confined.

The memory worried her.

"I don't know if a woman is what Kiffin really needs,"
Toby said, still pacing, "but we all need money. The
way I have it figured we'll be very lucky to make it to
Christmas."

"If things get really rough I could probably borrow
something from daddy—"

Toby halted in the middle of the room and turned on her
suddenly. There was still enough light for her to see a flush
cross his face. She had never seen him display the slightest
signs of anger before; high emotion was so against his natural

way and watching him now she became fascinated. "Listen,"
he said coldly. "Let's get one thing straight right now. We
are not taking any money from *daddy*."

"We're taking this house from your mom."

"That's different."

"What's different about it? We're just getting started and
as I understand it most young married couples have financial
problems. We'll come out of it."

"Sure we'll come out of it. But meanwhile I can't do
anything except fly an airplane and I've got a wife to
support."

"Does that make you resent me? I could go to work."

"Nuts. I don't go for that."

"Why shouldn't I contribute my share to the household?"

"This is Nebraska. People wouldn't understand. They would
say Toby Bryant's wife had to go to work because the bum
couldn't support her."

"You're not a bum and I resent the fact that you feel
obligated to support me. I can handle that very well myself,
thank you." A bit on the snippet side, she thought, but they
might as well get this all straightened out right now. "Do you
care so much what other people think?"

"No. I don't really give a damn . . . but it's just against
the nature of things. My mom never worked, and her mother
and her grandmother never worked. Why should you?"

"Because times have changed. People change."

"Not the Bryants."

Lily's voice rose. "Oh don't be so goddamned narrow-
minded. This is 1919—"

"I ought to tell you to go wash out your mouth with soap
and water. Ladies don't use that word."

"Are you saying that I'm not a lady?"

"No, I didn't say that. All you dames are alike. You twist
things around so a guy doesn't know what he's saying half
the time."

"I am *not* a dame. A dame is a British woman of some
distinction who has been honored by the empire."

"Thanks for the information. *We* are still in Nebraska."

"Well, I hate Nebraska. The goddamned wind blows
morning, noon, and night and—" Her voice had risen still
higher.

"Stop talking like that. I'm not a very religious man but it's not right . . . the good Lord saved my life too many times for me not to show him some respect—''

"Jesus! This really *is* Bible-thumping land. I can't believe what I'm hearing . . .''

They were standing only a few feet apart now and she thought she must be losing her mind. Fighting with Toby of all people in the world? Was it the wind? Or Kiffin? Or just money? It was a shock to realize so suddenly that because of her upbringing money had never been a matter of importance. Yet here it was and very little question about it—at least the partial cause of this frightening interlude with the man she loved. He was feeling guilty and so was snapping at the world. And you, she thought, are standing right in his line of fire.

She looked up into his eyes and saw there was still anger in them. It was time, she thought, for contriteness; she had taunted him without intention and she should be big enough to swallow her words. "I'm sorry," she said. "I'm awful. The devil made me do it."

He reached for her and pulled her to him. He kissed her gently. His voice took on a much softer quality when he said, "In Nebraska as elsewhere in these United States we use the term dame to describe a beautiful woman. If she has a brilliant mind to go with the body she is sometimes called a special dame or a great dame. Any red-blooded American male would have to think of you as a very special dame."

They were still holding each other in the darkness when there was a step on the porch and Kiffin charged through the door. "You two knock that off," he shouted. "We have come to the promised land."

Kiffin went directly to the kitchen where he poured himself a glass of milk and started making a peanut butter sandwich. They followed him into the kitchen as he said, "I'm starving. It's a long way to Omaha. And the prices they want for food on that train are only for the very rich, which we are about to be." He rolled his eyes toward the ceiling and said solemnly as if taking his words from on high, "It is written. It is written in stone that all will soon be well. Pity the poor to come unto me and they shall find salvation."

He took a huge bite out of the peanut butter sandwich, leaned against the wall and began munching happily.

He smiled tolerantly. "Bless you, dear friends. If I seem a

shade arrogant it's because I've just concluded the greatest business deal in the history of Nebraska . . . at least eastern Nebraska.''

Lily put down the urge to say the rest of the state was all Indian tepees but decided she had already said too much for one day.

"You are looking at the president of Draper's Great Flying Circus," Kiffin said. "We feature the finest and most daring aviators in the world . . . not to mention the most accomplished daredevil aviatrix. Step right this way, ladies and gentlemen. Satisfaction or your money back.''

Toby glanced warily at Lily and she saw that he shared her opinion. Kiffin was not drunk.

"It is this way,'' Kiffin went on. "This morning while I was fixing the sink I was thinking, which is very necessary during times such as we have here. And I remembered reading a few days back about an auto dealer in Omaha who had bought two surplus airplanes from the government on a sealed bid auction. And I thought, auto dealer? The man drives a Buick and he thinks he's going to fly an airplane? Just like that? Now here is a guy, I thought to myself, who has a real problem. Unless he happens to be one of us what is he going to do with not one but two airplanes? I thought it safe to assume he didn't buy them for firewood. What now would be the next step? Difficult because the news item failed to give this man's name. Still, how many auto dealers are out buying airplanes? By such logic did I take myself the whole sixty miles to Omaha and there after only one false lead found a man named Rudolph Piper, who did not submit any bid to the government as the item stated. His Kiwanis Club did the bidding and to help the club he bought a ticket in their raffle. No one was more surprised than Mr. Piper when he won and when I told him what a great ace you were and added certain shy admissions on my own heroic actions in France he was more than willing to sell me the airplanes. So I bought them both, a brand new Jenny still in her crate with an OX-5 engine built by my old employer Glenn Curtiss . . .''

.For a moment Kiffin was lost in an erotic memory of Bessie Stringfellow, then continued . . . "The second airplane is a brand new DH-4 with a Liberty engine and some spare plumbing also still in its crate. The total amount of the purchase free and clear for the whole lot is one thousand dollars.''

Kiffin paused in his munching long enough to extract a paper from his hip pocket. ''There's the contract. Read it yourselves. I'm tired. It's hard work being a genius.''

The ''letter of agreement,'' which was typed on ''Omaha Motors—Pierce-Arrow and Moon Automobiles'' stationery, stated that Kiffin Draper together with his Associates would pay Rudolph Piper one thousand dollars in exchange for two aircraft to be assembled immediately and placed in first class flying condition by the undersigned.

''How are you planning to come up with a thousand dollars?'' Toby asked.

''That still has to be worked out. Rudy and I will come to an understanding.''

Lily allowed a certain dryness to creep into her voice when she asked, ''How is it your new friend Rudy didn't ask for a deposit?''

''He waived it when I told him we'd go up to Omaha tomorrow and start work.''

''Doing what?''

''Just like it says . . . assembling the airplanes.''

''We don't know anything about assembling airplanes and neither do you,'' Toby said. ''You haven't even been in the air for more than two years. What do we know about rigging an airplane . . . how much dihedral in the wings and how much downthrust on the engine, for starters?''

''All will be solved in time. Fear not. Trust in Kiffin. Meanwhile, pack the bags.''

Both instinct and experience told Toby that trusting in Kiffin was always a gamble. Ths time, it seemed, he might be onto something that might have a reasonable chance of success. For Rudolph Piper proved to be an amiable man who had never seen an airplane except in photographs and his fondness for Kiffin was unmistakable. ''I consider it an honor to be associated with Lieutenant Draper,'' he said to Lily soon after their arrival. ''He breathes fire, that young man.''

Lily noted that Kiffin had promoted himself.

Rudolph Piper was so taken with the young people who had descended on him that he even lent the assistance of his mechanics in the process of assembly, which took place in back of his sales lot. Fortunately manuals for assembly were included in the packing boxes.

The fuselages and engines were mated first, followed by the wings, which would be transported separately to the Omaha airport. As the work progressed, Piper became fascinated and after listening to Kiffin he readily agreed to a change in the sales agreement. Instead of the flat payment of one thousand dollars he would take twenty five percent of the gross receipts of Draper's Flying Circus until he received a total of fifteen hundred dollars. According to Kiffin's enthusiastic projection the amount would be available within one month of commencing actual operations. He used the word "operations" in such an impressive way both Toby and Lily had trouble reconciling their more realistic hopes with such grandiose prospects. They knew only that they would be barnstorming the airplanes throughout the towns, villages and hamlets of the middle west and summer was already on the wane. From the viewpoint of the cheap hotel where Toby and Lily lived and the Y.M.C.A. where Kiffin lived, it was difficult to visualize such a high potential income. Lily, who pitched in and became particularly adept at placing the seizings on turn-buckles and flying wires, also did some calculating on the side of one of the big boxes in which the beautiful big wooden propellers had been preserved. "It's just impossible," she insisted. "We sell airplane rides for one dollar a minute. What are we supposed to live on if there's not a steady stream of customers?"

Toby told her not to be so pessimistic. Kiffin said they should be able to sell a few loop-the-loops every day at twenty-five dollars a lop. He added that this major attraction had yet to be revealed. "The public will go crazy," he promised while favoring Lily with his most engaging smile. "We will have to go into consultation about your wardrobe. I have much more in mind for you than just selling tickets."

Actually it was a summer for aerial gypsies who scattered across the land like lost birds seeking a safe nesting area. It was the time of flying men like Al Williams, Clyde Pangborn, the inimitable Casey Jones, and Frank Hawks, and Jimmie James. In the beginning their airplanes were almost entirely the residue of war and so were ill-suited to the new demands made on them. With the OX-5 engine flat out and turning 1,400 revolutions per minute even the best of Jennies flew slightly faster than seventy miles an hour and were slothful in all maneuvers. Intended as a training airplane for the Signal Corps it carried only one adult passenger, a disadvantage any sound businessman would have known immediately was not economical. The barnstormers were not business men. Flight itself, not money was the appetite to be served; the perpetual talk of money brought about by its normal absence was merely subterfuge, a way of convincing themselves that barnstorming was an honest way to make a living and convince normal people that such enterprise was not entirely futile. The OX-5 engine in the Jenny was reasonably reliable although it developed only ninety-two horsepower when running at its utmost—just barely enough to clear trees when ascending from a farmer's field of a hot afternoon. The Jenny could be spun and would enter one reluctantly, yet even when properly handled it would emerge with little grace. Therefore spins were not recommended. Nearly all of the Jennies flown during these first years by the barnstormers were still painted a drab khaki and smelled of nitrate dope, engine oil, and sweat. Partly because of their slow speed the Jenny controls were mushy. Response to control movement was unhurried and very much subject to the immediate atmospheric conditions in which they were flown. If the air was rough a few hours herding a Jenny around a pasture could become trying to man and his muscles. The barnstormers rarely complained because few of them knew any better.

The Jenny's greatest virtue was simplicity, which accounted for its long survival and ubiquitous presence throughout the flying fields of America. The OX-5 engine was exposed in nearly all its departments and hence was easy to work on with only the most basic tools. It was fueled with automobile gasoline available at any station. The fabric of the wings and fuselage suffered the stones, sand, mud and manure of countless pastures and dirt roads with tolerable resistance to serious damage and could be repaired with patches applied by inexperienced hands. While the wood and wire and fabric construction of all airplanes contemporary with the Jenny made them lethal in a bad crash, the Jenny was remarkably forgiving in a minor collision with an inflexible object.

Jennies were not pretty to look upon, rather they suggested a praying mantis suffering from a spine distortion. Yet in the eyes of the barnstormer they at least were capable of flight and that was the be all and the end all. The woe of a barnstormer who had left his machine in a pasture overnight was pitiful to be observed and word soon spread that it was asking for calamity. Cows, it was discovered, were inordinately fond of the taste of doped fabric.

The de Havilland was of British design and showed it in all its massive parts, disregard of aerodynamic drag, and general ruggedness. It had served the English well as a light bomber during the war and was of somewhat larger wing area than the Jenny. The rate of climb in both airplanes left much to be desired and on very hot days could be critical. The American built DH-4s were equipped with the powerful twelve cylinder Liberty engine, which made a sound when turning over like sweet music to the ears of barnstormers. The Liberty engine was water-cooled and as a consequence it was cursed with occasional plumbing problems. Even so it was a very simple engine and could be maintained with basic tools and only limited knowledge. Kiffin, manning the chain hoist he had borrowed from Rudolph Piper, eased the Liberty down to the engine mounts on the DH-4 and with even more than his usual exuberance declared it "the greatest engine ever built!"

The two airplanes were ready for their first flight by the middle of August, and they agreed that because of the difference in their personal weight Toby would fly the DH-4 regularly while Kiffin would fly the Jenny. Both test flights however would be flown by Toby because of Kiffin's relative rustiness in the air.

As it has always been with men who were more than ordinarily fond of each other, their daily banter was frequently spiced with disparagement and disdain. Toby would say, "I've heard that a gorilla can be taught to fly, but there are some men who can never learn."

And Kiffin would counter, "If I am going to take a refresher course it shouldn't be from some old man who spent his whole career floating around the sky in Caudrons. It's my understanding that those contraptions flew themselves and the pilot just went along for the ride."

Or, when they stood at last on the field at Omaha and regarded the visible evidence of their enterprise. "Good God," Toby said, "who rigged those Jenny wings? They look like a seesaw. You couldn't have been sober when you took your measurements. No man with normal eyesight could be satisfied with such work."

"Those measurements are down to the thousandths of an inch, my friend. They are right on according to the rigging manual—all assured by the sharpest pair of calipers in the business."

"It will be a miracle if the poor thing leaves the ground and returns in one piece. I'm not at all sure I should even attempt to test it."

"It's not the airplane, it's the pilot I'm worried about. Maybe I'd better go along with you in case your clumsy hands get you in trouble."

"You stay on the ground. Look after Lily if I make her a widow."

Lily was always left out of these exchanges and not quite understanding their male conceit sometimes wondered if their abrasiveness was genuine.

Toby tested the Jenny for one hour and found no fault except for its tendency to keep turning left. There were two king posts atop the Jenny's upper wing and they made a small adjustment to the left flying wire which terminated at the post. "I covered my eyes when you landed," Kiffin said. "It was more than I could bear to see all of our work so abused."

"If you don't watch you'll never learn. My landing was a nice combination of glycerine and glass. I'm not even sure I'm really down."

Testing the DH-4 was next and the roar of the Liberty engine prompted Kiffin to seize Lily in a bear hug. "Ain't she beautiful!" he shouted above the sound. "There, by God, goes an airplane with balls!"

When the Great Draper Flying Circus finally rose into the air, bound west in the blaze of the morning sun, the fuel tanks of the Jenny and the DH-4 were full and the pockets of their pilots nearly empty. Lily, appointed as treasurer, announced that their collective resources amounted to twenty-seven dollars, making it imperative that they land and take in some money before they could refuel.

Navigation was easy. They followed the railroad toward Fremont in the northwest. Kiffin flew the Jenny and Toby the DH with Lily riding in the front cockpit. She now wore a helmet and goggles of her own—the gift of Rudolph Piper, who said only half in jest that he was concerned for the safety of such a nice young lady and he wished she had chosen to stay behind and wait for her husband.

They flew in very loose formation. The Jenny was so much slower than the DH. Toby was obliged to throttle back and fly just above the edge of a stall, but he took some satisfaction in convincing himself that by using less power he was also putting the fuel-hungry Liberty engine on a diet.

Their meager personal belongings were divided between the front cockpit of the Jenny and such room as Lily could spare in the DH. She flatly refused to share her limited space with Kiffin's violin so it was left behind in care of Rudolph Piper. Of necessity their equipment was minimal, six cans of beef stew, a small alcohol stove, half of a pup tent, wooden stakes and rope for tie-downs, a five gallon tin of engine oil, linen, glue, and dope for patching fabric, a box of simple tools, and a box of spark plugs for the OX-5 engine. There were also two moth-eaten tarpaulins intended to protect the exposed rear cockpits from night rains, a cigar box, a roll of tickets, and a banner advertising "Airplane Rides—$5.00." Except for their toilet articles everything then was for the airplanes, a discipline which was to become their way of life until the final catastrophe.

On this particular morning they were all three of great heart, laughing and waving at each other as the scorched ochre of the prairie unfolded beneath them, convinced that at last they were embarked on a challenging expedition which would surely bring them bounteous reward.

Toby was twenty-four, Kiffin twenty-five, and Lily just turned twenty.

The clean prairie air etched the horizon all around the compass and everywhere they looked there was excitement and the zest of discovery. Thoughts of defeat were given no quarter even by Lily, who was still not sure what her role would be in this new life. Since it was her first time aloft she found much to awe her and she kept looking back at Toby in delight. Now, she thought, she understood at least in part how the two men she knew best were so devoted to flight.

Their "battle plan," as Kiffin proscribed it, was uncomplicated. Once over Fremont they would fly down the main street at the lowest possible altitude, say a hundred feet or so, and repeat the initial pass once more. The DH would lead and the Jenny would follow. If the population failed to turn out in satisfying numbers then they would make a third pass. Next they must find an open field as close to the town as possible. They would land and while they waited for curiosity to draw potential customers to the field Kiffin would offer the farmowner a free ride in exchange for the use of his real estate. "There should be nothing to it," he prophesied. "Who could turn down a free airplane ride?"

They arrived over Fremont just before noon and indeed caused a commotion. People came out of the shops and buildings along the main street and stood mouths open as they watched two airplanes snarl past just above the electric light poles. Toby found a fine field less than half a mile to the west of town and landed in the stubble of fresh cut alfalfa. A few minutes later Kiffin landed in the Jenny and taxied toward a farmhouse situated on the corner of the field. As he cut the engine a man came out of the back door of the house. He was chewing vigorously on something and his heavy chops were smeared with grease.

Kiffin swung up and out of the cockpit as quickly as he could. When he touched ground he was tempted to climb back in the Jenny—the man was long and lean and cold-eyed and there was no welcome whatever to be seen in his manner.

"What you doin' here?" the man demanded.

"Forgive us our trespasses," Kiffin said, taking a chance.

"Smart aleck, huh?" The man stopped chewing and Kiffin watched in fascination as a lump of something made the long passage down the man's exposed throat and seemed to bypass his Adam's apple. The man stuck his thumbs in the loops of his suspenders and rocked back slightly on his heels. He flicked his bald head sharply to drive away a fly. He glanced at the Jenny and made a rosette with his lips. "Got yourself a flyin' machine, I see."

"I'm sorry," Kiffin said, "if we disturbed your dinner."

"Decent folk always eat at noontime. I ought to get the sheriff out here."

"I would guess he's coming anyway." Over the man's shoulder Kiffin saw what he assumed was the man's family, a woman with her hair in long braids, and several children.

The man stared at the Jenny. "You coulda killed one of my beasts," he said. "A good cow is worth a lotta money these days."

"I didn't see any cows."

"They is over there under the trees, brushed up like they always is in the heat of the day."

Kiffin tried his most engaging smile. "Mister, how would you like a free airplane ride? Take you right over your farm and you can have a look at it from an eagle's point of view."

"There ain't no eagles around here no more. Died off with the Indians. And I wouldn't ride in one of those contraptions for Criminee sake. A man belongs with his feet on the good earth God give him."

Beyond the farmhouse Kiffin saw a trail of dust rising. People would be coming out from town. "Maybe some of your family would like a free ride?"

"I wouldn't allow it. Get them things out of here before I have you arrested. This ain't no amusement park. You got yourself mule nerve comin' in here, mister, and I don't like mules."

Kiffin was aware of a movement just behind him and he heard Lily's voice. "This surely is a beautiful place you have here, sir. I don't think I've ever seen a better looking farm."

Lily stepped forward until she was nearly between Kiffin and the farmer. She was wearing breeches and boots, a white shirt and a red bandana around her neck—all as Kiffin had prescribed.

Some of the iron seemed to leave the farmer's face as he said, "Thank ye, ma'am."

Lily pulled off her helmet and shook her short dark hair. "It looks to me, sir, like you're a good businessman, the way things are laid out. We'd like to use your field to make passenger flights this afternoon. How much would you charge?"

An almost instantaneous transformation occurred within the farmer. He raised one of his bony hands to shade his eyes and looked down curiously at Lily. He shifted his gaze then to the tail of the Jenny striped red, white, and blue. His tiny eyes, almost hidden in folds of leathery flesh, took on a new gleam. He worked his mouth around and around as if he were seeking unsuccessfully for a lost morsel of food. "How much you figure you could pay?"

"How about five dollars?"

"Ain't enough."

"Okay. We might go for seven-fifty."

"Make it ten. You kill a cow and I take your airy-planes."

That night, a sample of the many they would spend in a similar fashion, they tried to sleep beneath the wings of the DH. It was a restless night interrupted by many unfamiliar distractions. The cows became curious about the airplanes and threatened to tear the fabric with their nudgings and scratchings. They dropped their dung everywhere which made it messy to move about in the darkness. And along with the grunts, snorts, and blattings there were the founts of liquid splashing nearby as the cows urinated mightily. Dark shapes were everywhere it seemed until Toby decided they would have to stand sentry duty "like we did in the Legion." For a moment he was astonished to find himself longing for the company of Sergeant Delacroix. Ah, that was an easy life.

The ever present wind whirred softly beneath the stars and passed with an almost hypnotic sighing through the flying wires of the two airplanes. Frogs, apparently in complete dominion over the prairie, took up a raucous chorale that lasted until dawn. Mosquitoes whined and mewed in the crenelations of their ears all the night long while prairie fleas competed with nibbling ants for right of passage across their blankets. "So much for the romance of a gypsy life," Lily murmured as she returned from a nocturnal call behind a distant patch of thorny bush. "There has to be a better way to make friends with a rattlesnake."

Yet she knew already that there was not a better way, for the economics of their first day's "operation" were discouraging.

It was not until twilight when the little primus stove failed to function and they dined on cold pork and beans that they came to an accounting. Swarms of people had come out from the town of Fremont, proof enough that their method of attraction was correct. They came by car, horse, bicycle, and foot, most of them professing their wish to go aloft. Lily stood near the barbed wire fence urging them to buy tickets. But one dollar a minute? Ain't that an awful lot, sister? Why, that's half a day's pay for some men. How about trading a piglet for a ride . . . good little porker.

There were hundreds of people but few paying customers. Between shortly after noon and evening when all the customers and even the curious vanished toward their suppers, Toby and Kiffin took up only twenty passengers. No one felt affluent enough to buy a "stunt ride" and only two men wanted to fly more than five minutes. The reckoning against the estimated operating expense of the dollars per hour for each airplane, the ten dollars to the farmer, and one quarter of the total to Rudolph Piper left a mere fifteen dollars for the Great Flying Circus.

"Tomorrow will be better," Kiffin said. "We'll work our way out toward Broken Bow and find a little different type of customer."

Tomorrow was not better, nor was the next tomorrow, nor the next as the Great Flying Circus worked its way along a route that took them over North Platte, Ogallala, then down toward McCook, Nebraska, and into northern Kansas.

Flying out of a turnip field near Oberlin they took in one hundred twenty dollars, at Colby on a Sunday afternoon, eighty-eight dollars, at Great Bend using the parched beach of the Arkansas River as a landing field they took in one hundred forty dollars. They followed the same river down to Hutchison where landing alongside an old railroad track they had their very best of days—one hundred eighty-nine dollars.

Pressing on, they made the outskirts of Wichita. There, in anticipation of the Labor Day weekend, they hoped to greatly increase their fortunes. On the first holiday it rained steadily with the vicious squalls of an ugly Kansas cold front shivering the airplanes at their moorings. No one came to the empty field they had chosen which lay next to an abbatoir. The stench was compounded in the hard westerlies and soon became unbearable. Flying between squalls they found another field somewhat to the south and there spent the night harrassed by monstrous thunderstorms full of lightning and bellicose explosions.

They huddled as always beneath the lower wing of the DH because they could not afford the cost of lodging in the town, nor did they think the filling of their bellies with relatively expensive café food was proper just when every penny was needed to keep fuel in the airplanes. There were many times when either Kiffin or Toby walked a mile or more to the nearest filling station lugging back two five-gallon cans of gasoline so they could fly on to the next town, and they made those hops as short as possible because they produced no revenue and by now they knew that it was absolutely essential both airplanes must do better than barely make their keep.

Sometimes the locals were kind to them and offered them

shelter for the night, or brought gifts of food and sweets and good natured raillery about their chances of living out the afternoon, but usually the pattern was repeated day after day, and always they were treated as passing strangers not to be trusted and to be abandoned once what they had to sell had been seen.

Now the hours of daylight were becoming noticeably shorter. They had all lost weight, eating when they could and trying to make a major event of their nightly gathering around the undependable little primus stove. They were dirty, although they tried their best to cleanse themselves whenever there was a handy stream, a river, or a farmer's well. Toby and Kiffin's hands were always slightly greasy from working around the engines and their faces at night bore a fine film of soot from the constant outpouring of the exhaust stacks. Their breeches were spotted with oil and their shirts wrinkled and pungent with the aroma of themselves. Their boots, once so smart and polished, were now crinkled with use and often smeared with mud.

Toby now said more often than he intended that this was certainly no way to get rich, and Kiffin admitted there was something definitely wrong. He said the time had come for him to do some heavy thinking about the arrival of fall. Lily, engaged in a perpetual struggle to keep her one white shirt clean and herself as tidy as possible, kept her peace.

One evening when they were staked down in an oat field that had just been combined, she took out the little pad on which she kept their accounts and used three pages to write her father.

> . . . It's really very beautiful here. Rather stark, but at this hour there is a wonderful mellow quality to the prairie sun, it's a carmine instead of just red, very flamboyant, very huge, and very un-European. It's still hot during the day, but now the nights are becoming quite chilly . . . almost too much so since we have only one blanket apiece to protect us. Still, I have such joy to be alive, to be with the man I love with all the heart and passion I possess. . . . that is enough for this girl. I breathe deeply of each morning, always up and about before sunrise and we laugh a good deal and pretend we have to look at the Standard Oil road map (we'd be really lost without it), to remember where we are. My two boys are very

brave and determined, but I fear for our future unless Kiffin's new scheme works . . .

. . . should I tell you about it? Why not, since both Toby and Kiffin swear it's absolutely safe. And the funny thing is I'm excited about the idea . . .

. . . Kiffin says he was mistaken. Not enough people care enough about riding in an airplane to pay a dollar a minute, which is the least we can charge. This pasture flying just does not create enough interest so we must go where the "big money" is. (Kiffin talking). He says look at Roscoe Turner, Dick Grace, and Omer Locklear. They give flying *shows*, and they play the County and State fairs for a lump sum.

(Bless Kiffin's roguish heart. Sometimes I wonder if he's trying to get rid of me.) Now, don't worry, dear father, but prepare yourself. I am now to be known as the GREAT LILY BRYANT!, the so-called star attraction. I am what is known as a "wing-walker" . . . that is, I don't exactly go for a walk on the wings, but I do climb out of the cockpit of the DH, make my way to the end of the wing, which seems a long way you can be sure, and from my perch wave at the crowd as we fly by. I held on while Toby does chandelles and steep turns. It really isn't difficult and I suppose it looks quite spectacular. And for this you spent all that money sending me to Wellesley? . . . Now the *real* kick. Kiffin says we've got to be even more fancy and although Toby was against it in the beginning, he's sort of come around now and says it's safe as long as I don't get excited and try to do things too quickly. Tomorrow, or as soon as we have a calm day, I'm going to transfer from Toby's DH to Kiffin's Jenny. I've been practicing while the planes are on the ground and it's not going to be too difficult. I make my way out almost to the end of the wing and slip around the leading edge until I can get my legs into the wooden hoop that's on the underside of the wing. (It keeps the DH's wing tip from hitting the ground in a bad landing, which Toby never makes.) Anyway I'm very snug there (good I'm small), and I wait until Kiffin comes up from below in the Jenny. He has rigged a long bar on top of the king post and all I have to do is reach out and grab it, then slide on to the top of the Jenny's wing. All of this is done at about seventy miles an hour which makes for quite a wind, but the relationship between the two airplanes is deceiving. It's very slow and everything is easy to reach, almost as if you are moving from one chair to another. When I'm safe on the Jenny I hang on to a piece of heavy fence wire Toby and Kiffin rigged between the two king posts. I follow the wire until I reach the middle of the wing then I just drop into the front cockpit and the great plane change is completed. It sounds terrible, but there's really nothing to it if I don't look down. We are going to "head out east" (listen to me sounding like a native), tomorrow for Emporia, where there's some kind of a county fair and then on to Topeka for the big time. The wind will be mostly at our backs so we should save on fuel. I feel like a real circus performer . . .

Like all barnstormers they began to learn things that were never taught them in flying school. Starting the big Liberty engine on the DH after a cool night was in itself a major undertaking. They primed the cylinders individually then with Lily in the cockpit operating the magneto switch Toby would grab a blade of the huge propeller with one hand and extend his other hand to Kiffin. Thus they formed a "daisy chain" with Toby hauling on the propeller and Kiffin hauling on Toby. The engine rarely started on the first attempt and sometimes they pulled the propeller through for an exhausting half hour before they were rewarded with a series of explosions and a cloud of blue smoke.

Starting the OX-5 in the Jenny could also be frustrating in the early mornings, but at least the smaller engine required only one man to pull the blades through.

They learned that fence wire could be used for all manner of repairs to their airplanes and they learned that not filling the sump of the Liberty entirely full of oil cut down on the amount that somehow always escaped and streaked back to soil the DH fuselage, their passengers' clothing, and when in flight, their own faces.

They learned the value of a slanting field as opposed to one that was perfectly flat. If they could take off down hill and land up hill in the opposite direction the airplanes performed better and it saved taxiing time and fuel. In addition they could cluster their potential passengers at one end of the field and often have an additional chance to sway those who were indifferent to the value of an airplane ride.

They learned that clothing on a farmer's wash line was a fine wind indicator along with the ruffle of wavelets on a pond, smoke of any kind, and animals who had the good sense to graze with their backs to the wind.

They learned that morning ground fog was deceiving. From aloft you could look down through it and see exactly where you would choose to land, but once descended into it, you were blind for the last fifty feet.

They learned that an open cockpit airplane was no place to be in the vicinity of thunderstorms—unless you yearned to see your airplane destroyed before your eyes followed by the overture to your own funeral.

They were constantly reminded that cool areas, a stand of trees, a lake, a river, or a fresh green crop made for descending air and loss of lift when heavily loaded, and likewise they found that large parched areas roasting under the midwestern sun sometimes produced an air bubble that would provide a noticeable measure of lift. And in time they discovered that the reliability of both phenomena was initiated by other factors; in hot air the engines produced somewhat less power and the wings less lift. So they kept a sharp eye out for large birds of all varieties—the crows, ravens, buzzards, and eagles who were born to the sky—and they envied their ability to choose unerringly of the invisible thermals which would give them the blessing of lift.

They learned the true value of nose down side-slips when descending over tall trees for landing in fields they would previously have thought impossible to use. And they learned that sometimes a deliberate bounce on take-off would pry the DH or the Jenny out of a tight field on a hot day.

They learned to save every paper bag that came their way for the inevitable passengers whose metabolism insisted that vomiting was part of an airplane ride. And they learned to calm the occasional passenger who froze to near paralysis in fear and literally had to be hoisted out of the front cockpit. The spectacle was very bad for business.

Kiffin said that he did not have to be hit over the head more than once and therefore in the future Lily would do the negotiation with the owners of whatever fields they thought most suitable to their enterprise. The choice was almost always a compromise between convenience, temptation for customers, and the possibility that they might get in some fields but would never get out in one piece.

Almost invariably Lily was granted permission for their operation, sometimes at no charge. And at last when it appeared they had taken every local aloft who could be talked into it, and they disappeared east-bound over the horizon, they usually left a friend behind in the landowner. They were told, "Come back next year."

The one thing they could not seem to learn was how to make the Great Flying Circus show a profit. They all saw that something had to be done and that was when Kiffin began looking at Lily in a different light.

These were the days of "Tiny" Broderick, Gladys Ingle, Ethel Dare, and Gladys Roy—all wing-walkers, and tales of their exploits caused Kiffin to call for a meeting of the Circus.

" . . . Obviously we can't go on this way. We do have a choice if we want to keep flying." He pressed his lips together tightly and shook his head, all portents, they understood, signalled by Kiffin that something had gone wrong with one of his schemes and that worse would transpire if his latest modification was declined. "We can start flying booze up from Mexico that we can buy for ten or twenty dollars a case and sell for fifty dollars a bottle—"

"Forget it," Toby said. "I never saw a pretty jail."

"Or, our little friend here can come to the rescue." Kiffin smiled.

"In what way?" Lily asked.

"In a safe way. Rest assured that will be our only standard."

"Our? Sometimes I question your use of the editorial *we*—or is it the imperial?"

If Kiffin believed and Toby concurred, then Lily thought she was willing to do anything they asked and by the time they landed in Wichita, Kansas, word of her "daring plane-change" had already reached the fair officials. Kiffin was able to negotiate a contract for their performance at five hundred dollars an afternoon and he said, "Hallelujah!" every time he thought about it. He also kissed Lily frequently, on the forehead or cheek, of course, and declared that Joan of Arc was a hack compared to her.

The contract called for two performances, each to include no less than four loop-the-loops in the Jenny, chandelles in the DH and any other "dipsy-doodles" Toby decided on, the whole show climaxing with the "perilous" plane-change by Lily.

Kiffin saw to it that they were advertised as "Two Great War Aces" and "The Most Daring Young Lady in the World." Next year, he promised, they would wear some kind of a uniform. "We'll give them a show they can't forget. Para-chute jumpers, bombs in the air, a dogfight, maybe get some fireworks and do some night exhibitions like Frank Hawks, Jimmy Angel and those other guys."

Under Toby's watchful eye Lily had practiced the plane change for hours on the ground. Over and over again she climbed out of the DH's front cockpit then made her way to the end of the left lower wing. She wore tennis shoes to keep from slipping and she learned exactly where to step every time she put her foot down. Toby insisted that she learn the location of every hand hold so well that she could reach for it blindfolded. "Every minute and second you're out there I want you to have a firm grip on something solid. Never make a move without thinking what you're doing, what you've just done, and what you're going to do next. Don't be in a hurry. Pretend you've got all day. When Kiffin comes up for you don't be in a hurry to make the transfer. He'll wait. Give him time to position himself exactly where he should be. Remember he can see everything because he's looking up and there's nothing in the way. Once you go over the end of the wing I can't see you."

"When everything looks just right," Kiffin said, "I'll nod my head three times. Like this." He demonstrated with vigor-ous nods. "Disregard any other movement of my head. A negative signal will be just as easy to recognize. There's no way you can mistake my signals."

While the Jenny was on the ground Lily also practiced on the upper wing. One genial farmer allowed them to park the Jenny next to a shed with a flat roof about four feet higher than the Jenny's wing tip. It was not quite a true simulation because Kiffin could not get the wing close enough to put the king post where it would be in the air, but after fifty-odd "transfers" Lily said she felt very confident and was con-vinced she knew every inch of the route to the front cockpit.

They began air practice in the early morning and just before dusk when the air would be smooth. Lily was exhila-rated by her first attempt. "It was a piece of cake," she laughed. "It's the kind of thing you do in dreams, but you know it's real."

They held the most minute critiques after they returned from each transfer, exploring all the "what ifs" they could think of. By the time she had made three actual transfers Lily decided against using tennis shoes. "They're too clumsy," she said. "I'll be surer of my movements if I'm in my bare feet."

Their biggest problem was rough air, an unfortunate characteristic of the midwestern summer days. It was extremely difficult to fly the close formation necessary for Lily's transfer in airplanes that were unwieldy in the best of conditions and took an almost sixth sense of control when the prevailing winds blew hard or the thermals of the day had time to generate. Kiffin had given Lily the negative head wag on several occasions and easing the Jenny out of her reach signaled her to return to the cockpit of the DH. Both Kiffin and Toby could see each other before the transfer and had an understanding that either one of them could cancel it if they were not pleased with the way things were going. Likewise Lily could refuse by simply returning to the DH's cockpit.

They made one attempt at Hutchison, with Lily wearing a borrowed parachute left behind by a hot air balloonist who had lost his welcome to the local sheriff. She was no more than half way out on the wing when she returned to the cockpit. "It may have made you feel better," she said to Toby, "but it's much too clumsy. I was scared stiff it would be caught on a flying wire or hit a strut and knock me off balance. And besides there's something about parachutes I don't trust. People are always getting killed in them."

In fact there were very few parachutes available in the whole of the United States and their cost was far beyond the pockets of the average barnstormer. Toward the end of the war the Germans had been the first to use parachutes in actual combat, and now it was said that the newly hired air-mail pilots who were required to do so much night flying were beginning to wear them; but they were heavy, awkward, and too often packed by people of little experience. "Instead of a parachute," Lily said, "there's something I really want when the season's over."

"Name it," Toby said.

"And you'll have it," Kiffin said almost in chorus.

"I want to learn to fly."

If he had any lingering doubts Toby knew from that moment on that he had married the right woman.

The first day at Wichita was such a success the problems of the Great Flying Circus seemed to be over. The fair officials

were pleased, the crowd was delighted and the two performances were flawless. The late September sun shone brilliantly upon the dirt race track and the little grandstand which
became the center of all activity during the afternoon. The
finale left the crowd gasping and genial with a sense of
vicarious thrill. They watched the show with two faces, the
first because some latent and absolutely secret instinct compelled them to hope someone would be killed or injured and
the second praying they would not be witness to anything
unpleasant.

The DH and the Jenny flying in very tight tandem formation,
flew past at almost eye level with the crowd, only a few feet
above their waving arms. The sound of the band playing
"March Oriental" was obliterated by the roar of the passing
airplanes and the cheers of the crowd as Lily stood up in the
Jenny and blew kisses directly at their faces. It was not the
sort of thing seen every day in Kansas.

All went so well on the first day Toby and Kiffin and even
Lily became convinced that they had at last found the answer.
There was apparently no reason why they should not continue
through the rest of the year, working south through Tennessee,
Alabama, Georgia, and onward finally for a winter of exhibitions in Florida. They were so encouraged they began planning their route to take advantage of local holidays.

Yet Kiffin was not entirely satisfied. There was one detail
which troubled him and the morning of their second day's
performance at Wichita he went into the town in the hope of
solving his problem. The finale of their show was a single
pass above the audience with Lily standing in the cockpit
ahead of him and blowing kisses at the crowd. Now he
decided she was still not visible enough. There was too much
wing and fuselage in the way and somehow there was not
enough glamor in a plain white shirt. She was the star of the
show so she should have a spotlight on her at all times, but
what could compete with the sun? And during the actual
transfer her tiny figure against the sky was just not commanding enough.

Kiffin had considered the problem for several days without
mentioning it to the others. He wanted something that would
fix all eyes on Lily from the moment she left the front cockpit
of the DH until they landed. At Wichita he found the answer
in a small millinery shop.

"Wear this around your neck and their eyeballs will pop," he said as he draped a four foot red silk scarf around her shoulders. "It will flow back in the slip-stream and be beauty complimenting beauty."

Lily stroked the fine silk and was pleased. If she was going to do something then she should give it all she had and now her business was to attract attention. She experimented briefly with different knots to keep the scarf from tearing away and found that she could leave almost three feet trailing behind her.

For the third and last day they had not dared to hope for such perfect weather. The sun continued to bathe the area in a golden light and there was not a cloud or even a threat of cloud in the sky. The temperature was balmy instead of hot. The farmers and merchants, ranchers, and bureaucrats who came to the Fair all said they had never seen such a pleasant September and the sales of candy floss, hot dogs, pink lemonade, and corn-on-the-cob were most pleasing to the concessionaires.

There was no wind which was always helpful to the Flying Circus unless they were operating out of a very small field. When Toby and Kiffin took off they were pleasantly surprised to find the air as smooth as they had ever known it. Lily was also pleased because she knew the plane transfer would be cancelled if the air was rough and she was anxious to hear Toby's reaction to her new red scarf.

The DH held away some distance from the race track while Kiffin in the Jenny performed two loops over the center of the track and one directly over the heads of the crowd. Watching from above Toby saw that he was pressing things again, finishing his loops much too low to the ground. For the thousandth time he would have to ask Kiffin why he was always trying to kill himself. Why should he risk his neck for a mob of total strangers? He would be wasting his words. Even if he said it was the Jenny and not Kiffin's carcass that he really valued, Kiffin would go right on doing as he pleased.

When the loops were finished Toby brought the DH past the stands and climbed into a smooth chandelle. He did two, one at each end of the track and he knew Kiffin would be thinking that he flew like an old lady because he leveled out at least fifty feet above the ground. Toby shrugged his shoulders as he climbed toward the altitude agreed upon for the plane change—five hundred feet. So be it. He had just never been able to make himself take a deliberate risk.

Toby made a shallow bank into a circle while he waited for Kiffin to bring the Jenny up to his altitude. When they were in a line of echelon they made one pass from west to east adjusting their course little by little until they had the sun slightly at their backs and yet not so much so the crowd would have to look into it.

Below on a platform facing the grandstand Toby saw the Fair's master of ceremonies holding a large megaphone to his mouth. He would be repeating the speech Kiffin had written for him—" . . . And now the most dangerous and death-defying spectacle of all! Little Lily Bryant, weight one hundred pounds and not an ounce more, will attempt what most women would never even consider. . . . the transfer of her lovely body from one airplane to another at five hundred feet above the planet Earth. I must warn you that this maneuver is so tricky and must be so exactly flown by the two war aces they may not be successful on the first try. . . . so be patient and let us allow our hearts to soar on high and share the courage of that gallant little lady of the sky . . ."

Toby shook the DH's wings slightly and Lily turned back to glance at him. She smiled, pulled her goggles down and pushed herself part way out of the cockpit. The red scarf was caught instantly in the slip-stream and the end of it fluttered less than a foot from Toby's wind screen. He knew that just below the announcer's voice would rise as he shouted, ". . . . And there she is, ladies and gentlemen. . . . the famous Lily Bryant about to accomplish one of the most daring feats in aviation!"

Kiffin came up from slightly below and behind. As Lily left the cockpit and began her walk between the wings it was time to start a tear-drop turn to the right. Since she was working her way out the DH's left wing the upper wing and fuselage would block the crowd's view and the centrifugal force generated by the turn would make her footing solid. They had rehearsed and discussed these moments many times and by now Toby had developed a very exact feeling in his rump for the tightness of the turn. Too tight and Lily would have trouble moving; she could weigh twice her real weight. Too shallow and she would lose some of gravity's help.

Lily was a good soldier, he thought. She had been warned not to look back at him while she was actually moving along the wing. She kept her mind on her business.

By the time she had reached the end of the wing and the turn was completed they were more than a mile east of the stands and although Toby kept the Liberty throttled back as far as he dared with so much drag on one wing, Kiffin was left too far behind. Pushing the Jenny as fast as it would fly he was making a show of trying to catch up and slide into position.

The positioning was a deliberate tease. Kiffin said that no self-respecting acrobat ever accomplished his most difficult trick on the first attempt. He would miss a valuable chance to build suspense.

After passing the stands at the western end they eased into another right turn with Kiffin tightening his turn now and easing the Jenny just under and slightly to the right of the DH's tail. On the next turn when they started back for the stands, he would cut inside and climb into position.

There was no sense making the transfer a mile away where no one could see it. The timing had to be so exact it would occur right in front of them. Then, as she had now done so many times, Lily would be able to reach down and grab the long handles on the king post just as they passed in front of the crowd.

The transfer itself was relatively easy to accomplish. It was making these two ill-matched airplanes agree to marry without not quite doing so that became so frustrating. A minor brush of a wing tip would probably not do too much damage, but anything rougher could be disastrous.

If he had been flying a handy and sensitive little Nieuport in formation with another Nieuport, Kiffin remembered he could play this game to perfection, snuggling in against a comrade with only inches to spare, jockeying the throttle to a nicety as he saw the need to pull ahead or fall back. Now, with the Jenny and the DH precise control of the situation was much less likely. He was obliged to hold full throttle just to keep up with Toby. Reversing the standard and better procedure, it would now be Toby who would have to make the speed adjustments.

They settled down to a fixed relationship about a half mile

east of the stands and flew a steady course straight for the race track.

Lily sat down on the very end of the wing. She looked at Kiffin some twenty feet from her position and smiled.

She let her legs hang over the end of the wing and wiggled her bare feet at him.

He was satisfied that it would be nearly impossible for anyone below to ignore the red scarf as it whipped in the slip-stream. A feast for the eye. A bright scarf on a beautiful girl. At five hundred feet.

He saw that Lily was at ease.

He glanced at Toby. He was at ease. All was as it should be.

Beyond the rocker boxes of the OX-5 Kiffin saw the stands approaching. A quarter mile to go. And Lily was still smiling. Perfect air. Glass.

He saw Lily gather herself. In fifteen seconds, maybe twenty, she would grab the forward wing strut with both hands, make a half turn with her body and lower herself over the end of the wing. Her feet would contact the wooden hoop on the underside of the wing and give her additional support. She would wait, knowing exactly what was happening. She would wait for the final nod.

He glanced up at Toby. Positive or negative? Positive, of course.

He saw her turn and slip down carefully until she was half under the wing. She extended one arm to catch the king post bar.

They were nearly opposite the stands.

He brought the wing almost within her reach.

He was about to give her a nod when he saw it.

And he knew Toby had also seen it.

He eased the Jenny away. He had to think, and fast. How could he have failed to foresee that when Lily changed position the red scarf might not exactly follow her movements?

Now, somehow . . . God only knew how, the end of the damn thing, whipping in the tornado-like wind, had wrapped itself around the base of the rear strut. It looked like it might be jammed in a fitting.

He saw the puzzled look on Lily's face. She had been ready for the moment of transfer and was apparently unaware that she was still anchored to the DH.

And there was something else they had forgotten to consider during their sessions with "what ifs." Once all was just as it should be and Lily had lowered herself into final position she was committed to the transfer. It would take more strength than most men had in their arms to heave their body over the leading edge of the wing against the pressure of the slipstream. Somehow it had never occurred to them that Lily might want to reverse the procedure.

He saw now that she knew something was wrong. He was close enough to see the bewilderment in her eyes.

As the stands slipped past, Kiffin's mind tore at the alternatives.

Would it help if Toby put the DH in a steep bank to the right? He certainly couldn't take a chance landing with Lily perched where she was.

Could he stall . . . or approach a stall? The slip-stream would then be reduced to about fifty miles per hour. Negative. Bad idea. At best any abrupt maneuver was a bad idea because Lily would be subjected to unpredictable kinetic and gravitational forces. He might fall off into a spin.

Kiffin glanced up at Toby. He knew that he could see the end of the red scarf, but would be unable to see Lily.

For an instant a sense of helplessness nearly took him over.

He could not hear the sound of the groan that escaped him. He told himself to cool down and *think*. Lily would soon be chilled, but she could hold her position indefinitely. Continuing with the transfer was impossible. The scarf would choke her unless it broke away.

He moved the Jenny closer again, but not near enough to the DH for her to expect a second attempt. He made an elaborate gesture of tugging at his own white scarf hoping she would understand that she should try doing the same. Maybe the damn thing would come unglued.

He saw her yank at it several times. Nothing moved. He saw her try to look up to see the end of the scarf, but the wing blocked her view. And he saw that now she knew what had gone wrong. He saw a faint smile pass briefly along her lips and he found it impossible to meet her eyes.

They had left Wichita on the horizon and were now over the empty prairie. Precious minutes passing, without any solution. Kiffin remembered he had done some praying at

Landshut. He glanced instinctively at the sky and found nothing to cheer him.

He looked up at Toby. The old rock would come up with something. . . .

Their eyes met in despair and during that instant Kiffin knew very suddenly what he had to do. There was no other choice now and he had better damn well be fast about it.

He pulled the Jenny up until it was on the same level as the DH, then he gestured that Toby should continue straight on course. When he was certain that Toby understood, he pulled up still more and crossed over to the right side of the DH. The maneuver left him slightly to the rear, but he kept on full throttle and began a slight descent. Soon he was gaining slowly on the DH.

He reached for his seat belt and unclipped it. He took gunsight aim on the wooden hoop that extended downward from the DH's right wing and held it exactly between the rocker boxes of the OX-5 engine.

He waited, heart pounding. Jesus, could this really be done?

For a time it seemed that the Jenny would never move ahead in relation to the DH.

He flicked a glance at Toby, hoping he would throttle back just a trifle more. The Jenny started inching ahead and he knew that Toby understood what he hoped to do.

He moved the Jenny's trim tab until it took a little back pressure on the stick to keep it level. The air was still smooth, for which blessing, Kiffin thought, there would never be an equal.

The Jenny's upper wing was now only a few inches below the bottom of Toby's lower wing. The wooden hoop crept back over the Jenny's upper wing. When it was directly overhead he took a deep breath. It was like his first dog-fight, he remembered. The flow of adrenalin through his body caused him to actually tremble. If he missed, he knew there would be no second chance.

He allowed the hoop to pass a few inches behind him, just enough to keep it in his field of vision if he tilted his head. When at last the hoop appeared to be stopped in position he suddenly dropped the controls and got to his feet. As he reached for the hoop, the Jenny fell away from him, spitting out his legs. As if in resentment the tail struck the foot of his boot and nearly broke his grip on the hoop.

He hung for a moment gathering all his strength. His body trailed back slightly in the slip-stream and far below he saw the abandoned Jenny heading for the ground. A brown insect twisting down toward a brown field.

He was so exhausted when he finally hoisted himself over the leading edge of the wing that he had to lie still before he could move further. He saw Toby watching him and the urgency in his eyes forced him to pull himself up the leading strut.

He made his way along the wing to the DH's center section and tried to give Toby a reassuring smile as he crossed the empty front cockpit.

He moved out along the left wing as fast as he dared. Now he saw that the red scarf might as well have tied a knot in itself. The slip-stream had flipped one end under the other and Lily's weight had jammed the combination into the strut fitting.

Near the end of the wing he lowered himself to his belly and caught the toe of his boots on the flying wires that led down to the strut. He pushed himself forward until his waist was nearly on the wing's leading edge. Bending over he found himself looking directly into Lily's eyes. He reached for her armpits, felt her relax her grip on the hoop, and hauled with all the strength left to him.

When she lay beside him on the wing he found that he was too dizzy to move at once. He reached for her hand and squeezed it. He avoided looking at Toby.

When they were safely in the spacious front cockpit Toby turned back toward Wichita. En route they passed over a ball of fire on the ground and Toby circled it once. Now the Jenny was only a single column of black smoke.

They said nothing to each other then, nor for a long time after they had landed.

CHAPTER
8

Most of them died as they lived, undismayed, zestful, blind to the ordinary motives of life, utterly lost in what they were doing. An almost universal optimism was their only armor against defeat. At the time of Draper's Great Flying Circus' demise, there were some four or five hundred barnstormers scattered about the United States, all trying desperately to squeeze a livelihood from flying. No one was interested in the fate of aerial gypsies and they were not the sort to promote passionate interest in their welfare. Most barnstormers were aviators first and good fellows next, equipped with such easy consciences they went joyously a-whoring in every little settlement across the land. Even when they toured the really dry and Bible states like Nebraska, Kansas, Iowa and parts of Minnesota they found drink and they swore and seduced and sometimes fought with the locals who resented the intrinsic glamor they wore as comfortably as their leather jackets. A few of them were outright scoundrels and for one reason or another finished their tour in the local jail, but the vast majority were slaves only to the seductive power of flight and gave themselves to it.

They were rarely good businessmen and watched in awe as the life they had come to think of as uniquely their own began to wither. Instead of the accidents and deaths decreasing with experience, the toll mounted as their airplanes were asked to perform feats for which they had never been designed. Cockpits meant for one person were enlarged to hold as many as three and even four paying passengers and competition for the same customers became hostile.

Hoping to halt the toll, the government in a sudden display of interest, destroyed all the surplus Jennies together with their engines and spare parts. There was even talk of licensing the pilots. Barnstormers used whatever came to hand to keep their airplanes flying; baling wire here, garden hose there, a scarfing of spruce with a bar of the local pine, all accomplished with much cursing and natural ingenuity. Yet violent death took many, and economics spreading among them like a disease reduced their numbers still further. A new airplane like the Standard, built especially for the trade, was far too expensive for most of the young entrepeneurs.

It was not long before a new and most insidious regression appeared, and the public developed an increasingly morbid interest in dangerous stunts. A new breed of barnstormer appeared on the scene and several of them took over where Kiffin, Toby, and the dashing Lily were obliged to stop. Like Kiffin the newcomers recognized that aerial entertainment was the key to their immediate survival.

Ivan Gates, an acerbic man who could not fly himself although he usually claimed he was "too busy," became the most successful of all aerial circus promoters. He saw the wisdom of hiring and publicizing "the greatest aviators in the world" and he paid them fifty dollars a week. Among those who found their way to his headquarters at Teterboro in New Jersey was the colorful French ace Didier Marson, "Upside Down" Pangborn, whose specialty was inverted flight, "Tommy" Thompson, who was a master at shutting off his engine, making aerobatic maneuvers, and finally gliding down to a precise dead-stick landing, Cy Bittner who would attempt almost anything, and "Whispering Bill" Brooks, who attached giant sparklers to the ends of his wings and performed aerobatics at night.

Jimmy Angel's Flying Circus was a rival to Gates' outfit, featuring Eddie Angel who jumped from a Jenny at night carrying two flashlights and postponing opening his parachute during his "Dive to Death" until he could see the ground. Walt Hunter, who had his own flying circus, hung from the landing gear of a Jenny and dropped into a haystack without any kind of chute. And there was Mabel Cody, the rough and tough niece of Buffalo Bill Cody, who managed and performed in her own flying circus. A shrewd business sense combined with unlimited gall enabled her to survive where so many others had been forced to surrender.

While the barnstormers struggled and so often perished in their determination to fly there were other more important developments throughout the western world which brought

enewed life to the skies. The first airplane with a retractable
anding gear flew in 1920, the same year that Handley-Page
a England introduced flaps and wing slots for more efficient
anding approaches. While in Germany, even though the
ation was still on its war-weary knees, they managed to
roduce the Zeppelin-Staaken E-4/20, an eighteen-passenger,
our-engine metal airplane which they hoped would serve as
n "airliner." Elsewhere a La Pere biplane set a record
ltitude of thirty-six thousand twenty feet, the United States
ost Office inaugurated a scheduled mail flight from New
ork to San Francisco, and the Pulitzer Race was won by a
'erville-Packard at 156.5 miles per hour. American movies
reated new interest in drama aloft with pilots like Omer
ocklear, Paul Mantz, Shirley Short, and Roscoe Turner
oing much of the flying. Movie director Cecil B. DeMille
nd Charlie Chaplin's brother became fascinated with avia-
on and for a time competed in all kinds of aeronautical
ctivities at two different Los Angeles fields located at the
orner of Wilshire Boulevard and Fairfax Avenue.

Toby and Lily Bryant could view these excitements only
rom a distance, and Toby blamed himself for his seeming
nability to pry himself away from his native state. Finding
vork became an obsession with him. The Standard biplane
vas being built in Lincoln, but orders were few and their only
ilot position had been filled while Toby was away barn-
torming. There was no other local flying activity. "Maybe,"
'oby said with a new note of apology in his voice, "you
narried the wrong guy. I'm sure not earning my salt around
ere."

Lily was becoming increasingly worried about her husband.
heir little spats too often developed into long silences and
here were times when she thought she could almost see the
esentment rising between them. One evening she asked Toby
vhy he didn't go back east and try for a job with the new mail
ervice. Even as she asked the question she knew the timing
vas awkward, but she persisted because, she thought, I'm
uman and this is the moment to jab at the person I love the
nost.

All three jobs Toby had applied for that day had been taken
y the time of his arrival and his voice took on a new edge
vhen he turned on her.

"Because we damn well don't have enough money to pay

the rail fare plus a place to sleep and eat while I'm trying to get past some government bureaucrat who doesn't know one end of an airplane from the other! You stick to your business of keeping this house and stay out of mine."

Lily could not believe what she was hearing. She compounded the tension by pointing out that there had just recently been a time when Toby had welcomed her to his business. She aggravated the matter still further when she added, "At least Kiffin had the gumption to go out in the outside world and find work . . . wherever he is—"

She saw at once that she had struck her man a vicious blow and wished she had been less direct. Too late. Only a week after their return an envelope had arrived bearing a Brownsville postmark. It was empty except for a folded sheet of paper and a hundred dollar bill. "Kiffin," Toby said immediately. "No one else is that crazy."

"I'd call him a psychic angel."

"Where does he get this kind of money?"

"Out of his conscience, I suppose. I think losing the Jenny really broke his heart."

Since then envelopes arrived every month, always with postmarks of the far south and always containing a one hundred dollar bill.

Now Toby said, "Sometimes I wonder about your feelings for Kiffin. If he asked you to jump over the moon you'd give it a try."

"Don't be crazy. I'm in love with you. I'm trying to help you because I know you're unhappy." The rock was crumbling before her eyes, she thought, incredibly the mighty Toby, the strong man who had been so dependable ever since the first moment she saw him, was losing control of himself. Every morning he sat in their tiny living room and read the employment ads very carefully, marking those for which he might qualify and then spending the balance of the day tracking them down. Yes, before her eyes his stoop was becoming more pronounced and he seemed ever more reluctant to smile. He was beginning to look much older than his twenty-five years.

Now when Lily was alone she often spoke a curse on the head of Rudolph Piper, for the once genial automotive man had turned into a villain after the loss of the Jenny. He had demanded immediate payment and had instructed the sheriff in Wichita to chain the DH-4 to the ground pending settlement of their agreement. Eventually Toby had been able to persuade Piper that he should continue as long as he was bound back in the general direction of Omaha, where he promised to deliver the airplane. He had taken advantage of the two weeks of fine autumn weather to give Lily flying lessons after they had exhausted the local supply of paying passengers. There was no more wing-walking, and Toby performed only the most conservative chandelles over the towns to attract attention.

The heart was gone from them and they barely made expenses.

The disappearance of Kiffin troubled them and they found themselves talking about his sudden departure more often than they would have liked . . . After they had landed on that dreadful afternoon Lily pulled off the red scarf and stuffed it in the pocket of her breeches. She had meant nothing by the gesture, but to the emotionally exhausted Kiffin it was a signal of rejection. As they stood in embarrassed silence beside the DH, watching the approach of the fair officials and each waiting for the other to say just anything, Kiffin finally bowed his head and said, "I'm sorry. You could have been killed. I think I'd better go away before I ruin your lives."

The fair officials arrived just then along with a covey of reporters who began asking questions at once. After only a few minutes of their attack which displayed a notable lack of understanding, Kiffin somehow managed to escape. Lily remembered that he kissed her very briefly on the top of her head and that was the last she had seen of him. It was not until twilight that they realized he had taken their unfortunate afternoon as a personal defeat and had deliberately removed himself.

Toby had spent part of that night looking for him in Wichita without success and they told each other he would certainly appear in the morning. During the next eight days they telegraphed Rudolph Piper concerning the loss of the Jenny and went every morning to look at the forlorn DH chained down and standing alone in the middle of the racetrack. At first they were certain that Kiffin would be unable to resist returning to the DH, but gradually even that hope faded. On the ninth day they took off toward Omaha. "I guess," Toby said, "kind of with our tails between our legs."

The final meeting with the disillusioned Rudolph Piper took place on a rainy morning in mid-October. There was a threat of snow in the air and the flat gloom of an early Nebraska winter did nothing to ease Piper's disenchantment with the flying business. "Where's your fast talking buddy?" he demanded.

"I'm not sure," Toby said.

"I trusted him and what have I got? One airplane instead of two. That make sense to you?"

"It was unfortunate . . . and unavoidable."

"Nuts. I heard all about it. He deliberately abandoned my property."

"He had no choice. He's a very brave man—"

"I'm not interested in bravery. You war heroes, if that's what you really are, have got to start behaving like real people. You owe me a pile of money."

Toby held his temper and refrained from reminding Piper that he had acquired the Jenny and the DH for almost nothing and had them assembled for flight at no charge. Instead he said, "If you'll let me use the DH I can still fly around Nebraska hopping passengers and maybe pay off some of our debt. If we could paint 'Omaha Motors' on the side of the fuselage in big letters, and maybe on the underside of the wings, it would be fine advertising for you. Texaco and Phillips Oil are doing it. Maybe I could tow some banners."

"And if something goes wrong and you abandon the de Havilland, then what? I'm out two airplanes, and no money. I'm going to sell the damn thing." Then for a moment Piper seemed to soften and looked at Toby quizzically. "You know you've got a nice little wife there and I would think it's about time you settled down to honest work. You're not a bad looking guy and you give the impression that you're sincere even though I have good reason to believe most of you aviators are not. Ever think about selling automobiles? I got a hunch people might believe what you tell them. . . . at least temporarily . . ."

Piper bared his caninelike teeth in what he intended as a smile and became disgruntled again when Toby declined his offer.

Later that day the rain began to freeze and the Nebraska wind spewed a glaze across the train windows. They were bound for Lincoln and the little house with a total of seven dollars and ten cents between them. "I'm glad we're not flying today," Lily said, blowing her breath against the window glass.

"Someone is. I just don't seem to be able to get off on the right foot."

"It will all work out, like they say, everything happens for the best—"

"You sound like Kiffin."

"I hope he's waiting for us in Lincoln."

"I thought you didn't want him around all the time."

"I don't. Just once in a while. He needs someone to look after him."

It was well into November before Toby managed to find a job as a plumber's apprentice, an employment he said should benefit him greatly if he was ever again lucky enough to sit behind a Liberty engine. Thanks to the unpredictable hundred-dollar-bills which kept arriving from various locations along the southern border of the United States and a belated wedding gift of five hundred dollars from Lily's father, they managed to survive. But the wedding gift confirmed Lily's belief that their monetary stress had disrupted Toby's normally solid thinking.

"I will *not* become dependent on your father," he insisted.

"Baloney. He sent it to both of us as a pair joined in holy matrimony and you're going to eat off it just like I am."

"I feel like a damned gigolo."

"Oh get off that Nebraska high horse. This is nineteen hundred nineteen, not a hundred years ago. You have to start living in the real world of today and that doesn't mean that you always have to be the patriarchal provider."

"Sometimes I don't understand you."

"Good. If you understood me all the time I'd soon become a bore."

"Fat chance. You're the most exciting person I've ever known."

For an instant she looked at him in disbelief. It was so unlike Toby to toss verbal flowers. She saw that he had made his declaration in absolute sincerity, exactly in the way, she thought, that Rudolph Piper had sought to exploit. And she saw again that there just was not a false note in the man she had married. My straight arrow innocent-of-innocents, she thought, may you always say nothing more nor less than what's in your heart. Also, I love you . . .

She went to him then and reached up to clasp her hands around his powerful neck. She pulled herself up until her face was nearly on a level with his own. "Thank you," she whispered, "for what you just said. Why don't you take me to bed and let me prove you weren't fibbing."

During the early 1920s a loose and distinctive aviation hierarchy was building in the United States. While the enormous influence of the Curtiss enterprises persisted Glenn Martin became the largest and most important aircraft manufacturer. The now very great man bore the stiff and somewhat pompous manner of a powerful industrial captain. Even so he reported home for lunch with his mother every day and shared with her the daily operations of his expanding factory. It was said that her invisible yet powerful influence caused talented men like Donald Douglas and Larry Bell to become restive as Martin employees and to found their own companies. And in Detroit, Henry Ford became so interested in the promise of commercial aviation that he instructed his engineers to design an airplane capable of flying at least twelve passengers.

As the flowering of the barnstormers and their stunts and circuses wilted, more serious endeavors continued aloft. The first flight around the world was made in two of the new Douglas "Cruisers" flown by Captain L.H. Smith and the jaunty Lieutenant Erik Nelson. The U.S. Navy took over the former German Zeppelin LZ-126 and christened her the *Los Angeles*. In England, Daimler Airways began to use cabin boys to look after the needs of their passengers. . . .

It was in Key West, Florida, where Kiffin Draper had drifted for the winter of 1922, that he encountered a writer named Montgomery. Their interest in each other sparked very suddenly in the writer's favorite speakeasy and a rapport was established almost at once. They rolled dice for drinks and Kiffin won twice and said he had risked enough and wanted to stop. "You're my kind of guy," Montgomery laughed. "Never give the other guy a chance to win."

Montgomery was a big solid-looking man and after looking Kiffin up and down carefully as if debating the outcome of an exchange of punches with him his eyes took on a sly look. "I would guess," he said as the alcohol began to cloud his diction, "that you have been to the wars."

"I flew a little for the French," Kiffin said, downing his rum. "But I'm really the world's finest violinist."

Montgomery was delighted with his own perception. "Bullshit to that fiddle playing. I knew damn well you were an aviator. I can tell by that cuckoo look in your eyes. Have another dollop."

Kiffin was more than willing. He had found that alcohol in almost any form helped to dissolve the memory of the afternoon he had parted company with the Jenny. The specter of what could so easily have happened to Lily haunted him until he could not shake it away. At last he had given up trying. Before the night was through he had told Montgomery the whole story and eventually, slurring their words back and forth, pontificating by the shovelful, and exchanging ever more soggy tales of wounds, prison camps, and the need for heroes in a world of weaklings, they agreed that they were both the finest fellows in the world.

"I got to fix it for you to meet my friend Mori," Montgomery said. "The poor bastard was at Caporetto. I know he needs a man to fly his airplane because the pilot he had is now in durrance vile."

"Where's zat?" The bar kept doing chandelles. His new friend said he was a writer, but did that mean he had to talk strong?

"I hope you never find out. But if you want to meet Mori I'll turn the key."

Mori proved to be a soft-spoken chain smoker who took a full minute of silence appraising Kiffin. Montgomery had warned him that no one knew Mori's last name and no one asked. "He's inclined to be a pain in the ass, but when he does speak he utters the truth. Just be careful not to antagonize him. He has a different view of the value of life than most of the rest of the human race."

Kiffin had always been willing to admit that he was addicted to hazard. Why not? "If you risk your neck and lose you'll never know it. If you escape without serious damage it's marvelous—like breaking away from a set of chains."

He was quick then in accepting Mori's offer to fly his Jenny on a series of lucrative missions. Again and again and always at night he flew back and forth across the stretch of ocean between Key West and Cuba bringing back as many cases of scotch, gin, and brandies as the Jenny could lift. His new job had a strangely perverse effect on his own drinking. Even on the clearest of starlit nights the ocean became a black dungeon. Before the dawn he would traverse over two hundred miles of total solitude. Except for his presence the sky was empty and like a lone hunter he wanted all his alertness to anticipate the unusual.

Kiffin found it hard to believe his pay, which came in the form of cash peeled off a roll of bills by the ever taciturn Mori.

"I'm worried," he told a lady tourist one rainy night when he had cancelled his flight. "Money is a disease. If you keep it then it's only a question of time before it ferments and forms a scum over the spirit. A lingering death is inevitable." Pretty flowery, he thought. I'm being corrupted by Montgomery.

That night the lady tourist relieved him of one hundred dollars and offered to relieve him of any sexual tensions he might have in the future for half the price.

After only a week of sallying back and forth he told himself that he was well on the way to becoming a millionairé. And if Mori could be visibly pleased about anything, then for him his approval of Kiffin was extravagant. He half smiled and said softly, "I like a reliable man."

By the second week Kiffin was willing to admit that he earned his money. He tried not to think what would happen if the rather weary Jenny's OX-5 engine suddenly decided it had flown long enough. Certainly no one would come to his rescue. His own knowledge of engines was very limited and there was no mechanic in Key West capable of making a thorough inspection, much less obtaining Mori's approval. "Three people on the Key know about this," Mori said. "Me, Montgomery, and you. Let it stop there."

The Jenny was kept in a small clearing almost totally surrounded by a palmetto swamp. It was far enough away from the settlement of Key West to make it unlikely anyone would hear the OX-5 on take-off and Kiffin was instructed to avoid flying over the populated area. On his return from Cuba he would come in very high to muffle the sound of the engine and once the clearing had been spotted he cut the OX-5 back to idle and made a long, nearly silent spiral down to earth. He usually arrived about three o'clock in the morning and Mori was always waiting with a powerful flashlight.

Gliding down from the stars Kiffin steered the Jenny toward a black hole in the darkness beyond the lights of Key West. As soon as Mori heard the slip-stream sighing through the Jenny's flying wires he pointed his light straight up and held it for a count of thirty. On most nights Kiffin spotted the clearing as the first shaft of light sliced upward through the darkness. Then he circled once more and lowered the Jenny's nose. When he blurped the engine once Mori would turn his light horizontally and aim it in the direction of the wind. The instant the Jenny's wheels touched the sand he would turn it off. The system worked perfectly, and if the ceiling was low it was even easier with Mori's light burning a bright hot spot in the bottom of the cloud level. If anyone noted the brief flashes of light they never troubled to investigate. "These here crackers is too lazy to get outa bed," Mori explained.

At least an hour before dawn they were on their way to Key West in Mori's battered truck. They had fueled the Jenny with gasoline brought to the clearing in the back of the truck and tied the airplane down to stakes in the sand. Mori was not concerned about the Jenny being discovered on the ground; the tortuous trail to the clearing twisted around itself several times before it melted into the main highway. In a rare expository moment Mori said, "The only people that's goin' to turn off on this path is not inarrested in airplanes. They can stop and fuck all they want without bouncing through chuckholes. And at these hours they can do it right on the main street of Key West."

Kiffin never asked where Mori went after he had been dropped off at his seedy little hotel. It was a damp and rotten place that somehow matched Kiffin's mood. Sometimes he paid his rent with a bottle or two for the proprietor of the hotel who in turn disposed of them to various local clients. The asking of questions on such matters could lead to embarrassments and possible trouble . . . prohibition had turned a nation of reasonably law-abiding citizens into technical criminals and most Americans accepted the sale and use of illegal alcohol as the normal way of life. While those who engaged in the trade were not greatly respected, neither were they ostracized; it was easy to make the acquaintance of a good bootlegger, and in the Florida keys, where smuggling had been a way of earning a living since anyone could remember, the relatively new source of income was easily tolerated.

So Kiffin was happy and content . . . when he could drive thoughts of Lily and Toby away. He slept much of the day and those few nights when he told Mori the weather was unfavorable for flying he joined Montgomery at his speakeasy or chose from an apparently limitless supply of the local young women who preferred his company to the sailors at the naval base. He did not lust for any of these women nor did his occasional pawing greatly arouse either his partner or himself. His rutting was merely to fulfill a basic need that came up so seldom he became newly concerned about himself. He regretted that thoughts of Lily had a way of intruding just when he believed they should be the least dominant. It was as if Lily herself was sometimes present, arrived via some invisible and silent flying machine to distract him from that very moment when he expected to become lost in the body of another woman. Too often it seemed, when the mouthings and caresses he exchanged with Suzie, or Melissa, or Wilma reached the point of feverish expectation, he became suddenly impotent. There was always Lily, staring down at him from the ceiling or whispering from some unseen corner of the room, draining and diverting him as surely as if she were present. His visions of her were followed by an overwhelming loneliness and he thought, "She's the wife of the best friend you'll ever have. You have *got* to put her out of your mind."

Yet when he tried and even when he succeeded temporarily, he was left with an emptiness the young women of Key West could not possibly ease. And there were times when it seemed to him that his twenty-six years had become twice as many.

After a month of flying for Mori he recognized that a new and totally unforeseen sensation had captured his imagination. Wartime flying was one thing. There was always the threat of another man in the sky who hoped to kill you. The devotion then was to the airplane as a portable gun, not a vehicle for transport. When every sector of the sky had to be searched constantly for first sight of your potential murderer there was no relaxation; certainly no time for assessment or appreciation of your lofty surroundings. Likewise barnstorming with its perpetual financial battles soured the exhilaration of flight.

Now he could almost feel his original infatuation with

flying returning. He had been back and forth to Cuba so many times he had come to think of it as the "milk run," but now he thought there must be better words to describe the discoveries he was making during his passage through the upper night. He bought a book on the stars and learned to identify the Pleiades, Capella, Rigel, Betelgeux, Castor and Pollux, and Procyon. It pleased him immensely to murmur the majestic names of all the more prominent bodies glittering so serenely in the subtropic sky. It was as if he was not moving at all, but could view himself suspended in a black void while perched on his own commonwealth in the stellar society. Gradually he came to regard the stars as viable friends along his route; their lack of movement was reassuring.

The nights were cool and the cockpit of the Jenny offered only slight protection against the seventy-mile-an-hour slipstream, yet he was comfortable wearing only the same leather jacket he had worn with the Flying Circus. There were no lights in the cockpit nor on any of the Jenny's extremities—he slid along through the night with only an occasional flick of his flashlight at the instrument panel.

Oil pressure steady.

Tachometer steady on twelve hundred.

Altitude one thousand—more or less.

Light off. It is presumptuous to compete with the stars.

When he had been in the air half an hour and the lights of Key West had vanished behind the Jenny's tail he sometimes fancied he was the last human alive—certainly there were no other airplanes out there where the sea joined the stars along an indefinite horizon and on some still nights turned the heavens upside down.

Navigation was easy. Once the lights of Key West sank with his climb to altitude a flick of his light at the compass gave him direction through the void. One hundred ninety degrees . . .

It was not a very good compass and the numbers were already yellowed with age. It oscillated mysteriously on some headings, but it was steady enough to compare with a star beyond it and so fix his course.

Soon after leaving the Florida keys he entered upon a region of total wilderness. It was like a great dark womb in which he felt inexplicably comfortable.

"I'm Kiffin Draper, human being . . . I may be lost below, but here I am at home."

The steady rhythmic rumble of the OX-5 became a mighty concert to him. The air, almost always smooth at night, provided no sense of movement or attitude, hence it was the stars alone that kept him stable. A touch of the stick to the left or right would move a star an inch or half an inch either way. A slight pull sent the stars between the Jenny's wings in a brief descent. Caught like a tiny organism in a huge black bowl, the ordinarily clumsy Jenny became a thing of dark and subtle beauty, its movements wondrously sensual.

There were special little pleasures that contributed to his nightly euphoria. Once aloft he pushed his goggles to the top of his helmet and allowed all of his face to feel the soft and humid air. The vague odor of engine exhaust, ill-matched to the beauty of the night, somehow attained a musky fragrance that was worth an occasional satisfying inhalation. There was a certain place on the joy-stick where he liked to move his thumb up and down slowly as if he were caressing the whole assembly of wood and wire and fabric in which he existed.

How long would the Jenny float if he came down from the night and was forced to land in the sea? No one knew. He supposed it might be as much as half an hour before the weight of the engine and fuel would press her down, but on the return flight from Cuba burdened with all the weight she would carry he knew the time before sinking would be much less.

Tonight, he thought with a shrug of his shoulders, it made little difference. Nor any other night. If indeed the OX quit then all was certainly lost. No one would know he had joined the stars' reflections except Mori, and no one in Cuba cared.

He found the prospect strangely tantalizing. Who needed artificial stimulation when here so close at hand was the ultimate discovery?

It amused him to pull a chocolate bar from the pocket of his leather jacket and consume it slowly during the flight back to the Florida keys. When he was done with the wrapper he would hold it up between two fingers and let it be whisked away in the slip-stream.

These little time-passers were important. During the period between land and land they kept him from brooding about Lily. . . .

According to his log book this was his twenty-ninth flight. He started his usual descent toward the loom of lights marking the town of Key West. A delay loading in Cuba had caused him to be later than usual—according to the luminescent hands on his wristwatch the time was three forty-eight. A headwind had also slowed his ocean crossing. He judged it would be another thirty minutes before he would be on the ground, perhaps another twenty unloading and tying down. Dawn would not be long beyond and Mori did not like the light of day.

All else was usual as he eased the Jenny down through five hundred feet and turned to avoid actually passing over the lights of Key West.

A thin shaft of light off to the north. Mori. He would want to know why the delay.

A slight turn toward the light and clearing. Steady. On course. Goggles down. Head over the side, eyes seeking the horizontal bar of light. It was needed now more than usual because the wind was stronger than it had been for some time.

There. Directly ahead of the Jenny's nose. The light blurred by the propeller. Mori, faithful to his investment.

A slow pass over the terminus of the light for orientation then a descending full circle to land along the path of the light. Touchdown—soft against the sand. The light is extinguished.

A blast of the engine to raise the Jenny's tail enough to make another half circle, then a fast taxi back toward Mori and the truck.

He cut the switch to the single magneto and the OX stuttered to a stop. Another night gone and another lucrative flight. He glanced at his watch. 4:05. Time enough. As he pushed up his goggles he heard a voice from just behind the cockpit.

"Good morning."

It was not Mori's voice.

Without turning his head Kiffin knew there was now more than one person between him and the Jenny's tail. Another voice said dispassionately, "Get out of there and keep your hands above your shoulders. You're under arrest."

As Kiffin pushed up his goggles a beam of light struck him full in the face and blinded him. And another voice said, "Your buddy is waiting for you over there."

CHAPTER
9

By the winter of 1926 the United States Air Mail service had partially recovered from the erratic dispositions of bureaucrats who knew little about aviation and were not overly inclined to learn. Postmaster Otto Praeger had mellowed and no longer insisted that a pilot be fired if he refused to fly in weather he considered too dangerous. Now the pilot could use his own judgment without fear of reprisal and there was some improvement in the flying equipment.

Although various other aircraft were used in flying the mails the aging de Havilland 4s were still the mainstay of routes east of the Mississippi. The same old twelve cylinder Liberty engines with their twenty-seven links of hose uniting the plumbing system still gave trouble and caused innumerable forced landings, but all pilots preferred them to the Junkers JL-6, an all metal plane of German design which an eloquent salesman had sold to the postal authorities. They soon proved to be dangerous firetraps and after a number of harrowing flights their use was discontinued.

Toby Bryant spent much of his spare time composing letters of application for flying jobs; even the most remote possibility was ticked off his list, but an eternity passed before a form notice came to the bungalow in Lincoln. It was from the Robertson Aircraft Corporation in St. Louis and if he could present himself at their offices between April first and the seventh they would be pleased to grant him an interview.

Trying to restrain his excitement Toby said it was probably an April Fool's joke. One of his plumbing friends must have learned that he wanted a different kind of work and thought he was being funny. "Some twisted sense of humor," he said.

"Nonsense," Lily said. "I don't see any April Fool's note

196

at the bottom of the letter. It's just signed by a C. Lindbergh. Do you know him?''

"Nope."

"Maybe he knows of you."

"He will. Soon as a train can take me there."

Toby was astonished at what appeared to be a flourishing enterprise built by the four Robertson brothers. And he was immediately ashamed of himself for staying so long in Lincoln. This was a grand and wonderful world, he decided, and one way or another he must become a part of it.

While the Robertsons had originally operated out of St. Louis' Forest Park, it was now established at a place they called Lambert Field, after one of their most enthusiastic local backers. The Robertsons operated a large flight school and were starting to build a three passenger cabin monoplane powered either with an OX or a Curtiss Challenger engine. It would be known as the Curtiss Robin and they hoped it would fill the need to carry aerial passengers in some degree of comfort. After buying four surplus DHs from the army at a hundred dollars each the Robertsons had won the bid on flying the mail between St. Louis and Chicago and had hired a wondrously clever ex-barnstormer, Harlon Gurney, to modify their military airplanes for civilian use. Two other barnstormers, E.L. Sloniger and "Slim" Lindbergh had now been flying for the Robertsons more than a year. Lindbergh had just been appointed Chief Pilot of the Mail Service.

By the time Toby arrived in St. Louis, Phillip Love and Tom Nelson had already been hired. When Toby entered Lindbergh's little office he was surprised to find so young a man. His host was formally polite yet he seemed to be secretly enjoying himself.

"Sloniger's from Lincoln," he smiled. "He thinks anyone who hails from there *has* to be hired. You agree?"

"I do."

"This is a starvation operation. We don't pay very much because sometimes the sacks weigh more than the mail." Lindbergh paused and glanced at a paper Toby recognized as his application. "You flew in the war, I see. I wish I had."

"You didn't miss much." While that was not exactly true Toby knew custom demanded he minimize whatever he had done. Pilots who might color their hangar stories were always suspect.

Lindbergh said, "We weren't going to hire anyone who had passed their twenty-eighth birthday. . . ." he hesitated again as if he was embarrassed to go on. Toby was certain he saw a flush pass across his face. Too old at thirty?

" . . . but we need pilots with DH-4 experience so in your case I'm going to ask Bill Robertson to make an exception. He wanted to get over to France but the war was over before he could. I have a hunch he'll okay you. Let me show you around while we wait a decision from on high."

There was that curious smile again, mischievous and wise. Toby felt suddenly at ease. This was his kind of man. They were the same height, although Toby weighed a good fifty pounds more. When they looked each other in the eye it was a straightforward exchange, with neither man seeking dominance or advantage.

Dehavilland   D.H. 4.

There were four de Havillands lined up outside the single hangar. The wings were painted the color of aluminum and the fuselage a dark red. Lettered in white along the sides was U.S. AIR MAIL. Below, smaller letters designated the route between St. Louis and Chicago, C.A.M. NO. 2.

Lindbergh explained that they would be obliged to do a lot of night flying and the Robertsons had petitioned the Post Office Department to build lighted beacons along the route. "I'd like to see them spaced about every ten miles like they now have on the transcontinental route," he said.

"What happens in bad weather?"

"That's the hitch. We won't see them when we need them the most. And we're probably going to have to do a lot of instrument flying."

Where he had been so at ease Toby suddenly became uncomfortable. Here indeed was a hitch and probably the end of a job he almost had. This was the kind of employment where trying to bluff your way through could be very dangerous. "I'm sorry to tell you that I don't know how to fly on instruments . . . I've been in a few clouds for short periods, but that's all."

"Don't worry. None of us know much about it. We're sort of learning from each other."

"There's worse. You might as well know I haven't flown for about two years."

He saw Lindbergh frown then the smile was back again. "Okay . . . tell you what. I've got a full day so go over there to the flight school and find Slonnie. If he's in the air wait for him to come down. Tell him you need some refreshing. If Slonnie says you can handle the job it's fine with me."

Toby found the modified DH-4 a far better and safer aircraft than the one he had flown barnstorming. The Robertsons had made a large mail bin where the forward cockpit had been and the once ill-famous "flying coffins" now placed the pilot far enough aft to give him fifteen feet of structural shock absorber should he collide with an immovable object. The fuselage was now plywood instead of fabric and the tail skid was controllable for easier taxiing. The original landing gear had been replaced by a stronger version and moved far enough forward to minimize the DH's inclination to stand on its nose and sometimes continue the tumble until it was on its back.

Sloniger proved to be an easygoing man who looked not unlike a full-blooded Indian and talked with his hands even more than most pilots who "flew" their conversations. Like so many others he had trained to fly in the Great War, but had come along just too late for assignment overseas. Toby's experience with the French combined with the fact that he was also from Lincoln had a strong influence on Sloniger. "By God," he said, "if you're a little rusty we'll polish you up no matter if it takes all day."

Sloniger took him aloft in one of the Jennies that served the school. "If you can get us up and down without breaking anything the rest is easy."

Sloniger was laughing as he lowered himself into the front cockpit. After a third landing Sloniger told him to taxi back to the flight line. "Hell, you don't need me," he said. "Go on over to the DHs and get reacquainted. I'll recruit some hands to pull your prop. Fool around upstairs until you feel comfortable and go to bed early. My guess is you'll be flying mail tomorrow night.'' . . .

Things had progressed so smoothly with his new life that Toby was not at all surprised when events reversed the pattern. An ugly cold front, particularly violent for April, moved across the route to Chicago on the following night. Lindbergh decided against asking his newest pilot to fly the route for the first time under what promised to be difficult conditions. He flew the trip himself.

The weather proved to be worse than predicted and Lindbergh found himself trapped above a solid overcast somewhere over Illinois. Every time he put the nose of the DH down he slipped into a tomblike void. Time and again he let down as far as he dared seeking a light or even the dim outline of something he might recognize. Even when his altimeter read five hundred feet he could see no indication that he might be approaching the bottom of the overcast. At last he decided his dead reckoning was not accurate enough to be sure of the terrain below; if he flew much longer he might even be over Lake Michigan. Nearly out of fuel, he sighed and gritted his teeth as he took the only alternative. He climbed for the stars and bailed out.

Soon after his parachute opened he was horrified to hear the Liberty engine pick up and saw the DH start a circle around him. In his anxiety he had forgotten to cut the ignition switch and the berserk OX, flying on what must have been the last residue of fuel, was now threatening to gore him. It was the third time he had been obliged to abandon an aircraft, and as the chilled night air struck him full in the face he decided he liked it even less than the first time. Later when he reported to the Robertson brothers on the loss of their airplane he said, ''Maybe I should take up some other kind of work. I apologize for being such an expensive employee.''

There was an aviation law, unwritten yet as solid as if it were chiseled in stone. It had gathered stature along with the growth of aviation, and in America at least it was respected by all who considered themselves professionals. It was a law that forbade one man from putting himself in the place of another during a time of danger and second guessing his actions. Although the auditor might disapprove of whatever a surviving pilot had done to survive the situation, a different action was rarely suggested. After all, the listener was not present at the critical moment, his life was not in jeopardy, and a hundred demands were not insisting on his immediate attention. There was no way to reproduce the raucous anger of Wotan at eight or ten thousand feet or imitate the brain-numbing cold of an open cockpit on a winter night when the listener was sitting in an office. So wise airmen judged others whose luck or skill had brought them through peril according to a set of standards that was both tolerant and severe. Stupidity was rejected without pretense of sympathy. Over-indulgence in alcohol was considered indecent although risk-ing an airplane in a foolish buzzing of a lady friend's house was tolerated as a minor aeronautical sin and easily pardoned.

When it came to a contest with the elements, only a silly man would verbally place himself in the same fix as the pilot. It was considered bad form. The critic was not there, his guts were not roiling and his brain clouded with a bombardment of possibilities, good and bad. The pattern was, "Glad you weren't hurt . . . God wasn't waiting for you . . . any sugges-tions so it won't happen again?"

On his part the pilot who had recently emerged from serious trouble did not spare his own self-censure. "I must have been half asleep . . . it was a dumb thing to do (even though it might have been the only correct action) . . . maybe I'd better find somebody to teach me how to fly . . ."

If the pilot was killed his peers were all the more forgiving. The certainty of official condemnation laid on such a de-fenseless head was always resented and thought to be more than enough.

The St. Louis night was heavy with midsummer moisture. During the afternoon gigantic cumulo-nimbus had formed all along the line of the Mississippi River, building on them-selves rather than diminishing as the day faded. In the last of the twilight new battlements, redoubts, escarpments, sally ports and crenelations were formed and some of the more bulbous projections blossomed with lightning. Below, on the land and all along the banks of the great river, the fireflies lit the way for the swarms of mosquitoes, and everywhere there was a sense of dead air. By nightfall the city was steaming; people sweated and fanned at themselves and swatted irritably at the insects of summer. Residents of St. Louis, gasping, slept on porches if available, or put mattresses on the floor where it might be a degree or so cooler than at the height of their beds. Near suffocation, the poor and the blacks drooped out of their open windows, longing for near-dawn when perhaps the cauldron would cool and allow them brief sleep.

As he walked toward his airplane Toby noted that the only hint of a breeze was self-created as he moved through the sultry atmosphere. He carried his parachute over his shoulder postponing until the last minute putting on anything over his soggy shirt. He carried his leather jacket on his free arm and wished he dared leave it behind. If I had my choice, he thought, I'd fly this trip balls-ass naked. That would shake them up when I land in Chicago.

He slowed his pace instinctively while he reviewed all that he might need for this night's flight. Two hundred pounds of mail were already stowed in the bin—not enough to make a profit for the Robertson Aircraft Company. Private contractors like Robertson who the Post Office paid by the pound were still experiencing very thin times, and it was said that some companies mailed telephone books back and forth to increase their revenue.

His pistol, an ancient and possibly unworkable weapon he had bought for five dollars in a pawn shop, hung from his belt. Post Office regulations. A severe fine for himself and possibly the company if he flew without it. The damned gun was a hangover from the Pony Express days and a nuisance unless you were flying the mails out west. There, in the event of a forced landing in the wilderness, a pilot might shoot his next meal. But here in middle America? If he was going to be ambushed in that black and lonely sky above it would not be by some mere mortal.

His flashlight was in one hip pocket and his wallet, at last decorated with a few dollars, was in the other. Pencil in his shirt-pocket. His leather jacket was draped over a small canvas bag containing his toilet articles and a change of socks and underwear for the next day in Chicago.

Toby no longer wore the breeches and boots of the barnstormer. During cold weather the mail pilots wore fur-lined boots and several layers of clothing insulated with newspaper beneath their "teddy bears." And they still came down from the freezing skies rigid with cold. During hot nights like this one they wore pants of cotton duck and ordinary shoes. Tonight, Toby thought, bare feet would be more appropriate.

His charts were tucked in the cockpit of the DH between a longeron and the plywood of the DH's fuselage. He knew the route now and if the flight went well it was doubtful if he would even glance at them.

He carried a small paper bag in the hand that clutched the parachute strap, a snack Lily had prepared for him. At his request it always consisted of the same thing—a single ham sandwich. She varied the menu by including a different type of cookie and a surprise in the form of a scribbled note, "I love you," or a cartoon she had drawn intending to illustrate her sadness at being apart from him, or a news item annotated with a saucy comment: "Anything," she once explained, "to remind you that I'm still here waiting for you and to possibly discourage you from looking too closely at some blonde in Chicago."

As if he needed a reminder.

His leather helmet was perched slightly askew on his heavy brown hair. He had not yet secured the chin straps and they flapped as he walked.

Two mechanics and a boy were waiting for him in front of the DH. The lead mechanic, a thin man with a radish-red nose said, "How about you take me along, Toby. Maybe I can cool down some."

Toby smiled and said he would be happy to take all three of them along if they didn't mind sitting on the wings. He knew radish-nose now and called him by name: "Evening, Paul."

He greeted the others by name also—Hector and Johnny, the boy. It was a part of his determination to give his all to his job and he made special efforts to learn as much as he could about his fellow workers. Paul had an arthritic wife and treatments had kept him near bankruptcy for years. Hector was a Canadian emigré with a high blood pressure problem. He spoke constantly and lovingly of "Canucks," the Canadian-built version of the Jenny. And he was right; it was a better airplane than the American product.

Johnny, the boy who did odd jobs around the airport, anything to be near airplanes, wanted to be a pilot some day. His family was violently opposed to his taking up such dangerous work and discouraged him at every opportunity.

Toby paused a moment. He did not know exactly why he
so valued his moments with his fellow workers, yet he knew
he must do more than simply climb in the DH and fly away.
He appreciated their efforts to provide him with a vehicle in
which he could enter another world and he knew they were
doing their utmost to assure his safe return. Toby slipped into
the straps of his parachute and looking up at the nose of the
DH asked, "Will it fly?"

"She's a good old bird," Paul said. "I don't think nothin'
will bust."

"If it does do I get my money back?"

"We don't make no guarantees. Myself, I like trains."

Toby brought the leg straps of the parachute up between
his legs and clipped the ends to their D-rings. He wriggled a
bit to settle the straps in place, then waddled around to the
cockpit with the chute pack bouncing against the back of his
legs. Johnny took his leather jacket and canvas bag and
handed them to him as he settled in the cockpit. "Have a
good flight," he said, and went back to the others waiting
under the nose.

Toby held the flashlight between his teeth while he secured
the paper lunch bag and his canvas bag on the cockpit floor.
There was a bank of four landing flares in the bottom of the
fuselage. He could release them one at a time by pulling a
toggle. He did not expect he would have to use them.

Fuel? Full tank and valve turned on.

Magneto switch? Turned to "off."

He called to the vague figures by the nose. "All set?"

He heard Paul repeat his query, then reached for the handle
of the wobble pump and sent fuel surging to the Liberty
engine.

He waited until he heard Paul yell "contact," then turned
the magneto switch to "on" and advanced the throttle a
trifle. He felt the DH tremble as the three men pulled the
huge wooden propeller against the engine compression. It
took their combined strength . . . but nothing happened.

"Goddamn," he heard Paul say, and then "off!"

"Off," he repeated as he turned the magneto switch.

He waited while they pulled the propeller through two
more turns. He knew they would be puffing now and the
sweat would be rolling from them.

"Okay! Contact!"

"Contact," and he turned the magneto switch to "on."

Again the DH trembled as they pulled the propeller through. The Liberty stayed inert.

A storm of blasphemy erupted in the darkness beyond the nose.

Again they repeated the entire procedure without the encouragement of any sound except a metallic clicking from the Liberty and their own hard breathing. Paul spat on the ground. "I'm a son of a bitch if I know what to do next . . ."

Toby waited helplessly while they regained their wind. This Liberty on DH Number 108 was notorious for being balky, but once energized it was supposed to perform nicely.

Toby called toward the darkness ahead. "Try some sweet talk. See what happens."

After a moment he heard Paul's voice, husky now with frustration. "All right, you stubborn sonofabitch . . . take fire this time or I'll set you on fire. There's a sweet bastard—"

The DH shook as they swung the propeller again and a series of loud explosions followed. Acrid smoke from the exhaust filled the night as the Liberty belched, then subsided to a throaty roar. While Toby waited for the Liberty to warm he switched on the single landing light that the Robertson Company had installed on the right upper wing of all their DHs. It was helpful although not absolutely necessary since the airfields at Springfield, Peoria, and Chicago would be illuminated by large military surplus searchlights when he was due to arrive.

He saw Paul and the others waiting at each wing tip. They were still breathing hard and mopping sweat from their faces.

He saw Hector and the boy duck down and disappear beneath the lower wing. They would be pulling the wheel chocks, so he made sure the Liberty was at idle. When they reappeared holding the wooden chocks he pulled down his goggles, taxied the DH a little way from where they were standing and added more throttle until the Liberty snorted to full power. The tail rose as he pushed forward on the joy-stick.

Moments later the DH became airborne. He switched off the landing light and was refreshed by the cool slip-stream. As the city lights fell away he turned toward the northeast and continued to climb.

He felt a strong sense of liberation as if he ascended

through a long, soft, never ending arterial. Somewhere in this infinity he would find another arterial that would lead him on.

He decided to fly higher than usual this night . . . say six thousand to begin with, and from the vantage of this altitude better perceiving the character of the clouds ahead. Better too for finding avenues leading between the barriers and beyond and then to the next, and the next . . .

Now it appeared that it would be impossible to hold a straight course for Springfield. There directly over the nose stood a line of "flashers," quiet for long periods and then erupting in a long barrage of pyrotechnics as if each inspired the other. "Beautiful," he muttered, and squirmed slightly in his seat. "And nasty."

Maybe he could make a swing around to the west, then double back on the other side of the barrier where there might be more air room . . . maybe an even higher altitude would reveal an occasional canyon where he could weave his way toward his destination without detouring too far . . .

No one knew much about thunderstorms, except to give them a wide berth. They were reputed to be the summation of enormous forces that could easily crumple the stoutest of airplanes, but only mail pilots had even passing acquaintance with them and that had been gotten from as much distance as possible.

He could, he told himself, turn back to St. Louis. It would also have been nice to stay at home with Lily, then when the morning was young and the thunderstorms had dissipated, amble off to work like normal men.

But the schedule demanded the mail be transported through the night. If he and the others who flew this route turned back from every challenge there would soon be no route and no job. Still, the "flashers" weren't inviting and seven thousand feet did not seem to improve their disposition.

He remembered a recent conversation with Lily . . . "I'm glad you have the job, but take care . . . I'm too young to be a widow." She didn't smile when she said it.

When Lily said this two mail pilots had just added their names to the list of those who had already been killed. Johnson was crushed between airplane and stone in the fog-bound Appalachians. Hadaway was impaled in a Colorado forest and the fire following his crash left just enough to identify him.

Since they were flying for other companies both men were strangers to Toby, but he knew they had not taken off that night with the intention of dying. And he knew there would be more.

The delicate balance between pressing on and survival was too often memorialized by the bones of those who were sure they knew when to retreat. . . .

The lights of a town named Alton passed below, and the vague outline of the great river slipped beneath his wings and was gone.

He glanced at his watch. Midnight. The world was asleep below. There was no thundering of a powerful engine in the dreams of ordinary folks—

Flashes again along the horizon. Toby found this attraction almost hypnotic. He wanted to ignore them but felt compelled to stare at the erratic and brilliant display before him. One minute the DH would be flying in total darkness, the next the wings and flying wires and struts were silhouetted against the rumpled line of cloud. And then darkness again. Thunderclaps followed each flash, he knew, but they were inaudible against the constant rumble of the big Liberty. Until he was closer, he thought, then maybe he would hear them. . .

He reviewed the weather reports that had been handed to him before he took off. Springfield . . . clear. Thunderstorms to the south. Peoria . . . overcast . . . light rain. Visibility five miles. Chicago . . . overcast. Visibility unlimited.

An encouraging report, but also deceiving. It was always comforting to be told that good weather prevailed at his destination but there was rarely any reliable information about the flying conditions en route. Who was there to report? How valuable was a telephone call to a farmer who was inclined to report, "Not bad for this time of year. I can see my barn." The only practical solution was to "have a look"—a process requiring an equal mixture of hope and ignorance. Do I take a chance and try to slip through underneath the cloud or should I stay up here above it all and pray some kind of a hole will open before it's too late to turn back?

What about the wind? Here aloft, no one knows either its direction or velocity. Looking down over the side of the cockpit I can judge that there's a drift to the right or the left . . . or if my progress over the land appears to be slower than usual there's wind on the nose, or faster, the wind on my tail.

At night, unless there are many lights below, it's difficult to make judgments, and if there's a deck of cloud below, then day or night it is impossible. So put in a little extra fuel for Mother. . . .

Now the alternately dark and then livid monuments of cloud were much closer. Five miles? Less? There were canyons between the towering summits, then caves and caverns and tortuous halls sufficient for the passage of an airplane. They were all tempting in various degrees. The tendency was to choose the largest gash in the barrier while discarding the most convenient.

If Springfield was still in the clear with thunderstorms reported to the south, Toby figures this line of hostility must not be very deep. Once penetrated, the trip through shouldn't take too long . . .

He breathed deep and hunched his shoulders. When the lightning flashed again, the canyon he had been heading for was no longer there. Had he turned or had some magician slammed the gate? The nocturnal deception aloft of now you see it, now you don't. Hello. Here was another and better by-way.

He continued threading his way, the DH banking and turning like some frightened winged insect flitting through corridors of gigantic pavilions. It passed around grand terraces and hanging gardens of cloud all for an instant illuminated with such blinding clarity there was nothing to be seen for moments afterward. When vision returned there very suddenly were pendant cornices, fractured and torn, then scrollheads, pilasters, bannisters and baroque colonnades all intertwined and connected through vast galleries.

Hello. Here's another promising alley. Or is it? More likely a dead end.

He flashed his light on his compass. He was flying only a few degrees north of west. Not so good. Somehow he must average more toward the north.

He flew on.

What had happened to the lightning? Minutes, which had become a very long time, had passed since he had seen a flash in any direction. It was unnatural. How could the bombardment have ceased so abruptly? Something was wrong.

He looked all about him. The darkness was absolute. Suddenly he knew what had happened and cursed his preoccupation with the cloud forms that had been so distracting he'd failed to mind his real business.

He switched on the landing light to confirm his belief.

Yes, the wings of the DH were enveloped in heavy cloud. He was flying blind . . . "I'm not ready. Maybe Slim can handle it, but I'm still unsure . . ." He tightened his grip on the joy-stick, then forced himself to relax. He considered reversing his course, changed his mind. With no point of reference all of his sense of orientation was lost. He had to depend on the DH's simple instruments—the altimeter (fairly reliable), turn-and-bank (reliable), air speed indicator (reliable), and magnetic compass (reliable but capricious in rough air or while turning). At Lindbergh's urging he had experimented occasionally, making a turn without looking outside the cockpit. All those attempts had been reasonably successful, in clear weather—at least he'd not spun in, but here, when he was really blind . . .?

He now had to deny the very senses that had served him so long and so well. And he knew he wasn't alone. Some pilots, when caught in a similar trap, pulled the nose of their aircraft up until they fell off in a spin and waited until the earth showed up below the cloud so they could regain control. Hardly advisable under the present circumstances. Seven thousand feet below earth and cloud might be as one.

Was the air becoming rougher or was it because he was trying to refuse the message his senses were sending. He *must* believe only what the instruments said. His flashlight revealed their immediate news . . . altitude seven thousand, a little more. Turn and bank? Wings level . . . ball in the center. Air speed? Steady on one hundred and five. Compass? The numbered card floating in liquid was doing a slow little dance . . . too much to the west and not enough to the north. Difficult to be sure of his true course.

He thought momentarily of Lily. She would be asleep now, unaware . . . Kiffin. Where was Kiffin? The one time "family" was scattered to the winds . . . by the wind.

Where, by-the-by, are *you* now?

Twenty minutes flying time north or northwest of Alton, the last certain fix. The rest was guesswork, say, somewhere over Green County, if that far.

He was persuading himself that if he was patient and simply allowed the DH to more or less fly itself for a little while he would soon break out of the cloud . . . If indeed Springfield was still relatively clear with only a light rain to contend with, then he must come to it sooner or later . . .

A small boy whistling in the dark?

He was still trying to encourage himself when the DH was seized as if by some monster's hand and tossed violently on its side. Again and again it was jostled, pressed down and shoved up until he was sure he'd never be able to regain control. As it lurched from one attitude to the next the Liberty snorted and roared in complaint, dust and debris rose up from the cockpit floor and was spewed in his face. His maps, dislodged from where they had been so tightly secured against the fuselage, clattered and hissed past his head—never, he was sure, to be seen again. The compass had obviously gone crazy along with the altimeter which indicated he had very suddenly climbed to ten thousand feet although he had done nothing to cause such an impossibility.

The air had taken on a penetrating chill. Sniffing at it he thought it had taken on a peculiar almost acrid smell.

He heard a sharp, flat crack of thunder close by and then was nearly blinded again by a flash of lightning. Thunder before the fire? Another impossibility.

He flew on, trying to quiet the pandemonium in his stomach. The DH was a very strong airplane, but no craft built by man could withstand such abuse for long. If a wing root buckled? . . . if the tail feathers were torn apart? . . .

His hand went instinctively to the D-ring of his parachute. Slim had said jumping wasn't half bad—it was the landing that was tough.

He shivered. How could it suddenly turn so cold?

He considered pulling a flare. Maybe with the sky illuminated he would find a way out? He decided against it although he wasn't sure why. He wasn't sure about anything now. It wasn't because of any skill on his part that the Liberty was still roaring away or that apparently he was still right-side-up.

The monster's hand struck again with even more ferocity and a new noise assailed his ears. He heard the sound of a thousand snare drums and felt a sharp pounding on his shoulders and leather helmet. Puzzled and hurting, he switched on his flashlight. The beam struck the cockpit floor and his lap revealing half a hundred hailstones dancing on the surface.

He ducked under the wind screen and the cockpit cowling as far as he could, then almost at once felt a new sensation through the joy-stick . . . it was rapidly becoming mushy, as if it was losing all connection with anything, including himself.

The DH began to shake until it was near-impossible for him to see anything clearly. Afraid that the hail stones might smash the glass of of his goggles, he pushed them above his forehead. Now huddled as far forward in the cockpit as he could move, he turned the flashlight on the left wing and saw the glistening horizontal lines of white stones sliding through the flashlight's beam. A thousand bullets had penetrated the fabric of the wing just behind the leading edge. He could see the ribs and main spar clearly. No question, the wing's fabric covering was disintegrating.

At the same time the Liberty began a startling vibration. The propeller, of course. The hailstones were chewing away at the wooden blades, soon it would come to pieces . . . Shipwrecked at ten thousand feet.

Seconds passed while he tried to reorganize his thinking. Easy now. What had to be done had to be done *right* . . . and the first time.

He tried moving the joy-stick, found it had become even less responsive. The DH was floundering through the sky like a badly wounded bird.

He pulled all the way back on the throttle. The Liberty quieted. Perhaps with the propeller turning much more slowly it would survive a few more minutes.

Should he try adding the DH all the way down? Pull a flare when he was much lower and hope for some kind of a controlled crash? Only a few months with the company and he was about to lose an airplane. Jesus.

Bailing out now would be suicide. If the hailstones went all the way to the ground they would certainly collapse an open parachute.

Suddenly the DH took on a tremendous shaking and he was thrown against his seatbelt. He knew he was in a spin but made no attempt to stop it. The quick way to the bottom of this dark ocean.

He broke out of the cloud just long enough to be dazzled by series of lightning flashes, saw that he was flying a skeleton with parts of every bone revealed. The hail had stopped but it was too late. The carcass of the DH had already been consumed. It was time to leave it.

More out of curiosity than hope he took a few seconds to waggle the joy-stick. Nothing. He waited another few seconds for a flash of lightning and turned to look at the tail. Bones.

Surprised at his new calm he unclipped his seatbelt, pulled down his goggles and took a deep breath. He placed his hands on the cockpit cowling and pushed himself up and into the slip-stream. He hesitated momentarily and realized that, like Lindbergh, he had neglected to cut his ignition . . . the Liberty was still turning. He'd also forgotten his flashlight, which might come in handy if he tried to avoid a tree or see the ground rising to meet him. At least he'd be more prepared for the shock of landing.

He bent down into the cockpit, pulled the flashlight from the box beside his seat and switched off the ignition, then stood up on the seat. The humming of the slip-stream, the dying backfiring of the Liberty and the long sad sighing of the flying wires all combined with the spasmodic claps of thunder . . . One damned noisy place . . .

He gathered all his strength, hoped for some help from God and shoved himself away from the DH as hard as he could. He fell in total darkness for a moment, then a flash of lightning revealed the DH far above him. It was already a fragile ghost becoming rapidly smaller and smaller . . .

He fumbled at his side searching for the D-ring. When his fingers closed on the cold metal he closed his eyes—and pulled hard. He heard a rumpling sound, then a flat popping like distant gunfire. The leg straps dug into his groin, his body was jerked upright so abruptly the blood left his head. He must have tumbled head over heels. He realized suddenly that his right shoe was missing. Now how in hell . . .?

An eerie silence followed, but even in the darkness he knew that his chute had opened. He looked up and grabbed at the risers, and when the next flash of lightning revealed the white dome above him he thought it was the most beautiful sight he had ever seen.

He looked down at only a layer of cloud. He had no idea how soon his feet would touch earth again.

The descent took much longer than he'd expected. He floated down through the deck of dank cloud and began to wonder if it extended all the way to the ground. He bent his knees slightly in anticipation. A flash of lightning revealed the gray sock on his right foot. The lace of that shoe must not have been taut. He'd bought that pair of shoes at Herpelshiemer's in Lincoln. Would they be willing to sell a mate for the survivor? The survivor?

It was dark again, although now he was able to make out the thicker black of land below. He saw a few dim lights off to his right. He braced himself, turned on his flashlight. The circle of light expanded rapidly.

Hello! The luck of the Bryants . . . He was descending without any visible drift into a plowed field, for God's sake.

He hit with a thud and fell on his face in deep mud. The parachute collapsed on top of him, and for a moment he wondered if he'd mistaken earth for water. He fumbled at the parachute's straps and buckles, then finally crawled his way from under the silk.

He stood up and felt himself. All there, it seemed.

He smiled at the night and wiped the back of his hand across his mouth.

He found the taste of the mud absolutely delicious.

CHAPTER
10

Kiffin Draper discovered that his previous incarceration at Landshut served him well in Federal Prison, Atlanta. Thanks to good behavior and his work in the prison library he was released six months short of his original sentence. He made good use of his time behind the walls, although his violin playing brought dour threats from his fellow prisoners. When their protests became too unified he indulged himself in nonstop reading—everything that came to his hand from Sinclair Lewis to Gibbon. Along the way he devoured what aviation news came to the library in newspapers and magazines. Goddard's experiments with liquid-fuel rocket flight fascinated him and he yearned to replace Floyd Bennet who piloted Richard Byrd on their historic flight over the North Pole. He read about the first flight of Henry Ford's trimotored all metal airplane, wondered if anyone could actually sell enough tickets to fill it and worried about a new air commerce act that would now require the licensing of all planes and pilots. In spite of the warden's favorable impression of him, Kiffin doubted that he would be allowed the use of an airplane. Did that mean he would be banned from flying once he was on the outside?

Kiffin was released on the same day Rene Fonck crashed on his attempt to win the twenty-five thousand dollar Orteig prize by flying the Atlantic to Paris. Like so many airmen Kiffin had also considered the flight, but in spite of his still intact whiskey savings he could not imagine financing such a venture, particularly if a potential investor inquired about his most recent address. Maybe in France he could find people willing to listen to an American who had served their country? After all, Orteig was a Frenchman and his rules declared that the prize was available only to nationals whose countries had fought on the "allied" side during the war. Germans, then, were excluded.

By the day of his release Kiffin's impatience was nearly out of control. The Atlantic flight had become such an obsession he took the train directly to New York, where he promptly boarded the *Berengaria* for Cherbourg. Arrived in Paris, he was overwhelmed with nostalgia and spent the first week in a small hotel located only a block from Lily's old flat. Every time he passed the building he threw the windows on the top floor a little salute, and when he recognized any of the local inhabitants he began, laboriously, to try to resurrect his basic French.

Not only was his comprehension of the language rusty; what he managed to say had little effect on anyone he could find who would at least pass the time of day. While he'd not expected a hero's welcome, he was a bit nonplussed that the French seemed so indifferent to the fact that he'd worn their uniform during a time of war—their war. Only eight years had passed since the Armistice, and if any of the French he met on the street remembered, he couldn't seem to find them.

He realized that finding anyone interested in sponsoring his Atlantic flight was going to be extremely difficult. He'd been impetuous, hadn't reckoned on the short memories of his fellow man, and was rapidly depleting his whiskey savings. It would take much more time than he'd anticipated to achieve his goal. Meanwhile, he decided, he'd better establish himself more firmly.

He began by moving to a small and much cheaper room on the Ile de la Cité. The building was ancient and in ugly disrepair, but his landlady was talkative and sympathetic to Americans. She said he should try flying for the French again, specifically one Didier Daurat, who was a distant relation of hers. If Kiffin would practice his French she would see what she could do in the way of an introduction. "Now everything in France is based on personal relations," she said. "Nothing else matters. And Monsieur Daurat is a very busy man."

Lignes Aeriennes Latecoere was created by Pierre Latecoere, a Frenchman with sufficient imagination and daring to suppose that there would be a reason for a line carrying the mails and eventually passengers all the way from France to South America. Latecoere's bold concept was far ahead of any even

dreamed about in the rest of the world, and to execute his
high-flying mission he had hired Didier Daurat, a tough
wartime escadrille commander who believed the job could be
done provided all who were engaged in it gave their utmost,
including if necessary their lives. It was he who set the face
of Lignes Ariennes Latecoere and it was he Kiffin had to
persuade if he was going to fly for Latecoere.

Unfortunately Kiffin's timing was bad. From Paris the new
route cut south through Spain, thence to Casablanca in
Morocco, and then another 1,700 miles to Dakar. The first
regular flights to Dakar had not even been attempted until the
previous year and had immediately met with unforeseen hazards and difficulties that even the finest aviators in France,
driven beyond themselves by the ever-demandng Daurat, found
terrible. Cille, Rozes, Gourp, Dubourdieu and Reine all met
with trouble while flying across the Spanish Sahara, and
capture by the roving bands of Moorish tribesmen who had
no love for either Spanish or French became such a common
risk that Daurat's pilots refused to continue flying the route
unless with another aircraft. Jean Mermoz, the much decorated war ace, forced down in the desert with a sick engine,
had been captured by the Moors and only fast work by Daurat
and a ransom saved his life. Guillaumet, another celebrated
veteran, also flew the line, and the roster of pilots since the
beginning of the line had been the elite of French aviation.

It was hardly an easy aristocracy to join for an American
whose French was halting and limited. St. Exupery, one of
the newer pilots Kiffin encountered in Daurat's outer office,
at least had the decency to smile and wish him well, although
he was far from encouraging. "I'm afraid," he said, "that
the great ogre may not smile on you. He is beset with a
thousand problems, as we all are . . . for example, I must be
off tomorrow for Cape Juby to convince the Spanish we're
just passing through and don't want to take over their colony.
Ridiculous, but then this whole thing is. I doubt Daurat will
hire anyone he's not known for a long time . . . at least until
he's seen us through our growing pains."

St. Exupery proved to be right. When Kiffin at last stood
before the scowling Daurat he was asked how much flying
time he had.

"There was my combat time in the escadrille . . . some

hundred hours before I was taken prisoner. Here's my log book—''

"I'm not interested in flying time inscribed by your pen. Have you ever flown a Brequet?''

"No."

"They are very different than a little Nieuport and the flying is quite unusual. There is much rotten weather between here and Dakar.''

"I've flown a Jenny, more than a hundred hours. And a lot of that was at night—''

"A Jenny? Ah yes, that American contrivance . . . It is very simple, Monsieur Draper. You do not have enough flying time of the sort we need. We have half a hundred French pilots who are better qualified, and since the French government is our partner it is only natural that they must have preference . . . And perhaps you now are on the old side for such flying? Do I make myself clear?''

Kiffin found a cutting edge in his voice. "You do, *monsieur*. I hoped you were hiring men, not boys.''

"When the opportunity comes we will hire boys whose flying experience has already made them men. *Adieu, m'sieur.* And . . .'' Daurat seemed momentarily to relent his harshness, "and *bonne chance*.''

"I remember hearing that same *bonne chance* stuff ten years ago. Right here in Paris.''

"That was ten years ago. . . .''

So Kiffin, increasingly morose, spent most of his days in cheap cafés, "luxuriating,'' as he chided himself, "in self-pity.'' His disappointment with the French turned to antagonism and for a time he even considered going to Germany in search of finding a flying job. He managed to sober up long enough to find out that the several small German airlines that might conceivably have offered employment were in the process of becoming confined into a single government sponsored line known as Deutsche Lufthansa and many German pilots of his own vintage were also currently out of work. Grasping at anything that might offer encouragement, Kiffin ignored that the sketchy German he had learned at Landshut would hardly qualify him as a pilot for his former captors.

Lonely, frustrated, shifting from moments of confidence to despair, he finally moved in with Marie, a deeply religious prostitute half again his age who lived in a former storage room for hides behind a leatherworking shop. Most of her earnings went for the now prohibited Absinthe which she drank as if it were well water and as a consequence often removed herself from the human scene. She was a strange woman, inclined to fits of depression, yet most of the time her devotion to the troubles of others caused her own to disappear. She was a woman who exposed her heart as well as her body, and though both had been insulted too often they had somehow survived without serious damage.

Something near-mystical occurred between Marie and Kiffin the first time they eyed each other from adjoining tables at the little café near the Place de la Republique, where they had both retired to lick their wounds. It was as if their troubled lives had collided softly, discreetly, both sensitive to the other's woes and careful not to inflict further abuse after so many recent defeats.

After a week of living together something deep and not unlike a love had developed between them, and almost unaware of what was happening, they fell into a mutual dependency and shared affection that had the overall effect of cheering them both. Marie was content to listen to Kiffin for hours, although she rarely comprehended more than half what he was saying. Mostly he spoke to her in a mix of French and English that even in his lucid moments was difficult to make out. "I am thirty-one years old," he told her, "and I haven't accomplished one damn thing in this world. I'm weak, I'm a little crazy . . . maybe a lot. I go for older women so I must need a mother although I've a perfectly good mother in Lincoln, Nebraska, who worries about me . . . Except for Toby and Lily I seem to have trouble getting along with most people . . . which leads me to believe there's something wrong with me rather than with them . . . If I can find out what that is then maybe I can find the match to set the world on fire, comprendez? Also unless something good happens fairly soon I'll have no choice but to shoot myself . . ."

The fact that Kiffin did not have a gun, much less any real intention of shooting himself, did not trouble him in the least. He offered the threat with the solemnity of a doomed individual and Marie accepted the prospect as inevitable. It heightened the feeling that this relatively young man, who hoisted her out of her melancholy so dramatically, had been ordained by God Himself to be her true love. And Kiffin responded.

He listened patiently while she regaled him with tales of her fall from what she claimed was a strictly religious upbringing, and he rubbed her feet most tenderly when she came in from a long night on the pavements. She could find in Kiffin no limit for his mercy, nor for his physical care when the last drop of Pernod had left her disabled. "I am sad for you," she would repeat over and over again before she lost consciousness. "Ah yes, I am so sad that you stay here with me when there is so much younger and better in the outside world. You must fly from here. You must find wings and go away to distant lands . . ."

Their bond was sealed when they both recognized that Marie's sacrificial rejection of his presence was as sincere as his promise to shoot himself.

Their relationship continued through the winter of 1927 without friction and with warmth and affectionate understanding between them. In their way, they were uniquely happy and would have been puzzled if anyone had inquired how such a combination could be so successful. They were sufficient to each other . . . "two basket cases woven out of the same reed," as Kiffin described their union and they began to regard themselves as far better off than those officially married couples who so often lived in a kind of despair.

Tragedy, though, struck on the eleventh of March at seven in the evening. It was raining and already dark when Marie left for her usual beat. She had intended to quit early this night because a friend who worked in the chorus line had arranged for her to see Josephine Baker in "La Revue Negre." The toast of Parisian café society who sang while clothed only in a G-string and a few odd bananas would, as Marie said to her American paramour, "be an amusement for you."

They arranged to meet at midnight, but when she failed to make their rendezvous at the kiosk on the Place de la Republique he waited an hour, then went to the police. He found that one Marie Blanchard, age fifty-one, had been struck down by a truck while crossing the Boulevard Haussman, and killed instantly.

Kiffin restrained his emotions long enough to leave the police station and start walking back to the grungy quarters he had shared with Marie for nearly three months. And he thought now that he had never asked Marie's last name; it had seemed sufficient to think of her as just Marie. He had declined the invitation offered by the police to view her remains, which were described as "in regrettable condition."

No, he wanted to remember her as he had known and appreciated the one person who had taken him as he was without question. Marie, a friend who had encouraged and been there for him when he thought he was finally lost. A whore with a heart of gold, some might scoff. Well, she really was one.

When he realized that he would once more be alone the tears did come, and then he forced himself to stop. Marie would not approve of him being sorry for himself. She, who had known a damn sight more loneliness than most, deserved a better good-by. He even tried to smile while he walked back through the rain to the only home he knew.

By morning he had a hold on himself . . . it was as if in death Marie Blanchard had left him her legacy of resilience. But he knew he couldn't stay in this place they had lived in together—somehow he had to get away and find his old self-reliance. Work was the ticket, he decided, and he only knew one kind.

Inspired by the exploits of Alan Cobham, he considered trying to find a flying job in England. Like the Germans, the British government had subsidized a combination of private companies to fly under one banner, Imperial Airways. They were already making survey flights through the middle east to India and soon were scheduled on to Australia. Maybe they could use an American pilot to help them link the Empire? At least they spoke the same language.

The business of finding a priest to officiate at Marie's funeral plus the bureaucratic maze involved in arranging her burial made Kiffin wonder if he hadn't been an exile too long. During the ceremony the following afternoon at which he was the only mourner, he decided there was little reason for him to linger any longer in France. And when the clerk-witness from the coroner's office, having sought unsuccessfully for a closer relative, handed Kiffin Marie's property, a single handbag containing lipstick, rouge, a comb, a vial of antiseptic liquid and thirty-one francs, twenty-six centimes, he tucked the bag under his arm and wandered away from the public graveyard. He rode back to the Champs Élysées with the wheezing truck that had served as Marie's hearse and asked to be let off near the American embassy.

He stood now outside the imposing structure for some time, contemplating the stars and stripes flapping in the wind of early spring and the stony face of the marine guard at the gate. He didn't go in. He just wanted to be as close as possible to the familiar . . . it was here he had first met Lily . . . here the solidity of the embassy seemed to represent the strength of Toby, and wherever they might be he was now convinced he should rejoin them. They'd be a "family" once again. He hoped . . .

By the spring of 1927 Toby had become one of the more experienced mail pilots along the route from St. Louis to Chicago. He now knew far more than he had the night he floated down through thunderstorms; he was both competent and confident that he could keep his DH rightside-up and flying a reasonably accurate course while entirely on instruments. Now, along with most mail pilots, he was convinced they must soon find a way of descending through an overcast and emerging beneath with at least some knowledge of where they were. He also realized that to accomplish such a feat with any degree of safety even in benign weather, more information had to be fed to the pilot. He needed to know what was ahead—would he be able to see the airport? Should he continue to "have a look," feeling his way down toward the unknown? Recently he'd learned that other mail pilots flying back east were experimenting with the radio, talking to the ground as they flew, but he was also told that it was not a total success. When most needed it proved almost impossible to establish two-way communication. There was a pressing need for better instruments inside airplanes. Most were of early design and still marked "Aviation Section, U.S. Signal Corps." Airspeed indicators were not to be trusted in heavy rain or snow. The turn indicator was activated by the slip-stream passing through a venturi tube that had a tendency to choke up in ice or heavy snow, and in rough air the magnetic compass demanded constant attention to keep a steady course.

Years before, Dean Smith, one of the earliest mail pilots, had been forced down in bad weather and had sent off a telegram . . . "Landed on a cow. Killed cow. Scared me."

As far as Toby could see, nothing had changed and the monotony he'd feared in flying the same route night after night had certainly not become a problem. It was wonderfully challenging work.

Toby also knew that his status as an employee at Robertson Aircraft had undergone a subtle change . . . he'd proved his worth during a tough winter of flying, and his patience and gentle if sometimes ponderous humor won him open approval from his peers. As a happy married couple, with interests in common with the employees of the Robertson corporation, Toby and Lily were invited to their social gatherings and soon enjoyed a cadre of new friends even though Lily puzzled the more conventional pilots' wives. They found it difficult to understand why Lily would enjoy flying, much less fly herself, and they weren't sure they liked the consequent easy conversational relationship she was able to establish with their husbands.

There was also the rumor that Toby Bryant might be appointed chief pilot for the mail flights as a replacement for "Slim" Lindbergh, who had taken temporary leave of his job. And his senses as well, they said, because he was preparing an airplane for a flight across the Atlantic. Now it was known that "Major Bill" Robertson had contributed a thousand dollars to the adventure and a Harry Knight and Harold Bixby who belonged to the St. Louis flying club had underwritten a note for an additional fifteen thousand. Not surprising that the airplane would be christened "The Spirit of St. Louis."

Lindbergh intended to win the Orteig prize and the twenty-five thousand dollars that would enable him to repay his backers. His original intentions had been to make the flight in a Bellanca aircraft, but he suddenly changed his mind, went to San Diego and chose a Ryan. Among the tight little aviation community in St. Louis his chances for success were not considered too favorable.

There was recent cause for such pessimism . . . The "American Legion" piloted by Noel Davis, who was trying for the same prize, had just crashed on the final test flight and killed a crew member. "L'Oiseau Blanc," flown from Paris toward New York by two fine French pilots, Nungesser and Coli, also in quest of the prize, had disappeared on the westbound flight. Many of "Slim's" friends in St. Louis wished he wouldn't make the attempt alone. "I've got my best friend with me," Slim would say. "My Wright engine never misses a beat . . . ''

Other possible backers had shown no faith whatsoever in the project. Coca-Cola and Lucky Strike declined offers to contribute even if Lindbergh agreed to carry their advertising.

Meanwhile, their confidence in the world and in themselves renewed now, Toby and Lily moved from the room they had been renting to a small apartment close to Lambert Field. There wasn't much to move, but with the memory of the bed in their Paris flat, they bought a secondhand one, two chairs, and a card table for dining. The rest of the furniture was mainly a collection of wooden boxes Toby had found in the Robertson hangar. Lily used them imaginatively, though, and when illuminated by a bridge lamp on loan from Sloniger the small apartment took on a distinctly cozy air.

Trying to restrain her enthusiasm, Lily raced around the bare wooden floors humming to herself, "Be it ever so humble . . ." And suddenly Lily grabbed her husband and pushing her head against his chest, began to cry.

"For God's sake what are you crying about?"

"I . . . I'm so damn happy—"

"And you're bawling?"

"Don't you understand? This place is all *ours*. Domesticity may not be my basic nature, but I guess deep down I've always wanted *some* kind of a home. I don't know why having her own place to roost is so important to a woman . . . I guess it brings out the primeval in our . . . or something . . ."

Soon after their move Lily wrote to her father:

At last I seem to be wrapped up totally in my man and my home, if you can believe it. I've always heard about those couples who are *divinely happy*, but I thought deep down that it must be a set-up to propagate the race or perhaps a device to lure men into a marriage and once captured, oblige him to follow tradition. Now I think I was wrong. Toby continues to be the most marvelous man ever invented, and if my ravings make you a trifle ill please believe that I really am very happy . . . Toby is what I call a true giver, of his time and his wisdom, and he gives so much of himself to me. At times I feel terribly selfish to monopolize such a stalwart but I'll be damned if I'll share him with any other female . . . His schedule is demanding. Twice a week he takes off about midnight and flies to Chicago—two hundred and seventy some miles. He stays in Chicago that day and tries to get some sleep, usually without much success. Then that night he flies back here with the southbound mail and lands about four hours later (on the way he stops in Peoria and Springfield), but with one thing and another he rarely arrives here at the apartment until well after dawn. I fix him a nice breakfast— can you believe, dear daddy, my cooking has yet to poison him? Shades of mother, or dare I harbor such a macabre thought. He's always beat when he comes in, but I've never heard him complain. After breakfast he goes to bed and sleeps until noon or so . . . Last week when he was in Chicago he met a man called "Speed" Holman who offered him a job flying for a brand new firm called Northwest Airways. They fly between Chicago and St. Paul, which is like Siberia in the winter time so I'm just as glad Toby said no thanks. Wouldn't you know after waiting so long to find a job he now has more than one offer? One of the reasons Toby wants to stay with Robertson is that we have several friends now. "Bud" Gurney is not only a fine pilot but a true charmer. Delightful man. So is Sloniger and his wife Johnnie. (Don't understand how she acquired that male name, and since she's rather a formidable person I'm afraid to ask.) Before he left for New York we saw Toby's boss "Slim" Lindbergh a few times. Strange man. Aloof at times and then just as friendly and warm as a puppy. (A lanky pooch.) He's given to playing practical jokes on people, but Toby says he likes working with *him* and that he's an excellent pilot. I think he's about to take off on his Atlantic flight and all of us here are praying he'll make it. Neat-o if he does . . . If you twist your head just right and stand in a certain place you can see just a little stretch of the Mississippi from this apartment. And there's a nice old elm tree in between. We also have a spare bedroom if you ever come this way, but frankly I doubt you'd feel comfortable there. At least for a while. For one thing there's no furniture at all—not even a bed. Someday . . .?

What do I do all day with myself? I'm ashamed to say not much besides trying to settle in. When we get a few dollars ahead I'm determined to do some flying myself out at the Robertson School, where they promised me a special rate. Meanwhile I'm reading a good book, *Lolly Willows*, by Sylvia Townsend Warner, which was sent by a new outfit called Book-of-the-Month Club. I joined because I hoped it would keep me more *au courant* than I seem to be here in Missouri. This is a lovely old city, but it's not exactly the culture capital of the world . . . at least not those I've met so far . . .

The lovely May afternoon was fading when Toby rolled over on his back and realized he was not really in the Tuilleries being shouted at by Sergeant Delacroix. He opened his eyes to see Lily pressing against him on the bed and shaking him gently. "Wake up, come back to real life, my pet. He *made it . . .*"

Toby groaned. "Made what? Who?"

"Slim! He landed in Paris! He's alive and well . . . it's official and the world is going nuts! Everyone is on the telephone."

Toby shook his head to clear his thoughts, grunted. "Well, I'll be damned—"

"Isn't it wonderful? I'm so proud of Slim."

"If anybody could do it he could . . . all the way to Paris. Bless that ol' Wright Whirlwind—"

"I'm so proud of Slim I could cry—"

"*Please,* not that again."

"You don't even seem excited."

"Excited? I think I'm stunned. We'll send him a telegram right away."

That night when Toby once again climbed toward the stars he found new satisfaction in what he was doing. Before he left the ground he had seen the same sense of achievement in Paul the lead mechanic, and Hector and Johnny. The clerk in the little operations office had also been jubilant; in spirit, each man had himself flown the Atlantic. Their friend Slim was no Admiral Byrd whose uniform and imperious style removed him from the common folk. Here was a simple guy who delivered the mail and now, so suddenly, he was a hero . . .

Those who had radios heard his name mentioned constantly, and a portrait of his familiar face was even on the front page of the St. Louis *Post-Dispatch*. Some said Slim sure as hell would never come back to flying the mail, others weren't so sure. Paul the mechanic, massaging his strawberry nose, said, "By God, if he does come back I'll bet he asks for a raise in pay."

That same night in the absolute solitude of his DH cockpit, at least a mile removed from the nearest human being, Toby thought there might be much more to Slim's flight than he or anyone else had bargained for. Ever since his own return from the war Americans had been indifferent to flying. It was considered a stunt for nuts. When he was barnstorming he'd met up with that attitude again and again—never mind where they had happened to land. No one took aviation seriously. Now . . . maybe?

He squirmed down as far as he could in the cockpit. The night was crisp and he was already feeling a chill. He took a last look at the sliver of lights marking a distant town on the horizon and glanced up at the Milky Way, which cut a diagonal swath of luminescence across his upper wing. The deep-throated roar of the Liberty engine sounded especially melodious on such a calm night, and for a moment he imagined himself a solitary sailor bound for the stars in a ship that flew with the speed of light. Slim had talked about such things at times . . . God only knew where he got some of his ideas about the future, but if you argued with him he'd give you chapter and verse on why it all had to happen.

Toby looked away from the sky and confined his attention to the few instruments in front of him. Ever since his night of the thunderstorms it had been his custom to practice flying solely by instruments for a full hour. And no peeking. It had taken several flights before he gained real confidence, but now he thought that he had the hang of it. Slim had been so attached to the little clocks he couldn't see a damn thing ahead of the Ryan. He must have flown only by the clocks all the way to Paris and all he could see would have been out the side windows. Okay, Bryant, forget the stars and get down to business. You won't always be alone up here.

CHAPTER
11

No one had foreseen, nor could many understand, the effect of Slim Lindbergh's flight on the aviation world. Or the world itself, for that matter.

When Toby and Lily and Sloniger and Gurney and the Robertson brothers saw him on the grand occasion of his welcome back to St. Louis, he was outwardly the same Slim who had left such a short time before. And yet he was not the same. He did his best to be so, but it was futile because no one, not even his old companions, wanted him to be. At first euphoric and then dismayed, he genuinely could not understand what all the fuss was about. The Army Air Service had flown around the world only three years earlier, and the exploit had almost been forgotten. The Italians, with Francesco de Pinedo commanding, had piloted a Savoia flying boat to Japan, Australia, and back to Rome. Few cared. The English had flown from London to Cape Town and back in a de Havilland 50. Little interest. But "Lucky Lindy"? The world went mad because he was a symbol of solitary courage and, as it turned out, he had the grace of a born prince. He laughed when they called him the "Lone Eagle" and explained to an impatient press that much credit was due to his aircraft and the backers who put it in the air.

He said he was sorry not to be coming back to Robertson Airways, and to Lily he seemed a little wistful when he finally flew away to keep appointments with the rest of the world. He told Toby to look after things along the route, and then suddenly Slim and his little silver airplane were gone . . .

It was Sloniger who sipped thoughtfully at his drink when the farewells were done and said that there was a time for everything—mostly the wrong time . . . "But hell, Slim didn't know beans about timing. He was just interested in beating all the other guys who were lined up on the beaches, like a flock of pigeons, most of them ready to go. But look what's happening because the timing was so absolutely right . . . just as if Slim had planned it. But he's a goner now. Hell, the bandwagon is rolling and they'll never give him any rest . . .''

Four days after Lindbergh landed in Paris, James Dole, the Hawaiian Pineapple King, offered $25,000 to the first pilot who managed to fly from North America to Honolulu.

In June Chamberlain and Levine flew to Eisleben, Germany. Also in June, Byrd, Balchen, Acosta, and Noville flew from New York to France. They splashed down short of their goal, but few really cared.

Sid Grauman, the Hollywood theater man, offered thirty thousand dollars for a nonstop flight from Los Angeles to Tokyo.

Maitland and Hegenberger flew from Oakland to Honolulu in a Fokker, but won no prize because they were lieutenants. The offer did not include the military.

The Dole prize became an air derby with thirteen entrants. Three were lost at sea, and the National Aeronautic Association condemned ocean flights when attempted only for personal glory. Even so, nineteen pilots were swallowed by the Atlantic Ocean during this year.

A Charles Lawrence well deserved his prize—the Collier Trophy, and the loudest applause came from Charles "Slim" Lindbergh, who had spent so many important hours behind Lawrance's faithful invention—the Wright Whirlwind Engine.

All of these events were the meat of conversation and gossip for flying people around the world. Now the Bryants heard only occasionally from Slim Lindbergh, although he did call with the news that he had been to Mexico City and had met a young lady named Anne, whom he intended to marry.

A few days later they received another call from New York—this time from Kiffin, who warned them to "get out of town, I'm coming your way."

The reunion of "the Family" reminded all three of them of a similar occasion in Paris, though there were differences. Nine years had passed, and had left their mark. Lily was now twenty-eight, a striking brunette inclined to laugh at her

Imperial Airways—"Hannibal"

own stubborn individuality. Toby had changed the least physically—a few extra pounds were lost in a man of his bulk. Now his confidence was renewed. He moved with the dignified calm of a man in command of himself and absorbed in his work. Here and there the sun and the winds aloft were beginning to mature his face—there were new fan wrinkles about the corners of his eyes. His easy smile only added more positive lines to the texture of his face as he complained of not getting enough exercise.

Kiffin had changed the most; if possible he looked more emaciated than when he had come out of Landshut. Unsure of his reception, he had obviously been drinking heavily. At times his eyes still sparkled with intelligence and mischief, but his face was drawn and there was a new stoop about his shoulders. He still moved with the grace of an animal when he was sober, which he announced somewhat defiantly was less than half the time. Unlike Toby who stayed clean-shaven, Kiffin had grown a thin moustache in keeping with the custom of many pilots, and also like them, he was a chain smoker. . . .

A telegram had come warning of his arrival by train, and on the way to the station Lily said, "I was afraid putting that bed in the spare room might be a mistake."

"I'm not sure I follow you." Toby knew very well what she meant, but thought the time had come to squelch a possible source of trouble.

"Some people don't know when to go home. And you know about fish after three days—"

"I take it you're referring to Kiffin?"

"Could be."

"May I remind you that it was Kiffin who kept us in bread and beans for months?"

"I'm aware of that, and grateful. But the man has no sense of time. He might stay for years. Toby, we've been through this before . . . several times. Maybe it's selfish of me, but I *like* the privacy of my home and the one man who is supposed to be in it. Is that such an outrageous notion?"

"Hardly."

"I know, I know . . . he's your oldest and best friend. Well, I like him too, but enough is enough—"

"Try at least to be civil, I suspect we're the only real friends he has. . . .

There was the same back slapping and shoulder pounding, the same laughter and expressions of gratitude for the other's continued survival, and Kiffin said over and over again how time had only increased Lily's beauty. Driving back to the apartment he took a flash from his pocket and offered them a "tote of genuine Scotch made by a little old lady in the mountains of Kaintuck . . ."

They declined and their conversation limped along for the rest of the ride. It had been Toby's plan to take Kiffin out to the airfield and show him the Robertson operation but he decided against it. The aroma of the "genuine Scotch" could be sensed from some distance away, and Kiffin was in a garrulous mood. He told them about his disappointments abroad and later about his sentence to Atlanta.

"Have you got your flying license yet?" Toby asked.

"No. Do I have to have one?"

"Yes. Tomorrow I'll take you over to the Department of Commerce and they'll issue you one."

"Just on my word?"

"And mine. If the inspector wants to ride around the field with you I'll arrange to borrow a Jenny from the school."

"Flying is going to hell."

"No outfit will hire you without a license. It's the law—"

"Damn the law, I don't want to be a mailman."

"Suit yourself. Flying jobs aren't so easy to find."

"Let's take Lily and go out on the town for a celebration tonight. I've got a little money left and we might as well spend it—"

"Some other time. I have to fly tonight."

"Hey, you really turned out to be four square. I guess you always were and I just never saw it."

Toby said nothing. Anything would have been too much.

The dinner of steak and french-fried potatoes was enough to rally Kiffin from the semi-stupor that had held him ever since his arrival in the apartment. Lily and Toby both marveled at his apparent ability to cast off the effects of alcohol and behave as if he had never touched it. As quickly as some people became drunk he somehow managed to reverse the process until by dinner time his quick-witted charm was once again riding high. He had his hosts choking with laughter as he described the petty frustrations he'd met on his return to France and his recent passage back across the Atlantic as an attendant to a herd of pure-bred Charlais cows. "Other men fly the Atlantic, I shovel it full of manure. I fell in love crossing the Atlantic . . . full moon, stars . . . among all the girls on board I chose one Monique, after all, she had the biggest, most soulful eyes you've ever seen." He closed his eyes, as if visualizing a moonlit deck. "She also had four tits. No question about it, one of the loveliest ladies I've ever known, gentle and even fastidious when you got to know her. I played my violin for Monique once and she gave me the ultimate compliment. She went to sleep just standing there in her stall."

"Where is your violin?" Lily asked. "You didn't bring it."

"Disappeared at sea . . . somehow. I think Monique ate it . . . or maybe one of the crew threw it overboard. There were complaints. . . ."

After dinner Toby went to the bedroom for his pre-flight nap. Kiffin stayed at the table and talked with Lily for a while, telling her something about his affair with Marie and the deep sadness he'd felt at her death. Then he excused himself for yawning, said it had been a long train ride and went to the spare room.

Lily decided she had been mistaken. No matter what she might have thought about Kiffin it was very difficult not to admit that he was still an enchanting man, combining as he did that rare combination of masculinity and sensitivity that so many men lacked, topped off with an exciting imagination. Delightful Kiffin, Kiffin the good man, bad boy, successful failure . . . citizens, lock up your daughters!

Lily hoped he would not stay more than a few days. . . .

But a week passed, and then another. And still Kiffin occupied the spare room. He came and went unpredictably, but as often as possible in company with Toby, who, Lily thought, certainly seemed to be enjoying his company. He made no demands on either of his hosts and to Lily's surprise not only helped her with the household chores but was remarkably discreet about intruding on her time with Toby. What he did with many of his evenings remained a mystery, although he said that he had seen the film *What Price Glory* twice. He also said it did not bear much resemblance to the war he had known. He followed the events leading up to the Dempsey-Gene Tunney fight with special interest and cheered when Tunney won. Since he was quite drunk by the end of the fight, he also wept because Dempsey lost.

Meanwhile Lily had made a private vow that if Kiffin stayed another week, she was leaving. Besides, as much as she loved Toby it was time for a visit to dear old dad. And at once she discovered a new problem . . . when would be the best time to warn Toby? And would he be moved to ask Kiffin to leave, explain things man to man . . . that sort of thing?

She disliked presenting Toby with any unpleasantness when he came home in the early morning, sometimes terribly weary if the weather had given him problems, the mail had been delayed or something had gone wrong with his airplane. She was also reluctant to say anything that might upset him before he took off at night. It seemed unfair that he should carry any domestic troubles aloft with him. She knew one of the mail pilot's wives who gave a constant example of how not to behave . . . When her husband came down from his flight she could hardly wait to assail him with problems that had developed since his departure . . . the furnace had failed, the toilet was stopped up, their dog bit the neighbor's leg and he was about to sue, the plaster on the bathroom ceiling was falling off . . . the same dauntless lady waited until just before he left on a flight to warn him that a check she had written would probably bounce, that a prowler had been seen on their back porch during the last night her husband had been away and that their son age twelve had been kicked out of the Boy Scouts for giving instruction on masturbation to another member of his troop. The other mail pilots were sympathetic when her husband became lost for more than an hour one beautiful morning while flying a route he knew as well as the front lawn of his home. . . .

Lily waited until Toby had two nights and a day off before she touched on the subject, and even then as they started to bed on the second night she made only an oblique approach . . . "Darling," she said, "if Kiffin is going to stay much longer I'll have to buy new linens for the bed. What's there won't last forever—"

"He won't be there forever. As a matter of fact he brought the subject up just yesterday, said maybe it was about time he got on his way."

"What did you say?"

"I told him there was no rush, that there was plenty of room here. I confess I never thought about the linens."

"Perhaps you should do some thinking about *us?* I can't stand this much longer, Toby. Do you realize what his constant *being* here is doing to us as . . . as man and wife?"

"Nothing, I hope." He grunted and eased himself into the bed, picked up an account describing the first variable pitch propeller and said the idea was damn interesting.

Lily slipped in beside him but remained nearly arms-length away. She gave the brass headstand a caress, withdrew her hand quickly and wondered what had come over her . . . she should be caressing the man she loved. Change of tactics, lady. Sugar, not acid.

She eased her way slowly across the bed, closing the gap between them. She kept her voice to a near whisper, made it as suggestive as she could. "Sometimes I think if we were completely alone, we might make love more often . . ."

Toby said nothing, but she saw him smile. "Has that ever occurred to you?" She reached out and placed her hand on his leg.

"I thought we were doing all right," he said. He went on reading, but pressed her hand. She was encouraged. "Sometimes when you make love to me I feel like yelling out loud for joy. That's kind of hard to do when you know someone is just across the hall . . ."

"I doubt if he could hear you . . ." He put down the pamphlet, and she was further inspired.

"If I really let go he would."

"Hmmm. An interesting prospect."

She moved closer to him until her body was tight against his. Her instincts took charge as her hips began an undulating motion that was still slight but distinctly inviting.

"Hello," he said, rolling slowly toward her. "I like what you're doing . . ."

"Why should I feel almost naughty?" she whispered. "I can't *believe* that after all these years my damned Puritan upbringing still gets in the way—"

"Maybe it's because your neck is getting cold." He reached for the hem of her silk nightgown and pulled it slowly upward until it was bunched below her chin. His hand wandered downward in a long and slow caress. "Hello again," he said.

"I'm going to want to yell," she murmured. "I can feel it coming on."

"I'll fix that," he said, and covered her mouth with his own. Almost immediately she forgot everything that had been on her mind.

The commercial flying fraternity was still small and at times behaved both good and bad, in the manner of most small families. The mail pilots at any base always knew each other, often intimately, and they knew each other's wives, children, and sweethearts, often by name. Whatever their base might be—Newark, Cleveland, Chicago, San Francisco, or Omaha—they all shared common problems and a passionate involvement in their work. For these men life insurance was almost impossible to buy, their paychecks were more often late than on time and their social life was normally confined to their own tight little society. So the mail pilots flying out of one base at least had a speaking acquaintance with those flying out of another base, and even when far removed knew each other by reputation. Likewise news of death or mishap traveled with the speed of their wings, and the gradual changes in their technical progress was distributed throughout the fraternity.

There were enclaves of other pilots, most all of whom were struggling to twist a living from the life they loved. There were still a few barnstormers, the majority now with bigger airplanes capable of carrying more than one or two passengers. Yet they were less inclined to the gypsy life and more often confined themselves to hopping passengers out of fixed bases, where after a very loose fashion they advertised their services in flight instruction, banner towing, aircraft repairs and the sale of fuel and oil. It was a hand to mouth business, with the local bank and sheriff often becoming the unwilling partner. The fixed-base operators within a state usually knew each other, but since they were rivals for very scarce dollars they rarely displayed the trust more common to other clans.

There were also the test and demonstration pilots employed by various aircraft manufacturers who considered themselves an elite if only because their educational level was generally higher and when testing they often risked the unknown. They were a very small society, and the majority knew each other from their time in military flying.

A fringe of dreamers and inventors, despite a toll of accidents, persisted in the development of contraptions intended to make flight easier, faster and more practical, including such inventions as the ring engine cowling for radial engines, the slotted wing, catapult launching of aircraft from ships, rocket power, helicopters and ornithopters, and huge parachutes designed to be released in an emergency and lower the aircraft gently to earth.

There were the lighter-than-air people who were dedicated to their way of flight and whose faith was shaken by the crash of the ''Shenandoah'' but renewed by the marvelous performance of the German commercial zeppelins. And there were the military, soldiers first and airmen second, who lived in their own protected world during these times of peace, and because they were not obliged to show profit or to risk their savings were able to engage in research and development far beyond civilian means. Their discoveries and feats contributed enormously to the fresh blossoming of aviation.

Kiffin applied to all of these except the military in his search for a flying job. In addition he had written a letter to an Edwin ''Ted'' Parsons, a man who had also attended the Curtiss Flying School during those long ago days before the war. He had seen Parsons once when he was flying in the Lafayette Escadrille and at the time Parsons had given Kiffin his address in California. It was very old now and he supposed Parsons would have moved, but he sent the letter off anyway. After weeks of waiting for the mailman to bring him at least an acknowledgement of his many inquiries, Kiffin realized there were not going to be any for the same reason Toby had not been able to help him with Robertson. He hadn't enough *recent* flying time and what he had was considered of dubious value in the current environment. Most upsetting of all was his gradual understanding that too many of his thirty-one years were too much of another time.

Kiffin's natural optimism left him. And now there was no Marie. There were times when he stayed in the spare room all day, emerging only at night for the evening meal with Toby and Lily. Now conversation at dinner lacked the old sparkle and it was clear that at times Kiffin had been drinking heavily. He always appeared well-groomed, but the decay was creeping over him mentally; his thinking was slow, his speech often halting. He had developed a slight tick on his left eyelid that made him squint, and there were touches of gray in his heavy shock of hair. One day Lily gave him a much needed haircut and instead of thanking her he looked in the mirror and said grumpily that she had made him look like a prisoner again. The next day he apologized for his surliness and brought her a cleverly fashioned bouquet of brilliant autumn leaves he had gathered in Forest Park.

It was now early fall in Missouri, and Kiffin's deterioration was becoming so obvious that Toby knew he must try some kind of rescue. Maybe Lily had been right from the beginning . . . they couldn't just stand by and watch his self-destruction. Maybe in a new atmosphere he might come out of his melancholy altogether.

It was Toby's night to take the mail north, and he had suggested to Lily that she might find something else to do while he had his talk with Kiffin. "That's easy," she said. "There's a new Greta Garbo film at the Palace. *The Mysterious Lady* . . . something like that. I should be back in plenty of time to make your midnight lunch. Good luck . . . for his sake you have to do it."

Lily had been gone less than fifteen minutes before Toby said to a surprisingly sober Kiffin, "Maybe it would be a good idea if we had a little talk. You know sometimes things sort of get out of hand—"

Which was the moment the telephone rang. Robertson dispatch office was calling from Lambert Field. The voice of the clerk was matter-of-fact. A cold front, the first tough one of the year, was reported advancing rapidly on the St. Louis area. Heavy snows all through the west. Arrangements had been made to close the mails early. If Toby could leave immediately he might beat the weather.

"Why all of a sudden are we bothering about a little snow?"

"From what we've been told everything to the southwest is down to zero visibility. Either you leave now or we'll have to train the mail."

The bait, Toby thought. No one liked the idea of having to put the mail on a train. It was not only bad for the solvency of their employer but a reflection on their competency. "All right," he said, "I'm on my way."

He told Kiffin he would like to pick up their little talk the day after tomorrow when he'd be back from Chicago. He grabbed his little overnight bag, slipped into his leather jacket and threw his "teddy bear" over his arm. Tonight he would need it. He scribbled a note to Lily and left it on her pillow.

> Had to go. No midnight snack but too fat anyway.
> Toby-Kiffin talk not held. Patience. I love you.
> Back day after tomorrow morn as usual.
>
> T. Who else?

Kiffin went with him to the door and stood hesitantly for a moment, then smiled and held out his hand. "Good flight."

"Thanks. If I can get out of the area fast enough it will be. If I don't it won't."

"I'm pretty sure I know what you want to talk about. Funny, I got a letter today from Ted Parsons. I was just planning on leaving town but I'll wait until you get back."

"No big problem." He gave Kiffin a swat on the shoulder and left. . . .

Still charged with the glow of Garbo, Lily returned to the apartment just before ten. As she let herself through the door she felt her euphoria slightly diminished by a sense of guilt . . . she'd sat through half of the second showing of the film just to enjoy more of Garbo's subtle reactions. Now she would barely have time to make Toby's lunch and kiss him good-by.

As she opened the door she heard Kiffin's new violin. He had sent away for the confounded thing after reading a Montgomery Ward catalogue—some kind of a bargain sale. Right, she thought. You get what you pay for. Worse, he was playing something that sounded like he might have composed it himself.

She saw that the door to the spare room was closed and that the living room was empty. She entered the bedroom, found Toby's note and chastised herself for lingering so long at the movie. Damn. Taking a man for granted was a good way to lose him. Who said that? Mother?

She kicked off her shoes and went into the bathroom. She was still in a dream world with Garbo and was afraid the spell would be broken if she talked to Kiffin. She brushed her teeth, returned to the bedroom, hung up her dress and slip. The violin playing stopped in the middle of a bar. Had Kiffin heard her come in?

She slipped into her nightgown, turned to the night table and paused momentarily while she considered the two books she had been reading, *Stamboul Train,* by a new English novelist, Graham Greene, and Bernanos's *Sous le Soleil de Satan,* to keep up on her French. She chose the Greene book (she'd had enough of Satan's doing lately, thank you, and settled down against the pillows. Now more than at any other time she missed Toby . . . his big, powerful body beside her . . . Her eyes began to close after only a few minutes. Greene could be absorbing but tonight he was competing with the abiding image of a fabulous Swede—and losing.

By the time she reached for the light and turned it off she had become very drowsy.

Some time later, she was not sure if she had actually fallen asleep, she heard a tapping on the bedroom door. She waited a moment, wondering if she'd been imagining the sound. She hard it again, this time a definite knock. Suddenly she became uncomfortable, and she knew a flash of fear.

" . . . Is that you, Kiffin?"

"Who else? Or were you expecting company?"

"What do you want?" She was finding it difficult to keep her voice calm.

"I want to talk to you."

"Not now. I'm asleep . . . or was. It's late . . . we can talk in the morning."

"This is important."

She had never thought to lock the door. Was there even a key to it? And Kiffin was scrambling his words. She was sure he had been drinking again.

"I'm sorry, Kiffin, I just don't feel like talking now. Go back to bed—"

She heard the latch on the door sliding, saw the door open. It was too dark to see his figure.

"It's no fun celebrating by yourself," he said. "I'm lonely . . ."

She reached for the light and turned it on just as he slumped down on the edge of the bed. His eyes were half-closed, and she saw that he had indeed been drinking heavily.

"Get out of here, you stink of whiskey—"

"I told you I'm lonely. And I'm celebrating. Maybe I have a job."

"Good. Now *beat* it."

"Lily . . . I've loved you ever since I first saw you," he said simply, flat-toned. "I don't care who knows it—"

"Go to bed, Kiffin, you're drunk." Could he hear the fear in her voice? "My *husband* happens to be your best friend, in case you've forgotten."

He reached out for the light, she knocked his hand away.

"Now, now, I'm not going to hurt you . . . this is me, Kiffin . . ."

She held her breath. She wanted to jump up and run, but her body seemed strangely paralyzed. She saw him moving closer to her, very slowly, and still she could not move.

"Aw, come on, be nice, Lily. Be nice to me and I'll be nice to you. I've been waiting too *long*," he said, his voice rising.

"Kiffin . . . please . . ."

"I need you, Lily, now . . ."

He tore away the covers and pinned her arms down. "Lie still, I won't hurt you—"

"You're *insane* . . ."

"Yes, I guess I am . . ."

She stopped fighting, pretended to cry. Maybe tears would distract him. It was a mistake. For a moment his hands were free . . .

"Oh no . . . Oh *God*," she groaned. This had to be a nightmare.

"Quiet, little one . . . quiet, my Lily, *there* . . . finally . . ."

"No . . . no. Oh God, Kiffin, *stop!*"

CHAPTER
12

Toby discovered that the lusterless dawn brought with it the strange illusion that he could see the curvature of the earth, a feat he knew to be impossible from an altitude of only six thousand feet. Yet there it was, a curving line of light along the horizon where before there had been only darkness. St. Louis was just over the horizon, and he knew he was about to enjoy a reunion with the real world. A long night flight, alone in an open cockpit airplane, was like sitting in an icebox for the equivalent time with the door locked.

Now with the dawn Toby found that he was flying above an almost solid overcast. He wasn't concerned. There were occasional breaks in the cloud deck below and soon he would choose one for his spiral down. The DH hung in limbo while he waited for minutes to pass. He wondered how many other mail pilots would be greeting the new day in the same fashion. They would be flying Route 1 from Boston to New York. Colonial Air Transport with a twenty-six year old man in charge—Juan Trippe. Toby figured he must be an interesting man to know. He was said to be mixed up in something called Pan American, a flying boat operation to Puerto Rico and the Panama Canal Zone.

And there would be Clifford Ball Airways. Pittsburgh to Cleveland. Only a hundred and twenty miles, but the area could be tough going and it only took a few miles to transform a pleasant flight into a bear.

Out west along Route 5 Varney Airlines . . . or was it Airways? . . . was flying a long route over some very rough country in Nevada, Washington and Idaho. Varney would only take pilots who felt they could match the environment. Maybe that would be the place for Kiffin? Maybe he could try to talk to Varney on the telephone. Maybe if he began, "This is Toby Bryant, Chief Pilot for Robertson . . ." Varney would listen. "I have a very fine pilot for you. The only reason we can't use him . . ."

What *was* the reason? We know him too well . . .

Now there were more than twenty commercial carriers of the mail. From Chicago all the way to San Francisco was NAT's prize, and out west was Varney and Pacific Air Transport, where he had heard they were flying the new Boeing 40 B-2 airplanes. Toby had seen a photograph of one and decided they made his old DH look like an oxcart. Kiffin had told him about the French mails, and there were the English and the Germans. Italy? Probably not. Country too small. Russia? Too underdeveloped. No matter. It was still satisfying to realize that after such primitive beginnings so many men like himself were also aloft on this gray morning—

He saw a hole in the cloud deck off to his left and banked toward it. Unlike most mornings when he returned to St. Louis he pushed the nose of the DH down somewhat reluctantly, knowing this might not be the best of days. Somehow he had to convince Kiffin to get off his ass and join the world. And keep his friendship. Old friends, he reflected as the hole swallowed the DH, were irreplaceable.

It was murky below the overcast, and the snow-covered fields on the fringes of St. Louis appeared cold and barren. The first snow of the year. He must remind his pilots about taxiing and landing in the snow . . . watch for gray sky and flat snow, a combination that could destroy depth perception on landing or low approaches. Once down, watch for catching a wing tip in a drift or banked snow. Mechanics . . . Have a care about swinging propeller for an engine start, be sure of footing on snow or ice. Pilots . . . No flights in freezing rain. If you're caught in it, don't fight it. Land while you still have a choice. No descents for a look-see unless bottom of overcast at least three hundred feet. Raise it to four hundred if visibility less than a mile. . . .

When he landed at six-fourteen and signed off the mail manifest he walked stiffly to his Chevrolet, an elderly vehicle he thought that some day, with a little more money in the sock, he'd maybe take out his mail gun and shoot squarely between the headlights, and then buy a new one.

Just after seven o'clock Lily saw him park the Chevrolet in the alley behind the apartment and ran to the bathroom mirror to make doubly sure there was no outward sign of how she felt. She must appear the way he liked—the "band-box" look he so valued. All right, Mrs. Bandbox . . . how will it be? Are you going to indulge yourself, weep on his shoulder and ruin your marriage? You must *not*.

She touched at her hair then ran back to the kitchen window and watched him throw his "teddy bear" over his shoulder and start up the outside back stairs. He looked so *weary*, as always after flying all night. The combination of noise, cold, and tension must take a lot out of a man . . . and now, are you going to greet him with the glorious news that his best friend has—? Go back to bed and pretend to be asleep. Greet him like some of the other wives with your hair in curlers. Anything but the truth. Don't do that to the man you love . . .

Abruptly it struck her that it might not even have been all his fault . . . maybe she'd said something, done something, made some unthinking gesture that Kiffin's soused mind had taken the wrong way . . . Maybe they'd been alone too much lately, talking . . . keeping each other company, she not realizing how something unseen and unspoken was developing in his mind. Oh God, she felt so unclean . . .

He hardly had the door open and she was rushing into his arms. As he held her tight, she caught herself wanting to cry. She turned her face away, steered him to a chair at the kitchen table. She turned her back to him so he would not see the moisture in her eyes and asked him if he wanted his eggs as usual " . . . petrified or raw?" She couldn't manage a smile when she said it. Did he notice?

"Where's Kiffin? Isn't he having any breakfast? Don't tell me he's still asleep."

"No. He's gone . . ."

"That ding-a-ling. He told me he would wait until I got back so we could have a talk about his future. I had to leave in a hurry . . . You think I hurt his feelings?"

"I wouldn't think so." Please, God, help me change the subject. . .

"Guys out of work are bound to be touchy."

"Yes . . . I suppose they are."

"Did he give you a forwarding address?"

"No." She wondered if she would be able to do it—this pretending, and this clinging, totally undeserved sense of guilt . . . *totally* undeserved? Yes . . . it took very little to set some men off, but was that *her* fault? Was she responsible for Kiffin's ego, his built-in belief that he was born the world's greatest lover? Still . . . Kiffin of all men . . . give him a few too many drinks and he was bound to believe he was irresistible . . .

She brought Toby a plate of toast. He said, "I hope you two didn't have one of your fallings out—"

"Oh no, everything was fine. You know how he is. He just . . . took off." I can't stand this . . . I'm hating myself and that man, I absolutely *have* to change the subject . . . "Did you have a good flight?"

"Well, winter's coming . . ."

Keep it light . . . remember, he's your husband's best friend . . . whether you like it or not he's family to Toby . . . Toby loves him . . .

She attempted a light laugh. "Why can't you fly for Pan American? They're always down in the warm sunshine."

"You know I can't swim."

"Do you know how much I love you?"

"At this hour of the morning? Old grubby face? You can do better."

"Sure I can, but I'm stupid. It seems I'm in love with that grubby old face, broken nose included."

She brought his eggs, which, under the circumstances, had turned out miraculously well. He caught her hand and kissed it. She felt the stubble of his beard against her skin and badly wanted to cry again. Weeping willow, Lily. Knock it off. Pretend it never happened. *Do* it, if you want to save the best thing that's ever happened, will ever happen, in your life.

Kiffin strode along Chicago's Michigan Avenue oblivious to the biting October wind. He passed the Field Museum, thought of going into it, changed his mind. This was not a time for museums.

He was wearing his leather jacket and carried a small kit-bag on one shoulder. My total possessions in my new existence, he thought. Everything he could carry away from the apartment by hand had been sold—his violin, his medals that had brought much less than he had hoped for (so much for glory), and an exquisite ivory miniature he had bought in Paris soon after the Armistice. It was a portrait of a seventeenth-century woman. At the time he had thought it resembled Lily.

He couldn't count the hours he had studied it. Well, the Lily he had known had been destroyed and shortly after his own self-destruction duly committed. Kiffin the drunkard was dead. Kiffin the vagabond, the rapist, the loathsome bum was dead. Good riddance. The snake had shed his skin. This was another life.

Kiffin could not explain even to himself exactly how the transformation had taken place. When he had left Lily's bed his disgust with himself was so overwhelming there had been no room for any other thought or emotion. Like a rat, he thought, he had scurried away. When morning came and he sobered up, he found himself on the train to Chicago without the faintest notion of how he came aboard or how he had managed to pack his few belongings. The very business of selling his personal effects became so like the actions of a trustee he was temporarily haunted by the impression he'd died and was attending his own funeral.

The letter from Ted Parsons had at least broken the ice. It had arrived on the very day he had given up hope. Don't even try looking back. His telegram to Parsons had read: "DELIVERING BODY OF FORMER SERGEANT KIFFIN DRAPER IN PERSON."

Parsons had also learned to fly at Hammondsport and they had spent a few evenings together. When Parsons left the Glenn Curtiss School he had gone to Mexico and trained pilots for Pancho Villa. After the uprising failed he made his way to France and eventually joined the Lafayette Escadrille. There, soon after Kiffin's own arrival, they had a reunion. One hell of a guy, Kiffin remembered, but it had been a total shot in the dark when he had written to him. Now Parsons was a technical advisor on a film called *Hell's Angels* to be made in California. If Kiffin showed up he could probably have a flying job. "Why should I hire strangers who've never flown Nieuports or anything like them?" Parsons had written.

By the time Kiffin reached the Wrigley Building he knew he should turn back and make his way to the Union Station. In one hour he would be on his way west, and tonight while the train rocked and hooted across the plains he would be transported even deeper into the new life. Not a drop of alcohol no matter what the temptation. No cigarettes. No feeling sorry for himself. No brooding over past mistakes. Just every day being grateful for still being alive . . . And maybe someday, a long while down the line, he might prove to her, and to Toby, that he was worth knowing again. Maybe.

Now with the wind at his back he stepped out briskly. His shoulders were straight. The constant sound of taxis squawking and later the roar of the elevated snaking through Chicago's Loop inspired him to an even faster pace. Heads turned as they watched the tall, bare-headed, handsome man in a worn leather jacket making his way through the crowds and crossing the street intersections with such verve. They saw him smiling, which was somehow incongruous in a man in a hurry, and while some considered him demented there were others who were curious about the special secret he seemed to be only half concealing. . . .

The train took three days and two nights to reach Los Angeles. Kiffin went directly to the Roosevelt Hotel in Hollywood, where he found Parsons occupying a suite. Parsons explained that he had hired a special group—Kiffin's kind of people: Roscoe Turner, Frank Clarke, Ira Reed, Jimmy Robson, and a wild plump aviatrix known as "Pancho" Barnes.

"This could be worse than the war, but at least we'll eat better," Parsons said. "Howard Hughes isn't the easiest guy to work for, but he's a damn good pilot and he wants to do things right no matter what it costs. I just hope we don't kill anybody in the process."

Kiffin remembered that Parsons had been an ace with the escadrille and knew what he was talking about. "Best you just fly your airplane and if Howard tells you to do something . . . do it. Forthwith. Is that clear?"

"Clear."

Throughout the western world there was now a great reaching for new endeavors in the skies. In England Alan Cobham wan knighted for his exploits in linking the Empire by air. The Dutch Koninklijke Luchtvaart Maatschappij, (the Royal Air Traffic Company), under the redoubtable Albert Plesman began flying between Holland and Java.

The Germans began the construction of a gigantic aerial liner with ten engines intended to lift passengers across the oceans in the utmost luxury. The Germans had by now a well-established air service between their country and the

Soviet Union and were even flying the route between Konigsberg and Kaliningrad at night. The Germans were also established in South America, particularly Brazil, where the Kondor Syndikat flew both mail and passengers.

American services lagged far behind the Europeans. While passengers dined on white tablecloths and drank fine wines aboard Imperial Airways' London-Paris flights, adventuresome American passengers were lucky to buy a seat on a mail bag and a box lunch.

Toby had said, "Sure, we'll fly passengers someday, but we're getting three dollars a pound for our mail now. We'd have to charge a hundred-and-fifty-pound passenger four hundred and fifty dollars for a ticket. No one in their right mind would go for that."

In the far west, though, an enterprising man known as "Pop" Henshue headed Western Air Express. His pilots flew between Los Angeles and San Francisco and on to Salt Lake using Douglas M-2 biplanes. Henshue's little airline made money from the start, and when the mail loads permitted he would take a passenger or two, providing leather flying outfits to protect against high-altitude temperature, as well as parachutes.

Northward along the Pacific coast Vern Gorst, whose sense of adventure had led him to the Klondike gold rush, had established a line known as Pacific Air Transport whose route was between San Francisco and Seattle. He hoped to carry the mails on to Alaska. It was a tough route, soon marked with the blood of three pilots who crashed to their deaths. Gorst had bid too low on the mail contract and almost immediately ran into such financial difficulty he began paying off his pilots and his creditors with Pacific Air Transport stock. One pilot in a less than sober moment took out his airmail gun and used his certificates for target practice.

Later when Gorst tried his persuasive powers on the Wells Fargo Bank he met young William Patterson, who had a keener financial temperament, and it wasn't long before Patterson brought order to the line and the Ryan monoplane, not unlike Lindbergh's, proved itself an efficient mail carrier.

The renewed Kiffin Draper, striding down Chicago's Michigan Avenue, was unaware of the willingness shown by investors, entrepreneurs and ordinary adventurers to become part of the flying world. After the postwar depression and subsequent doldrums America was at last invigorated and the enthusiasm of Wall Street was infectious. There was Ford Air Transport, Varney, National, Stout, Boeing, Colonial, Southern Air Transport, and Northwest Airways. There was Robertson Aircraft, Universal Aviation, Maddux, Standard, Western Air Express, Embry-Riddle, and Clifford Ball. All of these proudly flew their own flags, and the people involved soon resembled small families, each with similar loyalties, worries and triumphs.

The action and rambunctious nature of the flying world made it difficult for Toby to force himself away from it, even on the few occasions when he wanted to. Every day there was some new development, he told Lily, so that he was afraid to spend much time away from the airfield out of fear he would miss something big and exciting.

But inspired by an unusual mild spell in early December, Lily said he should try to divide his passions and try living with earthlings for at least a few days. "You need a vacation, so why not take me fishing in the Ozarks?"

Lily had a further reason to pry her husband away. Somehow, in a relaxed atmosphere, she had to find the right moment to tell him the fact of life that now obsessed her. So far she had barely managed to acknowledge it herself, and the dread she had known for weeks had become almost intolerable.

They drove the Chevrolet to Arkansas and found a place on the Caddo River where the fishing was supposed to be good. The fine weather held, and when the sun reached its zenith they had a delightful picnic on the riverbank.

They hadn't had so much as a nibble, yet it had been a magic morning of great tranquility, during which the long silences between them as they worked their rods only seemed to enhance the communion between them. Lily was fishing off the bank, and several times Toby's attention wandered from the tip of his rod to her. Once she caught him watching her and she laughed and her voice echoed along the riverbank as she called out, "I love you . . ." and he called back to her through the sunlight, "Thank God!"

Later when they'd finished their sandwiches and drained the thermos of coffee, Toby apologized for their empty creels.

"It's not your fault, you didn't build the river."

"Using my superior knowledge of fish I chose it. Unforgiveable." They were lying on their backs staring up at a streak of dabbled cirrus in the sky, and Toby was surprised to discover that he was not even caring what the winds were doing up there or how long such fine visibility would last. At least for now, he thought, it was enough to think of something besides airplanes and pay more attention to the woman at his side.

He reached for her hand and held it.

And almost at once he sensed something was wrong. The feeling was so strong that he turned his head to look at her and saw that she was frowning at the sky. "What's the matter? Got a bellyache? Headache?"

"Sort of."

"I really am sorry about the fish, maybe they'll come this afternoon—"

"I don't *care* about the fish. I'm happy just being with you." She squeezed his hand and met his eyes.

"What's your problem?"

"Well . . . I guess you might as well know now as later."

"Shoot. Nothing can spoil this day for me."

" . . . I'm pregnant."

She waited through his silence, then asked finally, "Do you want to throw me away?"

Somewhere in the trees behind them a bird screeched, and then there was silence again.

"Well I'll be damned," he said quietly.

He pushed himself to his knees and looked down at her. "A mother? Is that what you want to be?"

"I don't know, I've never tried it before. But if you don't want to be a father I suppose it's not too late to do something about it . . . remember, babies aren't all cute little toe wigglers all the time. They wail and scream. You'll lose more sleep than you do now. They throw up. They wear smelly diapers. It will take a lot of me away from you. We'll be back living with a third person for a long, long time . . ." She looked at him closely, very seriously, as though searching his face for the answer to a deep problem . . .

A smile touched Toby's mouth. He reached out and tweaked her nose. "Sorry . . . you can't talk me out of it. I will be very proud, *very* . . . And now, mother, with your permission I think I'll go try to catch a fish."

She watched him stroll down to the stream, wade into the water. There was no retreat now, she thought. No matter about the dark visions that so often assaulted her mind, she had to convince herself that it would be his child.

Charles Tobias Bryant was born June 14, 1928, at the St. Louis Memorial Hospital. According to the doctor the boy was several weeks early in arriving, but no one counted too carefully. There was some unspoken debate about his resemblance to other human beings, but no one pressed the matter. On inquiry, the grandparents were advised that he looked like himself.

CHAPTER
13

The filming of Howard Hughes' *Hell's Angels* employed more pilots than most of the individual airlines in the United States. Day after day the air battles of the Great War were re-fought, often so realistically some pilots quit in fear for their lives. Mid-air collisions were frequent and the attrition rate among both men and airplanes dismayed even the veterans.

Unlike many of the others, Kiffin Draper was in his element. He soaked himself in the project, and because Hughes noticed his genuine enthusiasm he remained constantly on the payroll and was even assigned a bit part. He flew German aircraft as well as Allied and on one occasion managed to save a valuable Fokker D-VIII despite a collision and the resulting loss of part of its lower wing. Hughes saw to it that he received a bonus.

Now it was sometimes difficult for Kiffin to believe that he had ever led any other life, since most of the day he wore the same accoutrements he had worn in France, he flew the same airplanes and even experienced a momentary mixture of fear and challenge when a German aircraft came at him. On certain days when the light and atmosphere were just right his flights were often so realistic he had to look at the camera-airplane to make sure he wasn't dreaming. During the inevitable periods of waiting between camera setups he often had time to reflect on his desolate years—now little more than painful memory . . . Landshut, Paris, Lincoln with Toby and Lily—all gone. Barnstorming and the running away from defeat—only vaguely recalled. Then Paris again, and so much of those times obscured by alcohol. Lily—and disaster. That last, impossible to erase . . .

Howard Hughes spent more than two years filming *Hell's Angels*. Now during the last week of the flying, Kiffin found it difficult to believe that he had been involved so long and that in almost every sense he had become a new person. Except was that possible?

He had not touched alcohol or tobacco since that terrible day he had left St. Louis. He called his abstinence "my penance," but he would never elaborate on the cause. He had put on a few pounds, which gave him a more solid look, but those who bothered to look into his eyes saw a wild quality that refused to be subdued, or tamed. It was this apparent need for taming that had a distinct effect on the many women who somehow felt obligated to humble and control such an exciting male presence. All were unsuccessful in bringing him to heel, although thanks to Hughes and the environment Kiffin worked in, there were a great many of them.

While Kiffin had forsaken two of his potentially most destructive habits, he had also refined his tendency to risk his neck. Soon Frank Clark, chief pilot for *Hell's Angels*, was calling on him to do some of the most dangerous flying in the film. Kiffin was paid extra for such simulated catastrophes, during which he suffered a non-simulated broken arm and six smashed ribs—much worse damage, he wryly pointed out, than he'd suffered during the actual War.

When he was not actually flying, Kiffin joined his hard-drinking, hard-living colleagues in various celebrations that sometimes lasted an entire weekend. Amid such company his puritanical non-drinking style made him suspect for a while, but after he had safely delivered a few comatose friends to their dwellings their regard for him changed to . . . "Good ol' Kiff will take care of it," whatever "it" might be, including seeing a wife or girlfriend home when her escort was *hors de combat*. On such occasions a certain mystique about Kiffin developed. While the others caroused noisily and often profanely, he remained ever the quiet gentleman. Roscoe Turner once said, "The sonofabitch should join the priesthood." What Turner and the others failed to notice were the looks of longing fired across Kiffin's much abused profile by almost every female within range. Their advances ranged from bold to diffident, but the fundamental message was the same, and at times Kiffin accepted what was offered with a kind of sexual *noblesse oblige*. These liaisons were so many and so varied that Harlean Carpenter, a platinum blonde actress whose name had been changed by Hughes to Jean Harlow, found it absolutely necessary to explore why he seemed so much in demand. She arranged a rendezvous, and her enthusiasm for further clandestine meetings became so bold her agent warned her she was risking the displeasure of Hughes and her entire career for a "damn gypsy in a leather helmet."

Harlow saw the wisdom in her agent's message and thereafter restricted her activities to an occasional hand squeeze and a whispered, "Hi, Loverboy."

Those who predicted Kiffin would be captured permanently by one or another of those who devoted themselves to the task of forming a lasting attachment with him were proved wrong. When the film was finished and Hughes' private air force disbanded, Kiffin was still a bachelor. And as suddenly and as quietly as he had arrived, he disappeared from the Hollywood scene.

It was an axiom of the trade that no one who had made any kind of reputation for himself in the air ever forsook it for more conventional occupations. This wasn't entirely true, but the number of established airman who took up an entirely new type of work was extremely small. There was perhaps no common-sense reason for this reluctance to leave a way of life usually far from lucrative and crisscrossed every year with ugly accidents and frequent deaths, and because of such hazards aviation people of the late twenties tended to become increasingly clannish; often they knew the doings and fates of each other although such events may have taken place on the opposite side of the continent.

Kiffin nearly escaped the information net when he considered going to work for "Slim" Fawcett in Peru, where he would be flying back and forth from the sea to the high Andes in the crude airplanes Fawcett built using native labor. It was a high-risk operation, and poorly paid, but Fawcett had such a winning personality few pilots could refuse his invitations. Kiffin was sorely tempted, but found himself drawn to an event even more exciting, in his own country.

And so his name was listed among the participants in the first National Air Races held at Cleveland, which event brought together the hierarchy of aviation: Tex Rankin, a superb acrobatic pilot; Roscoe Turner, who had flown with Kiffin in *Hell's Angels;* Thea Rasche, a German, Louise Thaden, Phoebe Omile, Blanche Noyes, Ruth Elder, and a young woman of great determination, Amelia Earhart. "Speed" Holman, who at one time had tried to persuade Toby he should be flying for Northwest Airways, was also on hand, along with Clarence Chamberlain and Waldo Waterman.

The National Air Races were intended to be far more than a social gathering and the search for greater speed in the air was only a by-product of the whole event. The intent of the meet was to demonstrate new types of aircraft, engine and what could be done with imaginative modifications. Contestants learned from each other and the manufacturers had a splendid chance to parade their wares. Enthusiasm and hope was to be found everywhere about the vast flying field at Cleveland . . . this was the summer of 1929, and no one could foresee anything but a booming future for the country and particularly for aviation.

Nearly all the racers were sponsored by various companies who hoped their name and logo painted on an airplane would enhance the sale of their product. Kiffin's entry was no exception; his all-white Waco bore the name and insignia of the Bellflower Oil Company, Tulsa, and he had carefully planned his dramatic entrance. Just before closing time for further entrants he came glistening down out of the sun and made a high-speed pass along the spectator stands. When the roar of his three hundred horsepower Wright Whirlwind engine had caught the crowds he rolled the Waco on its back, pulled the release of a sack he had fixed to the upper wing, and two thousand posies drifted down to the ground. Later, at the spot where Kiffin parked the Waco, a saucy young lady in the pay of the oil company presented a flower to all who came to inspect the airplane. The response was far beyond the oil company's hopes, and word of Kiffin's presence soon spread throughout the area.

Kiffin, impressed, made a slight bow when a tall man he thought he recognized stopped by to say hello. "I'm Glenn Martin and I wish you good luck today."

Martin! Did he remember that evening at the Nebraska when two young football players had helped him disassemble his airplane? Now Martin was the world's largest aircraft builder, and one of the few who had made a fortune in aviation . . . He looked the part, Kiffin thought. Light linen suit to ease the humid summer heat of Cleveland, hard collar, watch chain and conservative tie. He wore a straw hat placed four-square on his head and what appeared to be the same rimless glasses he'd worn in 1915.

Martin's austere poise eased somewhat and indeed he nearly smiled when the girl from the oil company pinned a posy in his lapel.

"How's your mother, Mr. Martin?" Kiffin asked.

"Very fit, thank you. Nice of you to inquire."

Kiffin watched in amusement as Martin retreated into himself, tipped his hat to the flower girl and moved on. Had it really been thirteen years since they'd last met? Kiffin wasn't sure whether he was pleased or disappointed that the great man had so obviously forgotten him.

At four o'clock that afternoon Kiffin sat in his Waco with the big round engine grumpling at idle. He was in line with four other contestants waiting for the starting flag—"Speed" Holman in a Laird, Freddie Lund also in a Waco, T. A. Wells in a Travel Air, and H. S. Myers in a Simplex.

Kiffin was having trouble convincing himself that he could win. His competitors were all terrific airmen, their airplanes looked sleek and fast. The race would be around two pylons standing at opposite ends of the field, and according to the regulations at no time were the racers to climb above five hundred feet. The rule made Kiffin laugh. If at all possible he would never exceed an altitude of *fifty* feet even when turning around the pylons. "Stay low," he kept reminding himself. Down on the deck he would gain the benefit of "ground effect"; like certain birds the airplane would achieve slightly more lift when in close proximity to the ground, and the Wright engine would develop its absolute maximum horsepower. All the racers were aware of the phenomena, and Kiffin was sure they would all be competing for the same few feet of airspace. That should add some spice to the afternoon, especially since none of the competitors had much experience in pylon-racing. He took a deep breath to ease his tension and asked himself if this wasn't better than working for a living . . .

Now his attention was concentrated on the checkered flag which was held erect by a gray-haired man in a white suit. The start was already forty seconds late. What was the starter waiting for?

Kiffin squirmed in his seat. Would he ever reach the age of

gray hair? Ohio in the good ol' summertime. God, it was hot! Come on, mister, drop the damned flag. The band is playing. Can hear the horns and drums over the idling engines. What the hell is everyone looking at?

Every head in the stands, he noted, was turned toward the sky . . . even the gray-haired man with the flag seemed to have forgotten what he was doing. Hey, let's go before we fret ourselves crazy . . .

There was Charles Lindbergh standing near the starter. Looking up. Toby knew Lindbergh, Lily knew him too and liked him . . . what if they were here? Would Lily look through him or just turn her back? Lily . . .

Kiffin knew his hands were trembling. His feet were dancing lightly on the rudder pedals. Patience, man. Something was wrong . . . what the hell was the *delay?*

He glanced at the sky and understood why the gray-haired man had not dropped the flag. That huge gray object sliding so majestically across the field was the *Graf Zeppelin* on her last lap of a flight around the world. He'd been told it might appear some time during the afternoon but had been so absorbed with the race he'd forgotten about it. Impressive, yes, he thought, but just another gas bag, so let's get the hell on with the important events . . .

Another minute passed as he alternately watched the flag and the sweep second hand on the Waco's clock. He wondered if the officials knew how their air-cooled engines were overheating. Delay was hard on sparkplugs and souped-up pilots. Freddie Lund was the only one who knew what he was doing in the racing business. Hang on to his tail and then take him on the last few laps. Dreamer.

Kiffin smacked his dry lips. Sweat was beginning to steam up his goggles. The back of his shirt was already soaked through. Were they going to sit here all day?

The gray-haired man took out a handkerchief and mopped at his brow. And still the flag remained erect. It shivered a little with his movement as he returned the handkerchief to the pocket of his jacket. No wind. Good medicine, because judging precisely when to turn around a pylon if there was any wind was very tricky. One hundred degrees in the shade. Beautiful Ohio.

Kiffin stole a glance at Holman, who was on his left. Toby

knew him too, Toby knew everybody . . . How could Holman look so damn calm?

Just as his attention returned to the flag, he saw it snap down. He jammed the throttle full forward, kicked right rudder to compensate for torque and brought the Waco's tail up. The sooner he was airborne, the better. The stands became a blur, the Waco left the ground. The distance around the pylons was eight-and-one-third miles. He could see the first one in the haze ahead.

Something on his right. Holman in his Laird. How the hell did he get over on that side? He was sure not keeping the legal separation of one hundred and fifty feet. But then, no one paid much attention to the regulations. Officials looked the other way.

Holman was sliding ahead . . . pulling away. Everybody at full bore. Hot wind. Smashed bug on the windscreen. A quick end. Same for anyone who goofs.

Half a mile to the pylon now. Holman pulling ahead. Where was Lund? Above you. Oil along the bottom of his Waco's fuselage. He would dive for the pylon and pick up speed that way. Maybe pass you? Stick to your guns. Slide around in a vertical bank just high enough off the ground to miss catching a wing tip. Wells and Myers not a problem. Far back . . . maybe a hundred yards?

Horizon is shaking in the haze. The Whirlwind vibrating? A head mirage? Maybe you. Okay, *hit* it . . .

Kiffin rolled the Waco over in a vertical bank, pulled hard on the stick. His cheeks sagged, his rump pressed against his parachute. Three "g"s. His body weight of a hundred and seventy times three. Kiffin Draper now weighs 510 pounds. Lead legs. Doing this fifty times was going to be hard on the ass. In combat you did it easier to keep the wings on a Nieuport. And only a few times before it was all over. Either you got away or you were dead.

Vertical bank. He jockeyed his feet on the rudder pedals, keeping the Waco's nose moving exactly around the vague horizon. Summer haze. Hard to judge altitude when playing with a few feet. Playing? For six hundred bucks to the winner?

On the straightaway now. Where the hell was the other pylon? Where was Lund? Where was everybody? Holman is a sliver of dark against the haze ahead. Too far ahead. Must catch . . .

His hand instinctively pressed forward on the throttle, but it was hard against the stop. Get down on the grass. Ground effect . . . ground effect. Next time around the pylon make smoother turn. Ease into it gently. Too many "g"s defeat. Waco shakes in near stall—takes time to move mass up to speed again. Watch Holman. He knows.

There's the pylon, red-and-white against some dark trees. Holman already around and coming back the other way. Maybe his engine will blow up . . . maybe master rod will let go. Maybe anything or the race is won, but lost to Kiffin Draper.

Now into the turn easy. Flip over not quite so vertical this time. Take more space but keep more speed. What the hell is this proving? That Wright engines are reliable. Cheeks sag again. Eyes pulled down. Tongue heavy. Balls heavy.

A shadow overhead. Lund diving on the pylon. Jesus, watch it Freddie. Can kill somebody cutting in that close. This is idiot work. Hot idiot. Cylinder head temperature against the peg. The Whirlwind on fire? Something would have to give sooner or later. Make it later, Lord.

Roll into the straightaway again. Smoother this time. Less control surface movement—less drag . . . .

It happened during the fourteenth lap as Kiffin was rounding the far pylon. Despite the slip-stream he was soaked through with sweat. As he went into the turn he sensed the shadow above him again. Lund. He was trying his diving technique again. So close. Hey—

He's spooking me, Kiffin thought. He doesn't realize how close we are. If I pull up, my prop will saw off his tail. Nowhere to go but down and only inches of that.

And even as it occurred Kiffin knew what was happening. The heat reduced wing-lift. The Waco was shuddering into a high-speed stall. Bank too steep and tight. Trying to stay out of Lund's way. Maybe catching some of his prop-wash.

An instant, part of a second as the left wing tip scraped the ground. Horrible noise.

The Waco bucked violently, he was sure it was going end-over-end. Someone else's nightmare.

He saw the lower left wing crumple and bend back. Controls useless, just going along for the ride . . .

The Waco slewed toward the pylon, missed it by inches and bounded on the left landing-gear. It spun completely around and flopped noisily to earth, its nose pointing in the direction it had come from. Almost hidden in an explosion of dust and debris, it slid backward for some twenty yards before careening to a stop.

Kiffin regained consciousness once in the ambulance and then decided he was going to die anyway so he might as well get on with it. The next time he opened his eyes everything kept going in and out of focus, but he was fairly sure he was looking into a pair of green eyes sparkling beneath the bangs of a page-boy bob. And on top of the bob was perched a small white hat shaped like a paper boat. He watched the freckled face below the paper boat and liked the way it smiled.

"I'm Erin, your nurse," the face said.

"I'm dead and gone to heaven."

"You're fine. You're going to be just dandy. Lucky you."

His eyes wandered away from the face and he knew something was wrong. Oh yes, the crash. Was that today or yesterday? He hurt all over his body and especially in his legs, but that wasn't the trouble. Something was screwy . . . he reached to feel his head and neck. Was he dreaming?

"You're sure I'm not dead?" he said to the eyes.

"You should be, but you're not. Count your blessings."

"Where did you get those eyes?"

"Bought 'em at the five and dime."

"Gorgeous."

"Say that when you come out of sedation and I'll be your slave for life." She stuck a thermometer in his mouth and took his pulse.

He was having trouble organizing his thoughts. There was a window behind the white cap and green eyes. The ceiling was painted a light tan. He had a vile taste in his mouth.

He ran his tongue along his teeth and discovered a gap. "What'd I do. Lose a tooth?"

"Yup. I would have put it under your pillow for the tooth fairy but I couldn't find it. When you get out of here they'll fix you up with a false one and nobody but me will ever know the difference and I won't tell anybody, you'll be handsome as ever. Now I have to ask you some questions, since you weren't exactly too communicative when you arrived. Who should we notify?"

"I thought you said I wasn't dead."

"We have to notify somebody in your family that you're here."

"Why? Let's just keep it a secret. Where am I and when do I leave?"

"Doctor Heath will tell you."

"Why can't you?"

"It's not my job, and besides, I'm sure not even the doctor knows."

"Are you trying to tell me the doctor doesn't know where we are?"

"No. But I doubt if he can say when you can leave."

There was a long pause, and Kiffin closed his eyes. His ears were ringing. Let's see now, there was a hell of a noise and everything was bouncing around and dust everywhere . . . drowning in dust—"What's wrong with me?" he asked suddenly.

"Stop talking with that thermometer in your mouth."

"I want to know what's wrong with me. Something's fishy here . . ."

"You want me to take a rectal temperature?"

"You better not, green eyes or no green eyes."

"All right, then. Behave. Are you hungry?"

"How could I be? I smell ether."

"You should. But sometimes after vomiting patients are hungry. I could let you have some broth through a straw."

"Who's vomiting?"

"You were. It's perfectly natural, it's the ether."

"I don't remember anything like that."

"Good. Now I'll be leaving you for a few minutes. I'll be just down the hall, so press the button if you need me. Remember my name is Erin."

"Erin who?"

"Cassidy. It's an old Jewish name. And I don't have a phone."

"Are you trying to make me laugh? Damnit all, just tell me what's wrong or I'll chase you down the hall. I'll get up and leave right now if you don't tell me why I ache so bad."

"Dr. Heath will be here in about an hour."

She was gone before he could protest, but he decided that

if he had to be in a hospital, with a nurse like Erin it couldn't be too bad . . . A very neat package, the right curves everywhere, saucy manner. Full lips, red hair—wait a damn minute. How could he be thinking about such things when everything hurt so much. Nature, old boy. You're still alive and kicking. To prove it, try a few.

He saw that the white sheet was spread over a high hump in the middle of the bed. He could not see his feet beyond the hump, and when he tried to raise his head even slightly the pain forked through his body like chain lightning. What the hell was *wrong?* Hey, Erin, come back and tell me I'm alive. I think I need help . . .

And as suddenly as he had revived he became utterly weary. His tongue sought the gap between his teeth and he closed his eyes. All about his groin there was this excruciating pain. Then, gratefully, he slid down a staircase and sank beneath wavelets of bright green water . . . .

When he woke up he saw the green eyes again and remembered her name was Erin. She was holding his hand.

"There you are," she said. "You've been away a long time."

A man was standing beside her, and he heard her say he was Dr. Heath. A thin man with a warm smile and a Carolina accent. He was bending down now and peering underneath the mound in the center of the bed. "You're doing remarkably well," he said, "considering . . ."

"Considering *what?*" By God he was going to have some answers around here and right now.

Dr. Heath's smile faded. He took off his glasses and wiped at them with a handkerchief. "I didn't see it happen, but those that did say it's hard to believe you're still alive."

"I feel in fine shape except for my tooth. A little stiff . . . naturally."

"Naturally. I must tell you that you didn't come out of that crash exactly undamaged . . . I'm sorry to say it was necessary to remove your left leg near the top of the femur . . ."

Kiffin felt his hand being squeezed, then with her other hand Erin was caressing his brow and for a moment what the doctor had said failed to register. "You said . . . you took off my leg? You're joking, I can feel it—"

"It was unavoidable, Mr. Draper. It was completely destroyed. They said most of the engine was resting on what was left of it. It's going to be tough for you, but we've made a good deal of progress in artificial limbs since the war and in six months you'll be able to get around quite well—''

"But I still *feel* my legs, and they hurt. Everything hurts."

"That's not too surprising. Unfortunately you've suffered further damage and I hope it will be of some comfort if I remind you that it's a miracle you're alive at all . . .''

"I'm not sure I want to be."

"You took a bad whack in your groin. Your penis suffered severe lacerations, but we were lucky again. We made the best repairs we could. There will be some effect but I think eventually it will be fully functional—''

"Functional for what? Is that what that tube is for down there?"

"Yes. A catheter for urination."

Kiffin stared straight up at the ceiling. "How about . . .?"

"It's too early to be sure, but I'm optimistic."

For a moment Kiffin kept quiet, then only mumbled. "Well, well . . .'' And then in a barely audible voice, said, "I guess I got what was coming to me . . .''

Dr. Heath said that he didn't understand.

"Don't try . . . Will I be able to fly again?"

"I don't see any reason why you shouldn't."

Kiffin turned his head slowly until he focused on the green eyes. "Erin? What would you, or anybody, do with half a man?"

"Half of some men are worth ten of some others. Maybe when you get well I'll show you."

The doctor jammed his stethoscope's auditors in his ears. He listened to Kiffin's heart a moment. "You're one tough specimen . . . sometimes I think they've stopped making people like you."

The next day Erin admitted a visitor. He was a short, stocky Oriental with intense black eyes and an authoritative manner. He was wearing a seersucker suit and a straw boater placed level on his head. He introduced himself as Colonel Art Lym of the Cantonese Air Force and he spoke in a leisurely basso. "I was born in San Francisco and learned to fly at North Island . . . 1913. Curtiss Pushers . . .'' He took out his wallet, flipped through it quickly and found a paper. "Here is my Federation International Aeronautique license.

Notice the number 245? Very old now. Me too. Oldest living Chinese aviator before I'm forty. Some honor. Full of kinks. Basket of snakes." He chuckled merrily and added, "My people are crazy but brave. Like you, very brave."

"Colonel, you must have the wrong room or the wrong patient. Brave, I am not."

"Ah, but I was at the races and saw what you did. You would have killed the other man if you had pulled up, but you did not. That was very brave." Cocking his head from side to side he regarded Kiffin as if he were appraising a piece of statuary. "You're wondering why I'm here?"

"Now that you mention it."

"First, my sympathies. Back in 1914 when I decided to go back to my native rice bowl, I had a bad crash. Shock and shattered hip. Bad, bad. I was a long time recovering."

"You seem to get around all right." Kiffin thought he might be having another one of the strange dreams that had come to him so often since he had found himself in this hospital room. Most of his fantasies were so wild he could easily recognize them for dreams, but this . . .?

"I'm in the United States to buy airplanes for our little force in Canton . . . Probably they will be Boeing P-12s, but I'm dickering with Curtiss and the matter is not settled. Maybe a little of both because I like the Curtiss Hawk. Which do you think the best?"

"I've never flown either one."

"I'm hoping you will. You're the kind of man we're looking for as instructors. Good pay and living conditions. Lots of trouble in China now, but we'll survive. When you feel able to fly write me a letter. Here's my card." Colonel Lym plucked a card from his wallet and placed it on the pillow beside Kiffin's head. "I don't like surprises so I did a little checking on you. You pass. You'll like China."

"I didn't say I was coming."

"You will."

Lym smiled and said he hoped they would meet again very soon. He glanced at Erin near the door. "It appears you're well taken care of, which should speed your recovery."

Still smiling, he moved past Erin, bowed slightly to her and let himself out the door.

Erin said, "You're not supposed to have any visitors, but he's so distinguished and all I figured he must be some kind of ambassador. Besides, he gave me a ten dollar bill just to show him your room.''

Kiffin reached for his card and read:

> Lym "Art" Fu-yuam
> Colonel, Cantonese A.F.
> Canton

He handed the card to Erin. "Did he know I have only one leg?''

"No. I don't see how he could know.''

"Then keep the card. We won't bother to tell him.''

Later when she had left he felt disgust at his behavior. It seemed every word he said these awful days were loaded with phony bravado. He was going to be stumping around like a wounded duck for the rest of his time. A stiff wooden leg and a limp prick . . .

He pounded on the bed sheets with his fists and wondered how he could kill himself. Jump out the window? First he would have to crawl to the window and if he survived that he would have to jump over the sill. With one leg?

He stared at a brown spot on the ceiling. Something leaking on the floor above? Something wrong with the plumbing? Broken like Draper's plumbing? Maybe he could get a job in a carnival sideshow. See Kiffin Draper—ex-wild Bull of the Pampas . . . see the ruins of a once man. Free admission for unaccompanied ladies . . .

He yelled his frustrations at the brown spot on the ceiling and almost immediately Erin came hurrying through the door. "What's this, what's this?'' she demanded. And then she saw he was crying.

She went to the bed and took him in her arms, and although he was nearly incoherent she understood him when he tried to say, "I'm feeling sorry for myself and that's the last time ever. I promise you, I promise anyone who gives a damn, and most of all I promise myself, I'll never do it again.''

CHAPTER
14

While this was the year of the first National Air Race and the Thompson trophy, Kiffin found that other events were now of more interest to him. All of the contestants had now gone home and he tried to think about his accident and his missing leg as little as possible. He deliberately overcrowded his mind with thousands of miscellaneous mental adventures and discovered that he found relief in juggling the trivia of odd statistics. It pleased him to wait for Erin to arrive and bombard her with assorted facts he had picked up during her time off-duty. Was she aware that during the *Graf Zeppelin*'s flight between Tokyo and Los Angeles the twenty-four passengers consumed 160 bottles of spirits and 63 quarts of fine wines? Did she realize that the German Dornier flying boat had a gross weight of 115,000 pounds and could carry 169 people? Or how about the world's record for loops in an airplane set by Speed Holman? One thousand and ninety-three . . .

"What does that prove?"

"Nothing maybe . . . except that both airplanes and men are damn strong. Did you know an airplane called the *Question Mark* stayed in the air for 150 hours? Refueled 43 times. That *proves* the Wright engine is reliable."

"I'm more interested in your temperature," Erin said, shoving a thermometer into his mouth.

"What the hell has my temperature got to do with my missing leg? I don't have pneumonia—"

"We don't know that until we prove it."

"You're a real smart ass."

"You bet." She bent down, pulled the thermometer from his mouth and kissed him. When she seemed to be satisfied she put the thermometer back between his lips.

"Now I *do* have a temperature."

"Good. If I give you what you need then you won't take off."

"I'm going to China."

"Not if this Cassidy girl has anything to say about it."

"You won't."

"I will. Who else would marry you?"

"I wasn't aware our relationship had gone that far—"

"You are now."

"When did this happen?"

"Yesterday. Your new leg comes tomorrow and I decided I'd better trap you before you get too mobile." She took the thermometer out of his mouth, glanced at it, kissed him again. She slipped her hand down beneath the sheets, whispered. "We're going to get all departments going again." She pressed her breast against his cheek. "A little therapy here and there will speed up recovery. We'll set our own record."

"You're crazy . . . and I love it."

"Are you baptized?"

"I suppose so. Why?"

"I'm Catholic. I've already spoken with Father Muldoon. Under the circumstances he says that if you promise to take six weeks of instruction in the Faith he can marry us right away. He also wanted to know if you wanted to stand or sit during the ceremony."

"You work fast, lady . . . I'll stand."

"That's what I told him. Now give me your mouth again."

One month later, when the winds of October rippled the sullen surface of Lake Erie along Cleveland's waterfront, Father Muldoon made the sign of the cross as he repeated the names of Kiffin Draper and Erin Genevieve Cassidy, then pronounced them man and wife and congratulated Kiffin on his acceptance of the Faith. He added that life was full of handicaps and that Kiffin should regard his artificial leg as a symbol of his struggle to reflect the face of God. Kiffin politely thanked him, though his heart was not in it.

A vast assembly of Cassidys from all branches of Erin's family attended the ceremony, much of which took place without the bridegroom's full attention since he had been well-fortified with whiskey by several male Cassidys. The loss of his leg had resulted in an abrupt reversal of Kiffin's attitude toward booze, a venture endorsed by Erin, who turned out to be a rather dedicated tippler. Nor was the bride entirely alert to the proceedings, and for the same reason, except the donors of stimulant were various female Cassidys, who noticed that her freckles had paled alarmingly while she was donning her bridal array and promptly sought the handiest cure.

At the church and for the next three months Kiffin presented a stunning portrait of a man laden with the vicissitudes of life and surmounting all. There was a certain nobility of manner about his carriage; he moved with great difficulty, dragging rather than stepping out with his heavy artificial leg. Even so he managed to create an aura of dash in the business of merely crossing a room. His limp combined with his naturally rugged look and the thin line of his moustache to give him the air of a fine gentleman, not too well treated by life and yet triumphing. Erin's friends at the hospital, where she continued to work, whispered their approval of the match and particularly of her new husband. Those who knew her best said that such a splendid male should displace her affection for alcohol, hoped that now she would refrain from quick snorts of the pure stuff to be found in the hospital laboratory.

Kiffin was generally unaware of his wife's indulgences, since most of his waking moments he was removed from reality . . . The interminable changing of scar tissue to calluses on the stump of his leg caused him both excruciating pain and valleys of depression that he sought to alleviate with slow but near-constant applications of alcohol. He would spend all morning grooming himself for a walk from Erin's apartment to the end of the block and back, but there were many days when he abandoned the expedition out of fear of falling down and not being able to get up again.

The wedlock endured this way for eight months, without much passion or promise, since most of the time both parties kept to their own secret world. Their finances were a shambles of unpaid bills and uncashed checks both from Erin's work at the hospital and the disability insurance payments from Kiffin's crash. Money was spent only when they needed it for what little food they ate and to keep their credit at the local bootlegger.

Suddenly, as if he had passed through some invisible

gateway, Kiffin awakened one morning clutching a firm re-
solve to stay sober for the balance of the day. And what he
observed shook him. The apartment was a mess of discarded
clothes, half-eaten food, dirty dishes, and cigarette butts.

All of this, he thought, because of hydraulics. They had
tried everything they could think of to consummate their
marriage, but the failures of his cock to fully respond in spite
of Erin's efforts had left them exhausted, and remorseful. For
a while Erin had claimed her lack of satisfaction did not
really trouble her and, increasingly in dread of the next time,
repeated the claim. But they both knew they were lying and
they ignored the rapid deterioration of the humor that had
attracted them from their first meeting. After a while there
was no humor at all. Only increasing recrimination . . . .

On the morning of his decision Kiffin waited for Erin to
return from working the night shift at the hospital. He was
dressed and his possessions were packed in a single bag.
When Erin asked what he thought he was doing all dressed up
with no place to go he said he was on his way to China.

Erin went to the kitchen cabinet, pulled down a bottle of
Irish whiskey, took a sip and gargled. In the past she had
explained that she had always cleansed her throat after being
exposed to the thousands of germs in every hospital. Usually
she swallowed the whiskey, and if Kiffin was handy offered
him a similar prevention. This time she said, "You sonofabitch,
you can't do that to me."

"I'm sorry, I can't sit here the rest of my life—"

"Why not? You're in my apartment, sleeping in my bed.
You sit on my furniture and you walk on my rugs. You eat
off my plates and drink out of my glasses. What are you
complaining about? Look, I've been up all night and I'm
feeling lousy but I'll bust your pretty nose if you try to desert
me—"

"Erin, I'm not a damn lap dog. I'm sorry we can't screw
but there doesn't seem to be anything I can do about it. Or
you either. I have to get out and do something before it's too
late . . . I'm thirty-four years old—"

"You want to go to China or back to your fancypants
friends? That Tony and Lily you're always talking about?"

"His name is Toby."

"Whatever."

"And no, I'm not going to see them. But I think it would be better for both of us if we . . . if we got a divorce—"

"No divorce. I'm a Catholic, remember? So are you . . . almost."

"There must be some way to handle that."

"You can be excommunicated and go to hell."

"I've sort of been there . . . and don't feel like I'm out yet."

The conversation gained momentum all through the next two hours. They argued in bursts, usually acidic, although at moments a remembered tenderness would surface. Erin's Irish wrath flared only once when, lacking any handier weapon, she threw her shoes at Kiffin. A heel struck him on the cheek and opened a cut. At once Erin became the nurse, stopped the flow of blood and attended him. She did not, however, apologize.

Finally she took the whiskey bottle and dropped onto the couch. She held the bottle by the neck, caressing it, licking at the top with the tip of her tongue. Her eyelids were half-closed and she stared at the opposite wall.

Watching her, Kiffin decided it was now or never. He stood in front of her, leaning on his brass-headed cane. He carried his small suitcase in his free hand and was wearing his old leather jacket, which now appeared large for him. "Well . . . good-by . . ."

Erin's gaze momentarily rose to meet his, but it was as if she was looking right through him.

"I said good-by, Erin."

Still no response, and he wondered if she was asleep with her eyes open.

"Well, hell, kid . . . we did have some good times . . . I guess. I'll write and tell you all about China. I left a hundred dollars on the dresser for my share of your rent."

No response.

Kiffin completely lost the balance of the year 1930. He had even been unaware that the American stock market crashed in October of '29 and thirty billion dollars in capital disappeared from Wall Street, its accompanying lamentations audible throughout the world.

In fact, he was unaware of almost everything that was happening except his need to escape the weight of his handicaps and the gnawing fear that he would never again be capable of copulation. His unconsummated marriage to Erin haunted him, and whereas he had so recently been happy amid the admiring females who had been drawn to him, he now did his utmost to avoid any contact with them.

He wandered across America, always telling himself that the next week and the next week he would sober up and apply to Colonel Lym for a job. He was drunk for a year, well into 1931, and his residence varied from modest hotels to flop houses and even Christian missions when his disability payments failed to catch up with him. He rarely ate more than one meal a day and that usually a skimpy one for a man his size; he moved like a mechanical man with broken parts, and he emphasized his grotesque appearance by growing a beard and disdaining a haircut. While most of his thoughts were thick with confusion, he remained remarkably clear on one geographic matter—he would never allow himself to approach anywhere near St. Louis or any other place where even by chance he might run into Toby or Lily.

He did, though, experience very occasional periods of relative lucidity, and during these times he would make an almost frantic effort to stabilize the gyroscopic spinning of his thoughts and rejoin the only world he knew. Vincent Bendix had formed an aviation equipment company, and he thought he might find a job of some kind there but he never got around to applying. When he learned that C. E. Woolman, a former crop-duster, had started Delta Air Service with three six-passenger Travelaire monoplanes he considered trying for a job and almost immediately convinced himself that people would never fly with a one-legged man. The same attitude governed his actions when he learned that Pan American Airways had started daily flights between Miami and Havana—his old very personal territory, he thought. "What the hell right did they have flying down there when he'd pioneered it with an airplane full of whiskey . . .?" Happy days.

He spent time in the tanks of various jails as an indigent, a common drunk or a public nuisance, depending on the area in which he was locked up. His confinement was never long enough to sluice the mud from his brain, and as soon as he was released he found a way to get drunk again. In time he became a regular inhabitant of public places—tolerance for individual behavior seemed greatest there—and sometimes he wandered into libraries, where, full of whiskey, muscatel or whatever he could buy and hide, he would try to read. Once he stumbled on a copy of *All Quiet on the Western Front* and became so taken with it he gave up alcohol until he finished it. The book reminded him of his vow not to feel sorry for himself. He decided he was not so unhappy with this life. It was, after all, the only one he had. He had at last pretty well persuaded himself that as long as he stayed out of other people's lives he couldn't do any damage . . .

He did miss fiddling but had enough awareness left to realize a violin would soon be lost or smashed by his kind of vagabond existence. As a substitute he would often try to play "The Desert Song" in his mind or whistle a few bars of "Broadway Melody" while he savored a tasty muscatel.

As Kiffin sank ever deeper into a morass, the very society he had abandoned lurched toward its own maelstrom of bewilderment, anxiety and fear. The sale of automobiles collapsed. In Detroit almost half the workers were laid off. Hunger marchers, part of America's eight million unemployed, petitioned the White House for guaranteed employment at the minimum wage, and failed. President Hoover presented Congress with an emergency plan for a Reconstruction Finance Corporation and greatly expanded public works to relieve the desperate national condition.

And as if in direct defiance of the universal mood of depression, a posh speakeasy named "Jack and Charlie's" opened at 21 West 52nd Street in New York City. Almost immediately it became a haven for Eddie Rickenbacker, Reed Chambers, Douglas Campbell, and a boisterous coterie of aviators, aviation entrepreneurs and manufacturers. Howard Hughes, Richard Barthelmess, Clara Bow and the young Douglas Fairbanks, Jr., all of whom acted in flying movies, found comfort and escape at the "21" club, where, like Kiffin in his fashion, they could shut out the miseries of the real world outside.

And in aviation there was a unique and apparently dauntless spirit of optimism. In England Frank Whittle took out a patent on what he called a jet engine. Also from England a young woman, Amy Johnson, flew her tiny airplane all the way to Australia. Not even the loss of the Royal Airship R-101, which included the British Minister of Civil Aviation among the forty-eight people who perished, could dampen belief in lighter-than-air vehicles elsewhere. The *Shenandoah*, the *Macon*, the *Los Angeles*, and the *Graf Zeppelin* were all criss-crossing the United States and the oceans. Aerial explorers like Wiley Post, Martin and Osa Johnson, Admiral Byrd and the Lindberghs were flying over new horizons and shrinking the planet.

One of these directly involved Toby Bryant. While Kiffin was still convalescing, Toby received a call from Los Angeles. From his old friend Slim Lindbergh, who began as bluntly as he always did . . . "Would Lily be unhappy with me if I tempted you to come to work with us?"

"Who's us?"

"Transcontinental Air Transport. I've been appointed chairman of the technical committee and I need your help."

"You sure as hell get yourself into a lot of strange situations. I thought you didn't like committees."

"I don't, but this one is necessary . . . temporarily."

"Is the job temporary?"

"Not for you. We're about to start coast-to-coast passenger service in Fords, but of course we're only authorized to fly in daylight. We've still got to move the mail at night in the small planes and need a dependable man who knows his business to take charge. The pay would be six hundred a month and you'd be based in Kansas City."

"Are you talking about flying a desk?"

"No. You'd be flying the mail just like you are now, but you'd be chief pilot of the division. The other pilots and their troubles would be your baby."

"The people I work for now might not be too happy about this . . . can I have a little time to talk it over with Lily?"

"Sure. Give her my best and call me back in an hour."

A whole hour, Toby thought, to decide a future? The Robertsons had been nice people to fly for, but they'd shown little interest in expanding, and lately there had been rumors the company might merge with a new and much larger combine called American Airways. Everyone in the business was merging because Postmaster General Walter Brown wanted fewer but stronger companies, and because of the McNary-Watres Bill that had just been passed by Congress, reducing the maximum mail payment to $1.25 per plane-mile and providing permanent route certificates for operators willing to fly a such rates. It was one method to force the more unstable small operators out of business while encouraging the others to expand and operate larger airplanes. Brown was convinced no one would carry passengers if it was more profitable to carry just the mail. So Western Air Express and Maddux joined with Transcontinental Air Transport, American Airways absorbed Robertson and Southen Air Transport, and eventually National Air Transport took on Pacific and Boeing Air Transport under the banner of United Airlines.

Toby quickly decided that he would tell Lily they'd better move with the times. He also figured that some watchful angel must be arranging the schedule . . . While he was talking to Lindbergh, Lily was taking a flying refresher from Sloniger in an old Jenny. It would be her first time aloft since the arrival of Charles ("Flip") Bryant, now almost two years old, and she'd been especially excited about the challenge.

Toby's son was never called Charles or any other name except "Flip," a handle he had acquired through his ability to do quick snap-rolls in his crib. Motherhood had not come naturally to Lily; she had been obliged to work at it, and Toby thought she'd succeeded admirably. "Flip" had a very good nature and seemed eager to share his enjoyment of becoming part of humanity with all who paused long enough to smile at him. Ninety percent of the time they saw their smile returned, and Toby suspected that Lily's habit of taking him wherever she went must have something to do with his sunny attitude. She'd said that as soon as he could understand who was in charge she was going to take him flying . . . .

Toby was waiting now when the Jenny taxied toward the hangar. He saw Sloniger in the front cockpit and knew he'd never let on no matter what Lily might have done wrong. The telltale was Lily herself in the rear cockpit, grinning, and Toby knew instantly that the flight had gone well. Next year she planned to fly with Amelia Earhart and the other women in the second annual cross-country race—the so-called Powder Puff Derby—and it looked like she'd be more than up to it.

When Lily climbed down from the cockpit and whipped her helmet off Toby found himself watching her as if he'd never seen her before. By God, the girl had *style* . . . whatever she did was accomplished with true élan. And now there was even a hint of swagger in her walk as she came toward him, wearing her little-girl grin as if she'd just swallowed the last cookie in the jar. That face, he thought, with the small pinkish marks left by her goggles around her eyes and on both sides of her nose might not be the sort to launch ships, but it was still the most striking and delicious he had ever seen.

She came to him, stood up on her tip-toes and kissed him quickly.

"You look about fifteen," he said.

"What do you want for that kind of blarney? Something's on your mind. I can smell it."

"Our famous friend called," he began, and told her about the offer he had received. As she listened Sloniger joined them and put his arm around Lily. "This here lady of yours is some aviatrix. If the mail sacks weren't bigger than she is I'd recommend we put her on."

"Maybe she can take my place," Toby said, and repeated the news of the offer he'd received from Slim Lindbergh, adding that leaving the Robertson brothers was bothering his sense of loyalty.

"If it makes you feel any easier," Sloninger said, "I've been thinking about going with American. Sooner or later they're going to take over anyway . . ."

New York's Pennsylvania Station was jammed with the curious, assorted opportunists, publicists, press people, grinning dignitaries and local politicians being hearty despite their uncertainty about the occasion and what it might mean to them personally. Now a new system for crossing the vast North American continent had been conceived. Using both the conventional railroads and airplanes a passenger could travel from New York to California in two nights and two days.

The roster of corporate officials attending the inauguration of the new air-rail system was as incongruous as the participation of their vehicles, for here was the Pennsylvania Railroad momentarily joining hands with the Atchison, Topeka, and Santa Fe Railroad to launch a coast-to-coast air service via Transcontinental Air Transport.

As the huge locomotive of "The Airway Limited" panted and emitted little sighs of impatience at the head of the train all was in readiness for dancer Dorothy Stone to christen the platform of the observation car with a bottle of legal grape juice and cut the ribbon that tethered the train to the station's vast assembly of marble and concrete. Aviatrix Amelia Earhart had earlier performed a similar task on the Ford Trimotor *City of New York* which had been assembled within the station for public viewing. Newly appointed as special assistant to TAT's general traffic manager, she now stood ready to be a passenger on the train through the night. Arriving at Columbus, Ohio, in the morning she would transfer along with the other "first timers" to a TAT Ford and fly through most of the day to a place called Waynoka in Oklahoma, near the Cimmaron River and with a population of just over one thousand souls. Not one of the honored guests who gathered for photographers on the train's observation platform had ever been to Waynoka where they would entrain again and rumble through the second night to another outland destination, Clovis, New Mexico. After a hearty breakfast at the Harvey House, Clovis, they would board yet another TAT Ford for the balance of the flight to Los Angeles. The total time coast-to-coast, if all went well, would be forty-eight hours, and many predicted they'd never achieve anything like that time.

The details of this inaugural enterprise had been carefully orchestrated to reflect an historic accomplishment and obtain maximum attention from the press. In Los Angeles Charles Lindbergh was ready to push a ceremonial button that would send the train grunting out of Pennsylvania Station, and in Washington Secretary of Commerce Lamont would press a similar button to signal the take-off of the Ford Trimotor *City of Los Angeles*. In that city the attendance of dignitaries and functionaires was lent considerable color by the presence of Colonel Lindbergh, actor Douglas Fairbanks and his famous wife Mary Pickford. In Columbus, Ohio, actress Gloria Swanson was poised to christen another TAT Ford *City of Philadelphia*. Aviation's unique relationship with the movie crowd was thereby even more firmly established.

All those concerned with Transcontinental Air Transport's future were pleased with the new Fords. The three engines gave a powerful if somewhat deceptive sense of safety, since if one engine ceased to function the fully loaded aircraft became a handful for the pilots. Otherwise it was easy to fly, although the heavy control response became very tiring after several hours in rough air, and sometimes the center engine was inclined to spew oil vapor over the windscreen, making it more opaque than transparent. The Ford cruised at one hundred and twenty miles an hour when rigged to perfection, with the average slightly slower. The instruments that advised the pilots on the health of the engines were on struts outside the fuselage and could be viewed through the cockpit windows. The flight instruments were basically the same as in the open cockpit mail planes still flying for the line.

Like so many mail pilots, at first Toby was amused by the comforts offered TAT's passengers . . . The wicker seats reclined and a box luncheon was served by a male courier. The passengers were served chewing gum to relieve the pressure differentials as the aircraft climbed or descended and were given cotton to protect their hearing against the drumming of the engines. The toilet in the tail was a straight drop through to the surrounding atmosphere, and the door was locked when flying over cities.

The coordination of train and plane arrivals and transfer of the passengers from one type of transportation to another via the Stout-designed Aero-car was complicated by the Ford's flight limitations. There were no navigational devices in the cockpit except the magnetic compass, so the successful completion of every flight depended on the pilot's personal knowledge of the terrain and weather along the route. If the weather turned sour and he was unable to see ahead or down, the flight was delayed and the train obliged to wait. For the same reason lack of lights along the route precluded flight after dark.

As if to emphasize his importance, the pilot was now called "captain." Usually they were ex-mail pilots of about three thousand hours experience. The majority of the co-pilots were chosen from graduates of the army's Kelly Field, Texas, and their so-called assistance in flight was not always appreciated by their more independent-minded seniors.

Although Toby would not be flying the Fords until the mail planes were phased out, Lindbergh wanted him qualified to fly all of TAT's aircraft. So Toby spent a week in familiarization flights, and when he was finished he told Lily, "The damn things fly like a lazy cow but they're just a beginning . . . sort of like the square-rigged sailing ships were to the sea. Slim says the Fords are already obsolete and a whole new era is already on the drawing boards. I just hope he's right . . ."

While Toby found flying a multi-engined aircraft interesting and in some respects challenging, for the present he was content to stay with the mail flights. The hodgepodge of airplanes he had inherited plus breaking in new pilots to replace those who had left to fly the Fords demanded his constant attention. The airplanes were the leftovers from the consolidation of the smaller lines—Stearmans, Boeings, Douglas M-2s and even a Fokker F-14. Toby knew as well as the rest of the mail pilots that those nights when there were only the stars, God and themselves aloft would soon be only a memory, but for that very reason many of them were reluctant to shift their allegiance to the larger airplanes. Who the hell wanted to play nursemaid to a bunch of passengers? To do that meant a drastic change in their whole feeling about flight. Rough air had to be avoided or the passengers threw up all over the airplane and made a stinking mess. You were supposed to smile when in the presence of passengers lest they conclude something was wrong. The precious, although unwritten, right of pilots to bitch and grouse about petty annoyances was threatened when in the vicinity of passengers. You were expected to answer questions with a patient smile. *When will we take off?* You did not say God alone knew, or when the mechanics found out why the right engine was backfiring . . . *Promise you won't go near any storms?* You did not say, madam, I cannot change the route to suit the whims of God . . . *Why are we flying so high?* Because there is a mountain in the way. *Why are we flying so low?* Because there is cloud above. *Are you ever afraid?* Not *all* the time.

Although everyone recognized that the future of airline flying was in the transport of passengers, Toby sympathized with his proud and self-reliant colleagues, who were more than willing to postpone the future as long as possible. As a consequence of his understanding and his constant devotion to the various causes of both his neophyte and veteran pilots, as well as his knack for remembering the names of their wives and even their children, he soon became a very popular boss.

Toby had even less time for his own affairs when four single-engined Fokker F-32s inherited from what had been Western Air Express were put into service flying cargo between St. Louis and points in Texas. They were big high-wing monoplanes, and despite the large cabin in the fuselage the pilot still sat aft in an open cockpit, a position that appealed to some of the older pilots who were never quite comfortable in flight unless they were able to feel the slip-stream on their faces. Toby didn't sleep at the airfield, but the demands of his job as chief pilot made him think maybe he should.

Meanwhile, there was Lily . . .

After fourteen years of marriage Lily was finding the insti-tution not exactly as she had originally envisioned it. Some-how the little girl who had married the dashing aviator in Paris had been replaced by a slightly used woman in her thirties with a hint of crow's feet about her eyes and a suggestion of broadening about her hips. With a husband who spent very little of his time at home.

The hitch was the competition, which, thank God, was not another woman but was his passionate affair with flying. Damn Slim Lindbergh anyway for boosting Toby out of a nice easy-going job flying the mail and saddling him with the problems of thirty pilots and their airplanes.

The truth—how difficult to face squarely—was that Lily Cranwell Bryant was also just a bit of Mrs. Spoiled Brat. Her father, she forced herself to admit, had begun to spoil her as soon as her mother died, and Toby had taken up the torch while she was still in her teens. No question, her domestic inclinations were now running barely a hair above zero . . . Was every woman bound to become so restless when she reached thirty . . .?

She was sitting now in the living room reading the *Literary Digest* and trying to absorb the meat of an article on President Roosevelt, who had just announced a New Deal for the American people. Yet her real attention was on when Toby would come home. How many times had he called to say something had come up and he would grab a bite at the airport? It would be, she thought, like a cheap magazine story if when he finally arrived home he smelled of liquor, perfume—or both. Which was never the case. He'd always been working and always apologized and explained what it was that had kept him at the field. And it had become understood between them that any reliable man would have done the same thing. What did she want—some unstable so-called romantic like Kiffin?

And then there were the emergencies that came along frequently enough to remind anyone who faced reality that airplanes could, after all, kill you. TAT had received a terrible set-back when the Fokker crashed and killed Bob Fry, Jessie Mathis the co-pilot, and among the six passengers the famous football coach Knute Rockne. The newspapers must have had nothing else to write about. Toby was gone for a week while he sifted through the gruesome wreckage trying to find out what had gone wrong . . .

Lily left her magazine, crossed the living room and turned on the radio. Ethel Merman was singing "Life is Just a Bowl of Cherries." Indeed, Miss Merman . . . sometimes, yes . . . But my life seems to be reaching that dividing line between young matron and dowager. I'm restless. Restless, or a little desperate? But not hausfrau, not if there was some way to wiggle out of it, thank you very much la Merman.

She walked slowly into Flip's room, and for no reason she could identify her thoughts turned to Kiffin. He happened along with some frequency, and was most likely to occupy her mind when she least expected it. She no longer considered his momentary presence as a phenomenon or even a mental aberration. It just was.

Now he was out there somewhere—that is, if he was still alive. It should have been easy to hate the man, necessary even, but it hadn't quite worked out that way. She didn't excuse him, but she now was quite convinced that somehow her original fondness for him must have shown through and been taken the wrong way. Drunken male, unaware female. Bad combination . . . Toby was always hoping for some word from Kiffin but it never came. And Toby had done some worrying why. One of these days he was likely to do some dangerous wondering—and, God forbid, guess the truth . . . He knew how much time you and Kiffin had spent together. You would like to protect him, but suppose Kiffin, with customary unpredictability, showed up on the horizon some day with a new-born conscience? And suppose those two old buddies had one of their heart-to-hearts . . .

Better concentrate on today's pleasant reality—Flip, jolly as ever, the baby who did far more laughing than crying. She saw him focus his lively blue eyes on her and she listened while he began telling her a long story. She was pleased that she'd acquired such fluency in gibberish and thought she must be the only mother in the world who was told bedtime stories by her offspring. No Winnie the Pooh for this character. He was himself a rider of the purple sage, his own Zane Grey. As she listened and watched his warm smile she was grateful that in spite of the everlasting question in her head of his father's identity, he certainly seemed to reflect Toby's easy disposition . . .

She kissed Flip, retucked the covers around him and told him to go to sleep on the nearest cloud, then closed the door softly behind her, smiling at her action because she knew that was the traditional way all doors to all children's rooms were closed and had no effect whatsoever on how the child actually behaved once the parent had disappeared. Did any fond parent ever *slam* the door after himself or herself? As a sort of go-to-sleep exclamation mark?

She knew her mind was wandering almost in exact accompaniment to her sleepless pacing of living room. This restlessness was new, she reminded herself, and she seemed incapable of dismissing it. Amelia had been the spark, she thought—go on, blame Amelia. How dare she fly the Atlantic so successfully, and with such élan? That scrawny wonderful social worker with that mop of hair, how dare she make so many lesser women envious of her accomplishments?

As if Amelia wasn't enough of a troublemaker there was Louise Thaden winning the Powder Puff Derby; Blanche Noyes, Ruth Elder, and the rest of those women flyers who had banded together in something called the "99s." How did they get away with it? Where were their husbands and families? Why aren't *you* a 99?

The worst of all, she thought as her pace quickened, was her old school mate Ruth Nichols, that gorgeous creature with her portrait on the cover of *Vanity Fair*, no less. There she was, big as life, lovely as ever, the girl known as "Porky" at Wellesley because she loved sausages, now so grownup and fancypantsy in her custom-made purple flight suit with that majestic face rising above the collar. Wellesley takes to the air! Same class as the Cranwell girl. Set a new women's altitude record, crashed somewhere up north trying to fly the Atlantic . . . but *doing* things. And where was Lily Cranwell, also of Wellesley? In Kansas City waiting for her peripatetic husband, who dropped in for a slumber party now and then. Something had to be done.

"I," she said aloud to the empty room, "can also fly."

As if her voice had summoned him, she heard Toby crossing the front porch.

Out, out, damned spot, she thought as she ran to greet him. Evil, ungrateful, selfish, bitchy thoughts, get out of my Lady Macbeth mind . . .

She threw herself into his arms and they stood locked in a tight embrace for a moment. "The devil made me do it," she said.

"Do what?"

"Think bad thoughts about my life. I don't deserve you."

"No, you don't. You deserve better, but I'm handy."

She pushed away from him and looked into his eyes. She asked if he was hungry and when he said he was ravenous she said the finest ragôut of lamb outside of Prunier's only needed to be warmed for his majesty if he would just give her fifteen minutes . . . Lily back on track, or so she told herself . . .

With the now steady improvement in their finances after their arrival in Kansas City they had made several improvements to their lifestyle. They no longer dined at a card table, the whole house was carpeted and featured one of the new architectural innovations—a breakfast nook. They sat in it now, washing down the ragôut with a glass of Dago Red, a burgundy that Antonio, who supplied their modest alcoholic needs, assured them had originated in that province. Giving the liquid some kind of label other than South Kansas City made everyone feel better—including Antonio, who was a man of very good nature haunted by the prospect that one of his customers might be blinded because of drinking his potion.

Toby leaned back, loosened his belt a notch and went on telling Lily about TAT's newest step forward, the installation of two-way radio in all aircraft. "We'll know what's going on for a change," he said. "We can keep better track of flights and if the weather changes we can advise the pilot while he's still in the air . . ."

Lily was more interested than usual in the technical details of two-way radio, but she also had a great deal more on her mind. "Do you believe," she said, "that it's possible for a woman to turn into a vegetable?" She paused and inwardly gasped. Was she really going to come right out and say it in so many words, the dream that had been scratching at her peace of mind for weeks?

"You have that look in your eye," he said.

"What would you say if I told you I'd like to be the first woman to fly the Pacific Ocean?"

"I assume you're talking about from shore to shore?"

"What Ruth Nichols can do, I can do."

"As yet she hasn't flown the Pacific. And if I have the score right that lady has managed to survive six crackups. I might also point out that she doesn't have a husband and a son—"

"And look at Amelia—"

"Amelia has George Palmer Putnam, who is a rich man, and what he can't spend to finance her flights he can promote. He's an expert at it."

"You don't like the idea," she said flatly. She should have known. How could she climb out of this tub of propriety before she drowned? Oh, adventure, oh, glamor, where the hell is thy sting?

"The idea is fine," Toby said. "But it's a tad impractical. Where would we find at least a hundred thousand dollars to make it work? Or do you know the location of a money tree?"

"I'll find one."

"Good. Meanwhile your timing isn't the best . . ." He hesitated, and she saw him attempt a smile. But it was a thin smile, and she realized he must have had a difficult day at the field.

He began uneasily . . . "There's something I haven't told you because I thought it might upset you. About a week ago Jim Doolittle dropped by to see Tommy Tomlinson. They're both experimenting with high altitude flying and I was invited to listen in on their troubles. I don't know why the subject came up but it did and Jimmie told me that Kiffin had a bad crackup at the Cleveland Air Races . . . and lost a leg. I can't understand why he hasn't told us or why we haven't heard about it before . . ."

"I can—" She said it before she thought. She was hugely grateful that Toby was so preoccupied he apparently hadn't heard her.

"And now we have this . . ." Toby reached into his shirt pocket and pulled out a folded envelope. He handed it across the table to her and she saw that it bore a Chinese stamp.

"Read it. And please don't say anything until you've had chance to think about it. I'd appreciate your opinion."

The envelope was addressed to Toby in a fine Shakespea ean hand. The letter itself was typed on the personal stati nery of General Arthur Lym. His Chinese chop decorated tl space for his signature.

> My dear Mr. Bryant:
>
> Your friend Kiffin Draper has been under my command since August last. He is a fine man and has done much to improve the quality of our pilots. He has also done much demonstrating of aircraft for the Cantonese Air Force as well as for General Chiang Kai-shek in the north.
>
> Sometime in September Mr. Draper contracted malaria and he is now seriously ill. Most of the time he is delirious, but he refers frequently to you and your wife and his great affection for both of you.
>
> Our surgeon general and I are very worried about Mr. Draper. As you must know the handicap of his missing leg pulls his resistance down and the additional fight against such a serious disease becomes all the more difficult for him. However, there seems to be more than malaria working against the survival of our mutual friend. Our doctors describe it as general malaise, and it is true that he seems to have lost the will to live. Under the circumstances our doctors assure me this is extremely dangerous. Therefore, forgive me dear sir, if you want to save the life of your friend, I must recommend that you make all haste and come to Canton . . ."

The balance of the letter, which Lily found difficult t absorb through the sudden and conflicting whirlwinds in he mind, concerned General Lym's offer to meet Toby on hi arrival and "render whatever assistance necessary."

"You're going," she said quietly.

"Of course I am."

CHAPTER
15

Toby had gone to Jack Frey, president of TAT, and asked for and received a two-month leave of absence. Now three weeks later, he stood on the porch of the Canton's Pokoi Hospital listening to the deep, sonorous voice of General Lym as he apologized for the oppressive heat. "Canton is not exactly a resort area. This is our hot and heavy season. For relief I recommend Tsing-tao beer."

Little more than half Toby's size, he was immaculate in his freshly starched khakis and carried an air of considerable dignity and power. "We were pleased to arrange a private room for our friend," he said, "the only one in the hospital, and it overlooks the Pearl River. Fortunately we have no sick generals. You will have much to talk about so I will leave you alone. His nurse speaks English. Ask her to telephone headquarters when you are ready to leave and I will send my driver for you. We will have lunch and tell a lot of flying lies. You will find Kiffin in the last room at the end of the corridor. How long since you've seen him?"

Toby hesitated. He couldn't remember if it had been two or three years—maybe more. How did you measure friendship, or its loss . . . "It's been some time," he said.

"Then may I suggest you prepare yourself for a shock. He may not appear quite as you remember him."

Toby walked slowly down a screened corridor that stretched along the outside of the hospital. Huge overhead fans spaced along the ceiling stirred the air in the corridor until it was nearly cool. As he approached the end of the hall he found it impossible not to think of Nebraska, and of what had to have been another life. It *must* have been two other kids who stood on that barn roof just as it must have been two others who sold *Saturday Evening Post*s, had paper routes, found that girls were constructed differently than boys, buried treasure on the

wasteland behind the State Penitentiary, smoked hay cigarettes
bet on who could walk the rails of the train track the longes
without stepping off and mouthed candy floss at the state fair
It had to be two other young guys who did everything as ;
pair, including moving a football against some of the bette
teams in the country. And it was hard to believe that a singl
meeting with a man like Glenn Martin could so influence th
rest of their lives. Who could have ever predicted that tw
Nebraska cornhuskers would wind up in Canton, China . . .

There was no door to the room, but a white curtain ob
scured the interior. Toby shoved it aside, entered, stood for ;
moment while his eyes became accustomed to the deep shad
ows inside the room. The revolving blades of the fan on th
ceiling made the room cool, although it failed to disperse th
strong odor of cooking. He assumed the kitchen must b
near, since above the whirring of the fan he could hear ;
continuous human soprano chattering and the frequent rattl
of pots.

He approached the bed slowly and stood looking down at ;
face he hardly recognized. Kiffin appeared to be asleep. Tob
glanced at the artificial leg standing on its own in the corner
He looked away from it, so ugly with its dangling straps, an
then his eyes discovered the lower part of the bed, where o
one side the sheet lay flat.

God, the man was so *thin*. There seemed to be nothing t
him except a fragile collection of bones. His skin looked lik
tanned animal hide.

Kiffin opened his eyes and stared up at the revolving fan
He watched it for a moment, then finally his eyes move
slowly about in their deep sockets and centered on Toby. H
frowned and licked at his dry lips.

"You?" he muttered finally. "How . . .? Am I seeing
things . . .?"

"It's me . . . just thought I'd stop by and say hello—"

"Go away." A thin hand came out from under the shee
and wiped at his eye sockets. He looked up at Toby again
"Go away, I said. You've got to be a ghost . . . am
delirious again?"

Toby reached out and put his hand on Kiffin's shoulder
"You sure go a long way to avoid old friends . . . we miss
you . . . Lily sends her best . . ."

Kiffin's eyes were clearing now. At last he seemed to understand his visitor was real. "I'll bet," he said.

A long silence descended on them. As they looked at each other Toby found the sound of the fan whirring and the chatter from outside a welcome relief. He found his thoughts slipping down a familiar trail. There had to be some reason for Kiffin's disappearing act . . . it just might have something to do with Lily . . .

"Kiffin . . .?" he said, and pushed such thinking from his mind.

"Toby . . ." Kiffin said almost diffidently, as if saying the name itself made him, Toby thought, strangely uneasy. "You didn't have to come all this way to see me kick the bucket, I can die on my own . . ."

Toby shook his head, then suddenly reached for his wallet, opened it and took out a snapshot of Flip. He handed it to Kiffin. "Here's a relatively new member of the family. A funny little guy with some strange habits . . . likes to do snap-rolls in his bunk. We call him Flip. What else . . .?"

Kiffin was a long time studying the photo. He turned it slowly around until it was upside down, then reversed it. His eyes moved back and forth from the photo to the ceiling fan to Toby. He started a broken chuckle, and then the sound in his throat became more a whimper. He dropped the photo and turned his head until his face was buried in the pillow.

It was some time before Toby realized he was crying.

Northrop Alpha

Lily watched the TAT Ford land and taxi to the boarding ramp. When the engines were stopped an attendant placed a footstool below the door in the fuselage. The door opened and five passengers descended and walked toward the new terminal building.

As Lily waited for Toby to appear she explained to Flip

that the Ford had come all the way from California and would soon fly on to Newark in New Jersey. Her son was far more interested in trying to climb the woven wire fence. Her mind had been in a jumble ever since Toby's telegram advising her of his arrival. Two months had become an almost intolerably long time. It was all very well to be an independent woman, but having Toby around, she realized, was the blood of life. Of her life, anyway.

She hoisted Flip off the ground so he could see over the wire fence. What was the holdup? The Ford's open doorway remained vacant, a dark oval gash in the side of the corrugated metal fuselage. Then suddenly she understood the reason for the delay—there was Toby stepping down from the door and helping a man she knew must be Kiffin descend to the ramp. Dear God, he had brought the wreckage home. "Oh, Toby . . . why didn't you *tell* me . . .?"

She shook her head, hoping what she was witnessing would go away. Leaning on Toby's arm was a skeleton of the man she had once known too well. The pair moved toward her very slowly. She saw that Kiffin's eyes were searching for hers. "Oh nooo," and then she immediately tried to concentrate on Toby.

She threw her arms around him and after a long, full kiss forced herself to smile at Kiffin and offer her hand. "Welcome," she said, trying to believe she meant it, trying to fight down the deep sense of uneasiness that came over her. Remember . . . he's a sick man. Don't let the sight of him disturb you so . . . She said, "Well, well . . . I guess life will pick up for all of us now." And she wanted to bite her tongue because she thought . . . dear God, make it *only* a thought . . . that she saw something in the inquiring cant of Kiffin's head that she had sometimes noticed in Flip. Imagination, she quickly told herself, pure devilish imagination . . .

She said now very crisply, "Here's our son Charles."

Kiffin took the boy's hand. "How do you do, Flip?" And Toby tried to laugh as he explained that he'd told Kiffin how the boy had gotten his nickname. Lily tried to go along with his good humor but couldn't shake the familiarity of the way Kiffin tilted his head, a sort of quizzical, challenging gesture unique to him. As they stood in silent embarrassment she couldn't resist searching the whole of Kiffin's face, seeking some additional clues no matter how devastating the result, and finding none, she managed to say coolly, "I'm sorry you've had so much bad luck, Kiffin . . . we'll get you back on your feet . . ."

Again she wanted to bite her tongue. No matter what he'd done, the man had lost a foot and was terribly sick. And supposing she *had* found another possible resemblance, something she might have seen in Flip? Would she go wild and insist that Kiffin was the father?

While Toby lifted Flip until they were eye-to-eye and spun him around to his screaming delight, Lily and Kiffin stood looking at each other, their eyes anxious, saying their fears without speaking them. And when Flip was screaming loudest Kiffin said softly . . . "I hope you'll somehow find a way to forgive me."

"I've forgotten everything," she lied, and found herself once again wondering if anyone else in the world carried their head in *just* that way . . .

She glanced quickly at Flip as Toby set him down. No, the notion was crazy! He held his head like Toby did, and the already burgeoning strength in his arms was all Toby. She must never think this way again— after a while thinking could be believing. No question—Flip was Toby's son. No question?

For the first week the reunion went along better than any of them could have hoped. Kiffin shared Flip's room and since they had their own bathroom there was no actual inconvenience. And they soon formed a relationship—man and boy communicated in a language of their own that seemed to satisfy them both. Likewise, they kept the same hours. They got up together, took naps at the same time of day and went back to their beds at the same time each evening. "We're sort of growing up together," Kiffin said. "When we haven't anything else going on I show him my pegleg."

Toby and Lily kept their separate thoughts.

Kiffin's health improved rapidly in the temperate climate. His fever was gone, there was a new glow to his skin and he put on weight. He began to venture out of the apartment during the afternoons, and Flip usually went with him. They went to the park and sailed paper airplanes, they were frequent visitors to the zoo and they often went down to the waterfront hoping to see one of the few remaining paddlewheel steamers on the river. In spite of everything, Lily couldn't help being somewhat touched. Once she asked Kiffin what in the world they talked about during their long sessions together.

"We're both pretty good listeners. We do a lot of hangar flying. Sometimes we talk about life. Quite a boy. The other day at the zoo he asked me what storks do for a living."

"He can't even speak a full sentence."

"Oh sure he can, whole paragraphs at a time. You just have to do a little interpreting. I told him the facts of life . . . that storks brought babies—"

"Kiffin, I won't have that."

"Would you prefer me to tell how babies are really made?"

"You know what I mean. I don't think you have any right to shape Flip's thoughts on *any* subject. That's Toby's and my job . . ."

As their eyes met there was a long pause between them. Finally Kiffin said, "I understand . . . I have no right . . ."

As he regained his strength Kiffin wrote more and more letters applying for employment. Every one of his considerable acquaintances in aviation except those in the airlines, where he knew his missing leg would rule him out, received a very well-drafted letter of application. "I'm trying to get out of your hair," he said to Toby.

"Take your time, I just wish we had something for you."

Actually Toby had considered hiring Kiffin to fly some of the test flights of the twelve new Northrop Alpha monoplanes the line had bought to fly the mail along with a further addition of seven Consolidated "Fleetsters." Both aircraft were still flown from open cockpits. He reluctantly changed his mind because the regular line pilots insisted on doing the routine test flying and also because his own status with his pilots was becoming uncomfortable.

His duties had recently been increased until now those pilots who flew the passenger planes in his division were his charge in addition to the mail pilots. The system of starting the new men on the mail and then as time passed promoting them to a co-pilot's seat in the Fords and eventually promotion to captain was his from the beginning to the end. Lindbergh was now off on many other projects, lending his name and talent to Pan American, and Toby's boss was now another veteran of World War flying—Paul Collins.

Now he rarely had a chance to schedule himself to fly anything but a desk. It occurred to him that if he'd been Kiffin he would have said to the company thank you very much but I think I'll just stay in the cockpit, And that if he had, his day might be a damn sight easier, and happier.

He had to wear a business suit and a tie every day—and, shades of his father, a *hat*. Snap brim. He had a secretary and an office overlooking the Kansas City airport *and* an appointment calendar. Sooner or later it seemed everything to do with running several thousand miles of an airline sifted down to him whether he knew anything about it or not. "Let Toby handle it," was becoming a very handy phrase.

Winter had arrived and as always brought new problems to the flying business. One of the worst kind had recently been dumped in Toby's lap. It made him wonder why he'd let himself be talked into what was politely known as "an executive job." Although a line pilot was paid almost as much and was required to make several executive decisions every flight, he actually flew only eighty-five hours a month and sometimes less. Sometimes when Toby found himself overwhelmed with paperwork he tried to think of some way to levitate his desk and make the same simple decision about where and when to land . . . .

This particular day Toby hated to go to the field because of his friend Bruce Babcock. A month earlier one of TAT's westbound Fords had crashed in a wheat field. Considering the cause of the crash and the condition of the wreckage it was a miracle the casualty list had been so low. Out of ten passengers aboard two were killed and six injured. Babcock the captain, and his co-pilot Plummer had both escaped with minor cuts and bruises.

This morning there would be a hearing on the matter before the federal bureaucrats who had multiplied like rabbits since licensing had been required. While Toby had done everything in his power to avoid prejudgment it was all too apparent that Babcock had used poor technique and the Department of Commerce was going to demand his head.

The situation was further complicated by the fact that Bruce Babcock was the most popular pilot on the line, which had caused him to be elected chairman of the new pilots' union. All pilots were extremely touchy about blaming "pilot error" for any accident and with some reason. Worse, the

Babcocks, man and wife, were good friends and occasional poker pals with Toby and Lily. Babcock was a family man, as devoted to his wife Julie and their four daughters as he was to flying. "They're my harem," he often laughed, "and I'm the richest pasha in the world." His whole family considered him hero who could do no wrong.

Only he had done a grievous wrong. Two people were dead who also happened to have families. And one of the survivors would probably never walk again. The financial loss to TAT combined with reputation loss was incalculable.

Babcock was waiting for him when he entered his office. There was a splatter of cuts and bruises about his usually ruddy face, but now his complexion was ashen and Toby noticed that he got up with difficulty. When he took his extended hand he felt it trembling. "Hi, Bruce. I hope you haven't been waiting long."

"No . . . just got here. I'm a little nervous. This waiting for the hearing is driving me out of my gourd. I can tell you for sure I haven't had a decent night's sleep in a month. Why does it always take so damned long for anyone who works for the government to do anything?"

Toby told him not to be so inconsiderate of bureaucrats . . . "they have to have their coffee breaks . . ."

He maneuvered around until he stood behind his desk. He was badly in need of something to give him confidence for what he was doing—some bulwark against the good friend who'd just let him know his extreme distress by his red and watery eyes. Toby thought he looked twenty years older than the last evening they'd spent together. It had been the night before the crash and they had all laughed at Toby's clumsy attempt to bluff his poker hand. He hadn't fooled anyone and had promptly lost twenty dollars. Babcock's wife Julie had said they should invite the Bryants over every night . . . "A few hours of poker with such babes-in-the-woods and we can pay off the mortgage . . ."

Toby was desperate to relieve the tension. "You must have known I can't win a poker game even when I cheat," he said, trying to smile. "You took me."

"Anybody who backs only two aces deserves it." Babcock scratched gently at a scab on his forehead. The light from the window behind him formed a half-halo around his unkempt hair, and Toby thought it was implausible that Bruce Babcock was actually ten years his junior. He found himself wishing Bruce had worn a sports jacket and a tie instead of an old sweater. Maybe a more conventional appearance might impress the damn bureaucrats and they'd be easier on him.

Babcock squinted at his watch and Toby was reminded that his friend wore glasses at home but would not wear them within miles of an airfield. Glasses were just not part of any pilot's self-portrait. They would willingly stumble around and squint for years before they would surrender to the idea that they might not be able to see like an eagle. Cy Bittner, one of the mail pilots who was also a graduate of Gates Flying Circus, was the only man he knew who just didn't give a damn about his image. He wore glasses *all* the time, even inside his goggles, and when and if the time came Toby was determined to do the same thing . . .

Babcock was saying that it looked like it would be about twenty minutes before the officials arrived and asked how long Toby thought the inquiry would last.

Toby's frustration suddenly got the better of him and he made a sarcastic remark he instantly regretted. "Why? Do you have something more important planned?"

"No . . . there's something I'd like to bring up before Plummer gets here."

"Plummer's not coming."

Babcock rubbed his fist across his rumpled hair. Toby thought it looked like he'd been doing a lot of that lately.

"Why not? What the hell kind of hearing can they hold without the co-pilot there?"

"They've already talked to him. Yesterday afternoon. They wanted to talk to you separately."

"Goddamned bureaucrats. How are they going to help anything?"

"That's sure open to question, but let's start out with the attitude that they're only trying to do their jobs. I suppose you realize that you're in trouble. You can't fly an airplane through power lines and expect everyone to look the other way while they pick up the pieces."

"I know, I know . . . I'm prepared . . . I didn't do anything wrong—"

"Come on, Bruce, you've got to be realistic with these government guys."

"Do you think they'll yank my license?"

"Maybe."

Babcock sighed, shook his head. He rubbed viciously at his hair, and gingerly touched a dark bruise on his cheekbone. "Jesus, Toby . . . what'll I do? I've got Julie and the family to think about."

"I know. But before we meet with the Feds you've got to get hold of yourself. What you told me the day after the crash and what I assume you're thinking of telling the Feds doesn't match up with what Plummer says. He claims you were disoriented, which you know as well as I do is a fancy word for lost. You might be better off if you just came out and admitted it."

"Bullshit. I knew where I was all the time. I just couldn't keep on the beam, that's all. It was swinging from a broad A to an on-course and sometimes I couldn't hear anything at all. You know how it is when it's snowing hard, Toby. It knocks everything out."

Toby certainly did know. The so-called Adcock range was a radio navigation system that offered the pilot four "legs" or beams to approach the station from as many directions. The legs were like highways with four pie-shaped sectors dividing them. In two of the opposite sectors an "A" (dot dash) signal could be heard in the pilot's headphones and when flying in the adjacent pair an "N" (dash dot) could be heard. The meshing of the "A" and "N" signals created a continuous monotone, and formed each leg. A pilot had only to follow the designated leg on his chart and let down along it for a safe approach to the station. His safe altitude over the station was also specified and was called passing through "the cone of silence." Directly over the station the monotone would build rapidly in volume until it became a high whine, then silence would follow for a moment. The pilot would note the time and start his final descent for the nearby airfield as the monotone built rapidly on the other side of the cone. It would fade gradually as he descended, still using both sound and his directional gyro as shepards home.

The Adcock system was very new and there were only a few installations across the country. Pilots had much to learn about their idiosyncracies; sometimes they offered multiples along the beam-leg so it was difficult to be sure of position, sometimes the beam swung back and forth demanding radical changes in course to the station. In the rain and particularly when flying in snow they were often nearly obliterated by static.

" . . . I couldn't get on the damn beam," Babcock was saying, and Toby noted a new plaintive tone in his voice. "I had it, then I lost it. It was swinging all over the place."

"Then why did you start your descent? Your co-pilot says beam-reception was good right up until the time you hit the wires."

"The kid is crazy. He wouldn't know good reception if he heard it."

Toby thought about Plummer. He was certainly not crazy, in fact he was a kind of somber, noncommittal young man who had done a good job flying the mail and had only recently been promoted to the right seat in Fords. He wasn't the type, Toby decided, to wander from the facts. There was little doubt that in a few years he would be flying as captain.

Toby looked at the ceiling because he could no longer bear to see the increasing agony in his friend's eyes. How the hell was he going to tell him what he knew he must be told? Right now, he thought, he would trade this job for one sweeping the hangar. And maybe he would be better at it . . . "If the reception was so bad, Bruce, then why did you turn off course and keep right on letting down? That's what the Feds will be asking you and you'd better have some believable answers."

"I was trying to pick up the on-course signal. For Christ's sake, Toby, I've been flying for ten years and I've never put a scratch on an airplane. I knew what I was doing . . . or, thought I did . . ."

"Bruce, listen to me. I know you're upset and I can't blame you, but two people are dead and a lot of others are hurt. Plummer says he warned you that you were off-course and too low but you ignored him. He said he was hearing a broad "N" in his headphones and no oncourse signal at all."

"He must have been imagining things."

"You really want me to believe that?" Toby hoped for a full confession, then maybe they could find some way to rescue the situation. But if Babcock stuck to his excuses? The captain of any aircraft was solely responsible for anything that happened aboard, damnit. He was paid and respected for that charge and Toby believed every captain should live up to it. He swung around in his chair until he faced a large chart of the area on the wall. It showed the airfield at Wichita; the four legs of the range leading to it were superimposed in red. It also showed the power lines crossing one of the "N" signal sectors.

Toby ran his finger along the approximate course Babcock had flown. "Obviously you had to be somewhere in here and you knew damn well there are hills and power lines in the area. Just give me one good reason why you continued to let down when you couldn't see anything and maybe I can go to bat for you. Before you turned away from the beam and went exploring on your own the field was only four miles directly ahead of you."

Babcock lit a cigarette and hung his head. He inhaled deeply, blew a column of smoke at the floor. Toby noticed that his hand was trembling slightly and he hated to watch what was happening to one of the finest men he had ever known.

Babcock mumbled something about not being quite sure why he had turned away at such a critical time, then became silent.

"I'll tell you why you turned away and the Feds will think the same thing. You were looking for a hole instead of relying on your instruments and the navigational aids you had. And when there was no hole you stopped thinking. You kept on letting down because you *hoped* you'd break out below cloud and see something you recognized. Having a look-see, just like we all used to do. And what you were looking for wasn't there. But some power lines were. That kind of flying has been out for a long time, Bruce."

The silence between them was so heavy Toby thought he could almost hear it. Then somewhere outside the hangar he heard an aircraft engine and somehow it made him feel better.

Babcock leaned forward. His voice became increasingly urgent. "I'll level with you, Toby, because you're the only person in the world I can go to. I guess I've been under a lot of stress lately. Julie is worried about our finances. We never should have bought all that furniture, you've no idea how expensive four kids can be . . ." He paused while he sought Toby's eyes. "You'll back me up, won't you, Toby?"

Toby stood up. He might as well get it over with or get out of the job. There were at least fifty pilots who would be disgusted with him, because in their opinion he would have sold out one of them. It was simply not done, and he realized it would be a long time, if ever, before he would again be on the receiving end of their good will.

"No, Bruce, I will *not* back you up. I realize it's going to be hard for you and Julie, but not nearly as hard as it will be for the families of those two people who are no longer with us. I don't think you have any business flying passengers for a long time. I'll be lucky if I can keep you on flying the mail . . . ."

CHAPTER
16

It was the year Adolf Hitler came to power as Chancellor of Germany and saw to it that a fire destroyed the Reichstag. Soon afterward he appointed Hermann Goering and Erhard Milch to begin a mighty revival of German civil and military aviation. Almost simultaneously Franklin Roosevelt took up residence in the White House and said of the woeful economic situation which had spread across the world, "The only thing we have to fear is fear itself."

Roosevelt responded to the threat of national panic by declaring a bank holiday, and a month later issued a presidential order demanding that all private gold holdings be surrendered to Federal Reserve Banks in exchange for currency. He also began "fireside chats" to restore faith in the nation's economic future.

This was also the year that the revolutionary airliner, the Boeing 247, entered service on United and Western Airlines and the rugged Junkers 52 began to serve Lufthansa. The two-position variable pitch propeller was now reliable enough to find general use, and the DC-1, an experimental prototype aircraft, was built by the Douglas Company at the urging of Transcontinental Air Transport. Toby Bryant was involved in the original design concept and like all TAT pilots he looked forward to its first flight.

This was also the year the airship *Akron* was lost in the Atlantic, a tragedy that shook the faith of even the most devout disciples of lighter-than-air travel. It was also the year the National Air Races were held in Los Angeles, and it was Kiffin's friend Roscoe Turner from *Hell's Angels* days who won the Bendix Trophy, flying his Wedell-Williams Racer at slightly better than two hundred fourteen miles per hour and winning five thousand dollars. The aristocracy of air racing had gathered for the events— Jimmie Doolittle, Art Chester,

Gladys O'Donnell, Wiley Post, Gordon Israel, Ruth Nichols, Benny Howard, Ira Eaker, Frank Hawks and many others. The presence of so many people he knew and admired compelled Kiffin to attend, although he was concerned about the reaction they might have to a man who so obviously walked with an artificial leg. The last time they had seen him he was hale and whole; now he wanted to avoid even the slightest hint of pity.

Kiffin felt that his time with Toby and Lily had gone along pretty well, considering the cloud that had hung over their reunion. He'd done better than pay his way financially; had served as baby-sitter and companion to Flip. Most important, he'd managed to conceal his indestructable love for Lily. Time and again he'd reviled himself over his desire for her, but he'd never been even half successful in erasing her from his thoughts, or feelings. He loved her, as a man loves his wife. Maybe there was another one somewhere, but for him, here on earth, there was only one Lily.

As for Toby the Rock, he was always there. It was a lucky man, he thought, who could have that stone marshmallow for a friend. Finally there was Flip, who was so unlike any child he'd ever encountered he hardly knew what to make of him. Little kids were supposed to be a nuisance, not a pleasure.

It pleased him now to reflect on their recent times. Toby had been promoted again. The guy was going to be president of the world someday—but never mind. Kiffin Draper would survive as long as the family survived. Sharing the same room with a little kid had become one of the most rewarding times of his life. The haunting sense of having peered into his own image, that peculiar sensation he'd known when studying the photo in Canton . . . gone now . . . must have been part of his delirium . . . in the flesh, Flip was more like Toby . . . Still, though, there *had* been moments when the light would catch his towhead just right, or he would strike an odd pose . . . and that peculiar sense of harmony seemed to settle down on both of them and he thought how the hell can you explain something like that? . . . Sometimes, watching Flip had sort of given him the creeps . . . there had been moments when he could have sworn he knew what Flip was thinking even though he'd given no sign or hint that he was thinking about anything at all. The little stinker had about sixteen thousand words in his vocabulary, although only a few of

them were any recognized version of the English language
Was it his extraordinary mother, his father . . .? Father
Kiffin had asked himself about that too many times, and, o
course, had not found an answer . . . .

He found the atmosphere at the Races very stimulating
constantly meeting old buddies from his pre-China days who
at least seemed to ignore his cane and leg. He tried to smile
when he found himself speculating on how they might react i
they could view his damaged penis. Never again a thing o
beauty, for certain, he thought unhappily, and then quickly
reached for his sense of humor to rescue him. "But beauty i
in the eye of the beholder . . ."

By now he had developed a fairly reliable technique fo
combating depression. He would lose himself in the neares
handy project, in this case the exciting spectacle of progress
and individual ingenuity presented by the National Air Races
Here they were improving the whole spectrum of aviation by
running men and machines through the most grueling tests
Unknowns were becoming knowns every day the events wen
on, and there was a general feeling that all the participants
were joined in a grand scheme that was worth their sacrifice
in money and sometimes blood.

Here too were gathered the highest horse-power engines in
the world, the latest forms of superchargers, new methods to
retract landing gears and wing flaps. Here was the proving
ground for much that was new in aerodynamic design, a vas
laboratory where the active men and women of aviation were
gathered to set new records and to learn from each other.

During the four days of genial gatherings and endles
discussions that were a vital part of the air race scene, Kiffin
met the renowned Wiley Post, who had recently flown non
stop from New York to Berlin in his Lockheed "Winnie
Mae" at a phenomenal average speed of one hundred fifty
three miles per hour.

Kiffin's handicap and Post's lack of an eye created an
immediate sense of camaraderie between the two. Post was a
stocky man and jovial. He affected the usual aviator's thir
moustache, and the patch over his left eye enhanced the
intense alertness of the good one. He was fascinated by
Kiffin's flying in the French and Cantonese Air Services and
kept pressing him for details. In return he shared some of his
own past and aspirations . . . "You'll think I'm crazy," he

aid, "when I tell you that I intend to take *Winnie Mae* to irty thousand feet and maybe higher. That's where we'll all e flying someday in pressurized cabins. It'll be just like tting in your living room . . ."

As the race events unfolded, Kiffin and Wiley Post spent ore and more time together. When Kiffin confided that he adly wanted a job but was diffident about applying because f his leg, Post insisted he come to work for Lockheed. "I'll x it so you're part of my crew, Maybe you won't do much ying for a while but you can start working on pressure suits. s soon as we can make one I can trust we'll take that irplane of mine a lot higher than anybody's ever been . . ."

It was the beginning of a real friendship. The persuasive ost talked Lockheed officials into hiring Kiffin as a test pilot ather than as simply a crew member. Post knew that once he as on the flying roster something would come his way. So iffin was soon involved in the upgrading tests of the Lockheed '10," the final tests of the "12" and the experimental work n the "14." Like Post's eye patch his laborious limp became a symbol of his presence. Instead of mistrusting his bility as he'd feared, people, Kiffin found, seemed coninced that if he had overcome his handicap thus far then he ust be very good indeed. His reputation grew even faster fter a few newspaper and magazine stories had appeared bout him, and with the permission of his employers he egan a series of tests for other aircraft companies.

It was while Kiffin was flying for Northrup on an experiental dive bomber program that his notoriety combined with is powerful urge to prove that all of his body was whole xcept his leg led him into some difficulties. Now, as one of ie best-known and popular pilots on the Pacific coast, he vas sought out by numerous Hollywood personalities and pparently never disappointed them. The aviation set—Wallace Beery, Henry King, Bill Wellman, Clark Gable—was always pleased when he could join one of its parties, and the starlet ypes who were in such abundance considered him just about ie *most* exciting man they had ever met. And Kiffin Draper ould be counted on to stay absolutely sober no matter what ie temptation, and to be an interesting conversationalist at he more formal affairs. Such was his new popularity that he vas even obliged to buy a tuxedo rather than rent one for ach formal affair as he had for some time, and since Gable himself arranged the tailoring he cut a very fine figure indeed complete with his brass-headed cane . . . .

He was so decked out and in fine form of an evening whe attending a party given by Howard Hughes, who was ver partial to fliers as guests, and it was there that he met buxom young singer called Candy.

Perhaps it was the jasmine around the swimming pool, o the half moon overhead, or Candy's soft crooning in accompa niment to an orchestra playing inside the house—perhaps i was during one of Kiffin's frequent encounters with loneliness which occasionally caused him to become bitter. Whateve for lack of a better audience on this lush night he wa persuaded to pour out his sorrows to Candy, and she at leas listened sympathetically. Her comforting included her eage volunteering to drop by his apartment on her way home which in turn led to curiosity about his bedroom. There, fo the first time since his crash at Cleveland, Kiffin discovere that except for the loss of his leg his injuries were no longe so grievous after all. The abrupt revelation did wonders fo his spirit, and as the last of his fears of impotence left him h was easily convinced that Candy could do no wrong. Withi a week of their meeting at Howard Hughes', Kiffin propose marriage and after scarcely a few moments of meditatio Candy accepted.

It took hardly more of a passage of time before Kiffi began to question how his marriage had come about, espe cially since he knew that he had been sober at the time of hi proposal.

His bride's spectacular bedside talents had been his undoing but how very blind he had been to her other passions. Every thing about Candy, including her raging gangs of insecuritie were offered to the world at large, unless an explosion wa inconvenient at the moment, in which case she surrendered t the darkest resentments until a full venting was possible Kiffin discovered that she was almost uncontrollably jealou of everyone, male or female, who came near her husband She was a scene-maker of formidable temper and performance given to melodramatic speeches, gesturing and acrobatics tha sometimes left Kiffin astounded. It occurred to him that hi bride might even be capable of murder if provoked at th right moment; that is, he reassured himself with what was lef of his humor, if she could be pried out of bed long enough t accomplish the deed. Only the best of parties kept Candy erect beyond midnight, and her preference was for retirement by nine o'clock. She did almost everything in bed, rising only out of necessity. Kiffin would be gone to the Lockheed plant in Burbank by seven in the morning while Candy remained in a semi-coma until almost noon. She would then perform a few household tasks, talk to her agent, who never seemed to have a job for her, and return to her bed for reading, manicuring, letter writing, until overcome by need for a nap. When Kiffin returned in the evening she was ready for action, which usually included a detailed interrogation about his activities, hour by hour, during his absence. He soon learned not to mention the names of anyone he might have been with or seen, man or woman, because Candy would zero in with her relentless suspicion and not let the matter drop until she was proved to her satisfaction . . . if she ever really did . . . that the meeting had been innocent.

Once Kiffin made the mistake of asking his new wife if she had been in Africa, where she might have contracted sleeping sickness. The subsequent tirade taught him to restrain himself in the future . . .

It was in this uneasy atmosphere that Kiffin proposed a small dinner party for Toby and Lily, who had suddenly arrived in Los Angeles. The DC-1 was being put through a series of flight evaluation tests by D. W. Tomlinson and Eddie Allen, two of the best pilots in the business. Performance reports were exciting, and the aviation telegraph worked so fast everyone recognized that a whole new era in transport flight was about to begin. Now it was Toby's turn to fly the DC-1 and make his recommendations for features to be included in the next version. It would be known as the DC-2 and TAT had already placed an order for twenty-five of the aircraft.

Those who knew Candy best, including her husband, were more than willing to admit that her skill in the boudoir was matched only by her endeavors in the kitchen. She was a serious and versatile cook, even willing to postpone a tantrum if it threatened to interfere with the cuisine. Kiffin had already considered a wry scheme whereby he might create domestic happiness by allowing Candy out of bed only long enough to cook dinner.

As with most cooks, Candy liked long and full notice

before entertaining guests, which it so happened Kiffin was unable to offer before the arrival of Toby and Lily.

"Snacks and fast food," Candy declared in her clarion voice, "are not my real bag. But come in anyway." She more or less hurled her greeting at Toby and Lily, who entered upon the newlyweds exactly at seven o'clock.

Kiffin risked a difficult scene by warmly embracing Lily and Toby. Remarkably, Candy kept her peace. In fact, she turned on her not inconsiderable charm long enough to offer them a drink. "Kiffin won't keep any booze in the place so name your poison. We have furniture polish, insect repellent, or would you prefer Clorox in warm water?"

They all laughed politely, and soon after they sat down in the living room she excused herself to "whip up a bite. And I know y'all have got a lot to talk about during those good old days when y'all were together . . ."

When she had left, Lily said, "Candy is . . . really very nice. But why didn't you tell us you were married to a southern belle?"

"I didn't know I was. Candy was born and raised in Wisconsin."

"Where did that 'y'all' come from?"

"Her last acting role. She had two lines in a movie set on a Georgia plantation, and every once in a while she sort of goes back to the Civil War again."

A lengthy silence followed, during which Kiffin thought that his bride was an active participant in a civil war right here at 2705 Redondo Drive in the year 1933. And for a moment he forgot his pleasure in seeing Toby and Lily while he envisoned Wife Number One, Erin, and Wife Number Two, Candy, both charging the barricades in their respective fashions. Then he broke into a laugh and said that while Toby was uglier than ever, Lily was certainly a sight for sore eyes. And he thought, maybe imagined, that he heard a snort of displeasure from the kitchen . . .

They proceeded to discuss the health and welfare of Flip, and Kiffin was shown the latest photographs featuring him on a pony in the backyard of their new house in Kansas City. Kiffin said that it was obvious to him that Flip would one day become president of the world, and they had a long laugh at

Kiffin's admission that a rolling stone might at least gather wives if not moss.

It was at this juncture that Candy sailed into the room in an aura of freshly applied perfume and scorn to announce dinner was ready. Beneath her smile Kiffin detected a frown that he attributed to her possible overhearing his reference to what rolling stones did and didn't gather.

Candy waved her hand languidly at the well-set table. "Y'all just have to take potluck so just kind of take a place wherever you like."

Candy's well-practiced frown deepened as she watched Toby and Kiffin collide in their haste to hold Lily's chair while leaving Candy standing. When Kiffin apologized she sniffed ominously and said it was quite all right, she did not mind waiting at all, at *all* . . .

Still, the meal that followed was memorable for its simple perfection, and as their guests "oohed" and "ahhed" over the crispness of the vegetables and the exquisite spicing of the beef, Kiffin thought he saw the clouds of irritation clearing at the opposite side of the table.

It was inevitable then that the conversation would shift from the qualities of the table to aviation. Toby told how it had been Slim Lindbergh who had insisted that the Douglas company provide an airplane that could maintain flight after losing an engine on take-off, and the DC-1 had done so admirably. The DC-2 he added would perform even better and probably have greater speed and certainly more passenger comfort than its only rival, the Boeing 247.

It was difficult to include Candy in the conversation, and she was beginning to show her impatience through a series of strategically timed yawns. Her ennui escalated after the dessert when they talked about how Pan American had just bought China National Aircraft Corporation and the steady march of Juan Trippe's airline around the world. The subject led them into further speculation on the merits of Glenn Martin's huge new four-engined flying boats which were still in the developmental stages. His mother, Toby heard, was still the power behind the throne.

Lily alone laughed when they slipped into a nostalgic mood and recalled their bold ignorance during their first encounter with the young Martin and his mother. Eventually they began to argue the relative merits and faults of sea and land planes which led them naturally to Lowell Yerex in Central America, who had made a bid to acquire any tri-motored Fords TAT might want to sell. From there they shifted easily to Jimmy Angel's disappearance in South America and the marvelous waterfalls he had discovered deep in the jungle and how his loss was regretted by so many friends. Candy, becoming ever more restless, interrupted. "Jesus," she said, without a trace of accent, "don't you people ever talk about *anything* but flying?"

Toby shrugged. "Only once in a while, I'm afraid. It's a curse of the profession. I suppose the movie people are pretty much the same and I don't know if doctors ever get very far off the subject of who died of what."

"Or survived," Lily said quickly. Kiffin saw her smile at Candy, saw Candy return Lily's smile, but the signals were mixed. The acid in her voice denied her smile as she said, "Y'all are absolutely fascinating. And I sure appreciate the way you have of expecting other people to care why so and so crashed and got himself killed and your yak-yak down to the last bolt and rivet why it happened. But who gives a damn? I mean, they're dead. And *I* may just die of boredom."

Kiffin rushed into the breach. "Take it easy, love," he said as calmly as he could manage, "these are our guests and my old friends—"

"Friends?" Candy turned her head slowly from Toby to Lily, taking her time, looking them up and down as if she had never seen them before. "In Hollywood we don't go beating around the bush. We say what we feel. And I'm only asking what gives here?" She stabbed a glance straight at Kiffin.

"*Maybe*, mine husband, you can be friends with Toby here, but what's with this friend business with the fair Lily? Y'all got some special arrangement?"

Candy paused and watched her audience twist uncomfortably in their chairs. Her attention went directly back to Kiffin. "All I've ever heard since the night I met you is *Lily*. I should have known better. It was Lily this and Lily that and Lily, Lily, Lily. Now that I've met Saint Lily and since so far she hasn't passed any miracles, I wonder what she's got that I haven't . . . *and* I've come up with a suggestion for you, Buster. You better make up your mind who you're married to. Either I'm the number one lady in your life or you can take your fiddle and your peg leg and shove it."

Toby and Lily looked at the tablecloth, then started to get up as Kiffin said, "Candy, I think you owe our guests an apology—"

Candy was the first on her feet. She slammed down her coffee cup. "Apology? For *what?* You invite these . . . These *aviators* to come here without even asking me. What am I . . . the *maid?* I'm supposed to keep my mouth shut while you slaver all over Lily telling her what a sight she is for your poor sore eyes and a lot of other crap I haven't heard since the last Claudette Colbert film. And what is all this so called *family* stuff I'm hearing. You aren't really related . . . you aren't real relations at all . . . !"

While she was still raving Candy's audience began to make their exits. Toby took Lily firmly by the arm and escorted her to the front door. Kiffin, moving with remarkable speed considering his handicap, limped into the bedroom and returned almost at once carrying a large briefcase and his leather jacket. As Toby and Lily went out the door he called after them, "Hey, wait for me!"

He passed Candy without pausing or a backward glance.

"Where the hell do you think *you're* going?"

"West by east a quarter east," Kiffin said as he passed through the doorway.

"I'll find you," Candy yelled as he closed the door, gently. "I'll sue you for non-support. You bastard, I'll make you pay for the rest of you *life* . . ."

And suddenly she began to sob and plead at the closed door. "Don't leave me Kiffin, please . . ." And when that clearly would not work she placed two fingers in the corners of her mouth, folded the end of her tongue between them and emitted a shrill whistle. "Come back, you gimpy bastard . . ."

But Kiffin did not hear her, he was too busy trying to squeeze himself and his clumsy leg into the front seat of Toby's car. He put his arm around Lily, who sat between them, and mumbled that he was sorry, terribly sorry . . .

"You sure pick some lulus," Lily said.

"You forgot your violin," Toby said solemnly.

"It wouldn't fit in my escape kit," Kiffin said, patting his briefcase. "It's been packed and ready for a month."

"Where are you going to stay?" Lily asked.

"I think I'll try the bull ring in Tijuana. It'll be more peaceful there."

And so ended Kiffin Draper's second marriage. Following an urge to be closer to his work, he restarted his life in a small furnished apartment near the Burbank airport and the Lockheed factory. And for the next year and long after a lawyer advised him that he was no longer a married man, he had no difficulty whatsoever in resisting the various temptations that came the way of a handsome and gallant bachelor of thirty-eight.

CHAPTER 17

Disquieting rumors had been seeping out of Washington for weeks. The whole of the American aviation industry had taken to walking on tiptoe rather than affecting the bold stride that had become so characteristic of the profession. Roosevelt's new Postmaster General, James Farley, had discovered that the awarding of airmail contracts to the various airlines had some nasty aspects. Now in the autumn of 1933 he went back four years and found that the airline officials had held a series of secret meetings in which they agreed to control their bidding and allocate mail routes to their mutual benefit. A special committee had investigated the situation and once it was proved there had been a "spoils conference," Farley advised the President to cancel all airmail contracts.

The swift action by the President stunned the airline industry. Confidence in its economic future collapsed. The mails were a subsidy, and without a subsidy it was doubtful if most airlines could continue operations. The President seemed indifferent and called in Benjamin Foulis, an army general and one of the first of the military to fly. Toby Bryant and all his colleagues were dismayed when Foulis said the army could fly the mails and the President believed him. Winter was coming on, neither the combat-trained pilots nor the miscellaneous collection of aircraft they would be forced to fly were equipped for tough weather. Yet the airlines were ordered to make their last mail flights on the nineteenth of February, 1934.

All of the airlines began furloughing their employees. The hangars filled rapidly with unusable airplanes. Toby listened as patiently as he could to the concerns of his pilots, who were ill-equipped by training or inclination to make a living in other ways. Winding down an airline, he found, was even more difficult than winding one up. Now there was only gloom to dispense, and many of his pilots, he knew, lived from paycheck to paycheck. On the last authorized day Jack Frye of TAT and Eddie Rickenbacker of Eastern Airlines made a surprising and quixotic gesture they hoped would at least swing public opinion their way. They loaded the still experimental DC-1 with mail in Los Angeles and flew direct to Newark, the airport for the New York metropolitan complex. Landing three hours ahead of schedule, they set a transcontinental flight record of thirteen hours and four minutes, and more importantly reminded both government and the public of airline efficiency.

Also, as Toby feared, the brave attempt by the army to fly the mails brought almost instant tragedy. Three army pilots were killed during their training in blind flying. The winter weather was cruel, and in one month a total of ten pilots had lost their lives. Washington became increasingly nervous at the accusations aimed by the press, and Farley, a political animal of great experience, hurried for cover along with all the others who had approved of the cancellation, putting out a call for the nation's forty-five operators to meet with him and discuss returning the mails to the airlines.

But he included a catch in his invitation to make new bids on the various routes. No officer of the companies that had been charged with the conspiracy or the companies themselves were allowed to apply. The only alternative was the complete reorganization of the companies originally involved and the dismissal of many officers. Everyone presumably turned over a new leaf. Toby, grateful that his duties had never required him to be anywhere near corporate negotiations or policy, now found himself doing the same job with most of the same people but working for a company with a different name. What had been Transcontinental Air Transport had suddenly become TWA, and Toby had to smile as he threw a desk full of TAT stationery into his office wastebasket . . . "Well," he said to Lily that night, "at least I finally managed to get rid of a lot of damn paper work."

By late spring the airlines were back in the mail business. It was also during that deceptively benign season that Toby Bryant very nearly terminated his life span. The originating factor was Bruce Babcock, who after strong urging by Toby decided to tell the truth about his accident and face the consequences. His penalty was a year on the ground and he had only recently returned to flight status.

Scheffler, the young man responsible for scheduling flight crews, called Toby. "Babcock was supposed to take out the eastbound flight, but about an hour ago one of his daughters burned herself in the kitchen and he had to take her to the hospital. It doesn't look like he's going to show so what do you want us to do?"

"Call whoever's on reserve like you always do. And tell Bruce to stay with his daughter and not worry about flying."

"There's been a lash-up somewhere in shipping and the new tires maintenance needed for number six-eleven didn't arrive. The aircraft isn't legal to fly schedule without them . . . so . . . the reserve crew took the airplane to Akron to get the job done because the CAA is breathing down our backs and insists we go by the book and—"

"When will they get back?"

"Not until after midnight would be my guess."

"Who was supposed to fly the trip?"

"That guy you just hired . . . Van Ausdale? He's the co-pilot and he's been here for about an hour and so has the stewardess. We haven't announced any delay yet but the passengers are getting antsy."

"Okay, don't. I'll take the trip and I'll be there in twenty minutes. Meanwhile tell Van Ausdale to make up a flight plan and I'll meet him at the airplane. How's the weather to the east?"

"So-so. Ceilings on this side the Appalachians are down and there's none through the mountains but Newark is reporting two thousand and three. So your destination looks not too bad . . ."

Toby looked at Lily, who had been in a strangely wistful mood this evening. When he asked her about it a new sense of mischief appeared in her eyes and she suggested that since Flip was already asleep they might take a fast nap themselves. "Misty nights like this get to me," she smiled. "I become a total voluptuary. As if you didn't know." He took her in his arms and held her for a moment. "If there are raindrops on the window, I'm not responsible for my actions . . . All right, all right, I realize you have to go, but . . ."

They were very close, entwined in each other. He felt her moving against him. He bent down to kiss her upturned mouth and stayed there exploring until they were both breathing rapidly. She turned her face away, whispered, "You've got to go . . . you'll be late—"

He reached down, picked her up and held her in his arms like a child. "Toby! Don't be silly, you'll strain your back."

He kissed her, then started for the bedroom. "Toby . . . people are waiting for you—"

"Let 'em wait."

"I can't believe this. After eighteen years? Could it have been something we had for dinner?"

"Shut up." He closed his lips on hers and eased her down to the bed.

"Toby . . . this is going to make you very late. Don't blame me . . ."

They were murmuring now, their words almost unintelligible. "You talk too much, especially on misty nights," he told her.

They fumbled at each other, she kicked off her shoes. "Darling . . . this is crazy . . . we can wait until tomorrow night—"

"He who hesitates does not good fornicate."

"*Toby!* What's got into you? You don't even sound like yourself. This is crazy . . ." as she delightedly pulled him down onto her.

Later, still breathing hard, they lay back spent. "Wow, I think we just passed through a time warp," she said.

"Meaning what?"

"Only teen-agers do it with their clothes on, they're all so in such a hurry—"

"Don't knock it." He reluctantly got up and pulled on his pants. "If I remember correctly you weren't much beyond being jailbait our first time in Paris."

"I've often thought we might have made a good living posing for those French postcards."

"If I don't get to the field right quick we just may be doing that. Good-by." He bent down, kissed her just as enthusiastically as before. "By the way, I love you ten thousand times more than I did then."

As he started for the door she called after him, "Toby, what's come over you? You're turning into a poet!"

"I better hurry up and turn into a pilot. So long . . ."

"Okay then, lover, beat it, but for God's sake, hurry on back, you hear?"

Toby smiled at the gyrating windshield wipers. He smiled at the traffic light that delayed his progress. A glance at his watch told him that he was already half an hour later than he had said he would be, and the fact delighted him. He felt easy and content, enormously pleased with his momentary disregard of duty. It was about time, he thought, that the rock showed a few cracks. Kiffin was the one who knew how to live. The sonofabitch wouldn't think three seconds about delaying a flight or any other sort of obligation if he could enjoy himself . . . especially in making love . . .

And now, in spite of his easy mood, cross-grained to it, the old, haunting thought returned to gnaw at his piece of mind. What had happened between Kiffin and Lily all these years ago? Something had seemed to snap—at least their relationship had never quite been the same. Their behavior was still not natural when they were in the same room together—too formal and stiff, as if Lily held some deep resentment, and Kiffin was aware of it and even was afraid of her. Or was he imagining such things? When he'd been flying the mail the two of them had been left alone on many a night . . . Had Kiffin somehow—?

Toby quickly discarded the thought. It was unhealthy, sick, in fact. He would avoid any such dreary destructive brooding in the future, and as he made the resolution realized that he had made the same resolution more than a few times before . . .

He went straight to his office, picked up his flight kit bag containing his charts, flashlight, railroad ticket forms if passengers had to be put on a train, and his airmail pistol, still required by postal regulations. The bag also held his toilet kit, a fresh shirt, and shorts and socks against the possibility of an overnight stay at either end of the line. The regular-line pilots now wore uniforms, but since they had come along with passenger flights Toby had never bought one.

For sure, the flying business had become mighty fancy, he thought as he started for the operations office. All pilots wore TWA wings on their uniforms, with two stripes on the sleeve for captain and one and a half stripes for co-pilot. Among the other transformations had been the hiring of "hostesses," who supposedly made life aloft more comfortable for the passengers. It sometimes amused Toby to visualize what he would have thought during his days of flying Caudrons in France if he could have foreseen what his professional life was like now. Tonight, for example, his mission was far less urgent than any he had flown on the western front, and yet it was quite likely he would spend the night flying on instruments with his navigation supplied by a series of electronic sounds. And he would have a co-pilot to help him. No one would be frightened, no opponent was going to drop out of the sky with intent to kill, and behind him, tagging along as if part of another world, would be several well-dressed passengers. Each of them would be bound on a personal adventure or they would not have chosen to fly. They would share their experience in a common unspoken agreement, sleeping as they pleased or taking coffee and snacks from a young hostess trained to make their flight pleasant. Their mood would be a reflection of all travellers since earliest times—expectation, occasional anxiety, and the spice of experiencing new things . . . It was curious, he thought, how that very sense of contributing to the needs of strangers gave him so much personal satisfaction.

He smiled now when he recalled that the hiring of "hostesses" had not brought entirely idyllic results. They were all nice enough girls and were even required to be trained nurses, but some of the pilots' wives viewed their presence with anything but enthusiasm. They didn't like the idea that their husbands would be sharing the experiences of their work with a strange and attractive woman, and they found even less to approve of in the long, better-paying flights that necessitated the crew's staying overnight at the opposite end of the line. Since the girls had been hired Toby knew of two marriages that had capsized and there were, by rough count, some twenty broken hearts. "I stay the hell away from that department as much as I can," he told Lily. "How can I explain company policy to a jealous wife or girl friend?"

CHAPTER
18

The Ford squatted like a huge insect in the dank night. She was illuminated by three spotlights on the end of the covered walkway leading from the terminal to the airplane. Eleven passengers stood beneath the canvas awning, talking in subdued tones, instinctively responding to the unusual closeness and quiet of the night itself. Tonight the air at Kansas City was pungent with the odor of stockyards and laden with moisture. Although it was not actually raining, there was so much dripping and peckling of droplets off the long canopy over their heads most of the passengers thought that it was, and they supposed the delay in their departure was due to the rain. A few regarded the Ford dubiously, impressed with its bulk but not entirely convinced it would soon be transporting them through the night sky. Those who were nervous about the prospect of actually flying were especially jocular and somewhat louder of voice than their traveling companions. There were two passengers who were veterans of previous flights and so enjoyed a distinct sense of superiority over the others.

Toby strode across the ramp toward the Ford. It looked old to him, a gigantic piece of corrugated scrap iron silhouetted against the absolute blackness of the night. He was spoiled, he realized, after flying the new Douglas DC-1. In a few months now the Fords would be gone . . . they had really become obsolete when they were still being built. They would be taken down to Mexico or South America where their short-field capabilities would make them worth patching up. They would become ghosts then, like so many other types, to be scrapped for their aluminum and a handful of instruments and sometimes their engines if there was still any life in them. The Fords represented an era almost passed, he thought. By fall TWA would be flying airplanes that would be much

313

faster and more economical because time aloft was cost to an airline . . .

Toby greeted the two mechanics standing under the wing, paused long enough to ask a standard airman pass-word . . . "You think she'll fly?" And the mechanics responded with the standard, "We wouldn't count on it."

"Well, we'll have to at least give her a try."

Such were the niceties that would transfer responsibility.

Toby hoisted himself through the rear door and started the ascent up the slanting aisle to the cockpit. Van Ausdale, the co-pilot, was already in the right seat holding a small flashlight between his teeth while he made new entries in the Ford's metal-bound logbook. He was an energetic young man, his alert face topped with a head of dark curly hair. He had flown the mail only a short time before being transferred to the right-hand seat of Fords. Toby thought he had unusual potential. If he was a bit on the over-serious side and therefore likely to have undue respect for regulations, Toby figured in time he would find a better balance, and then with a few years of seasoning he should make a fine captain.

"What kind of time en route are we thinking about?" Toby was always careful to use "we" when co-pilots were involved, and they appreciated it. Regular line captains were inclined to use an imperial "I" in all flight discussions, a custom that very nearly denied the co-pilot's existence.

"We should do pretty well, sir," Van Ausdale said. "Six-and-a-half hours flight time to Pittsburgh if the winds are on our tail like they're supposed to be. That should put us in Pittsburgh after sunrise."

"I'm glad you're learning nothing is ever as it's supposed to be." Toby buckled on his seatbelt and thought Van Ausdale must be the only co-pilot in the world who would bother looking up the dawn in Pittsburgh. Extra point for Mr. Van Ausdale.

When they received a wave-off indicating all the passengers were aboard, the door secure and the control locks removed, Toby used only the center engine to start the Ford rolling, then with just the right amount of left and right engine he kept it in a straight line for the opposite end of the field. The Ford's brakes were used only when absolutely necessary, partly because they were applied by heaving on a long rod extending upward between the pilots. It was the co-pilot's job to haul back on the "Johnson bar" while the captain moved the rudder pedals according to which wheel he wanted braked. Holding the pedals even resulted in equal brake pressure on both main landing wheels.

Toby barely had the Ford rocking when he said, "Would you like to make this take-off?"

"Yes *sir*."

"You don't have to sir me. She's all yours."

Toby threw his hands up in the air while Van Ausdale grabbed at the three throttles. He yanked open his side window as if to see better, and the rattling sound of the valves in the right engine riffled into the cockpit.

Moments later the lights on the perimeter of the field fell away as they climbed into the night. When Toby switched off the landing lights there was only a void beyond the windows. Both Toby and Van Ausdale wore headphones, since now all TWA passenger-carrying aircraft were equipped with radios and two-way communication between plane and earth was possible if not always probable. The headphones were heavy and uncomfortable to wear for long periods, but they did subdue the sound of the Ford's three engines.

Now their headphones crackled and spat with the unwanted electrical energies of some distant thunderstorm. And occasionally because of low frequency "skip" they would hear an airplane calling the ground on the east coast. Whining softly through the admixture of signals was the beam of the Kansas City station, fading rapidly as the Ford continued eastward.

The Ford, heavy with fuel, climbed reluctantly. Minutes had passed and they were barely through one thousand feet. Below, through tears in the cloud cover, Toby could see an occasional cluster of lights, but soon they were gone and the Ford was removed entirely from any visible relation with the earth. Unseeing and unseen, they roared through the night, suspended in a noisy cocoon, their hands moving occasionally to readjust their headsets or wipe at the condensation on the windows at their sides. They were waiting until they had achieved five thousand feet, at which point Van Ausdale would level off.

Neither Toby nor Van Ausdale allowed himself to consider the consequences to their passengers if through some foolishness or stupid misjudgment the Ford failed to arrive safely at its various destinations. Eleven individuals, innocent of techniques, personalities, and meteorological events had placed their trust in thousands of metal parts all flying in what they assumed was some sort of well-disciplined order, and they *were* apprehensive now because the air was rough and there was nothing to see out the windows. Sylvia the stewardess did her best to offer a comforting smile along with cotton for their ears and coffee in paper cups, but she hadn't been flying for long and had her own qualms to manage. She was a tiny person with doe-like eyes and a large, expressive mouth and had left nursing for the more glamorous life of a stewardess. Tonight she was not so sure she had made a good decision.

There was barely enough light in the cockpit for Toby to watch the wrinkles of concentration along Van Ausdale's forehead surge and ebb away. It was chilly inside the cockpit, and yet Van Ausdale was beginning to perspire and Toby noticed he held the Ford's big wooden control wheel so tight his knuckles were turning the color of ivory. "Relax," he said. "I haven't seen anyone yet who was strong enough to squeeze juice out of a Ford's controls."

Van Ausdale tried to smile. He stared at the turn and bank instruments and the airspeed. Toby asked if he had done much instrument flying in Fords.

"No . . . not so you could notice it."

"Sit back and let the old girl have her head now and then. You'll wear yourself out."

"She's so heavy, I'm not used to—"

"Don't your captains ever give you any instrument time?"

"Only when they want to go in the back and take a leak. And we've always been flying straight and level then . . . not climbing."

Toby had no way to determine their exact speed over the ground, the airway lights invisible in the murk below, but he made a rough guess at their average speed when they passed over the cone of silence at St. Louis and matched it with the distance and their take-off time from Kansas City. He was reassured some by his calculations, which indicated they had about a fifteen-knot tail-wind, and hoped the free boost from the hand of the night would continue all the way to Pittsburgh.

Twenty minutes after refueling at St. Louis they were in the air again listening to the TWA radio operator in Indianapolis reporting the weather along their route, his voice sounding like a bullfrog croaking in a distant swamp. Toby thought he recognized the man's plaintive voice, as if he had too much to worry about, and became convinced it must be Schumann, a dour fellow who had once done some barnstorming and in the process sired nine children, all of whom he felt obligated to support in spite of their geographic scattering.

Toby picked up his microphone. "How's all the family?" he asked, and Schumann croaked that a son he had never seen had died in Alabama of some unknown disease. Before he could say more, a bombardment of static assailed Toby's headphones and minutes passed before he was heard from again.

"Is this Captain Toby?"

"The same."

"Welcome to Indianapolis when you get here. Why aren't you flying your desk?"

"They unchained me for a night."

Toby thought about Schumann. Somewhere in the darkness ahead sat a man so confounded by his personal problems they even effected his voice on the job.

How different from his own position at the moment . . . here aloft a man's discouragements left him almost from the instant he began an ascent. Here in a noisy little world of jiggling instruments, metal and leather, new problems came up, nearly all of them having to do with the immediate environment. Bruce Babcock may have claimed that his unstable finances had contributed to his awful mistake, but he was really reaching for a crutch. He simply could not admit that here in this element so foreign to man he had simply lost control of his thinking. Here, everything could be simplified. You took off, climbed to a certain altitude and proceeded in a more or less straight line to a destination. You arrived. And that was the end of it. Whatever went on in the personal lives of the crew or the passengers usually had nothing to do with it. The Department of Commerce had seen to it that even if one pilot collapsed of a heart attack another pilot was on hand to complete the arrival.

Real complexities began when a flight did not arrive, and the reasons for failure were beyond the control of any man. There was a saying that if an earthquake opened a six-foot crack in an airfield and an airplane fell into it, the official cause would be "pilot error." In the autumn a flock of migrating fowl could come through the windshield and incapacitate the pilots. Whether the pilots were beheaded or merely blinded and lived to hit the ground made little difference. Structural failure in a Ford had never happened, but no one could deny that it could happen. Likewise, failure of all three engines in flight was so nearly impossible it was not worth considering. Only one thing in the airline flying business was absolute. Whatever went wrong was the captain's child.

Yet there was still one possibility that might be attributed to chance, and the Civil Aeronautics Authority was already working to make the odds against it acceptable. It was a big sky, and there were very few airplanes moving through it. Toby well remembered that only a few years back no one had ever considered that in peace time two civil aircraft might collide. It was still a remote possibility, and now that transport airplanes were equipped with two-way radios they were supposed to report their position and altitude over specified points to their dispatch offices. That position was then telephoned to a regional control office where blocks of wood inscribed with the aircraft's identity were moved according to each report so that when several airplanes converged over the same destination during bad weather they could be laddered down in sequence for an approach.

The procedure was crude, Toby thought, but it worked— most of the time. He had been been surprised by the sudden appearance of another aircraft on several occasions, and on nights like this when there was nothing to be seen he found himself wondering just how big the sky might be.

He allowed Van Ausdale to make the instrument approach into Indianapolis and coached him in an even voice as he descended on the range leg that extended west of the airport. Listening carefully they could hear the monotone of the "on course" signal tinged with a slight "A."

"Hang right in there now . . . you're in the twilight zone," Toby said. As the volume of the signal began to increase rapidly Toby suggested Van Ausdale steer fifteen degrees to the left. He would pass through the "on course" and hear a faint "N" signal. Then back to the right again ten degrees once more through the "on course" to pick up the faintest of "A's" again, then splitting the difference and hanging fast to the "on course" until the lights of the airport appeared. The process was called "bracketing the beam" and was much like a blind man feeling his way down a staircase. Once he had established where the wall and the bannister were, he could descend the middle of the stairs.

They broke out of the cloud at two thousand feet, and there almost directly ahead was the revolving green-and-white beacon of the airport at Indianapolis. Van Ausdale was soaked with perspiration from his efforts, and when Toby told him to keep the controls and make the landing he said "I've never landed at night before," in a high and unnatural voice.

"Might as well start now. First, don't worry about it. Next, remember there are only three ways to land an airplane. The wrong way, the company way, and your captain's way. You have to decide which is the right way. Just remember that at night you're going to be ground-shy and like everyone else you'll want to level off too high. Let it sink on down until you're sure you're going straight through to China, then make your flare. Don't try to three-point it, just let it settle on the wheels and ease the tail down."

Toby watched as a whole new break-out of sweat droplets blossomed on Van Ausdale's forehead. "Easy . . . easy," he said as Van Ausdale worked ever harder at the controls. "If you start a wrestling match the Ford'll win every time. *You* fly it . . . don't let it fly you."

A faulty pump on the fuel tank at Indianapolis made them almost two hours late climbing back into the night, and Toby was again reminded how the Ford's short range worked against it economically. There were three fuel tanks, one in each wing holding a hundred gallons, and an auxiliary tank of fifty gallons mid-wing. The three Wasp engines burned approximately thirty gallons each per hour, which left the tanks nearly dry after only one-and-a-half hour's flying. In contrast, the new Douglas transports would carry two additional passengers and burning the same amount of fuel as the Ford have a range of six-and-a-half hours with a few drops left for mother. And gallon for gallon it would cover sixty miles more for every hour in the air. The Ford used up far too much energy just getting airborne and landing for refueling.

It was three A.M. now and Toby was more than a little disgruntled at the delays. He rubbed at the stubble of beard that was sprouting on his face and wished he was home in bed. He sat staring at the windshield just in front of his face, watching thousands of bubbling water rivulets propelled horizontally across his line of vision by the slip-stream. There were always a number of leaks along the windshield framing, and this airplane ran true to form—the largest and most persistent being directly over the captain's left pant leg.

It was the little things like leaks, when it was not actually raining outside, that could irritate a man on extended night flights. Long before dawn the same clock-like instruments, each offering different information, began to say the same thing until they threatened to become one. Gradually the cockpit became smaller; Van Ausdale, who was not a particularly large man, now seemed to be taking up more than his share of the available space. It was such ruminations, so perishable once the flight was over, that came along near the tag-end of the night.

Toby flipped on a landing light and confirmed his belief that it was not actually raining. The lights simply stabbed through cloud so heavy with moisture that when collected on a small area such as the windshield and compressed by the speed of the airplane it became water. And there you were with your own private shower . . .

Here at five thousand feet there was the leaking windshield to look at and then a window at your side. And outside the window, subject to inspection by flashlight from time to time, was a Wasp engine turning a metal propeller, acting on the surrounding atmosphere like a corkscrew and so pulling the airframe along with it. If it should stop and was joined by the other two engines in a function-refusal, the airplane would continue to fly for a very limited period of time, after which it would also come to a halt. The terrain below was approximately fifteen hundred feet above sea level—higher for the hilly regions just west of the Appalachians. If all three engines quit, the Ford could be kept in a steep glide for about three-and-a-half minutes before it collided with the planet earth again.

Faced with such an awkward situation Toby decided to attempt a very slow landing and hope for the best. It wasn't going to happen, of course, but here were the post-midnight sillies again, an affliction known to most pilots who flew long at night and managed to reject in various ways . . . some smoked far too much and felt worse than ever; others relieved themselves in brief snoozing; some talked about sex; and some simply sat waiting in silence.

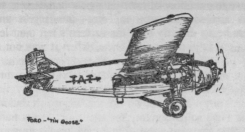

FORD - "TIN GOOSE"

It was easier on clear nights. Then there were the stars to observe above and the airway beacons flashing below. Now and then the distant loom of city lights or the outline of a small town established a reassuring connection . . .

To ease the slow passage of time Toby watched Van Ausdale, who had never been allowed to do so much of the flying himself. Obviously he was in his private heaven, his whole will directed toward giving a performance that would please his chief pilot. While they were waiting on the ground during the delay at Indianapolis, Toby had said to him casually, "If you don't secretly believe that you're the best pilot in the air then you ought to stay out of it."

Van Ausdale seemed pleased by this ancient homily, which had obviously inspired him to do his damndest. How young he was, Toby thought, remembering that when he was Van Ausdale's age some sixteen years ago (or was it more like seventeen?) he was trying to fly while someone was shooting at him . . .

After Van Ausdale had flown through the Columbus radio range cone of silence Toby relieved him at the controls, seeing that he was tired and his coordination was beginning to sour. "Why don't you take a fast snooze or go back and have a cup of coffee with Sylvia?"

"I'm fine, really."

"Beat it."

Van Ausdale rubbed at his eyes and rolled his shoulders to ease the long build-up of tension along the back of his neck, buttoned the collar of his shirt and pulled his tie into place. "I won't be long," he said as he went quickly through the door to the cabin. Toby noticed that just before he left the cockpit he slightly tilted his cap, gave himself a bit of a cocky air, which was the way of young co-pilots who hadn't flown very long. Charged now with new confidence after his long and successful time flying the big airplane solely on instruments and making a "greaser" landing, he would be inclined to bravado even though most of his audience must certainly be asleep. And he would take pains to let Sylvia know that it was he, not the captain, who had so far safely taken her through the night.

Alone, Toby settled down to the laborious business of flying the Ford in moderately turbulent air. Fords had a will of their own, he felt, and flying one was something like riding a more or less benevolent bull. Still, the rough air had been easing for the past half hour and he wasn't sure he trusted the change . . . rough air meant wind, and wind at least usually meant reasonably high ceilings below.

He found himself glancing down through his side window, looking for a break in the solid cloud. A single light in a barnyard at this point would be a welcome sight. He glanced at his watch. Four-twenty eastern time. According to his rough estimate of their position there should be a few breaks visible by now. The forecast had been for easy weather in the Pittsburgh area.

He couldn't account for his growing sense of uneasiness. This wind. What was it doing? He wanted at least some reference to the ground. It was impossible to guess wind speed or direction when the limit of visibility were the rocker boxes on the center engine, and at his side if he turned on a landing light the wing strut and the vaguely outlined profile of the left engine.

The forecast was for a tail wind, but was it? Too many times forecasts might as well have been based on the reading of tea leaves.

The radio range at Columbus was now lost in static. The beam leg pointing toward Pittsburgh had enabled him to set a trustworthy course, but until he could pick up the Pittsburgh range it was going to be dead-reckoning. He would be depending on the same navigational device the Chinese had invented thousands of years ago—the magnetic compass, which survived in the Fords and every other airplane. Of all the instruments, it was the one to be trusted.

He watched the compass swimming in its liquid, the numbered card unstable now in response to the turbulence, but it was not too difficult to average a steady and reasonably exact course. Below the magnetic compass was a directional gyro compass that gave a steady reading. But the gyro compass had no brains of its own. By turning a small knob it could be set to match the reading on the magnetic compass.

Toby was suddenly reminded of a dictum handed down by Keim, a veteran airmail pilot. Like so many of his breed he was fiercely independent, and when Toby had told him he would soon be flying passengers he took his ever-present five cent cigar from between his teeth, sighed the sigh of a man overloaded with the injustices of the world, and gave forth with: "Humph. Well, I guess if my ass gets there they will too . . ."

Now there was that flat rattling in his headphones again. It sounded almost like a human voice. So much for radios. They were no damn good when you needed them most. It would be nice to know the weather in Pittsburgh, but what he really needed was the welcome whine of the Pittsburgh range.

The sound came again, and now he was able to decipher several words. "Kansas City . . . alt . . . six thousand . . . okay . . ." The rest was gibberish.

"Skip" was at work again. The radio signals bounced off the ionosphere at an angle and happened to come down to bounce off the earth again in the same area he was flying. Like waves on the surface of the sea, the electronic impulses would continue to bounce back to the ionosphere and back to earth until finally somewhere in the world they would be too weak to identify. Toby remembered that when TWA had first started using radios the transmissions from one Ford had been picked up in Africa, and yet there were times when a station directly beneath the aircraft could not be heard. The alternate then was to relay the message through any station on the system that might be able to hear the pilot.

He watched the sweep second hand on the panel clock swing around the face. Nothing in the air, he reminded himself, was positive except the passage of time. Time was fuel. Time was money. Time was the interval between take-off and landing.

He took a brace in his seat and yawned. God, this was becoming one damn long night. Four twenty-one. Dawn should be along soon. The course was easterly into the sun, which should bring it up sooner . . . if there was still a sun, if there was anything but solid cloud in this aging airman's life—oh,

come the hell off it, Bryant . . . you're still under forty . . .
just . . .

He flexed his fingers on the control wheel. Van Ausdale?
He hadn't told him he could spend the rest of the flight back
there. By now Sylvia must be at the stage where she would
ask him if he was married. If he said yes he would find that
he suddenly ceased to exist. If he said no then all the coffee,
cakes, cookies and anything else on the airplane his little
heart desired would be his—

That rattling in his headphones again. It was different from
all the rest of the electronic pandemonium. Was someone
trying to call him?

Maybe there was something wrong with his headset? He
reached for Van Ausdale's and listened. The same.

He took up his microphone. Columbus was the nearest
station—maybe fifty miles behind. "Columbus? Have you
been calling Flight Six?"

No answer.

He tried again, the result was the same. "Indianapolis?
How do you read Flight Six?"

No response. He tried once more, then tried again after
switching to the day frequency. Nothing.

He had been told that dawn and twilight were the worst
times for low frequency radio transmissions. "Skip" was at
its worst then, but *someone* should be able to hear him.

He switched back to the day frequency and tried Newark.
Nothing except the static. Wait—he made out a better sound
buried so deep in the noise it was barely audible. He listened
carefully, heard the Morse letters "P" followed at once by
"T." If the sequence was repeated in thirty seconds he would
have the Pittsburgh range station and the rest of the flight
would be an easy slide home.

He watched the second hand on the panel clock move
through thirty seconds. Sure enough, there was the "P"-"T"
again, and he thought he detected the faint hum of an on-
course signal below everything else. Right on target. In less
than an hour they should be on the ground.

Strange, he thought, how quickly situations could change
in the air, and a large part of the change could be in the
pilot's mind. Now when he thought of his disappointment
with the two-way radio he realized it was a luxury he wouldn't
have missed a few years back, because, of course, it didn't

exist then. Sure, he'd been unsure of his position because the Columbus range had faded away and the wind aloft was unknown. In earlier times he would have known his position exactly . . . because on a night like this he would have been on the ground.

As he'd been watching and waiting the clouds had turned a soft gray. By turning the volume in his headphones far down until he could no longer hear the Pittsburgh range and then waiting until he could hear it come back and build in volume again he knew that at least he was headed in the right direction. As soon as the signal was stronger he would bracket the leg and nail a course down to the cone of silence. Full daylight by then. Pittsburgh visible below, smoke and all.

Van Ausdale came back to the cockpit, slipped into his seat and placed the headset over his ears without removing his cap. The bracket holding the phones pressed down the sides of the cap. It was a new cap and the top was still rigid. Van Ausdale would like to have it look like it had seen a lot of weathering, protecting the head of an old professional complete with spoked wrinkles fanning out from his eagle eyes. Don't worry, kid, Toby thought, it'll come soon enough . . .

"How's everything going, sir?"

Toby suppressed a smile. Van Ausdale was really asking how he'd managed without him.

"I thought I told you not to call me sir. And the way it's going is, no one seems to love us."

"I don't understand."

"I called everyone who might be interested in our progress but they don't want to talk. So I thought I'd turn the situation over to you."

"Me?"

"I don't see anyone else in this cockpit." Toby nodded at the windshield. "Comes the dawn. Okay, now tell me, where are we?"

Van Ausdale's face flushed. He reached for his chart. Toby caught his arm. "No. That won't do you much good, there's nothing to see. But you have other means at your service. *Think*, my friend . . ."

Van Ausdale's face brightened. He pressed the headset tightly against his ears. "I hear the Pittsburgh identifier . . . P-T. The first time is louder than the second."

"What does that mean?"

"We're in the 'N' quadrant. Obviously the southern 'N' quadrant and the bi-sector zone."

"How do you know it's in the southern quadrant?"

"Because the volume is building. If we had passed over the station and were in the north 'N' quadrant the signal would be fading."

"Go to the head of the class. By God, you'll make captain yet."

"Yes *sir*—"

"*Stop* that. You're driving me crazy."

After a chastened moment Van Ausdale said, "Looks like we'll be landing right about smack on our ETA."

Toby frowned. "Don't talk like that. It's bad luck. You're never sure when you're going to land until the wheels touch the ground."

Toby winced at his clichéd philosophy, but what the hell, it was true and he figured he could afford to indulge himself a little. The sky was brightening and there were breaks in the upper clouds; good signs that the weatherman's tea leaves for a change had not led him astray.

Suddenly they broke out of the clouds into breath-taking splendor. The sun was a vermillion orb floating in a jade sky extending to infinity. In every direction below was a flat deck of cloud that solidly filled all the valleys. Here and there like rocks in a vast sea, mounds and peaks of the terrain protruded above the cloud deck. "Beautiful," Van Ausdale said quietly.

Toby rose slightly in his seat to survey better all that could be seen below, and the longer he looked the more his lips tightened. He grunted unhappily and blinked at the sun. True, the air was glass smooth. Nothing was moving except a six-and-a-half-ton tin airplane with twenty-seven cylinders hammering away at five thousand feet. But its current master was busy looking for a nest that was presently invisible—and if he guessed right, would remain so for some time . . . how much time depended on the separation of the local dew point and temperature, the further the better. And wind? Where the hell was the wind to drive this stuff away? He reached for his microphone. "Pittsburgh, do you read Flight Six?" '

The static was all gone now; the operator's voice came through with only slight distortion. "Loud and clear, Six. We've been trying to call you. So has Columbus. We both tried every ten minutes for the last two hours . . ."

Goddamn radios. They lured you into trusting them and then left you hanging.

"What's your present position, Six?"

"About forty miles southwest of Pittsburgh."

"We're zero-zero here. Forecast to clear about noon."

Noon? The Ford would use the last of its fuel long before that. The tea leaves were running the show. "Well, why the hell didn't you or somebody advise? We'll go back to Columbus."

"They're down too. Ceiling one hundred, half mile visibility."

"All right. What have you got that's any good?" Toby tried, unsuccessfully, to keep the annoyance from his voice. There was a nasty smell to this, but it wasn't, after all, the Pittsburgh operator's fault.

"Newark is good. Two thousand five . . ."

Interesting, except that the Ford could never make Newark with the fuel still on board. Toby pulled back on the throttles and let the Ford's speed diminish to only seventy miles an hour. Less power, less fuel burned—a little late for conservation, but at least he had a sense of doing something.

The sun was now golden and blazing straight into their eyes. A lovely day. A beast in disguise.

Pittsburgh was calling. "We checked everywhere and haven't had much luck. Harrisburg and Scranton are the same as we are. Johnstown also the same. Can you make Elmira? They're in the clear."

Elmira? It was beyond Pittsburgh.

Toby took his pencil from his shirt pocket and did some quick calculations. He pulled the chart off Van Ausdale's lap and measured the distance between where he thought they were and Elmira. It had to be in excess of two hundred miles. Hopeless. Columbus, behind them, was actually closer.

He glanced at Van Ausdale's face, found it impassive. The kid was totally absorbed in the mechanical chore of flying the Ford. The possibility that the impossible might happen on this very morning, the very odd chance that all three engines could die of starvation had not yet impressed him. And when it did it would not be his baby.

This was the sort of thing, Toby thought, that got the adrenalin going. It had been a long time since he'd known the super-charged sensation, that incongruous combination of fear and invitation that somehow forced a man to exceed himself . . .

The Ford droned on toward Pittsburgh, a lonely speck moving through an enormous panorama of brilliant sky.

"We have a problem," Toby said more to himself than to Van Ausdale, then remembered that in this case the "we" was inaccurate. *I* have a problem . . .

He had three choices. He could hover over Pittsburgh hoping the ceiling would rise with the sun and then try to land down through it. With barely an hour of fuel remaining? The cloud deck below was thick and matted. Little rumples extended all the way to the horizon and there was no sign of the slightest break. From this altitude it appeared to be at least a thousand feet thick, there was no way the sun could warm it enough to dissipate it before noon. Strike Pittsburgh.

If he turned around immediately he could probably make it back to Columbus. On paper. But it would be a very narrow squeak and there was something he knew that the ground didn't. Some kind of a front must lie between here and Columbus. The turbulence earlier meant wind could be on the nose returning, and if it slowed the Ford even ten minutes . . . Maybe the Columbus ceiling would come up some during the intervening time . . . but enough? Three engines quitting while trying to make an instrument approach was an ugly prospect.

The third choice was based on a lot of ignorance and some hopeful reasoning—

"I think I see the smoke of Pittsburgh up ahead," Van Ausdale said. He pointed to the horizon, and Toby saw two columns of black emerging from the lower cloud and twisting toward the sun. "Turn twenty degrees left," he said.

"What are you going to do, sir?"

This time Toby ignored the sir. If he got out of this mess it might even be deserved. "We're going to the only game in town." Toby took up his microphone. "We're diverting to the Elmira area," he said. "Give me any reports you have on weather in that vicinity."

Pittsburgh came back after a long pause. "Sorry, we don't have anything except the Elmira report I gave you. I thought you couldn't make Elmira. Are you declaring an emergency?"

"Not yet. But stand by."

Now, after Van Ausdale had turned, the sun slid around

until it stood more to their right. Toby was rubbing his weary eyes when the cabin door opened and Sylvia appeared. "Good morning," she said brightly. "What time shall I tell the passengers we'll be in Pittsburgh?"

"Some time this year."

"Come on, captain, I have to give them an answer."

"That is in answer. Tell them we're not going to land at Pittsburgh. We're diverting to Elmira."

"Elmira, New York? I've never been there."

"Neither have I. Now would you please bring me a cup of coffee?"

"Sure thing." Toby was relieved when she was gone. Right now he didn't need any distractions.

He reviewed his reasoning. Elmira was beyond the range of the Ford, but the weather there was good. Like a long ago day when he had flown over it. Rolling hills around Elmira. Deep valleys. Lakes to the north, but not any he could remember to the south. And if the weather at Elmira was good, then there were fair odds that the weather in the general area should be similar. It was a beggar's choice. They would run out of fuel some fifty miles shy of Elmira, but maybe, just maybe, there would be a clear spot somewhere. It wouldn't take much, even a handy corn field would do, and anything was better than trying to make a blind landing.

And suddenly he thought of Babcock. He'd also been forced to make a choice, and had decided on the wrong one. And he, Toby Bryant, had sat in his comfortable office and passed judgment on the man. He could hear his own voice, ". . . you were looking for a hole . . . and when there was no hole you stopped thinking . . . you *hoped* you'd see something you recognized . . ." and then, Toby Bryant, great sage, had said, ". . . that kind of flying has been out for a long time . . ."

And what kind of flying was this? Back to barnstorming days, looking for a hole, looking for a nice corn patch to present itself on cue. The Pittsburgh radio range was now far off to the east and he could hear only a broad and lonely sounding "A."

Face it. Babcock had to believe he knew what he was doing. You don't really know if you're heading straight for Elmira. It has no radio range yet, so you're just sailing off across the land—hoping.

Thirty minutes' fuel left, maybe thirty-five. Don't wait for the engines to quit. It's a hell of a lot easier to land in a small field using a little power to slow the touch-down speed than to land with no power at all.

He looked at Van Ausdale. Still trusting, apparently. Would he feel the same if he knew the man who had condemned Bruce Babcock was taking an even longer gamble?

They could feel a little heat from the sun now. The white overcast below stunned their eyes. The sky above had become a proper blue, the long shadows of the hills projecting from the low cloud were gone. Toby had lost track of how many times he'd reckoned their remaining time in the air. The answer was always the same. He could control his thoughts, but not his body. He badly wanted to go back to the restroom, but he knew that as soon as he appeared in the cabin one of the passengers was sure to grab at his sleeve and ask questions he couldn't give straight answers to. If he lied they would see it, and if he told the truth they might panic.

He leaned across to Van Ausdale. "Listen to me. We're going to start a slow descent in five minutes. I want you to go back in the cabin and talk to the passengers. Try not to worry them. Help Sylvia give each one a blanket. If I don't happen to make the world's best landing it will at least give them a little protection."

"Aren't we landing at Elmira?"

"I wish. Go on."

Van Ausdale took a final glance out the window, and Toby saw that some of the cockiness had gone out of him. "It'll be all right," Toby said with more assurance than he felt. "We'll find a hole somewhere."

With Van Ausdale gone, Toby found the melancholy face of Bruce Babcock mocking him from every sector of the cloud deck below. The beauty of the morning was deceptive—at least Babcock had a snowstorm and bad visibility to give him a better sense of reality. Now Toby could see from horizon to horizon, perhaps five hundred square miles. There were swollen humps like the back-sides of sleeping giants scattered over a broad area, and Toby figured the projections concealed the rolling hills of northern Pennsylvania. He wasn't sure, though. Nothing was for sure this morning, except that very soon they would cease flying.

His eyes burned from the impact of the sunlight on the

white coverlet below. He couldn't make out a single dark gash or even a slit to reveal the terrain.

Five minutes more at this altitude and then the descent had to begin. Ten to fifteen minutes of fuel remaining? Or even less?

Things had snowballed. A wrong decision during an early part of a flight could accrete other mistakes. Things could begin simply, then become unbelievably complex. If he hadn't been so damn sure of himself . . . Would he have passed right over Columbus where the weather was admittedly not very good but at least there was some ceiling? He could have made a tight approach—any attempt to land with a hundred feet and half a mile was bound to be sticky, but if he'd sat right in the middle of the beam and had had Van Ausdale keep a sharp eye out for the revolving light on the field he probably could have made it . . .

Four minutes.

He'd made a mistake carrying on toward Pittsburgh without a current weather report—even though the forecast when he'd left Kansas City was for decent weather. He should have turned back to a known situation when he was out of communication and not have continued the flight on a vague hope. He'd grounded Babcock for a helluva lot less . . .

Three minutes and thirty seconds. The instant he left this altitude his view would be considerably reduced. The higher he could remain the more area he could survey for even a sliver of darkness against the white. As a last resort, even a dark smudge might be worth an attempt to land. There was nothing.

Two minutes.

He was sweating, the heat coming from inside although it was not over him, not the cockpit. He found his hand straying toward the throttles, anticipating the moment when he'd have to pull them back and let the Ford's nose drop below the horizon. Van Ausdale had better come back soon.

He rehearsed what he had to do. Don't be tempted to hold altitude until the engines starve and quit. Set throttles at about half power. Pull nose up and feel out stall. Hold steady a little above that speed all the way down. With this light load and some power still available it wasn't beyond reason to hope for a landing speed of fifty miles an hour. All right, maybe a little less . . .

One minute and thirty seconds. Line up between two humps that might indicate a valley and flat terrain. Keep the sun behind the tail. Pray for a little separation between the bottom of the cloud and the ground . . . at least enough to avoid slamming into a barn or anything solid.

The rest was up to God.

Van Ausdale returned, breathing more quickly. "I did like you said." He fastened his seat belt and hauled it tight. "There ought to be belts for the passengers—"

"There will be in the DC-2s . . . How are they taking it?"

"Okay. One guy was pretty unhappy, but Sylvia is sitting beside him and holding his hand. Nobody's saying much of anything. I guess they're thinking."

Thirty seconds. Toby had already chosen a depression in the cloud ocean that was off to his left. He thought briefly of his previous night with Lily. Was that really only last night? Was this really the next morning?

He reached for the throttles, eased them back but held the Ford's nose as high as he dared above the horizon. The air-speed indicator slipped from seventy to sixty, held there. The rate-of-climb needle said the Ford was descending at three hundred feet a minute. Few Fords, Toby was willing to bet, had ever been flown with such a light load, for which he was grateful . . . a light load slowed both their descent and stall speed.

He held sixty as they left four thousand feet, then eased back further on the throttles until the speed went to fifty-five. He felt a slight, unnatural quiver in the controls, and decided fifty-five was 'as slow as he dared go.

As they passed through three thousand feet he guessed it would be another thousand before they would be dipping into cloud. But how thick? The terrain here was variable, but he supposed the valleys would be two thousand above sea level. At most.

Suddenly he realized that this was not the first time he'd tried such a descent. Michaud. Little Michaud in the Caudron—a boy dying like a man. A long time ago.

Remembering Michaud gave him some new confidence. Goddamnit, if he could walk away from that landing in a forgotten stone quarry he ought to be able to walk away from this one, and according to the gospel of Kiem so would his passengers . . . "Call Pittsburgh, tell them we're going down.

Somewhere southwest of Elmira. About fifty miles tell them. Say that all's well . . . so far.''

Out of the corner of his eye he saw that the new tone in his voice had encouraged Van Ausdale. Someday he'd have to tell him about landing with Michaud when he'd known so little . . . someday—

Calling Pittsburgh would only keep Van Ausdale busy. There was nothing they could do with such a vague description of their trouble and location except worry. And this was hardly the time for an essay on pilot error. This time the verdict of pilot error would be correct—with some auxiliary help from the fickleness of modern radios.

Van Ausdale was still calling Pittsburgh when they were swallowed by the cloud. The rankling brilliance of the sun held for seconds, then dissolved rapidly as they descended into a clammy morass.

Toby allowed himself a quick glance down from his side window. Getting black fast in the depths. Mother Earth was very near. Ahead nothing.

"When we hit get on that Johnson bar and pull your arms out."

Van Ausdale braced himself. If he was afraid he wasn't showing it.

Never had a Ford's engines purred so smoothly. Never had the ground been so long in coming up. Michaud, if you're listening, pass a miracle and help us get away with a blind landing. The Ford was slow and strong. If they were lucky enough to touch the wheels in a clear area there was a chance. Like ten thousand to one, Corporal Michaud . . . 'Sing out when you see the ground."

"Yessir . . . I think—"

Toby held a steady fifty-five with the nose high. He wasn't going to change now. The big Ford wheels would hit first and he had to be ready for a bounce. If they nosed over, the center engine would come back in their laps and that would be that—

"*Sir* . . . wires and poles ahead . . ."

Topy looked up just in time to see a line of poles stretching across their flight path. Beyond, a clear field black with spring plowing. Furrows going the right way . . . almost. Slightly diagonal to course.

The wires barely visible.

Toby heard and felt a heavy thunking sound as the airplane tore through the wires. The Ford slewed off, he kicked hard right rudder to line up with the furrows. He pulled off the power and hauled the control wheel back against his stomach.

In spite of his efforts the ungainly Ford plunged nose-down into the field, bounced heavily and fell again, tail high, with the main wheels chewing along a furrow.

Lily opened her eyes just long enough to see daylight out the bedroom window. She was curled up like a rag doll, with a pillow between her legs as she always liked to sleep when Toby was away. She drifted in and out of consciousness, awaking long enough to revive delicious memories of the preceding night, then losing the image . . .

She buried her face in Toby's pillow and began choosing from various alternatives what she would make of her day. This cozy moment was always difficult to cut off, and at such moments she liked to consider staying right where she was until, say, an earthquake came along.

She heard the soft sound of Flip crossing the hall in his bare feet, and in a moment he had crawled in bed beside her. "Good morning, Mr. Bryant," she said. "What are your plans for today?"

Flip said he was going to build a balloon like the one he had seen in his new picture book and she agreed it was a good idea. They were discussing the backyard as a possible launch site when she heard the front doorbell ringing. At this hour? She glanced at the clock. Seven-fifteen. Who in the world was dropping by at this time of the day? A social call from the garbage man? The milkman? If it was one of Flip's friends she would send him packing.

She slipped into her bathrobe, told Flip to stay where he was and went to the front door. She opened it to see Bruce Babcock standing on the porch. He was wearing his old sweater (did he ever wear anything else out of uniform?). There was a strange expression in his eyes. She was saying that she was very surprised to see him when a sense of fright shot through her body. How well she knew that when anything "unpleasant" happened on an airline the news was never transmitted by telephone. An unwritten custom said that it should be a chief pilot like Toby or a close friend of the family who personally brought condolences . . .

" . . . Morning, Lily . . . uh, you know I wouldn't call on ou at this hour if it wasn't important—''

She shook her head. *No!* Bruce's coming here on this unny morning must be because of something else . . . some her reason . . . his daughter was in the hospital, *he* needed elp . . . *something* . . .

"Toby's flight's been missing for about two hours—''

"Oh God . . .''

"Hold on . . . that doesn't necessarily mean anything bad, t I thought I'd come over—''

"Sure, sure, Bruce. Come inside.'' It didn't mean anything? st the whole world gone. What was left was a dead rock.

Babcock followed her through the door, stood uncomfort- ly in the living room while she went to see that Flip was ccupied for the moment. When she came back he was still anding in the same place, thumbing through a copy of *ational Geographic.* She asked him to sit down, he shook s head. "I worry less if I'm standing . . . You ever been to ellowstone Park?''

"No.''

"It's a great place, you and Toby—'' he hesitated, closed e magazine and rubbed at his brush of hair. "Actually I'm ot much worried at all . . . weather's good back east and as ng as Toby's in charge I'm not really worried at all—''

"You're repeating yourself, Bruce. Please tell me all you now.''

"Not too much. When last heard from Toby was talking to ittsburgh. He said he was diverting up toward Elmira but he ever arrived there. The guys in operations figured he would ave been out of fuel about five our time. I'll phone them in a w minutes and see if they've heard anything more. Of ourse you can't trust these new radios—''

"How's your daughter, Bruce? I was going to call Julie is morning and tell her how sorry I was.'' Mother of God, ow could she be thinking about the Babcocks' daughter and er mother's feelings when her own world was threatening to ll apart?

"It really doesn't mean a thing . . . I mean, just not having eard from a flight . . . if anyone could get that Ford down in ne piece it would be Toby . . .''

Lily wondered why she was so much on the defensive, lmost resentful of Bruce's presence when she asked, "Are

you trying to convince yourself or me? It seems to me tha
after a couple of hours have passed and no one has hea
anything it's very damn serious—''

The telephone rang. Babcock started for it. "Maybe I'
better take that," he said.

"No thank you."

Lily took a deep breath, picked up the phone. All righ
She was ready. She said hello . . . and almost at once hea
Toby's voice saying he hoped he wasn't waking her up but h
thought he should before someone else did with some wil
stories . . . "I made sort of an unscheduled landing and I'
okay and so is everyone else—"

"Thank God . . . where are you, when are you comin
home?"

"As soon as I've gotten cleaned up. It's been a four-mil
walk through the mud to this telephone."

"You're sure you're not hurt?"

"I'm sure. A little on the beat side, is all. It's been a lon
night . . . started out just fine with you and ended not so fine
I did a dumb thing. Now I know how Bruce felt."

"He's right here. I'm sure he wants to hear what happened.'

She only half heard him when Toby said, "Just tell Bruc
Toby Bryant's pride has been so badly shook up it may no
survive. He'll understand. Now I've got to go, bunch o
unhappy passengers waiting to tell everyone they know they'r
going to be late arriving. Love you."

She heard a click and he was gone. She smiled thinly a
Babcock and ushering him gently to the door said she hope
he wouldn't mind if she excused herself.

Babcock said, "I hope I didn't upset you, Lily. I guess
did but I thought—"

"No, it's all right, thank you, Bruce . . . good night . .
oh, it's morning . . . well, good-by, you meant well," an
she shut the door, resisting the impulse to slam it.

Feeling dizzy, Lily ran to the bathroom. She stood for
moment, swaying uncertainly, and then she retched violently

When she had finished, pulled herself together, she went t
the bedroom, and gathering Flip to her side, lay face dow
and gave in to the tears of fear, and relief.

CHAPTER
19

Kiffin was not quite sure why he had such a desire to postpone the moment of reunion, yet he was reluctant to appear at the door of the Bryant house until he had a chance to readjust his own perspective. Some surprises were not always pleasant.

Too much had happened to the world and to him since their last meeting. Most people lived a reasonably predictable life, or at least thought they did, and tended to resent abrupt change. It was always difficult to reenter the past . . . in spite of themselves people never stayed the same. Rip Van Winkle was lucky; when he came back no one was around he could recognize. That old saw about good old Charlie being "just the same" was hogwash unless they'd been hermetically sealed in a locked container. Time made people different.

How different depended, of course, on what they'd done, or had been done to them. Last year, friend Amelia had made her solo flight from California to Honolulu. A first solo for anyone, let alone a woman. Was Amelia the same person she was before that? Of course not. No matter how subtle the effect or how modestly she carried it, she was different . . .

Toby and Lily had been together a long time now . . . eighteen years? They had changed together because they had stayed together. Apparently the transition had been easy. Or had it been?

How about yourself? The old rolling stone was sitting out here in a rented car, parked far enough down the street not to be noticed, close enough to see Flip playing with a wagon in the driveway that slanted down to the street. He was a pleasure to watch. He would haul the wagon up to the top of the driveway, climb aboard, give it a shove with his feet and zoom down the incline making a sound that to him represented a racing car at full throttle. Every time he lugged the wagon to the top of the drive and launched himself again he seemed to go faster. No quit in him, like his mother. Big for his age, like his . . . father?

Flip would be eight now, or was it nine? This was the tag end of 1936, and right there hiking up the driveway and dragging a little green wagon behind him was a human being who must be changing every day—just as his mother would be changed from the last meeting, as Toby would be. Which was all a damn good reason for easing back into the atmosphere instead of reentering with a terminal velocity dive. Surprises, maybe all right. Shocks . . .?

He glanced at his watch. Six o'clock, and Toby hadn't shown up yet? Come on home, Toby. Flip and your wife and Rip van Draper are waiting for you.

It would be ironic, he thought, if this was the day Toby decided not to come home until after dark, which it would soon be, or had he taken one of his fancy new DC-3s on a flight far from Kansas City. Reentry into the family would not be complete without Toby, especially now with the drastic change about to happen. After the disaster at Cleveland, after China, after testing for Lockheed and others, after Erin and Candy could anyone imagine that a few years later a peg-legged pilot would wind up . . . in Spain?

Sitting here was like watching a movie from a seat in the last row of the theater. At the moment the only actor was Flip, who would never behave so naturally if he knew he was being watched. Hey, kid, take it easy before you roll that wagon and bust your ass. Watch the car coming, for God's sake.

Never mind, it's slowing . . . and it's Toby.

Kiffin thought that it might be easier on him if he closed his eyes during the next few minutes, because he was fairly sure he knew what would happen. Incident would follow incident—and there it was happening just as he'd supposed. Toby drove up the driveway, stopped the car in the garage and got out. He was carrying a briefcase, poor hard working bastard . . . And there was Flip running to him and yelling something about his wagon he'd left at the bottom of the incline. The hug would follow—and there it was. Daddy's home from the office in the best middle-class all-American fashion. And where is the fair Lily? Come on, Lily, your cue was the sound of the car climbing the incline and the rattle of the garage-door when Toby closed it. You're late, Lily, or don't you bother to greet the breadwinner when he arrives home? *That* much change?

Whoops . . . there she is, full to her unforgettable eyes with that million-dollar smile. Now the everyday embrace. A trifle on the casual side? Change? Are they taking each other for granted now?

He watched them go into the house and wondered if he was one of those masochists he'd read about. Was observing Toby and Lily together, a not so subtle self-torture? Why should he play peeping Tom on a family that no doubt would go on for generations if Flip survived to beget descendents. None of his eerie loneliness for them; they weren't spectators sitting like hawks on a telephone pole watching three wonderful people going about their lives, changing their lives without the nagging feeling that something was basically wrong with the *way* things were changing. They were secure. If something happened to her husband, Lily would be fixed for life because Howard Hughes and TWA and the Airline Pilots Association said so. Their lives were bound up in a neat package with everyone working on the same team until the day they rode off into the sunset. Solid, predictable friends came over on Saturday nights for cards or a potluck feast with all assembled groaning about how they had eaten too much . . . The women, of course, in the kitchen, the men in the living room until they actually started chewing . . .

Now what the hell happened along the line to deny all this to Kiffin Draper, who presently sat on the outside looking in? Was there some kind of natural law that said no admittance—reserved for solid folk? Look what happened when you did try to join the crowd. Both Erin and Candy knew how to smash all the four freedoms in a single stroke. Stay ready to roll, old stone. Be sure all you own fits in one rucksack. Leave the moss gathering to others, you taste the sauce of change . . .

He started the car and drove the several hundred feet to the front of the house. He wished he could send an advance messenger to tell them that Uncle Kiffin hadn't changed so much, although some of the quirks they'd found annoying in the past were under better control . . . It occurred to him that men who were obliged to carry a cane were also partial to rucksacks. It left the hands free.

He strode toward the house, managing even a hint of swagger to his pace. It took years to develop the kind of calluses on a stump that could allow a man to stride out like this. The cane was an affectation and not really needed except when his good leg became unbearably tired or he had been standing a long time. They wouldn't care in Spain. They wanted fliers, whole or on the half shell, as long as they had experience.

Lily responded to his polite knock on the door. She gasped at the sight of him and said his name.

He smiled. "You know what they say about bad pennies?"

"What in God's name are you doing in Kansas City?"

"I must be lost. I thought this was Spain." He extended his arms and saw her hesitate.

Toby came now and pulled the rucksack off his shoulder and embraced him, and Flip came running and grabbed his good leg. They all laughed heartily, their voices rose in excitement as they exclaimed in chorus how very fine each of them looked and how they hadn't aged a day except for Flip who asked where Kiffin had left his violin.

They moved into the house still chattering, Lily saying Kiffin's timing was just about perfect . . . all she had to do was put an extra plate on the table and there was still more than enough stew for their dinner. Flip wanted to sit next to "Uncle Kiffin," and his small moist hand led Kiffin to the table.

As he lowered himself into a chair, Kiffin reminded Flip that they'd sort of grown up together. Flip smiled at that, like he understood.

The stew was outstanding, and they washed it down with a bottle of Tokay that Lily's father had sent from his new post at the embassy in Vienna. They toasted each other repeatedly, ignoring the chatter from the radio in the living room which went on and on about a new baseball player named DiMaggio, the recent Olympic games in Berlin, where a Negro named Jesse Owens had won four gold medals, and Joseph Stalin's great purge of his political enemies in Russia.

When they'd finished their dinner Kiffin sighed and said he felt very much at home here and hoped he would always be welcomed this way. And then he told them then that he was going to Spain because there was a war on and that was where he belonged.

Lily asked him what had happened to his flying job with Lockheed, implying, he thought, that a man with only one leg shouldn't give up a good thing. And maybe, he thought, she was right.

"I ran into a fellow named Whitey Dahl. He's some special sort of guy and he's already over there. He said if I had any life left in me I would be over there where the action is. I couldn't give him much of an argument."

Lily shook her head. Toby said, "I'm well aware what happens to any attempt to reason with you, but haven't you been shot at enough?"

"From a man who puts a Ford down in a cabbage patch and stops on the edge of an irrigation ditch he didn't even know was there I'd say you're sure an expert on pressing luck. Hell, Toby, you ought to be scared to step out the front door because you just might be struck by lightning—"

"From what I understand they have a mean war going on over there," Lily said. "One side is Communist, the government, the other side are Fascists trying to overthrow the government . . ."

"Why not let them settle their own war," Toby said.

"If you'd felt that way about France you'd never have met Lily."

"Touché."

"Look, I admit I don't know which side is right or wrong. I don't like Communists *or* Fascists. But Spain is where the flying action is these days. The Germans and Italians are in the thing with all the latest hardware in the sky. I'd like to know what's going on . . . what it's going to be like a few years from now. I think some guy once said look to the future and tomorrow will be yours—"

"Nuts. You may not have any future," Toby said. "You're forty years old."

"I'm in the bloom of youth."

"You don't even know which side is in the right," Toby said.

"If Mussolini and Hitler are on one side, I want to be on the other."

Toby held out his coffee cup for Lily to refill. He scowled into his cup. "Some dumb kid who learned to fly a few months ago will get the jump on you and give you a fifty caliber enema. I didn't haul you out of China to have you commit suicide. You owe it to us to stay alive.''

"I'm touched . . . I never thought I'd live to see Toby Bryant, Nebraska's star fullback, born hero, fearless flier of the mails, leader in the airline business turn into an *old lady*.''

The laughter that followed was somewhat more restrained than Kiffin had expected, and for a moment he wished he'd held his tongue. He'd been luxuriating in the feeling that they cared at all . . . especially that Lily did . . . and now he'd almost insulted them. Damn my big mouth, he thought. "Tell me more about the DC-3s," he said quickly. "How are you ever going to fill all twenty-one seats?''

"We will eventually . . . I hope. As soon as we can persuade the insurance companies to cover business executives we should open up a whole new market. As it stands now most policies are automatically canceled if the holder even thinks about flying. That makes it hard to compete with the trains.''

"Are they easy to fly?''

"Some of our old-timers are having a little trouble adjusting, but they'll eventually get the hang of more speed. I just hope the day never comes when I'll have to tell some guy I've admired for years that he's a has-been—''

"That's just what I'm trying to avoid," Kiffin said, grasping at an explanation that at least sounded like it made sense. God knows, the real reason for going to Spain had so far eluded him, and he was relieved to decorate this inner compulsion with at least some aura of logic . . .

Four months after Toby and Lily had seen Kiffin off at the Kansas City Airport they received a postcard from him. It carried a Spanish postmark and was ominously succinct. "This is a screw-up. Love. K.''

Via the same mail they received an invitation from George Palmer Putnam to a farewell party launching his wife Amelia's proposed flight around the world. "Wow," Lily said, "our little friend Amelia is getting so fancy. The Waldorf-Astoria. Whatever will I wear?''

Amelia, she thought, that incredible bundle of charm, poise, guts and home-spun beauty was the one woman in the world who gave her alternating hot flashes of admiration and envy.

There, she had always thought, but for Toby Bryant and Flip, would go I. Amelia had the nerve to set down some premarital reservations before she married Putnam, and she had not been shy about sharing her sentiments with Lily when they had last been together. She said that marriage was probably not for her, but if Putnam insisted on going through with it she would do her best. But she did not want to be bound by any "medieval marriage codes," nor could she guarantee that she would be content even in the most attractive gilded cage. There had also been something about how if they failed to find happiness together after the first year they could part with no hard feelings. Amelia was a woman who damn well stood by her convictions. Now she was going to beat the pants off the men pilots by flying around the world.

"I suppose it's going to be utterly utter if George Putnam has anything to do with it," Lily said. "That is, after he's made his usual bows to the press. I wonder if my blue rig will do . . ."

Toby, who had brought the invitation home from his office and had noted the asterisk followed by "Black tie" on the bottom of the card shook his head. "May I suggest your black number . . . the one with cleavage. You're a knockout in it—"

"Amelia might not like it. In some ways she's kind of a Girl Scout."

"Well, damnit, *I* like it. And George Putnam will like it, and Slim Lindbergh will like it, and Juan Trippe, and for sure Howard Hughes. I think the world of Amelia . . . we did a lot of work together when she was with TWA, *but* . . . and a great big *but* . . . I want my woman to look and act like a woman no matter what else she does."

"You're just one bearskin ahead of a Neanderthal. Come out of the cave, my darling."

"I'm not as stuffy as you think. We're taking a sleeper to New York."

"What's so modern about a Pullman car?"

"Not a train, wench. We have two berths on our new sleeper *plane*. You'll sleep above the clouds."

"Wow. Maybe I should buy a new nightgown . . . which brings me to another . . . can you and Flip manage if I'm gone for a month?"

"Oh, sure, who needs you?"

"Mrs. Anderson says she'll come every day and do all the cooking and cleaning just like she'll be doing for this trip. I trust her with Flip, but you two will have to do a lot of batching it together."

"What's up?"

"I had a letter from daddy today. He's not well, I'm worried about him. I think I should go to Vienna."

"What's the matter with him?"

"He says his blood pressure is way up and he hurts all over. I don't like the sound of it."

"Neither do I. When we get to New York why don't you just keep on going?"

"That's what I had in mind." And she kissed him for a thank-you.

The press conference, labeled by George Putnam as a "reception," was held in a small ballroom at New York's Waldorf-Astoria Hotel. Fiorello La Guardia was present, full of enthusiasm for a new airport that the city was building on the sight of an amusement park in Flushing Meadows. Ebullient as ever, he was telling everyone who would listen that at last New York City would have its own modern airport and the airlines would all be obliged to abandon their present terminals at Newark. Eddie Rickenbacker, the president of Eastern Airlines, argued that the move would be expensive, was not needed and he intended to stay where he was no matter what his competitors decided. C. R. Smith, president of American Airlines, said he had already contracted for hangar space at the new complex, as had Juan Trippe, who planned to land his Pan American seaplanes in Flushing Bay and dock them at a special ramp adjacent to the airport. Pat Patterson, who headed United Airlines, was still considering the change but was favorably impressed with La Guardia's claim that the new airport would be the greatest in the world.

Putnam was a master at press relations. He knew instinctively the result of combining one celebrity with another. He was a tall, rather slim man with a nervous twitch about his mouth due perhaps to the constant struggle between his ultra-conservative background and his near-genius for far-out exploitation. Scion of a noted publishing house, he was a man of thoughtfulness and courtesy; his energies among the famous belied his tendency to be ill at ease among those he

d invited to commemorate his wife's forthcoming flight. In
dition to the airline crowd, which included Toby and Lily
yant, there was Jimmie Doolittle, whose almost weekly
ntributions to the art of flying had become a priceless part
transforming it into a science; Benny Howard, an extraordi-
rily talented aeronautical engineer and test pilot; Roscoe
irner, who had threatened to bring the pet lion that had long
en his trademark; and Harry Richman, a Broadway enter-
iner with a passion for aviation, who had flown the Atlantic
e previous September with Eastern Airline's Dick Merrill as
s pilot. Richman had insisted on loading the wings of his
ockheed Vultee with ping-pong balls for greater bouyancy if
ey were forced down in the sea. Among the many others
ho came to honor the young woman who had already
come an international heroine were Bernt Balchen, the
nowned arctic pilot, Frank Hawks and Al Williams, the
ited aerobatic and racing pilots, Ruth Nichols, Viola Gentry
d Phoebe Omlie, who held their own share of flying records.
oward Hughes appeared just long enough to shake Amelia's
ind, smile at Lily and ask Toby what he thought of moving
WA's eastern operations from Newark to the new airport at
ushing. Then he disappeared.

There was no formal reception line; rather Putnam saw to it
at Amelia was kept moving as the guests drawn by particu-
r interests or experience formed one little social island after
other. She was not encouraged to linger except with the
embers of the press, who were exacting their customary
bute in free hors d'ouvres and champagne. Yet when Ame-
spotted Lily and Toby she broke away from her escort,
rew her arms around Lily and said that next to a success of
r world flight she wished she could look as exciting as Lily
ways managed to and Lily said that maybe Amelia should
ive an eye examination before she departed.

The babble of conversation had reached such a high decibel
vel that any true conversation was nearly impossible, but
hen Amelia reached for Toby's hand he pressed a small
ird object into hers. She opened her hand, studied the gray
etal casting and frowned. It was a wreath encircling a small
ir of wings.

"What's this, Toby?"

"I wore those wings when I was flying for the French.

Would you mind taking them along with you? I don't thi
they'll overload your airplane.''

"Maybe they'll bring me good luck.''

"I can't guarantee that, but when you get back I'd li
them back to save for our son.''

Amelia's gray-green eyes became moist. She shook h
head as if to erase any undue display of emotion. Then s
looked at Lily and said, "Do you mind if I say that I ca
help loving a man who's not afraid to be sentimental?''

Lily laughed. "As long as you're going around the worl
be my guest.''

Amelia brought the wings to her lips, then holding the
tight in her hand moved on to talk with a group surroundi
the crooner Bing Crosby and his wife.

Toby put his arm around Lily and gave her a squee:
"When a nice girl starts taking her flying seriously it's
ten-ring circus every time she puts her foot on the ground
hope that's not what you want.''

"I want to come back from Vienna and spend my grour
time with the two best guys in this world . . .''

CHAPTER
20

The deep and ugly sounds of discontent that rose from the Spanish peninsula during the summer of 1936 were barely audible on the western shores of the Atlantic. By early autumn the Spanish generals, fearful of a political takeover of the government by leftists, resolved to make their own *putsch* and began their offensive by overwhelming the government's most effective military establishment—Spanish Morocco. Led by General Francisco Franco they then moved swiftly to the peninsula itself and with surprising ease conquered Oviedo in Asturias and Saragossa in Aragon. Soon afterward key points in the south fell to the insurgent troops: Seville and Cadiz, Burgos, Salamanca, Avila, Granada, Pamplona and Valladolid. By late October and November even Madrid, Barcelona and Valencia were threatened, and as a consequence a civilian army tried desperately to repel the invaders, who made no secret of their fascist persuasions nor of the powerful support they were receiving from both Hitler and Mussolini.

The elected Spanish government, a loosely held coalition of communists, anarchists and trade unionists pledged to a better life for the average Spaniard, appealed to the rest of the world for assistance, both military and economic. But only Russia responded; the rest of the great powers—France, England, and the United States—assumed a hands-off policy. Even Leon Blum, newly elected premier for the Popular Front government of France, gave in to the warnings of divisive conflict in his own country should he attempt to help the Spanish. He was also cautioned by the conservative British government that he would receive no support from England should he intervene.

The government in Spain, besieged on every hand and desperate for survival, took any support they could find as volunteers from all over the world found their way by various means to join the conflict. The majority were young liberals, still nurturing their idealism, who believed they were rescuing Spain if not the rest of the world from the curse of Fascism. It came as a surprise for many of them to find themselves actually standing in the way of death for convictions which had so lately been only lofty conversation. The purity of truth and freedom were often adulterated by the appalling atrocities they saw inflicted by both sides, the terrible executions of priests, landowners and ordinary middle-class Spaniards by the anarchists, and the brutal slaughter and grisly mutilations inflicted on Republican captives by the invading Fascist troops. The lamentations brought about by the loss of naive idealism as it shattered against the hard stone of Spain proved for some to be as grievous as any wound they might receive at the front.

Above all the rest, two men knew exactly why they had come to Spain, if only by proxy. These fast rising despots, themselves usurpers, were well aware of the values to be found in Spanish agonies. Nowhere else on earth could they take the present measure of their might so handily and effectively, nor could they so well assess elsewhere the true worth of what they both foresaw as a new and enormously powerful aid to their ambitions—the airplane. Urged on by their even more air-minded subordinates, Hitler and Mussolini dispatched their latest flying hardware to the Spanish peninsula, believing that the dividends they would reap from such adventures would far outweigh any losses. Both were dreaming of greater empires, and with only the relatively feeble aeronautical shows of the first great war as a guage no one understood the potential of aircraft as an instrument of destruction, nor were there more than a handful of airmen trained for their deployment in actual battle.

The policy of *blitzkrieg* and of *schreckichkeit*, intended to terrorize the civilian population of any nation that opposed the vaunted glory of either Berlin or Rome, began in Spain. To accompany his steel, Hitler sent such promising underlings as Generals Jannecke and Sperrle of the Luftwaffe as well as General von Richtofen. He also sent Admiral Canaris, General von Thoma and Heinz Guderian.

The Soviets were not to be outdone, and from their gray autumnal skies they sent to the sunshine of Spain such reliables as Antonov Ovseenko, who had led the Red Guards in

storming the Winter Palace during Lenin's long ago October
Revolution, and such military technicians as Zhukov, Voronov,
Malinovsky, Stern, Berzin, Rodimstev and Konev.

If Hitler and Mussolini could beat their hopeful drums,
then Stalin would dream of even grander things . . .

The rather frail looking young woman in coveralls with a
red band on her sleeve announced that she would be the
escort for those volunteers waiting in the reception center at
Valencia. She also informed the small assembly of English,
French, Dutch—and Kiffin, the one American present—that
her name was Estrella. Speaking passable English, she advised that the bus that would take them to their training units
would soon be ready for boarding.

"Most of you," she said, "will be assigned to the Fifth
Regiment, some to the Sailors of Kronstadt Company, some
to the Leningrad Company and some to the Primera Unidad
de Avance."

It was four o'clock in the morning and they had been
waiting in what had recently been a theological seminary
since four of the previous afternoon. They had been asked to
surrender their foreign currency and had been issued meal
chits after a thorough examination of their credentials. During
the long wait Kiffin had found that his French had become
almost hopelessly rusty (had it really been eighteen years?)
but he did gather from a French volunteer that a twelve hour
delay when involved with the Spanish Loyalists was nothing
special. "They have too many factions among themselves,"
the volunteer tried to explain . . . "the Unified Socialist-
Communists, the Trade Unionists who call themselves the
CNT, the POUM, who are Trotskyists, and the Anarchists,
who do as they damn well please. But all are very brave, you
may be sure, monsieur, though they are often confused . . .
as who is not, monsieur?"

Kiffin was not greatly impressed by his fellow volunteers.
There were no aviators, and so far he had found none of *the
joie de vivre* that had been so dominant during his early days
in France. Certainly he shared their scruffy appearance after
so long without a bath or shaving, but he was discouraged by
their apparently aimless shifting from fist-shaking ideological
nostrums to total apathy once one of them managed to buy
another bladder of wine, which they squirted into their open

mouths until nothing but air emerged from the spigot and then after a few bouts of drunken bravado lay down to snore like hogs.

Kiffin tried to view all this with detachment as he reminded himself that he was the oldest volunteer present and that it had been a long time since he'd tried to live with a group of other men.

When the girl who called herself Estrella arrived and began bustling about so officiously Kiffin could not be sure if it was her relatively refreshing appearance in contrast to the surrounding company or if she actually was as beautiful as she seemed. For such a small person (he was willing to bet she weighed no more than a hundred pounds), he found her manner almost intimidating, and while she involved herself in endless interviews and paper checking, all of which had been done before, he took considerable satisfaction, even pleasure, in studying her.

She had an aquiline nose, balanced by a lovely and, to him, very kissable mouth. Her skin was more copper than bronze. Her hair, which she wore short beneath an "overseas" cap, was ebony black. Her eyes, definitely Slavic in structure, fascinated him with their wild delft blue.

He guessed she must be in her late twenties and had been blessed with what appeared to be an unholy quotient of energy. Her movements reminded him of a stamp he had once seen depicting La Belle France in the act of starting a revolution or finishing one . . . he'd never been sure just what inspired her extravagant pose. And as Estrella transferred her fierce attention from man to man he suspected she was a sergeant-major at heart—sort of another Sergeant Delacroix . . .

His own interview with her had not been particularly harmonious. She had checked her clipboard, found his name and smacked her lips as if she had a bad taste in her mouth. "Ah, *si*, you are the American pilot. We really do not need such people."

"Then I've been misinformed and will take the next boat out. What's the problem?"

"There are good Americans and bad Americans and the pilots who have come to us are all bad. They do not take the war seriously . . . they make much trouble and only drink and play. We are going to send a Señor Acosta and his friends home. So behave yourself."

"I wasn't told this was a Sunday school picnic. And I don't much appreciate your hostile generalizations."

She had turned her attention to the papers on her clipboard, and only muttered, "I do not understand you . . ."

Kiffin intentionally maneuvered to be the last to enter the bus. He had jettisoned his cane before his arrival in Spain and was reluctant to have his companions witness the twisting effort he knew would be required to hoist himself up to the first step. He hadn't counted on Estrella standing by the bus door, once again ticking off items on her clipboard.

She found his name on a list. "Señor Draper? Your name is now Domingo. Do not forget it."

He tried to place her accent in English and failed, except that it was more British than Spanish.

"Domingo." He smiled, determined to soothe her. "I like that. Has a nice ring to it."

They had all been made aware that once members of the Loyalist forces they would be given new names that they were assured would avoid complications with their native countries. Kiffin considered it a silly attempt to pretend they were not there at all, but at least it was a less apparent ploy than the Germans'. They'd arrived to help the rebels allegedly as "strength through joy" tourists and promptly became members of the Condor Legion. Likewise the Italians, who were gathered under their own banner, "the Aviazone Legionaria."

"Did you hurt your leg?" Estrella asked suspiciously.

"Yes. I bruised it against one of those damned cast-iron benches we've been living on for the past twelve hours. They weren't in my contract."

"I still don't understand you."

"Never mind. What time do we get to Albecete?"

"Today . . . if nothing goes wrong."

"I like a woman who makes positive statements."

She shook her head. "Please enter the bus."

He chose a moment when she glanced down at her clipboard and swung up to the bus step with what he hoped was a minimum of display. In spite of the many broken windows, the interior of the bus was dark and smelled of urine, stale wine and onions. The driver was leaning against the window at his side, snoring softly. Kiffin slipped into the seat just behind him.

Estrella mounted the steps, shook the driver to wakefulness and spoke severely to him. He quickly started the engine as she took the seat beside Kiffin.

As the bus pulled into the deserted street there was a chorus of raucous cheers from the rear seats where the British had settled themselves. Kiffin saw Estrella frown, but she did not look back. Now she sat straight-faced, staring ahead and tapping her fingers impatiently on her clipboard. There was enough light for him to notice the large mole on the left side of her neck, and he was about to say it was the prettiest mole he'd ever beheld when the driver began a tumultuous clashing of gears.

The light of the bone-chilling dawn outlined the buildings of Valencia against the dismal sky, and Kiffin was grateful that Estrella had chosen to sit on his right rather than his left, where she might notice that the corduroy of his left pants was much smoother than where it rounded his natural leg. He hoped that his artificial limb would not be recognized until he was established—as long as he held a valid flying license and could prove himself in a coming checkout he had been assured the Loyalist government was not interested in his health. Using an old Pitcairn mail plane as a rehearsal hall, he had practiced climbing into and out of the open cockpit until he could manage it without help and with a minimum of commotion. He was confident he could do the same with any airplane the Spanish might offer, but he hadn't counted on such hurdles as bus steps before the eyes of an unsympathetic witness.

Near the outskirts of Valencia they passed several long breadlines, the people waiting glumly for the simultaneous arrival of dawn and the bakers. They passed a few private cars occupied by very young Spaniards and marked with large letters identifying the various political parties of the government . . . CNT, POUM, PSUC. They all blew their horns and waved at the bus.

Soon they were bouncing through a countryside that appeared dull, and frozen fast in the calcium light. They passed two burned-out churches and on the whitewashed walls of a village a sequence of posters warning that looters would be shot. Another series of posters proclaimed, "Less talk! Less Committees! More bread. All power to the Generalitat!"

Kiffin found it impossible not to stare at his seat companion; her present sullen composure intrigued him, and when she opened her eyes after a few quick naps it was like watching a beautiful mechanical doll come to life. She had been dozing for several minutes when she caught him watching her. "What are you looking at?"

"You. Domingo doesn't think you look very Spanish."

"I am half-Czech, but this is my country." They passed a crowd of refugees gathered at the intersection of two gravel roads who were occupying a little slope, hovering together, some sprawled in sleep and others warming themselves over small fires. A pair of *Guardia Civil* muffled to their mouths in their capes stood a little apart from them. "Those are my people," Estrella said solemnly.

"This looks like where I came in," Kiffin said.

"I don't understand."

"If you go to the movies and arrive in the middle of the film, don't you leave when the story gets to the part you've seen before?"

"You have seen war?"

"A little." He rubbed at the stubble on his chin. This *was* where he had come in . . . a long long time ago. Insanity. Why had he come back? Toby and Lily were right. He should be put in a loony bin.

"But you have not seen the war here. You will see terrible things."

He smiled at her and he thought to hell with this gloomy beginning. "I'd like to know you better."

She turned her head away and stared straight ahead. As the bus careened around one curve and then another, each time threatening to capsize, shouts of protest came from the rear. Then someone broke into the chorus of "Quinto Regimiento," and soon several voices were limping through the lyrics in chorus. They began passing wine bladders from man to man, and a Frenchman who was behind Estrella insisted she open her mouth for a squirt. To Kiffin's surprise she took it well enough, and as if the wine had crumbled her reserve she joined in a few bars of the singing.

"I was beginning to think it was against the rules for you

to smile," Kiffin said. "You don't have to be so serious.
We're here, we'll fight. Forget the propaganda."

"This is a serious time."

"You are one beautiful lady when you smile. The world
isn't coming to an end—"

"Mine can."

"Baloney. You're young, make the most of it."

"We have many young people in Spain. All fighting. We
also have the Abraham Lincoln Brigade. All young Americans.
They are very brave *and* well-behaved. They are not like you
pilots."

"Hey, wait a minute. I just got here."

"Tell me who is this Abraham Lincoln."

"Hard to say. He was sort of a . . . counterrevolutionary,
guess."

"A Fascist? Then I'm glad he is dead."

"He was definitely *not* a Fascist."

"A Marxist?"

"Guess again."

"He must have been very important to have a whole
brigade named after him. Was he a worker or an aristocrat?"

"You might say he was both."

"That is impossible. Then he was bourgeoise?"

"Not exactly. The only way to become an aristocrat in the
U.S. is to *do* something."

"What did Señor Lincoln do?"

"He kept the country from coming apart. It was something
like here."

Estrella kept silent. She fiddled with her clipboard a moment,
then said something to the driver and checked her wristwatch.
Finally she turned back to Kiffin, and it seemed to her that
some of her fierceness seemed to have left her. "I'm thinking
I do not understand why people like you leave America and
come to this old and sick place unless your country is also
sick from what the imperalistic capitalists have done. I cannot
find the true reason for you and the other Americans to
come."

Kiffin thought of the young men behind him, all so strangely
alike, all hard faces yet somehow lacking confidence in their
eyes, all nervous in spite of their continuous applications of
wine and tobacco. He lit a cigarette and made a face, because
after so many during the past twelve hours its taste was

awful. "Estrella . . . when you find out exactly why any of us came here . . . please let me know . . ."

If ever Kiffin had experienced confusion and disappointment it was during the first week after his arrival at the Loyalist military reception center near Albecete. He found that the place and the people were already sore from the ravages of the war, and that Franco's Moors were pounding at the gates of Madrid. He also discovered that he did not particularly like being addressed as "Comrade" by the few Spaniards he had any social contact with. He wanted to find Whitey Dahl, who was in a squadron to the south somewhere and was disappointed to learn that Estrella had been correct . . . the wild and wonderful Bert Acosta, who had flown the Atlantic as Admiral Byrd's pilot ten years earlier, had been sent home along with several other American pilots for being rowdy and unwilling to accept military discipline. Frank Tinker, also an American, was supposed to be in the vicinity, and Kiffin found out through Estrella that his pseudonym was now Francisco Gomez Trejo. But the man could not be located under any name.

Kiffin was shaken when he realized that the confusion during the war in France was nothing compared to what went on with the people who were supposed to pay him fifteen hundred dollars a month plus a thousand dollars bonus for every rebel plane he shot down. Worse, after waiting out an idle week of bitter cold and mud that reminded him of France he realized that chance of *collecting* any bonuses was almost nonexistent. So far he'd only seen a few seedy looking Breguets, a French biplane designed not long after the Great War. Compared to the German and Italian airplanes now slicing through the sky they were antiques.

Albecete, once a provincial city barely awake even during the noon hour, a backwater of the old Spain where only recently old men and crones had sat on park benches and talked of oranges, figs, grapes, madonnas and the religious education of grandchildren, had been transformed into a garrison with three times it normal population crowding its dusty streets. The winds whipped down off the nearby Sierra de Alcaraz and chilled them all, soldiers and civilians alike, and since this was a major staging area for the dispatch of recruits to Loyalist Units on all fronts there was an overwhelming atmosphere of indecision and transience. Commanding the

base was André Marty, a party-line Stalinist whose liquida
tions of Spanish citizens simply on the basis of class ha
earned him the title of the Butcher of Albecete. An Italia
Communist, Luigi Longe, served as inspector general, an
another Italian, Giuseppe de Vittorio, was the chief politica
commisar. Also attached to the Loyalist headquarters a
Albecete were a number of Russian advisors who kept almos
entirely to themselves. Kiffin was grateful he had nothing t
do with any of the Loyalist brass.

On a sunny and relatively mild December afternoon he wa
escorted for a very brief interview with General Hidalgo d
Cisneros, the chief of the Air Force, who wanted his phot
taken with a foreign volunteer. Kiffin found him a pleasan
man with a real appreciation of the government's pitifu
aeronautical position. While two photographers snapped innu
merable poses the general explained almost apologeticall
that he was just passing through Albecete on his way t
Madrid and wished he could spend more time with a pilot o
Kiffin's experience. He also said that if Kiffin objected to hi
photos being published he would personally see to it the
would not be released.

Kiffin was not sure why he had been chosen, since he ha
not as yet been issued a uniform and in his own opinion h
looked only a little smarter than when he had been release
from prison camp in Germany. He wondered if he had bee
so honored with the interview because Estrella seemed s
omnipresent or simply because he was the handiest American

At Estrella's urging Kiffin told the general of his shoc
when in addition to the Breguets he had seen several Nieuports
the same type of airplane he had flown in France.

"We only use them as trainers," Cisneros pointed out
"we do not take them seriously."

Kiffin told him that the Breguets, which were being use
as bombers, were almost as antiquated and wouldn't stand
prayer against the German and Italian machines now see
occasionally slicing across the sky.

"Be patient," the general said. "The French writer Andr
Malraux is doing what his government refuses to do. He ha
raised the money to send us thirty of the latest fighters. W
have many friends, soon you will be flying the Russia
Chatos and you will not be afraid."

"I'm not afraid now. I'm just scared silly to even leave the ground."

The general smiled and put a hand on Kiffin's shoulder. "A man who will come here with one leg cannot really be afraid of anything." The General thanked Kiffin for coming to Spain and walked away.

Kiffin turned on Estrella. "How did he know about my leg?"

"I told him."

"Well, damn you. You want me grounded?"

"You will not be grounded. I have orders from the general to take you to Captain La Calle. You are assigned to his squadron and so am I."

"What are you, some kind of a bolshevik nursemaid?"

"I am a lorry driver and I was before I ever saw you."

The interview with the general together with a continued spell of fine weather somehow established a new relationship between Kiffin and Estrella. One evening he asked her to go for a walk and, to his surprise, she accepted. As they approached the Plaza he looked for anything to talk about except politics, finally settling on a more personal note. "If I'm called Domingo when I'm really Draper, what's your real name?"

"Estrella."

"But what's your *real* name?"

"It was Gomez because I was married to an *asalto* and he was called Gomez. But I am not married to him now and no one but a Czech can pronounce my born name so I have, how do you say it . . . junked it?"

"What's an *asalto?*" Kiffin wasn't sure he trusted Estrella's sudden shift toward him, but he saw no harm in going along with it—and besides, she *was* a spunky little woman who could at least talk English . . . more or less.

She told him that an *asalto* was a policeman.

"You? A communist married to a policeman? No wonder you didn't get along."

"Oh, many *asaltos* are communists. So are the *Guardia Civil* with us. Because they are both loyal to the government, and we are the government of Spain."

"I'm never going to get the hang of all this. Let's kiss."

"What? I do not understand you."

"You never understand me unless you want to. I suggested we start off with a kiss."

Estrella shook her head in disbelief. "You're crazy. Right here on the street? You make a joke of the war?"

"I don't make a joke of the war. I just want to kiss you. And that's no joke. I realize it's not a normal military request and won't be rendered in triplicate, but I'm overcome with a desire to kiss that mouth of yours. Right now."

He halted abruptly, pulled her to him and kissed her. She twisted away.

"Just as I thought," he said. "You're frigid. What a damn shame."

"Frigid? What does that mean?"

"Cold. Cold as ice. Seems like you don't know how to make love. You're so full of propaganda you've forgotten you're a woman."

"That is what you think?"

"Yes," he said solemnly. "After an emergency meeting of the Draper Committee on Wasted Womanhood a decision has been reached. Your blood is ice water. And *don't* say you don't understand."

"You want to sleep with me?"

Kiffin swallowed. A question or an invitation? "Not especially. Who wants to sleep with a cold fish?"

"A gold fish? I am *not* a gold fish."

Real anger in here eyes now. He found himself loving it.

She said, "It is against regulations for two people in the same unit to make love. The Soviets say if we take the war seriously there will be no time for anything else."

"And you believe that?"

"Of course."

"Okay. Then leave me alone." He walked away, deliberately exaggerating his limp. As he moved along the dusty litter-strewn street he crossed his fingers and hoped his solitary progress would not last too long.

Suddenly he heard quick steps behind him, felt her hand take his arm, and he knew the war was about to take a distinct turn for the better . . .

CHAPTER
21

Kiffin's squadron, still unnamed, was made up entirely of foreign pilots except for the commander and the native Spanish ground crews. Captain Andres Garcia La Calle, a fine officer and one of the majority of Spanish Air Force pilots who had remained loyal to the government, was in command. The majority of professional ground officers had gone over to the insurgents because their entire careers were identified with certain regiments, but the pilots had been chosen individually on the basis of their aptitude and ability. They had not been committed to particular regimental flags when they had accepted assignments to the air force. Most flying officers were inclined to be of liberal mind, although they had trouble adjusting to the extreme methods and thinking of the communists and anarchists and were uneasy when addressed as "comrade" by anyone. Only their loyalty to the government and disapproval of fascism kept them from defecting to the rebellion's army.

The squadron was based east of the Madrid-Saragossa Highway near Estobel, a small town of white-washed structures leaning against each other for support in their old age. There was a rolling plain three kilometers from the town, which served as a satisfactory aerodrome except for the small rocks resembling potatoes that sprouted from the hard earth.

During inclement weather the entire squadron, pilots and enlisted men alike, were turned out to pick rocks from the airfield and toss them into the squadron's three trucks. Kiffin was amazed as were the other foreigners at the hopelessness of their clean-up efforts. Within a week of removing every visible rock from the surface an entirely new crop would sprout and Captain La Calle would make them have at it again. One of the English pilots said the recurring appearance of the rocks was a harbinger of spring. If so, Kiffin thought,

there. was damn little other evidence of it. The area was
exposed to the high winds and often freezing rains pounding
down from the distant Sierras, and their tents and the few
buildings including a schoolhouse and monastery the squadron has appropriated, were impossible to heat. The food
served twice a day was a monotonous ration of rice, goat and
mule meat, turnips, bread and occasional jugs of heavy red
wine that some claimed was the father and mother of all
vinegars. The squadron quenched their thirsts with a more
exotic and less distressing liquid. By some bureaucratic twist
of supply the squadron had received a full truckload of tea
that had been confiscated from Moorish insurgents somewhere along the actual fighting front.

While Captain La Calle never openly betrayed his reluctance to order sorties in the lumbering Breguets Kiffin noticed
that he used any excuse of weather or technical problems to
keep them tied down in the shelter of their revetments. Such
missions as the squadron did perform were straight bombing
runs that were not very effective and occasional strafing
attacks on insurgent ground troops that were. Only once had
hostile aircraft been sighted—a trio of the new German Messerschmitts flying so high they apparently never saw the
Breguets. Even so Captain La Calle ordered a hasty retreat
for home.

While the rest of Spain was choking on the blood of
Republicans and rebels alike the various military ground actions almost always included large numbers of civilian
casualties. In contrast the little group of mercenary aviators
quartered near Estobel seemed to be deliberately withheld
from the more violent actions. There were daily rumors of
vast preparations in the north where Franco was said to be
assembling fifty thousand Navarese, Moroccan and Italian
troops for an attack on Bilbao, Santander and Guernica. The
troops were reported to be very well-equipped and the German and Italian aircraft in full command of the skies, yet
Estrella told Kiffin that the miserable fascists would meet
better than their match when they came up against the
Basques . . .

Now all along the escarpments of limestone surrounding
the bleak dung-colored aerodrome there appeared soft hints of
green. There was an occasional touch of warmth in the sun
and a few larks flew up from Africa. Along with such pallia-

es to the edgy tempers and low morale of the squadron
me eight Russian Chatos, and every man in the squadron
t transformed. The stubby little biplanes were reputed to be
ong the best fighters in Spain, and with them visions of
rvival along with even possible dividend payments arose
ce more.

Even Perez, the commissar assigned to the squadron, was
iled upon, and the man became so unnerved by such a
neral display of approval that he sat down to write a
ok-length report to his superiors recommending the squad-
n be given the name "Jarama" after the area involved in
e current heroic defense of Madrid. Anxious to cover all
ssibilities, Señor Perez wrote an article for *Solidanidad
brera,* the anarchist daily, in which he described in glowing
rms the bravery of the squadron pilots. The fact that they
d as yet to engage in actual aerial combat and that his sole
servation of their conduct had been from the ground and
any kilometers away from what little action they did see
ubled him not in the slightest.

Only two of the Chatos were new; the rest were hand-me-
wns from Russian squadrons. The Soviet pilots were now
ing supplied with the Polikarpov I.16 Mosca, a high perform-
ce little monoplane with a fully retractable landing gear.
iffin discovered that while his Chato had been manufactured
Soviet Russia, the engine was a Cyclone, and manufac-
red by the Wright Company in New Jersey, in the good old
.S. of A.

Along with his squadron-mates Kiffin was granted one
ur at the Soviet fighter base to acquaint himself with his
w airplane. His Soviet guide spoke no English and showed
tle desire to transfer even by gesture the faults and qualities
the Chato.

Kiffin stood back to assess the little machine as he had so
any others in his flying time, reminding himself that an
rplane usually flew like it looked. Visibility directly for-
ard along the gull-like dip of the upper wing would be
cellent, a definite plus in combat. It should be capable of
ick turns with its stubby configuration—another plus in a
ght and something to be kept in mind on landing. He
arned himself to watch out for a ground loop, particularly
nce his artificial leg was a shade slower on the rudder
dals. Climb looked like it might be very good—3,000 feet

per minute according to the mimeographed sheet of statist
he had been handed. Top speed 228 miles per hour? It look
to dive even faster and appeared strong enough to take
Four 7.62 millimeter guns made a victory almost a sure thi
once he could maneuver into position. It was an ugly lit
monster of an airplane, and yet in the eyes of any profe
sional pilot its design might well appear beautiful.

To protect the Chatos from possible air attack they h
constructed special revetments of the stones that were sc
tered over a considerable distance and as far apart as possi
to minimize the effect of bomb blasts. Kiffin's revetment w
nearly a mile from headquarters. Mechanics, ammunition a
fuel were brought by truck, sometimes driven by Estrella a
occasionally by Señor Perez, who in a rare unbureaucra
moment complained he hadn't enough to do.

JV 8781 Condor Legish. Spain.

After some debate with himself Kiffin decided to paint t
name "Lily" along the Chato's engine cowling. He render
the name in red to harmonize with the green fuselage and t
red bands and tri-colored stripes of Loyalist Spain across t
rudder. He had just finished the job and was standing back
admire his handiwork when Estrella drove up in a truck. S
spotted the name almost at once. "Who is this Lily?" s
demanded.

"A friend of mine. Why?"

"*Where* is this Lily?"

"In America."

"You have not tell me about her. You love her? W
would you paint her name if you do not love her? Tell me t
truth."

"Of course I love her." Kiffin tried to hide his amusemen
By God, no matter what their politics or nationality, t
female antennae were still fine-tuned to the primary signals

reat from others of their sex. "She's the wife of my best
iend," he said with a straight face. "What else?"

"I do not . . . I cannot understand you Americans."

Apparently unable to quash her doubts, Kiffin saw the
outh he had come to treasure display the hint of a pout.

"Maybe you'd rather have your name painted there?"

"That is impossible. All the squadron would know about
."

"I thought they all did. You think they've been blind for
/o months? Or are you suddenly ashamed of me?"

"It is very difficult," she said. "They all know you are
ot even a good socialist."

He could see she was still displeased, but by now he knew
at Estrella's upsets were like a summer squall. She could
nange from gloom to gaiety in moments . . . "I'll admit I
aven't done much for the cause so far, but now that I have a
ecent airplane that will change. And what do my politics
ave to do with me?"

He was certain of her answer, and equally sure that the
orm clouds would quickly dissipate.

She said, "I have told you a thousand times you do not
nderstand the needs of the working class. You are like a
ttle boy who listens to fairy tales and thinks that what is
ght will win without a struggle. We must fight hand in
and, with nothing else in our hearts, or the fascists will rule
s all. Look what we have done already . . . just in Catalonia.
/e have taken over the factories from the capitalists. The
amways, electricity and gas and water are all nationalized.
ents for the workers are lower. All things are better for the
panish workers. You must understand all this to understand
1e."

Kiffin wondered what sort of magic had been at work to
1ake him so confident that in this little volcano in baggy
overalls he had discovered his own Lily. In this tough
ountry she had emerged from the unforgiving atmosphere
nd revitalized him; all of his bitterness and lack of confi-
ience left him when she was near him. Now he thought it a
iamn shame that such a bright mind should be so stuck in a
ingle viewpoint. There were moments as he watched her
vhen he was sure he saw a sadness in her face, and he
vondered if some deep sorrow she hadn't yet decided to
hare with him haunted her. And then, presto! For no discerni-

ble reason she would become an ebullient, and confident little girl once more. As for him, he had two compelling passions . . . win over Estrella completely, and stay alive until the day he could take her away from Spain . . .

"Why don't you get off your soapbox?" he said, smiling.

"I don't understand you again. I am not standing on a box. But I bring you one as you request. It is in the truck. You want soap? There is no bath here."

He had forgotten that he'd asked that an empty ammunition box be sent to the revetment. The Chato's cockpit was relatively high off the ground and he had great trouble even with a hoist from his mechanic and armorer in maneuvering his artificial leg past the rim. If he could first get on a box, he thought, his entry could become much easier.

"Let's start all over again," he said, ". . . with I love you."

"I love you, but you make me angry."

"I make a lot of people angry. I think it's called building character. But I really am doing my damndest to behave like a standard-issue human being. I'm not sure, but maybe I can even make a baby. I'm getting better . . . by the time this war is over maybe I could even make a good husband."

"Do you say you desire to marry me?"

A new warmth was in her eyes.

"For all I care you can have a hammer and sickle ring and wear it for the rest of your life."

"I am so happy!" she said, and she embraced him fiercely. "We will start a revolution in America!"

"Hold *on* now. Don't get so carried away. Before you burn down the White House at least take time to get acquainted."

And suddenly they stopped talking. They stood in the sunlight holding each other. She reached up to caress the side of his face and he thought that the best thing he had ever done was to come to Spain because at last he had found a woman who was as rebellious and as unconventional as he was. At least life with her would never be ordinary, or boring.

They broke apart only at the sound of the approach of the second truck.

"That will be the miserable handful of ammunition for my guns," Kiffin said. "Tomorrow maybe you can arrange to bring it . . . ."

During the first week the Chatos were with the squadron they flew hardly more than an hour each day. There was an inexplicable shortage of both fuel and of ammunition for the new 7.62 guns, and the old ammunition would not fit either belts or muzzles. Captain La Calle and Señor Perez had beseeched Albecete for immediate allocations but they met with little encouragement. All materiel went to the Soviet squadrons first, and if there was any left over then the Loyalists might share. So their flights were still training flights, which did little more than give the pilots time to become better acquainted with the Chatos and to sharpen their fighter techniques. Captain La Calle was careful to avoid those areas to the west of Estobel where insurgent aircraft might be encountered.

The relative idleness that prevailed because of their limited operations left the squadron pilots frustrated and quick-tempered. It must be the same in all wars, Kiffin thought . . . the peak of enthusiasm and dedication was always missed because of some damned unforeseen hitch in the military *system*. Generals belabored their maps and logistical charts, isolated from reality by protective staff officers and the relative comforts of their headquarters. Meanwhile their men marked time and their units lost precious energy while everyone waited for reality to catch up with grandiose plans.

Finally, though, the squadron had been promised the arrival of ample fuel and ammunition on the next day and ordered to prepare to use it. They were to attack and strafe Italian ground forces marching along the Madrid-Saragossa Highway toward Guadalajara. As additional targets they were to attempt to "neutralize" insurgent air squadrons on their airstrips near the Sierra Guadarrama. The weather forecast for the operation was pronounced ideal for the Loyalist airmen. Freezing rain and snow plus heavy cloud were already moving across Portugal and western Spain. The columns of vehicles manned by the insurgents would not be expecting air attack in such weather and their airplanes would be conveniently on the ground. No one bothered to explain why the Chatos could fly while the Fiats and possibly the Messerschmitts of the Germans could not . . .

In any case, the forecast promised to be accurate. During the preceding afternoon a threatening bank of cloud was already approaching the Plain of Estobel, and what was left

of the sun created almost solid-looking shafts of light that
dappled the distant mountains and the Plain of Estobel. Kiffin
decided to make one final test of his Chato's turning radius at
full power. Because of the previous fuel restrictions he hadn't
been able to test its ultimate performance, which he knew he
would have to use if the squadron met any opposition.

He climbed to six thousand meters, as high as he wanted to
go without oxygen and marveled at how cold a Spanish
March could be—the outside temperature was minus ten
centigrade. He looked above, making sure he was alone in
the immediate area, and looked below for some odd aircraft
that might have slipped between him and the aerodrome. He
made a few easy turns to clear the sky at his own altitude.
This was no time to be caught napping. There were exactly
forty rounds all told in the Chato, ten for each gun. Full belts
would be fitted during the night.

He kept the aerodrome at Estobel within sight below and
made two "5-g" turns, one to the right and one to the left.
As his body sank against his parachute pack and his cheeks
sagged with the multiples of gravity he saw his face in the
rearview mirror and didn't recognize himself. I look like a
dying ape, he decided, and thought with a mixture of discomfort and approval that the Chato was capable of pulling his
balls right off their moorings.

He straightened to level flight, and as the blood surged
back to his head he felt confident that the little Chato was
capable of doing exactly what he needed . . . if jumped by a
faster aircraft, say a Messerschmitt, he was sure now that he
could turn inside his adversary and reverse the advantage.

He made two more turns, firing a quick burst of his guns to
see if it would make any difference. The Chato shook rather
violently in response, but otherwise he couldn't fault it . . . it
turned with almost equal ease both to the left and the right.

Although an errant shaft of sunlight sparkled momentarily
along the Chato's tips he saw that it was already twilight
below. He was hungry and looked forward to the evening
meal, when all the ranks ate together. The hot Moroccan tea,
maybe even a glass of the terrible wine and Estrella would
make a pleasant end to this day. He was damn lucky . . .
whoever was in charge beyond those shafts of mellowed
sunlight had blessed him beyond understanding . . . how
many other one-leggers had the opportunity to fly an airplane

like the Chato? More, how many other half men could share a war with the likes of a woman like Estrella?

He took a final glance at the sun, pale behind a torn patchwork of dull gray and amber clouds, and for an instant was convinced that here aloft he really did sit in the lap of the gods, all of whom had been forgiving of him. He thought of Wiley Post, now almost two years gone, and all the other friends who for one reason or another were no longer alive to enjoy such skyscapes. Toby could have his predictable old airlines. *This* was the good life—all the rest diminished in comparison. Now add to it all the love of a great woman . . .

He pulled back the throttle and the "Cyclone" rumbled easier. He rolled the Chato onto his back and with the earth above him pulled on the stick. The Chato's nose fell away until it was pointed straight down. The slip-stream screamed past the cockpit canopy as he gathered speed in the "Split-S." The airspeed needle wound around until it was pegged, and he knew he was exceeding its highest reading.

At a thousand meters he leveled out in a relatively gentle "3-g" recovery, then whipped the Chato around in a full one hundred and eighty degree turn and glided down for a landing. He taxied toward his revetment and saw a truck waiting for him. He saw his mechanic standing in the back of the truck with two armorers. Estrella was in the driver's seat, and as he taxied past the truck he saw her smile and wave.

Inside the revetment he shut down the engine, opened the canopy and sat listening to the tinking of hot metal as it contracted.

Estrella came carrying the ammo box and placed it at the trailing edge of the Chato's lower wing. Grunting with the effort, he hoisted himself up until he could stand on his parachute pack, then carefully lowered his artificial leg to the box until it supported his weight. He reached down to place a hand on Estrella's shoulder. She put her arm around his waist and steadied his descent to the ground.

As the armorers and the mechanic rotated the Chato, Kiffin walked slowly toward the truck with Estrella at his side. When they were concealed from the others by the revetment he pulled her against him and kissed her. She responded with the abandon he now knew and appreciated so well.

"You're crazy," she whispered. "We will be shot if they see us."

"Baloney. No one is going to shoot a valuable truck driver. Tomorrow I'll be shot at by experts. I just want you to know I love you. And long live the proletariat."

"You make me so—"

Her words were lost against the roar of a diving airplane and the sharp staccato barking of machine guns. Kiffin looked toward the oak trees behind the revetment and saw an Italian Fiat coming straight at them. He saw the twinking of four gun muzzles against the bronze sky and shoved Estrella away from him. "Quick, *run*. Under the truck . . ."

She had some twenty paces to go. "Don't wait for me—"

She started to run, then halted and turned back for him. "*Beat* it," he yelled. "*Quick.*"

Moving as fast as he could he threw his hands up, motioning her toward the truck. He saw her continuing on toward him, shaking her head—then just before she got to him, as if in a nightmare, he saw her propelled backward, followed by an instant blossoming of dark red spots, three across her forehead and mouth, another three across her breasts, a final pair at her stomach.

He caught her as she collapsed and dragged her underneath the truck.

He tore at her coveralls. He wanted rags, anything to stop her hemorrhaging. He was smeared with her blood, and as he tried to straighten her head saw that her face was unrecognizable. He began to weep and curse and begged her to look at him and kissed her bloody face and he called out for her to say *something* . . . "Baby . . . baby . . . please, no . . . please . . . *please* . . ."

Still holding her tight he beat a fist against the hard ground. "I *told* you not to wait for me . . . goddamnit I *told* you . . . Oh God, Estrella . . ." and he said her name over and over while he rocked her body in his arms as if she were a sleeping child . . .

Finally he knew she was dead. He stared at what was left of her face, bent to kiss her. Somewhere, breaking into his horror, he heard the airplane coming back for another pass, and he rolled over until he was on top of her lifeless body, soaking himself in her blood, determined to protect her . . .

It was nearly dark before the armorers and the mechanic left the safety of the revetment and found them still locked together beneath the truck. Kiffin said nothing when they pulled them apart, nor did he seem to react as they put Estrella's body on the floor of the truck and helped him into the cab. It was, they told the others during the mess that night, as if the American was a stone man, dead himself.

CHAPTER
22

Captain La Calle intended to ground Kiffin at least temporarily the following morning, but after he looked into his eyes he thought better of it. The weather for the squadron's first real attack was filthy, and La Calle supposed that a man who had suffered so much only the evening before would have been far too unnerved to be of use. Until he saw only cold fury in the American, a controlled, frightening intensity. To play it safe, guard against erratic behavior, La Calle said that he would fly as Kiffin's wing man . . .

When the mission was done he appointed Domingo, formerly known as Kiffin Draper, as his deputy squadron commander. From that day on, as the air and land battles raged around Madrid and to the north of Guadalajara the squadron flew every day, and with such style and determination that their reputation spread throughout what was left of Loyalist Spain. La Calle credited the American called Domingo with at least part of their special inspiration . . . the man was obsessed with killing Fascists, whatever their nationality, and regardless of any danger to himself.

By the end of March Kiffin-Domingo had accounted for two Fiats on his own and had shared with La Calle the kill of one ineptly flown Heinkel. When not actually flying or involved with some maintenance for his Chato or experimenting with ways to make it and himself more effective he kept to himself almost all the time. He joined his squadron mates at meal times but spoke only when necessary. The others understood. They watched him in the evening when he took his customary stroll and saw that he always went toward the oak trees and then directly to the place near his revetment where it had happened. He'd made a knobby cane from one of the oak branches and used it more frequently now, and they realized he needed it because it was a long limp for him

rom the mess to the revetment and back. For a while their
ielplessness in trying to cheer him made them uncomfortable
until they learned to accept his moody behavior, and they
eminded each other that two rounds from the attacking Fiat
ad gone right through his artificial leg without any damage
except for the holes. His good leg hadn't been touched . . .

Kiffin's dedication to his business was not a pretty thing to
vatch once he had an enemy aircraft in his sights. He held in
dangerously close and poured ammunition into his victim
until there was no possible chance either man or machine
could survive. Once engaged in a fight he seemed blind to
any other activity around him—which all-absorbing concentra-
ion was his undoing on a certain gray afternoon of April the
seventh . . .

He had been engaged in a long chase almost down to
ree-top level after a Fiat that exploded in front of his eyes,
but he kept right on firing into the ball of flame until it sank
but of sight beneath the Chato's nose. Only then did he haul
back on the stick to regain altitude. But instead of looking up
nis eyes stayed focused on the pieces of the Fiat twirling and
tumbling down to earth.

Suddenly he sensed a shadow above him. He glanced up
just in time to see the gear and belly of a Junkers 52. He
jinked hard to the right but collided with the Junkers' enormous right wing. The Chato jerked violently and he saw both
his left wings swept back at an odd angle.

The Junkers continued on, apparently unseeing and unharmed, but the Chato threatened to roll over on its back.
Soon Kiffin discovered that the only way he could keep it in a
controllable glide was to bring the engine back to idle. Lacking enough altitude to bail out he aimed the descending Chato
at a winding gravel road, the least cluttered area available. He
couldn't raise the left wing as he flared for a landing, the
Chato caught the gravel hard, slewed into a low bridge
abutment and finally came to rest upside down in the thick
bushes bordering the road.

Kiffin was unhurt but furious with himself. He was fairly
certain he'd come down in enemy territory. He released the
canopy latch, relieved to find it hadn't jammed. Then, very
slowly and carefully, he released his flying-harness, closed
his eyes and fell out into the bushes.

He somehow managed to pick himself up, floundered through

the bush in the direction of the road, and almost immediatel⸴
found himself looking down the gun barrel of a squad o⸴
Moorish soldiers . . .

After a week had passed and no one had spotted a downe⸴
Chato nor had there been any word on the fate of its pilot
Captain La Calle was obliged to report that a pilot known a⸴
Domingo had probably been killed in action or was possibly ⸴
prisoner of the insurgents. An enterprising American reporte⸴
picked up the story while visiting Albecete and somehov
learned "Domingo's" real identity. He thought that he saʋ
an opportunity to expose the use of false identities to protec
Americans fighting in Spain from the penalizing action o⸴
their own government. Giving the story a romantic twist, h⸴
wrote about "one lone American's sacrifice in the cause o⸴
democracy," never mind that Kiffin Draper was also a pai⸴
mercenary. The reporter, only trying to do a day's work
succeeded beyond his most souped-up imagination. The stor⸴
was syndicated throughout the world and enlarged upon itseʟ
as it was further revealed that the noble American had gon⸴
into battle handicapped by an artificial leg. Packs of journal
ists of every nationality seeking more information about th⸴
missing American appeared before the press officers of botʜ
the Loyalists and insurgents.

Several days later Kiffin was recognized when he wa⸴
brought before a military court in Salamanca and sentenced t⸴
be shot as a spy. It was explained that General Franco and hi⸴
Falangist troops were closing in rapidly on the Loyalists an⸴
victory appeared to be only a matter of weeks. One o⸴
Franco's firmest objectives was the complete elimination o⸴
all Soviet influence and of all people who might be of ⸴
socialist or communist persuasion. His ruling included *everyon⸴*
who had fought against him, including in particular thos⸴
"disgusting mercenaries" he considered even worse than th⸴
Russians.

Along with every other major newspaper and magazine i⸴
the world the Kansas City *Star* carried the story of Kiffi⸴
Draper and even managed to dig up an old barnstormin⸴
photo of him taken at Wichita. Toby, reading the story witʜ
his breakfast, immediately put in a call to Lily at her father'⸴
number in Vienna. Surely, he thought, her father or some o⸴

his colleagues at the embassy would be able to do something about this incredible business . . .

It was early evening in Vienna when he finally reached Lily's father. "How are you feeling, sir?"

"Ever so much better, thanks to your good wife. She hauled me off to a Viennese specialist who gave me some pills which I suspect are dynamite, but they've done the trick. All departments are back to normal and I'm anticipating a long life."

"We've been worried about you."

"It's awfully nice of you to call but I'm afraid I must disappoint you . . . Lily took off for Spain yesterday."

"Then she knows about Kiffin?"

"Yes. To what avail I'm not at all sure. Franco has a bone in his teeth these days. The feeling here is that he smells complete victory in a very short time. So do the Soviets, who are already pulling out . . . rats leaving the sinking ship . . . we Americans backed the wrong side to win . . . which doesn't make us very popular with the Generalissimo. I'm afraid your friend Kiffin is in serious trouble. He's considered as a spy, not a healthy position to be in. It gives Franco's people a semi-legitimate excuse to thumb their nose at Roosevelt and the United States. Our Lily is capable of moving mountains if she puts her mind to it, but I can't hold out much hope that she can do anything to help this situation. On the other hand, she's awesome when she gets an idea in her head . . . as you must know—"

"I do, I sure do . . . do you think she's going to be in any danger herself?"

"I doubt that or I should have done my utmost to keep her from going . . . not that I actually could have stopped her. With a little maneuvering we managed to set her up with a diplomatic passport so she should be able to get about in spite of everything. She says she's forgotten most of her Spanish, but I'm sure it will come back. No, I don't think we need worry about her . . . she's very resourceful, as you also well know, and incidentally, looking really smashing these days. You've taken good care of her."

"It's the other way around . . ."

Toby spent the rest of that day and most of the following trying to reach his old friend "Slim" Lindbergh, who he'd heard was at least on speaking terms with some of the higher

officers in the German Luftwaffe. God only knew what a ma
like Slim was doing with such people, but maybe he coul
persuade them to put in a word to Franco and keep Kiffi
from a firing squad.

Toby called Pan American offices in New York, calle
Juan Trippe, called the embassy in London where Lindberg
was supposed to be in seclusion, and tried desperately t
contact him on an island off Brittany, where he was als
rumored to be in hiding.

All of his attempts ended in failure.

Thirty-six hours after Toby had talked with her father, Lil
arrived in Salamanca and went directly to the headquarters (
the Second Moroccan Regiment, now occupying the Ayunta
miento and other buildings of the municipality. Immediatel
on arriving she made inquiries and learned that a Colone
Calvo Asunsolo y Toledano was commanding both the cit
and the garrison.

Lily hoped she didn't look as weary as she felt after tw
sleepless nights en route, but she'd managed to find a hote
room, take a luke-warm bath and partially revive herself. Sh
had decided against trying to see Franco himself, who wa
said to be in Valladolid, because she was afraid it would tak
too long even if he agreed to a meeting. She would begi
with the officer directly in charge and work up as an opportu
nity presented itself. Memories of her days as a diplomat'
child reminded her that most professional Spanish officer
fancied themselves gallant gentlemen, and she prayed Colo
nel Toledano was no exception. With that in mind she'd pu
on her best black dress and spent more time than usua
applying a hint of makeup around her eyes. She slipped on
pair of white gloves she had bought in Vienna especially fo
the occasion. Examining herself before a mirror she though
. . . aging, but not too repulsive.

Certainly her theory on the nature of Spanish officers hel
true in the Colonel's outer offices. The members of his staf
were punctiliously correct and elaborately polite. "If th
señora would be so kind as to wait . . . ?"

Lily was careful in fielding inquiries on the purpose of he
visit, vaguely inferring that she wanted to discuss the disposi
tion of American Red Cross aid to refugees once the hostili
ties were over. Using the merest hint of an aristocrati
Spanish lisp, she implied that she approved of the war's nov

obvious outcome. In less than twenty minutes she was admitted to the large office of Colonel Toledano, and winced inwardly at the echoing tap of her spiked heels as she crossed the tiles toward his desk.

The colonel stood up from his huge mahogany planning table and smiled. The battle flags of the Moroccan regiment were grouped behind him along with the flag of Nationalist Spain, and the morning light from a very high window slanted down to bounce off his bald head. He stood very tall and thin except for a notable paunch, and as she came closer his interest in his visitor appeared to increase rapidly. He came around the table, bowed slightly, took her extended hand and kissed her white glove. He waved her to the chair in front of his desk and stood for a moment with his hands behind him, rocking back and forth from the toes to the heels of his polished cordovan boots. When he removed his glasses Lily saw the shrewdness in his eyes, and the approval of what he saw. Good. She could use that approval . . .

Keeping to the lisp, she began in her most formal Spanish, explaining that she had come from the American embassy in Vienna, relying on a foundation of truth before it was necessary to color the facts, and all the while fingering the small cross she had brought from a street peddler outside the hotel, hoping that Toledano, like many of the Falange officers, was a Catholic.

She also worried that she had already lost his attention when he strolled around to the chair behind the table, removed his glasses and began wiping at them with a spotless handkerchief. Maybe the man was anti-church or anti-clerical; from what she'd been able to gather there were several split factions among the so-called Nationalists who had flocked to the banner of the Generalissimo . . . "You are very kind, colonel, to give me a few minutes of your very busy day. My father has met General Franco. I will tell him of your kindness and I'm sure he will pass it on the next time they meet."

If the implication that her father was more than a middle-status functionary in the foreign service was an exaggeration, well the cause was a good one. Her father *had* said he'd once met a professional Spanish officer named Franco in London but wasn't at all sure it was the same man. Never mind . . .

Colonel Toledano held up a warning hand and lowered himself carefully into the huge chair that emphasized his

stature. Was it cunning that she saw in his eyes now, or was
her fatigue building imaginary devils?

"My dear señora, it is not necessary that we speak Spanish
. . . in truth I would prefer that we do not." He glanced at a
side door to the room, a cautious reflex?

Lily was relieved. Her brain was nearly exhausted from
trying to resurrect her Spanish, and she was not at all sure she
could have continued. "You'll appreciate that I have come a
long way, colonel. I wouldn't have done so if my mission
was not very important."

"So? You have come to speak of the Red Cross. I can
assure you the Generalissimo intends to continue cooperating
with that fine organization—"

"I've also come to speak about an American pilot . . .
Kiffin Draper?"

Colonel Calvo Asunsolo y Toledano sighed and studied his
polished fingernails. "Alas . . ." he said almost inaudibly.

"You've already won the war, colonel. Everything will be
over in a few weeks and you can start to build your new
Spain. What possible good will it do you to shoot one
American? You'll only bring down the disapproval of the
world, especially the United States, for such an act. It could
have far reaching effects . . . even influencing the future
attitudes of international bankers, and certainly Spain will
need money for rebuilding its economy. By shooting one man
who has now been so well publicized you may risk being
considered barbarians . . . the very word you have used to
describe your enemies. I beg you not to follow the communist
socialist way of killing anyone who might have the slightest
difference of opinion. I can only believe that honorable officers such as yourself are above such petty and vindictive acts.
I beg you not to disillusion the people of my country, of the
rest of the world that is also watching you—"

"Señora—"

"Please, colonel. It is *señorita*." Lily said it before she
realized she'd forgotten to take off her wedding ring. Thank
God for the white gloves. If she had the Colonel pegged right
he would be far more interested in listening to a *señorita*
than a *sēnora*.

Colonel Toledano had gotten up from his chair and, taking
his time, sauntered around to her side of the table. She

noticed that he affected a pronounced slouch now, as if he was anxious to shed any suggestion of military stiffness.

"You are very eloquent, Señorita Cranwell. May I inquire your relationship to the prisoner?"

She'd figured that there might be some initial advantage in using the same name as her father, but the sound of it now came as something of a shock. She had gambled so far, now how much further must she go?

The answer was easier than she had expected. Lies were always a gamble, but now that she had Toledano's attention, somehow she must hold out a promise—something that would intrigue him . . . "I will confide in you, colonel. I'm in love with your prisoner and we plan to marry as soon as he's released. Would you take that chance for happiness away from me?"

She lowered her head, considered wiping away a few tears and decided against it. The colonel was no fool. She must be extremely careful to arouse his interest but not his suspicion.

Instinct, and a slight change in his melodious voice gave her some hope. Well, you seem to be playing the right music, she told herself.

"Señorita Cranwell," he was saying, "do me the honor of viewing this regrettable situation from . . . how shall I say, our advantage? No? . . . I should say our obligation. We are bringing law and order to a Spain that has been torn apart by insane revolutionaries. Your friend was hired by them to kill the good people of Spain. He employed a powerful weapon to do his work and we have no idea how many hundreds of Spaniards he murdered . . . military and civilian. He was captured wearing civilian clothes. As a consequence he stands outside the international conventions of war. The military court had no alternative but to condemn him as a spy."

Colonel Toledano half-sat on the edge of the table, seemed to find his polished boots of passing interest for a moment and then turned his attention back to Lily. Their eyes met directly and in the long silence that followed she saw a trace of a smile. He reached behind him and his hand sought and found a box. He opened it without taking his eyes from hers and offered her a cigarette. She declined but picked up the lighter on the table, flicked on the flame and held it out to him. "*Gracias*," he said, and for the first time turned away from her long enough to blow smoke at the high ceiling. "I assume you do not smoke?"

"No."

"Good. I try to stop many times but I am a coward." He shrugged his shoulders and made a face—a face that combined the softness of libertine with the hard lines of a professional soldier . . . huge nose, deep olive skin, mischievous black eyes, heavy expressive eyebrows arched over the sun wrinkles lining his face, like exclamation marks for his mobile features. She thought she detected a certain melancholy when he said, "I am sympathetic to your problem, señorita. I have also known what it is like to be . . ." He hesitated, then said, "Please understand that I am not solely responsible for the decision in your lover's case. After listening to you, please be assured that were it within my authority I would try to think of a reason to release him."

He began blowing smoke at the ceiling again, keeping silent now, letting what he had just said sink in. Lily crossed her legs in as provocative a fashion as she dared and was satisfied to see Toledano's sudden melancholy leave him. "Would you at least allow me to see him?" she asked.

"I'm afraid our prison is a very gloomy place. You will find it depressing . . ." He hesitated, rubbed his strong chin. "I will arrange for you to visit him at five this afternoon. One of my staff will come to your hotel and escort you to the prison. May I suggest that after your visit you will consider reviving your spirits by dining with me?"

Lily had never been in a prison. She hoped this one would be her last. While it was cleaner than she'd expected it still had the rank aroma of prisons everywhere, dominated by a powerful smell of ammonia. Along with her escort Lieutenant Sandoval, she was led by a Moorish soldier up flights of worn wooden stairs to the third floor. She was surprised the soldier was armed only with his keys. When he opened the heavy wooden door to a cell the lieutenant said he would wait at the top of the stairs.

Kiffin was sitting on the end of a canvas cot—poised, was more like it, like an animal about to pounce on its prey. He didn't look up when the door opened. Suddenly he threw himself at the middle of the cot, grabbed at something and threw it out the barred window. "Got ya," he yelled in triumph.

He turned around now and saw Lily. "My God . . . what are you doing here? How? They told me someone would be coming but—"

And then they were in each other's arms.

"I can't *believe* it," he said, "I just can't believe it . . . God, Lily, am I ever glad to see you . . ."

He hugged her again and his words ran away with him as he muttered over and over again how happy he was to see her and how he probably smelled bad and how in the world had she found him and . . .

She wiped at her eyes in spite of herself, said she was just trying to save him and then, trying to lighten matters, added that she wasn't sure why.

"I always said you had more guts than any woman I've ever known. More guts than sense coming here. Hey, this is really my day. I just got rid of my last cockroach, which makes the score Draper sixteen, roaches zero. I can die happy now—"

"Don't talk like that."

"I guess I have to." The smile disappeared. "I better get used to the idea that *mañana* . . . well, I have to get it all out. I keep looking for someone to say even an obligatory few good words about this sinner. Say he wasn't a born rat, or a rapist . . ." He looked seriously at her. "It's been on my mind ever since that awful night that I can't forget. I want you, Lily, of all people to know that I've lived in my own special . . . self-made hell ever since . . ."

He limped to the window, then came back to her. She saw he was trying very hard to put on a brave front now and found it difficult to believe this was the same man she had flown and lived with during their barnstorming days . . . God, how he had aged . . . hair nearly solid gray now, stooped as if in constant pain. Time, she thought, had not been so good to dashing Kiffin Draper. But even so, there was still something remarkably magnetic about him—could it be, she wondered, and not for the first time, that she might have been at least a little in love with him and had just refused to recognize it, acknowledge it? He was a hard man to hate for too long, even after what he had done to her . . .

"How's Toby?"

"Fine. He knows about you, of course. I think the whole world knows . . ."

Kiffin frowned, his eyes going dull. "Not about us, I hope. I've always hoped you would never tell him—"

"I never have and I never will. Why hurt him . . . or us . . . What I meant was that you're all over the newspapers, I'm sure Toby knows that you're in this awful trouble, and by now he's called my dad and been told where I am.

"Trouble. I'm an expert at making it for myself . . . seems to be a habit."

He moved to her, put his hands against her cheeks for a moment. "Before I become either a good or a bad memory I want to say what I suspect you've known anyway . . . I love you, Lily. Always have. Dead man's confession. Sort of cheap, I guess, but at least it's honest. A nice change of pace for me . . ."

She kept her silence, realizing he desperately needed unwinding.

"What kind of surprises me," he said, "is that I'm so damned scared. I'm no Toby . . . never have been half the man he is. And you were right about that being a war hero stuff . . . I never got over it. I guess I expected you to fall into my arms like the others. Sounds like some last confession, doesn't it? Well, it is, even if I'm not a Catholic. One thing I'd like you to understand . . . Before the Generalissimo uses up his leftover ammo I want you to know that I'm . . . I'm terribly sorry for the grief I've caused you. Please believe that . . ."

"Kiffin, we haven't time for this kind of dramatic nonsense—"

He smiled, shrugged his shoulders. "Sorry, but just now I'm acutely aware of the passage of time."

Lily warned herself that she was talking with a man who was convinced he was going to die within hours, and maybe he was right . . . but was it cruel to give him some hope even if it proved out to be false? . . . If I promise Colonel Toledano you'll leave Spain right away will you do it?"

He went to the window, took hold of the bars with both hands and looked down. "The view from here is very interesting. I'm looking directly down on a barracks with two tiers of balconies. There are always twenty or thirty troops lounging around this time of day. They're mostly Moors.

Below the barracks is a courtyard where they drill once in a while . . . as if they didn't give a damn. But the courtyard is where they put on the big show. The bullets have scarred up the stone wall at the far end. I don't know if they give their targets this view on purpose or if it's just an accident—''

"I asked you a question, Kiffin."

"I heard you. Sure . . . if I had a chance to leave Spain under any circumstances I'd probably take it . . . my survival instinct is stronger than my guts. What I'd really like to do is lie on the beach at some place like Almira and try to figure out why a guy who has had forty-two years of life and loved two women . . . never really had either one—''

And suddenly Lily knew what she had to do. She crossed the cell to him, spun him around and slapped him hard as she could. "Now you *listen* to me. Stop that goddamn caterwauling self-pity. You're going to do *exactly* as you're told for a change because you're going to stop thinking about yourself and consider your family. You heard me. Family. That's us. Toby and Flip, and, yes, me. All for one and one for all. Remember? Now I'm going to leave you because I have a date for dinner and I'm going to be a long time getting ready for it.''

"I'm not going anywhere."

"Yes you are," she said grimly. "You're going home."

And for the moment he almost believed it.

The wine was from Jerez de la Frontera. Toledano smacked his lips after his first sip. Lily congratulated her host on his perception—he had chosen exactly the right wine to match her mood, which she described as "venturesome." She was wearing the same dress she had worn to Amelia's farewell party. If "Colonel T.," as she now addressed him, was interested in cleavage he had an eyefull.

They were dining in the colonel's quarters, a modest, pleasant house protected from the street by a high stone wall. Two sentries stood guard at the wrought-iron entrance gate. Since the evening was warm, Toledano had suggested they dine on the patio. It was apparent that he had instructed his batman and his cook to provide the best available.

"I apologize for the rather sparse menu," he said, "but the disruption of agriculture has made a proper Salamancan meal very difficult. Fortunately that inconvenience has not been suffered by our wines.''

So far Toledano had behaved exactly as Lily had hoped; the Castilian gentleman playing gracious host. It was remarkable, and fortunate, she thought, how men of most any nationality could be so easily led into a narration of their life story. Toledano was proving to be no exception as he regaled her with tales of his youth at the family estate in the province of Cadiz, where his interest in the breeding of fine horses had been ''all consuming.'' Eventually he'd gone to Harrow in England for part of his early education, then to Germany for a while and eventually to a Spanish military academy. He had followed a line of Toledanos dating back to the sixteenth century who had been ''soldiers of Spain. Strange''—he smiled—''most of my forebears were sufficiently vain to have their portraits painted, one by Velasquez himself. They all had spade beards.'' He fingered his clean-shaven chin. ''Perhaps there is something lacking here. Do you think it would improve matters if I grew a bit of foliage?''

''I would suggest you leave things as they are,'' she said, and meant it in more ways than one, especially so far as the two of them were concerned.

Toledano laughed, then abruptly sobered. ''I'm afraid things are never left as we would like.'' And he told her about his wife, and how she and their son were killed in a train accident. And how lonely he had been ever since . . . Lily wasn't sure, but she thought he sounded genuine in his show of misery. Never mind . . . she hadn't come to Spain to commiserate with a Fascist colonel. She had a mission, and needed to concentrate on the role she had to play to accomplish it.

She spoke carefully. ''Colonel T., since you understand loneliness so well, I wonder how you could inflict the same on me?''

She hadn't finished the question when she knew she'd been premature. She saw his eyes grow cold and for the first time since they'd sat down he looked away from her. Damn, she thought, Damn her impatience when just the opposite was needed.

Toledano reached for his wine glass, took a sip, but he still avoided her eyes. Just as she became convinced she'd lost him entirely the batman arrived and took away the dishes, then returned almost immediately with a decanter of port and a wedge of cheese. A hundred phrases flashed across Lily's mind; she groped for anything that would regain the ground she was sure she'd lost. Everything that came to mind sounded artificial or banal, likely to drive him even further into himself, which could mean the disastrous end of the evening.

As he raised a knife to carve the cheese she was terrified that she had somehow offended the one man in Spain, other than Franco himself, who could save Kiffin. When she accepted the plate she decided she had to plunge ahead . . . "Your son," she said carefully, "was he preparing for a military career?"

Her words seemed to hang there between them. Then: "Try the port," he said, meeting her eyes once more. "I believe you will find it inspiring."

Inspiring for what, she wondered as she raised the glass to him.

She was relieved when he began to tell her about his son Phillipe, about his superior horsemanship, how they had ridden together since he had been a very small boy. But it seemed that Phillipe had decided there has been enough Toledanos in the army. Phillipe had felt that he might better serve his country in politics, or if not that then as a scientist . . . "Who knows," Toledano said morosely, "what wonderful things he might have invented or what mathematical treasures he might have left the world? It is the same with all young men who die too soon . . . they leave so much undone. A good officer, who must always deal with young men, must not think of such things . . . but then, sometimes I think I am not such a very good soldier . . ."

She watched him take a long draught of the wine and wondered if she'd heard right . . . if he had made such a surprising confession because of the wine or because he suddenly had decided to trust her . . .

Whatever the reason, she must not pass up the apparent opportunity. She told him she admired him for making such an honest statement and that she was pleased he felt he could trust her with such a personal confidence.

As he poured himself another glass of port she began to ease the subject of Kiffin back into the conversation. She assured Toledano that he was no ordinary mercenary, that his contributions to aviation had been very great and that he was

a renowned test pilot and had much to offer the future of
aviation if only his talents were not lost . . . "As a courageous man yourself you must admire a man who can do so
much on only one leg."

Then she dropped the subject, not wanting to press too
hard.

The flickering candlelight distorted Toledano's heavy features so that it was difficult even to guess what he was
thinking.

The batman came again and whispered something to
Toledano, who got up, then said, "You would think my man
was transmitting some great military secret when in fact it is
only the telephone. I am not only the commander but the
godmother of an entire regiment, not to mention the city of
Salamanca. They are probably having trouble with the sewer
system again."

As he walked away she saw that he was a trifle unsteady
on his feet, which pleased her.

She waited uneasily. Was this Lily Bryant, loving wife of
Toby Bryant? Damn right it was. She knew she'd put herself
on a nightmare course that soon might be irreversible, but if
she kept telling herself it was Kiffin's last chance, that she
and only she could give it to him, then maybe it would *seem*
like a nightmare . . .

And now, here it came.

When he returned Toledano had taken off his tie and his
uniform shirt. As if listening to a distant voice she heard him
say there would be no further interruptions and she saw that
his smile was no longer wistful or morose. She watched,
almost in a self-induced trance, as he poured himself a half
glass of port and tossed it down.

"One should not rush the drinking of wine . . . or anything
else," he said. "I hope I have not made a mistake, but the
Toledanos have never been noted for their patience."

He moved around the table and stood at her side. There
was, of course, no question about his meaning.

Face it. He knew, she knew. The game was over.

She forced herself to look at him, and he said quietly, "On
my honor, he will be released tomorrow."

He reached for her hand and she got up slowly. They stood
for a moment, their eyes on each other. "On his honor . . ."
It was all she had. He took her arm and led her away from the

able. They went up two steps, through an archway, down a hallway. They turned into a doorway, and she heard the door shut heavily behind them.

A candle was burning beside a huge canopied bed. She went to it and blew it out. Then, in the darkness, she began removing her clothes.

She had tried to nerve herself for this moment. She told herself that she was disembodied, that the body she was now exposing was not hers, that the body he would enter and leave would be only impersonal flesh, unrelated, unconnected to the real Lily Bryant. There would be no insult to it, no wounds because she would have departed from it long enough to complete a life-or-death bargain.

She moved beneath the sheet. "Remember your promise," she told the darkness.

She did not hear the wooden floor squeak as he moved across the room. She did not feel the weight of his body as he lowered himself onto the bed. She did not breathe as his hand reached out and touched her breasts.

"Please," he whispered, "be kind."

She did not say a word.

At zero nine hundred on the following morning the three officers who had sat as the military court on the matter of Domingo the Communist spy reported to the office of the district commander. Colonel Calvo Asunsolo y Toledano commended them on their promptness, they lit up cigarettes all around, a Moorish batman brought them coffee and they proceeded to discuss a situation which he had described as "awkward and disturbing."

Toledano ruffled through a modest stack of papers on his table. "Certain extremely confidential information has reached me which convinces it would be a mistake to execute the man known as Domingo. In fact the Generalissimo himself has become interested in the problem and urges you to reconsider your verdict. I agree. Such an act at this time would do far more harm than good for our cause. May I suggest there are two solutions." Toledano made a church steeple with his fingertips. "First, the man we hold is Kiffin Draper, not Domingo, but an American citizen. While it was true that he served in the Republican Army he was not shot down but deliberately crashed his aircraft so that he might desert." He brought his fingers down to make a flat roof and knocked the tips together. "Second. The accused could not have been on a spy mission since he is not Domingo. We do not know what happened to Domingo. Therefore, as represented by his Excellency General Franco we have no jurisdiction over the individual except to make certain he leaves Spain. You may wish to revise your conclusions." Toledano blew smoke at his favorite place on the ceiling.

The three officers put their heads close together, conferred in low tones for a moment, turned back to Toledano and advised him they had reached an agreement. The official papers pertinent to the release of the American would be ready by noon. The colonel would naturally wish to sign in the name of the Generalissimo.

At fourteen hundred hours Lieutenant Sandoval presented himself at the door of Lily's hotel room. He saluted with a slight bow and handed her a large thick envelope. "Inside you will find two exit visas and two first class reservations for Irun. I have been instructed to inform you that your friend will meet you at the train which departs at seventeen hundred hours."

Lieutenant Sandoval placed a small white envelope on top of the large one, saluted again and turned down the hallway.

Lily closed the door and stood looking at the small envelope. It was not addressed, but it was sealed on the back with a coat of arms. She broke the seal and pulled out a card. Inscribed across the face of it in an elaborate hand were the words, "Bon Voyage." Below the words were the letters "Q.B.S.P." She turned the card over, expecting to see Toledano's signature. The card was blank. Then an almost archaic Spanish phrase of courtesy she had not thought of since she was a very young girl came across her memory. "Q.B.S.P?" "*Que beso su piedres.*" Who kisses your feet.

The seal on the envelope was enough signature. As she dropped the envelope into a wastebasket she found some satisfaction in knowing she at least would never see that seal again.

CHAPTER
23

Toby Bryant's world was changing so rapidly there were times when he wondered if he was the same man who had learned to fly in 1916. To the consternation and bemusement of line pilots there were now occasional "uniform inspections," a ceremony that caused those who had not been trained in the military to twist their white uniform caps askew and neglect to shine their shoes. They asked, with what Toby thought was some justification, what shoe polish had to do with their skill in flying airplanes.

There were more far reaching developments which Toby knew must have a profound effect on his professional world. The magnificent *Hindenburg* had been lost at Lakehurst in a flaming debacle that had horrified the world, and its gigantic cindered wreckage had become the funeral pyre of all hope for the future of rigid lighter-than-air ships. In contrast, a Pan American flying boat produced by the same Glenn Martin who had first inspired Toby to fly completed the first commercial flight across the Pacific to Hong Kong.

Every day it seemed that aviation leaped ahead and new frontiers were discovered. The full-feathering propellers installed on the new Lockheed "14s" cut down drag and greatly improved the safety factor if the power of one engine was lost. Toby heard of an Englishman, Frank Whittle, who had progressed far enough in the development of a turbojet engine actually to start it, but there were many reservations about its possible use in powering aircraft. There were no designs suitable for even an experimental attempt to use such power.

There had been aeronautical triumphs and defeats everywhere in the world where the same sense of urgency seemed to prevail. While the boundaries of the oceans had been charted to the most remote coves and estuaries and the great

surface ships transported travellers with little fear of the wors
gales, international air travel was still a miniscule percentag
of the whole. The Russians in a desperate and brave adven
ture to prove they were capable of outstanding aeronautica
achievements made a successful flight from Moscow t
California.

Other attempts ended in tragedy, one of which directl
affected Toby and Lily; it was less than two months afte
Lily's return home that Amelia Earhart Putnam had gon
down in the Pacific and had never been heard from again
Her husband had managed to persuade the navy to launch a
intensive sea-and-air search for his wife and Fred Noonan
who as navigator had been supposed to find little Howlan
Island. Their Lockheed had vanished without a trace.

Along with Otis Bryan and Tommy Tomlinson, Toby wa
now heavily involved in five new aircraft which TWA ha
ordered from the Boeing Company. These were four-engine
transports, the first to be pressurized and therefore capable o
flying passengers high enough to avoid much of the ba
weather over the continental United States. These aircraft
which involved so much that was new and innovative, wer
not without many problems and Toby found that he wa
spending more and more of his time away from both his des
and his home. Unlike the early times the airline now operate
twenty-four hours a day from coast to coast, the unions ha
moved in with continued demands and restrictions, the gov
ernment air bureaucracy was expanding even faster than th
airlines while framing new regulations every day, and th
public's expectations of one-time dependability in all weather
was becoming ever more difficult to satisfy. As one of th
newly appointed directors of flight operations Toby was face
with all manner of details from the design of new boardin
ramps for the larger aircraft to the cleanliness and variety o
food served to the increasing number of passengers. Ameri
cans seemed to have decided en masse that traveling by ai
was not only for the very rich or for an emergency visit to
dying relative.

In the United States, there were disturbing winds. Th
country had barely recovered from the Great Depression an
had slithered into an era of apparent prosperity such as peopl
had never experienced. It was a fickle prosperity, though
touching some and leaving most unaffected. The rabid mouth

ings of Germany's new leaders and the bombastic rantings of Italy's Mussolini stirred up feelings and with them, increasing fears of a new European war and possible U.S. involvement.

There were echoes in the Orient, where Japan was striking an ever more belligerent pose since its successful military adventures in China and Manchuria. Even so the prideful strutting of the Japanese went relatively unnoticed by the average American, engaged as he and she was with the Satanic pogroms of Hitler and the theatrical posturing of Mussolini after his triumphs in Ethiopia and North Africa.

To Toby Bryant's dismay and many others who had known and had flown with "Slim" Lindbergh, they listened via radio to repeated arguments offered by their old friend who had recently surveyed British, German, and Soviet air power. Slim declared that England could not possibly win a war in Europe even with full aid from the United States. As a result of Lindbergh's continued championing of isolationist stands it became Toby's sorry duty to see that the words "The Lindbergh Line" were removed from the fuselages of all his company's aircraft. While he found it difficult to stop admiring the Lindbergh he knew, he found it difficult to believe that a man who had done so much for aviation and who was so intelligent could continue to advocate a policy of non-intervention.

It was while he was heavily preoccupied with the daily operations of his rapidly expanding airline that Toby received a summons from his real boss. He was to see Howard Hughes at his bungalow in the Beverly Hills Hotel at noon on the following day. He caught the first westbound flight out of Kansas City. He had just enough time to call Lily, ask her to pack a few clean shirts and send them to the airport with Kiffin. Then on impulse he said, "And tell him to bring a

angler DC-3.

few shirts for himself. I'm going to give myself the treat c
watching a reunion between Howard Hughes and Kiffin.''

Lily said, "Maybe Hughes will give him another job
Anything to get him out of this house!''

The next afternoon in California Toby and Kiffin entere
the Beverly Hills Hotel and passed through the lobby to th
gardens beyond. They followed along a winding path to
bungalow secluded by surrounding foliage. As they approache
the entrance a statuesque woman with bright red hair emerge
from the doorway and passed them without a glance. Tob
said, "You'll find Hughes hasn't changed much except tha
he's losing his hearing. So speak up. Just keep in mind ho
much he's done for aviation and is going to do. He's about t
fly around the world and for sure he'll break all record
Don't give him any malarkey about what you've been doin
since *Hell's Angels* because he probably knows more tha
you think. I've no idea what his stand on the Spanish wa
might have been so don't talk about it unless you're asked. I
you want to work in our flight engineering department this i
the guy who can do it in ten seconds. Any questions?''

"I feel like I'm about to be judged by Saint Peter.''

"He's no saint, but we both know he's one hell of a fin
pilot.''

. . . A husky man in a black suit was lounging on th
porch near the door. "Bodyguard," Toby whispered. Th
man surveyed them but made no challenge. Instead he took
small notebook from his coat pocket, glanced at it, and took
sudden interest in the shrubbery. When Toby said "nice day
he only grunted.

Toby pressed the button beside the door. They heard th
sound of chimes and an Oriental in a white coat appeare
almost immediately, held the screen door open while they le
the brilliant sunshine and entered the bungalow. Inside, all c
the curtains were drawn.

They blinked at the darkness, and it was a moment befor
they saw Hughes sitting on a couch at the far end of th
room. He was wearing pajamas and a slouch hat. Reports an
newspapers littered the area around him and he was staring
what looked like an over-cooked cabbage on the coffeetabl
When he saw Toby he looked up and smiled, although he di

ot get up. He said, "Who's that character you've got with ou? Looks like Kiffin Draper to me."

Hughes now did stand up, took Kiffin's hand for an instant. t was a rare tribute because he was obsessed with the notion hat handshaking spread disease. "Welcome," he said. "Glad ou got out of Spain with your ass in one piece. Sitdown, oth of you. Have some coffee? Tea? Milk? Whiskey?"

He pointed to the coffee table. "How about a chunk of Haggis? Friend sent it to me from Scotland . . ."

He reached for a knife and sawed off three slices of the Haggis. "It's terrible stuff. Pig's bladder stuffed with things hat grow in the dark, guaranteed to make you foam at the mouth. Better than rhinocerous horn, they tell me . . ." He chuckled and handed them each a slice. They chewed in silence until Hughes asked Toby how things were going in Kansas City.

"Good. We could use a few more airplanes, but of course we'll need crews to fly them. The military is calling a lot of our reserve pilots back into the service. The same is happening at all the other airlines."

"Where are you getting new pilots?"

"We're beating the bushes . . . and some of the applicants don't have much time."

"Do you think we'll get into the war?" Hughes seemed to have thrown the question at both of them. Kiffin said he hoped not, that he'd seen enough wars to last him for a while.

Toby said, "I don't think so . . . the way things are, Roosevelt could never swing it alone. Too many people are against him."

"Do you think this flight around the world I'm about to make is a nutty mistake?"

One of the things Toby liked about Hughes was his way of firing off an unexpected, direct question. There had been times when he had felt like he was dodging a cannon ball aimed at his belly. "If you're going to make it this may be your last chance for a while," he replied.

"You just said you didn't think we'd get in a war."

"If they're shooting in Europe it may be sticky trying to fly a nice new Lockheed between bullets."

Kiffin said, "The Germans and Italians have made some big improvements in their aircraft, Mr. Hughes. They learned a lot in Spain. We really don't have an edge on anyone."

"You went with Lockheed after *Hell's Angels*, righ Testing?"

"Yessir. And also at Northrop."

"How come you're still not at either place? They fi you?"

"No, sir. I have an itchy foot."

"You seem to get around fine. How is it flying with o leg?" He'd heard about that too.

"The flying's okay. It's the getting in and out that take some preplanning."

"Would you like to work for us?"

Toby thought he must be dreaming. If he had fed Hugh the words things couldn't have fallen more in line. He hea Kiffin say that indeed he would like to work for Hughes if could be a flying job.

"It would be a damn shame to have a pilot with yo experience flying a desk, handicap or not. Toby . . . see to that we take him on in flight engineering, where we ha problems. We've got to do something about our dam Stratoliners before they bankrupt us. We've got to stop t engine failures, fires, and delays for every damn little thin that can happen to an airplane. I like to be progressive, b when every flight we make with those airplanes becomes a experiment it means either we're doing something wrong Boeing is so busy trying to build bombers with the same wir they goofed on us."

Hughes rose stiffly to his feet, almost as if he was rheumati Toby thought. Or maybe he'd just had a hard night.

Hughes padded the length of the room in his bare feet, the returned to Toby. "The air corps has asked us to start multi-engined flight school. Can we handle it?"

"Sure. We may have to scratch around for instructors."

"Then start scratching. Albuquerque would be a god place for training. Mostly fine weather there."

Hughes took off his hat and tossed it at the piano in o corner of the room. He picked up a report off the coffee tab and flipping through it, seemed to have forgotten their existenc

Toby nodded at Kiffin, they both stood up. There w never any question when an interview with Howard Hugh was finished. As they made their way quietly to the do Hughes looked away from the report long enough to sa "Good luck, guys. Come back next month with all o problems solved. Then I'll have some new ones for you. I've given Lockheed the go-ahead on building Constellations.''

Tendrils of fog hung from the tree branches and became so gathered to the sight at a distance they appeared to be growing parts of the forest. The stream in which they fished with such dedication dissolved into the gray sky only a few hundred feet away and nowhere in all their surroundings were there any sharp lines. The quiet was broken only by a soft whirring as they cast their lures.

The four had remarked on the fact that they were gathered as a family on holiday for the very first time, and they recommended to each other that they do more of it. Toby and Kiffin stood on the bank several yards apart with Lily casting in between them. Flip, very proud of a new pair of waders, stood up to his thighs in the stream and had been the only one to catch a fish.

Lily found the whole scene deeply satisfying and had lost almost all interest in the fishing itself. She was too entertained watching the differences in the way the "family" fished. Toby was deliberate and relaxed about every movement he made while Kiffin was impatient and erratic. Flip took his casting with total seriousness and had developed a style of his own.

When any one of them spoke it was in subdued tones as if they might scare the Arkansas wilderness rather than the very occasional fish.

Toby wiped at the mist which had settled on his features, making them all the more powerful and clean-cut. "At least in this kind of weather I can take the day off with a clear conscience." He smiled at the languid stream and said that on a day like this even the ducks canceled their flights.

Flip asked sotto voce, "Why can't the ducks fly today?"

"Because they need a horizon just like we have in our airplanes or they spin in. Nature forgot to give them an artificial device like we use."

"Okay. If you have the instruments why aren't you and Uncle Kiff flying today?"

"Because the ceiling is right down on the ground and we haven't perfected a way to land blind."

"Will we?"

"I expect so."

Later they found a reasonably dry spot under a buxom maple tree and Toby reminded Lily that it was very near this place where she had first told him she was pregnant. "Now look what've you've done," he said, and pointed out Flip slogging up the riverbank. He was reluctant to leave the fishing even for food.

When they had settled down to eating Lily asked Toby, "Why don't you pretend you're George Washington at Valley Forge and cheer up your troops?"

"I didn't realize you're depressed. The weather is lousy and the fishing is lousy but you're not supposed to actually *catch* fish when you go fishing. The real pleasure is in hiking much further than you intended, getting your feet soaking wet and hooking your fingers a few times."

"Don't forget," Lily said, "insect bites, even if the fish don't."

Kiffin said, "You could catch poison ivy in a place like this. I hear there's a lot of it going around."

Kiffin paused, regarded his sandwich thoughtfully for a moment and then looked directly at Lily and Toby. "You know, folks, lately I've been wondering if I might be a little crazy."

"Are you about to say something profound?" Lily asked.

"Maybe . . . maybe I'm beginning to understand that I don't really deserve you people. Any of you . . ."

"Granted that," Lily said. "What are you leading up to?"

"It's been three years since I came back from Spain. I've loved the work and the chance to be with you guys once in a while. But I can't keep this up forever . . . writing reports on why the Boeing's heating system has broken down again or why it rains in the cabin when there's not a cloud in the sky and why we haven't got the condensation problem licked yet . . ."

He put his hand on Flip's shoulder. "My friend, you should know there are a jillion different birds in the sky and they differ, just like people. You might say your dad is a pelican . . . maybe he's not so beautiful, but he's absolutely dependable, he's *there*, and one very fine flier. And then there are the cukoos—"

Toby interrupted. "Are you trying to tell us that you're about to take off again?"

"Well . . . there's too much going on in Europe. I feel left out of things. Now there's an outfit in England called the American Eagle Squadron.''

Lily said that it seemed she had heard this song before.

At almost the same hour that President Franklin D. Roosevelt met secretly with Winston Churchill aboard a cruiser off Newfoundland, Kiffin entered the Waldorf Astoria Hotel on New York's Park Avenue. He knew exactly where to go, thanks to a telephone call he had made to a "Colonel" Charles Sweeney in Salt Lake City, an addicted soldier of fortune.

Kiffin had been temporarily loaned to Boeing as a test pilot after John Tower had been killed flying a prototype of the new B-11 bomber. One night in Seattle Kiffin had met Tower, both men discovered their mirror image, and Tower had talked on through half the night about how they were both missing the big show in Europe.

Kiffin was ripe and ready for a change. Even if he'd wanted to join the pilot's union at TWA it would have been impossible since he had never been a regular line pilot. And Toby could do nothing to squeeze him into the all-important seniority list. "The hell with it," Kiffin had said, "I'm my own security, such as it is . . ."

. . . That was all behind him now and a new feeling of freedom inspired a swing to his limp as he crossed the Waldorf lobby. It was, he realized, a splendid sensation to be rid of *all* encumbrances, the very last of which had been a near calamity. Thanks to God, and Lily, who had finally taken a hand in the matter, he had missed becoming the husband of one Winsome Brockaway. Recapturing her face now he marveled at how much trouble a pair of well-placed cheekbones could manufacture; the more so since Winsome's face was normally vapid of expression and her voice had already soured. She also had an annoying tendency to tuck her lower lip under her front teeth on those rare occasions when she entertained anything like a serious thought and she frequently spiced her conversation with four-letter words.

Now, he thought, there was no rational explanation why he should have been so taken with such a creature and had actually considered marrying her. Had he just been hopelessly lonely or had his brief liaison with her been yet another example of the kind of woe a man could bring down on himself if he stayed too long in one place—Kansas City, his best friend's house, or elsewhere?

Some protective instinct, perhaps, had caused him to take Winsome to meet Lily, almost as if, he now realized, he were taking her home to mother. Lily, *mother . . . ?* Anyway, the meeting had moments of female hair-bristling that soon proved to be a salvation.

. . . Kiffin consulted the slip of paper he took out of his pocket on which he had written "Clayton Knight Committee—Suite 1455." Knight was the well-known aviation artist who believed the United States should be more directly involved in the war against Hitler and had formed a group to help American pilots join England's Royal Air Force.

As he gave the elevator operator the floor he wanted, Kiffin thought it a strange time to be remembering Winsome Brockaway, but her encounter with Lily would not leave his mind. The two women had not exactly become instant soul mates, and it hadn't been long before Lily had asked Winsome if she knew what she was getting into. The tone of her voice had not been particularly cordial, and Winsome's reply had been even more caustic. "I've seen worse husband material. Junior isn't my first and he may not be my last. I've been married three times and they were all sonsabitches."

Winsome's use of her favorite title, "Junior," had not exactly built a rapport with Lily. She'd said that maybe she was old-fashioned but she respected her husband and considered marriage a lifetime commitment. Which remark, in turn, had somehow prodded Winsome's peculiar sense of humor and she broke into a spasm of raucous laughter, saying something about a cat having nine lives and she'd surely favor another tumbler of bourbon, thank you very much. As the bourbon seeped through her veins she had warmed to her favorite subject—herself. She'd begun with a lecture on women as the playthings of men and how they should stick together to survive . . .

Now, standing in an elevator, he was amused to discover that he could recall almost verbatim the essentials of Winsome's speech. " . . . all you've got to sell in this world is your little ol' hootenanny so make the most of it. I come from a very fine family down Texas way and I've seen what happened to my mom when she didn't take a stand and tell my daddy to go fuck off when he annoyed her. Junior's all right, though. He comes to heel pretty good when he gets randy. I keep him hungry and just say *down* boy . . ."

Winsome had giggled for a full minute after sharing her wisdom, and had been so busy ho-hoing and slapping her thighs she had failed to notice the glaze that had passed over Lily's eyes . . .

A narrow squeak, Kiffin thought, as the elevator door opened and he started down the hall.

He was surprised to realize he was almost marching, swinging his artificial leg briskly forward, as if he alone could hear some inaudible band. What in the name of God caused him to repeat history in this silly way? For the third time he was about to become a volunteer.

Once again here was the same old American neutrality theme at work, although this time it was played to a different tune. The free French were established in New York's Berkshire Hotel with the presence of Madame Rene Pleven, who was making it easy for American pilots to join their Air Force. In spite of her charm, it was "no thanks," from K. Draper this time. The French had learned nothing since he had served with them and had proved it by sticking their heads in the mud and building the Maginot Line. The Germans had learned and remembered, created swiftly mobile forces that passed right around it. The British had also been mired in traditional military thinking, but here at the Waldorf they were still in business and needed all the help they could find.

As he crossed the parlor of the suite Kiffin did his best to strike out boldly. His artificial leg was made of a new plastic material and was much lighter and more comfortable than the old one, but it still made a slight ticking sound as he moved. He hoped the gray-haired middle-aged man who stood up as he entered was at least a little deaf, but a long developed instinct told him that he had noticed his limp when he first came through the door.

"Smeeton," the man said while holding out his hand. He was very tall and very British with a proper guardsman's moustache. "I've read about you. Please sit down. Make yourself comfortable."

Since Spain it seemed the whole damn world knew about his handicap. Make yourself as comfortable as you can with a pegleg.

They spoke briefly of the weather and of Smeeton's desire to some day visit the American heartland. Kiffin suggested he visit Lincoln, Nebraska, where he would find a warm welcome and the people straight-forward. They went on to the virtues of the United States' "Lend-Lease" program to Britain and the disadvantages of "pickling" airplanes and sending them to England by ship—it meant disassembling the wings and even the tail feathers on some models and exposing them to submarine loss before they had a chance to be used. Both men agreed that the Canadians, through of all agencies the Canadian railways, were doing the right thing by flying the Lockheed Hudson bombers direct to England. And they agreed that it was ludicrous to pretend the United States was preserving its precious neutrality because the bombers were landed just south of the border and towed across to Canadian soil on the end of a rope.

Smeeton pointed out that there was a pilot recruiting office for that otherwise admirable enterprise in the old Murray Hotel located further south on Park Avenue. "You might want to have a talk with those chaps. I understand the pay is excellent . . . much better than anything we could do for you, I'm afraid."

"I'm not much interested in pay, I want to be where the action is."

"My dear fellow . . ." Smeeton said, "I should think you'd have had enough of that sort of thing. Of course your past experience is invaluable but . . . if I may say so, you're . . . a bit long in the tooth for combat. We're looking for lads in their late teens or early twenties. You do look remarkably young, but—?" Smeeton held up his hands in a gesture of resignation.

"Hell, I'm only forty-four," Kiffin said.

"Dreadful, isn't it. Something we all have to accept, I fear." He hesitated then added, "However, if you're bound to get yourself into uniform, perhaps we could make some adjustments. Perhaps we could place you as a flight safety officer or in operations . . . the odd something along that line. The pay by American standards is, of course, abysmal."

Kiffin took a deep breath, shook his head, and muttered something about wanting a flying job. Then he said quite clearly, as if Smeeton had suddenly left the room, "Jesus. What happened? Suddenly I'm an old man . . .?"

CHAPTER
24

Now the clarions of the European conflicts echoed around the world, but in the United States a curious mixture of disbelief that such events were actually happening combined with the release of enormous energies to transform the country. Some Americans did trouble themselves to take the boasting of Adolf Hitler very seriously, yet the majority were still committed to a business-as-usual week and the self-indulgent life.

It was a long way from St. Paul to Berlin and from Memphis to Warsaw. The fate of countless Jews was not cataclysmic in the minds of the American population, except to the Jews, who were often torn between sympathy and tribal duty while at the same time reluctant to stir up possible resentment against themselves by advocating immediate intervention.

Even so, larger sections of the American people were becoming aware that something very big was now at hand and was threatening their daily lives and liberties. Many young men were being drafted, outfitted with the soup plate helmets of the first Great War and trained in a lackadaisical fashion at various army posts across the land. More and more reserves were being called into active service, including the majority of licensed pilots who were invited to take commissions or become military instructors. National Guard units were being transferred to active duty and although the atmosphere of the nation was anything but military, the restlessness of a people preparing—whether they knew it or not—for war was apparent to anyone who would take notice.

It was against this forceful undercurrent that Toby Bryant's old friend Slim Lindbergh now argued publicly and with some success. Disapproval of his theories and pronouncements were general throughout the aviation fraternity, a rejection from those who had previously regarded him as a true hero. His efforts were soon lost in the contagious excitement of threatened danger, agreeable prosperity and an enormous shift in population . . . Black people migrated from the south to the northern seaports of both coasts where the building of armadas jammed the shipyards; midwesterners of multiple job skills and some with none at all turned their backs on their birth-states and went to California and Washington and Maryland, where the once modest aircraft factories were exploding with commissions . . .

At last no area of the country remained entirely unaffected by the surge of national vigor, and soon the dynamic movements of people and goods became so compounded that the transportation services were hugely taxed. Trains were full both of passengers and freight and suddenly the airlines, so long the striving orphan, found themselves amid an unpredictable bonanza with such a demand for seats that a priority system had to be inaugurated.

Women of every description and often surprising backgrounds flocked to the new opportunities for jobs, and "Rosie the Riveter" was born . . . Indeed, Lily Bryant was among those who found the temptation to shake loose from the traditional housewife routine and join the fray irresistible. It was significant and a direct reflection of the newly emerging American woman that Lily did not inform her husband that she was taking a refresher course in flying at a small field near Kansas City. She continued until she had qualified as an instructor with the new government-sponsored Civilian Pilot Training program, after which she did, proudly, tell him.

Soon after his arrival in England Kiffin was posted to 71 Squadron Royal Air Force, otherwise known as the American Eagle Squadron. They were stationed at Kirton-in-Lindsey, and Kiffin found himself regarded with such awe by his very much younger squadron mates that he was almost continuously embarrassed. A pilot who had survived the first Great War? And Spain? It was soon an established fact that he had lost his leg in combat with the Baron von Richtofen. He let it be. If only they would stop deferring to him on every occasion, from mess-time to passing through a doorway . . .

"My job," he told them, "is to make sure you guys don't kill yourselves before the Germans have a chance at you . . ." Although he thought his assignment as squadron safety officer was much too placid for his taste, he was at least near the action. He usually welcomed new recruits in the briefing room, and often their anxious faces revived images of his earliest flying days in France. His opening address had become almost standardized:

"Consider how lucky you are. How many guys do you know back home who get to sit behind a beautiful Rolls-Royce engine and give it all it's got? The Spitfire is a very forgiving airplane, but if you're thinking about that girl down at the pub just before you land you may be in for a nasty surprise. Number one is, of course, remembering to extend what our British friends call the undercarriage or cart. Spits land nicely on their bellies, but the destruction of our own aircraft does not inspire official applause. Next, absolutely no monkey-shines on final approach to landing. That means no low-level rolls and no cowboy slips. Just set your power up for a comfortable rate of descent and stay in the groove until you touch down like a feather . . ."

Kiffin was popular with his squadron mates, but talks on ordinary flying safety was not particularly interesting to young men whose job was to contest the sky with enemy aircraft several times a day. When they yawned Kiffin could not blame them. He was much relieved when Smeeton appeared at the mess one noon wearing the stripes of a Wing Commander. He asked if Kiffin thought his leg would give him any trouble entering and exiting a Hudson bomber.

"*No.* I flew production tests on them when I was at Lockheed."

"Very fine. I suspect you could do with a bit of change in your routine. They're very short of ferry pilots in Montreal and we've a flock of Hudsons to bring over."

"I can be packed in sixty seconds . . . make it thirty."

"We'll worry about the paperwork later. There's a Liberator from Ferry Command leaving out of Prestwick in the morning. Fetch your kit and I'll see you get up there. . . ."

The English now found themselves in much the same situation as the Loyalist Spaniards when the hordes of Germans sought command of their air space. Except for the Spitfire and the Hurricane the RAF fighters were no match for the Messerschmitt 109s, which were now much improved thanks to the Spanish experience. The Germans were many and the aerial defenders of Britain appallingly few. Very brave young airmen did the best they could, and Bomber Command, flying huge old Halifaxes, fat Wellingtons and lanky four-engined Lancasters over Germany at night did inflict serious damage on the enemy. Still, their own losses were heavy and the demand for new aircraft and crews to fly them remained insatiable.

One of the main supply lines to satisfy the pressing need for more aircraft was the RAF Ferry Command, and the transfer of Lockheed Hudsons from Canada to the United Kingdom was already a well-established if sometimes harrowing operation. Since nearly all the flights were flown across the North Atlantic at night the threat of possible antiaircraft fire from German submarine was unlikely. The only real villain faced by all three outfits—RAF Ferry Command, Canadian Ferry Command and the civilian crews originally employed by the Canadian railway—was winter. From mid-October until mid-May the weather across the route was often filthy, and although the crews were skilled they sometimes wondered how much more nerve-wracking actual combat might be.

Kiffin made his first flight out of Montreal's Dorval Airport in mid-November. The Lockheed "Hudson" was a military version of the Lockheed "14" and had already proved itself a fine flying machine except for a quirk in its fuel system that caused the right engine to indulge in spasms of backfiring at unpredictable times. Kiffin remembered that all Lockheed test pilots were familiar with the fault and had given up on finding the cause. Endless modifications had been made to the fuel system, and still the problem persisted. Some pilots swore the fine Pratt and Whitney engines had a soul that found itself incompatible with the airframe and chose to protest at the most vulnerable times—at night in bad weather, when over large bodies of water or mountains, or when the pilot tried to take a quick nap.

Kiffin's first crew consisted of an eighteen-year-old Cockney corporal from East London who had done thirty-three missions over the continent in ancient Blenheim bombers and after being shot down and parachuting into occupied Holland had been given the ferry assignment as a rest. He complained about the lack of heat in the Hudson all through the night, swearing to God he would come down with pneumonia before they sighted the coast of Ireland.

Kiffin's navigator was a baby-faced twenty-year-old Welsh-man on his first solo flight. He had diligently prepared himself for his navigational duties by pre-calculating the shots he would make of various stars throughout the night. To his astonishment the entire night was spent in heavy cloud, and by dawn when there were a few breaks in the overcast, the stars had become invisible. His fears that they might become lost were not helped by Kiffin's casual remark that as long as they held a steady easterly course land would appear, eventually.

The day after turning over the Hudson to a domestic ferry crew in Scotland, Kiffin boarded another Liberator and returned to Montreal. The RAF crew, worried about picking up ice in an airplane notorious for lack of ability to carry it, resorted to a standard ferry command alternative; to stay above the worst weather they flew the entire trip at twenty-thousand feet. There was no heat in the fuselage of a Liberator. Their uncomfortable passengers, strewn like so many dead carcasses along the floor, endured twelve hours of bone-aching cold while fighting off total collapse from lack of oxygen. Kiffin said that even his artificial leg hurt.

Flying eastbound with Kiffin this time was Odansky, a gloomy Pole who had joined the RAF as the best outlet for his all-consuming hatred of the Germans. Kiffin's navigator-wireless operator was another eighteen-year-old. His face was splashed with freckles, and Kiffin found his Northumberland accent nearly incomprehensible.

This second eastbound flight in a camouflaged Hudson was far less comfortable than Kiffin's first. "Freckles" confessed that he had become disoriented less than an hour after they had reached a cruising altitude of nine thousand feet. Like Kiffin's previous navigator he had depended on better weather for his celestial sights and when he found himself in solid cloud he had become increasingly uneasy. Desperate for some rescue to his addled position reports, "Freckles" threw his total dependence on a series of direction finder bearings. Lacking experience he believed them even though he had been warned in Montreal of considerable aurora activity, which would affect all radio transmissions.

About three hours after they had reached cruising altitude the Lockheed began picking up ice. At first the rate of accumulation was slow and Kiffin was not too concerned, but in time the total load made it impossible to maintain altitude and a safe airspeed. He was obliged to start a descent and became so busy with the physical demands of flying that he was late in questioning Freckles' repeated course adjustments to the north.

At a thousand feet they were still in a cloud, still picking up ice, and sinking. Kiffin ordered Odansky to have the Hudson's little life raft ready at the door although he knew it was a formality. Accomplishing a successful ditching even in daylight and on smooth water was largely a matter of luck. At night in the huge seas of the North Atlantic, it was nearly impossible.

At last it became apparent that the signals Freckles had been relying on were false, and he came close to tears when he informed Kiffin that he had only the vaguest idea of their present position. There had been reports that German submarines were deliberately transmitting on the same frequencies as the stations in Iceland and Ireland, hoping to confuse navigators or lure them into the mountains of Greenland.

This December night the result was nerve-wracking. Still in cloud, fighting to maintain even a thousand feet, Kiffin knew they were far below the gigantic mass of Greenland. Yet now if he turned back there was not enough fuel aboard to make Newfoundland.

The longer they flew the more ice the wings and fuselage of the Hudson acquired and the greater the alteration of the air foil that kept them aloft. With the greatly increased weight, Kiffin was obliged to use more fuel and soon the rate of consumption was far beyond a tolerable limit.

Only one slight compensation: Kiffin saw that in flying at the lower altitude the rate of ice accumulation had decreased. He began to hope that if he could find a level where it might stop completely the loss of total weight in fuel consumed would help keep them in the air.

An hour later he was still using full power on both engines and beginning to wonder if they would have enough fuel to divert from course and try for a landing in Iceland.

The flat crucking sound of the ice flipping off the propellers and striking the fuselage like countless projectiles was nerve-shredding. Combined with the high RPM the noise was barely tolerable, and felt like being tossed around in an empty icebox. Now the Hudson had taken on a strange bucking motion that puzzled Kiffin. He wondered if the ice formed some kind of eccentric shape over the Hudson's tail feathers? Suddenly he was compelled to ease his frustration and as if he were addressing the elements directly he yelled, "One thing's for *sure*. I'm getting too old for this sort of thing . . ."

His comment failed to amuse Odansky and Freckles.

Banking the Hudson very carefully lest it get away from him and stall, Kiffin altered course to the south, but in spite of his caution he lost altitude in the maneuver. As the Hudson sank through five hundred feet and then down to four hundred, he did realize that here, so close to the sea, the temperature was just a few degrees warmer and that at least gradually the ice was beginning to flake off the airplane.

He ventured down another hundred feet and thought that he must be skimming along just under the surface of the cloud deck. The night was black. When the windshield had cleared enough to see anything, he switched on the landing lights, and caught his breath as he saw whitecaps only a few feet below. He yelled at the faces that hovered close to him. "We've got it made . . . if we don't run into a convoy . . ." Optimistic, he knew, but justified under the circumstances.

During the rest of the night Kiffin decided against trying for Iceland. Direction finder signals from the RAF establishment at Reykjavik operated erratically, and if for some reason they missed Iceland there would be no more chances. The squeaky choice was to press on eastward. There was an airfield at Nutt's Corner in northern Ireland that had not maintained a "neutral" status as had the southern Irish. It also had a powerful radio beacon that should soon start coming in.

Dawn revealed a gray boiling sea below, with nearly every wave streaked by long white tails of scud. Freckles had regained enough command of himself to be realistic and admit that although he had only the foggiest idea as to their position, Nutt's Corner, he thought, must be somewhere directly ahead. How far ahead that somewhere might be remained a mystery, since the cross-bearings he'd taken from stations in the Shetland Islands and Iceland made no sense. If the sun appeared at all it would be at least another hour before it would be high enough to shoot with his octant and at least try for a line of position.

And in another hour they all knew the Hudson would have consumed the last of its fuel.

Attempting to cut down on the rate of fuel consumption, Kiffin had reduced power as much as he dared. At least the ice was gone and the total weight of the airplane was much less because of the fuel consumed. At six pounds of weight per gallon the Hudson became 500 pounds lighter each hour. It was now flying well although not much faster, he thought wryly, than Slim Lindbergh had flown over these same waters nearly fifteen years previously.

The increasing light illuminated a sky strewn with multilayers of cloud and Kiffin debated climbing to a much higher altitude in the hope of picking up a favoring west wind. Yet a climb back to nine or ten thousand would require precious fuel and he decided against it. Here, practically on the surface, the wind was out of the south and of no help or hindrance. And down here in denser air he liked the way the airplane was flying. Maybe it was old-fashioned seat-of-the-pants reasoning, but on this grim morning he thought instinct was better trusted than wishful calculations.

During the next hour they made a meal of sandwiches and lukewarm coffee. They knew that within the next hour, give or take ten minutes, one of two events had to occur . . . either they would see the coast of Ireland appear out of the gloom, or the engines would quit and they would splash into the turbulent sea with little or no hope of survival.

Kiffin smoked continuously and was well into his second pack of cigarettes since the take-off from Montreal. He looked down at the thrashing ocean and irrelevantly remembered that smoking was bad for his health. So was trying to put a Lockheed Hudson down in the Irish Sea.

Freckles had tried repeatedly to raise any station with his wireless key, transmitting on five hundred kilocycles, the distress frequency. There had been no reply, and at last Kiffin had told him to give it up. "The Germans who are out here don't want to talk, and the English who are out here don't want to talk or the wrong party might say hello. But for sure they're both listening. So sign off by sending love and kisses from Shark Bait."

Kiffin ordered them to secure their life jackets. At least, he thought, it was giving them something to do during the next long long minutes.

The fuel gauges in the Hudson were of dubious reliability, and now they both read "Empty." They knew more exactly that there was not a drop remaining in fuselage ferry tanks. Kiffin knew the strain was beginning to tell when he found himself lighting a second cigarette before he had finished the last. Abruptly he saw a black mass fringed with a white collar of foam directly ahead. It had to be the coast of Ireland, and he yelled at the somper specter. "There you go! The auld sod!" And he thought that to a blind man even the sight of a garbage can could be beautiful.

Kiffin was surprised at the resilience of his so-called mind. Seconds before the sighting he had been preparing himself in every way he could for ditching and the termination of his life, since the sea had become rougher than ever. He knew that even if he could have landed without killing them all, crawling out of the airplane and into a small life raft successfully would be asking for a miracle.

Now here he was suddenly worrying only about whether the rapidly approaching land was the friendly Ireland of the north or the hostile Ireland of the south, where they would be interned.

Kiffin cut even further back on the power until the Hudson was barely floating through the air. As they passed over the huge breakers pounding the shoreline and slipped over vivid green fields, the needle of the direction-finder pointed directly ahead. Now, using the shore as a reference point, Freckles shouted that they had only fifty miles to go.

Kiffin brought the Hudson straight in to the long runway at Nutt's Corner. The engines died of fuel starvation before he could taxi to the little operations building. Odansky grunted dourly. "Fuck this. I'm going back to combat."

Freckles took out a rosary and kissed it.

And Kiffin lighted another cigarette from the nub of the one he had been smoking. Suddenly he was so sleepy he allowed the smoke from his cigarette to curl up and further torture his half closed eyes. He could not know, of course, that more than seven thousand miles away the Japanese had bombed Pearl Harbor.

CHAPTER
25

When President Roosevelt delivered his "Day of Infamy" address to Congress most Americans had already marked forever in their minds exactly where they were and what they were doing when they first heard the incredible news. There was, in effect, no other durable subject of conversation.

Within a few days helmeted Air Raid Wardens patroled the beaches along the Pacific coast and blackouts of huge areas were the law. There were public alarms and alerts of every description, nearly all of which were proved illusory. Japanese-Americans were herded into groups and transported off to camps. To the consternation of many American women an embargo on Japanese silk was declared, which resulted in a wild rush to buy every available silk stocking.

Unity for Americans was neither automatic nor easy. Even as General Douglas MacArthur was preparing for a last stand at Corregidor, the CIO ordered union members to strike against Bethlehem Steel, where many of the most vital components for the pursuit of war originated. The settlement was declared by the union as a great "victory." Most were patriotic, but some did seize on the war as a bountiful grab-basket.

As for Sourdough bush aviators like Orville Tosche, Noel Wien, Bob Reeve, Harold Gillam and Joe Crosson, they flew through the Alaska winter to help establish air bases in places most people had never heard of, and countless other fliers took off on a thousand different missions to various parts of the world; it was understood that Americans must collect themselves and expand their efforts at an even faster pace.

Now the frontiers of national interest were everywhere on earth. Patriotism was not sung in quite the naive chorus as it had been during the first Great War, but neither was it disdained by the majority. Hitler and Tojo were excellent targets for national anger. Mostly the country knew why it was at war, and wholeheartedly supported it.

As with all the airlines, the flight activities at TWA continued around the clock. Toby rarely had his feet on the ground long enough to spend any real time with Lily and Flip. The over-ocean flight services in flying boats to England and Portugal offered by Pan American Airways had become inadequate against the press of rapidly expanding logistics, and Toby's unit, known as the Intercontinental Division, began flying additional priority passengers and cargo in the new Strato-cruisers. As a result of the haste in which the service was assembled very little went as planned, and Toby found himself trying to pacify all kinds of people from statesmen bound for London to seismologists and bull-dozer drivers en route to some previously obscure locale where there was pressing need of an air base.

Lily Bryant now called on the ever faithful Mrs. Anderson to look after Flip when he returned from school each day. She tried to believe herself as she persuaded Mrs. Anderson with all the eloquence she could muster that since she could teach flying and Mrs. Anderson alas could not, their duty to their country was clear. Mrs. Anderson was one of the few remaining American citizens who still believed Charles Lindbergh was right in his isolationist stand. She had no way of learning that he had experienced a sudden change of heart after Pearl Harbor, and despite having resigned his commission in the Air Corps now volunteered his services for any duty including combat.

Thanks to her experience during her barnstorming days, Lily qualified as a flight instructor in less than a month, was hired by a small flight school near Kansas City and flew six days a week. At first she was assigned to primary training, which was easy enough since she had only to teach her students the basics in docile little Piper Cubs. The training was paid for by the government. Students were required to be enrolled in a college or university and when they were ready the Air Corps had first call on their services. Best of all, they were not eligible if they had any previous flight training, an ignorance that Lily found worked to her benefit. Challenged for the first eight hours with the new and strange business of taking an aircraft aloft, maneuvering it according to her demands, and bringing it down safely kept the students as easy to handle as the airplanes . . . they had no preconceived notions or bad habits to lose.

It was when she started giving advanced training in Waco UPF-7s that she ran into new problems. The Wacos were two-place, open cockpit fabric-covered biplanes with a 220 Continental engine. They were a good aerobatic airplane, and Lily delighted in the release she found in performing the basic maneuvers—loops, rolls and spins. Toby and Kiffin had taught her well, but now she found that her role as a flight instructor was affected by factors beyond her control.

Those students who hadn't been washed out for clumsiness or lack of aptitude during primary training knew they were at a critical point. Once again they were in danger of being rejected if they showed any tendency to be squeamish about the more violent maneuvers or hanging upside down by their safety harness. There were those whose stomachs refused to keep up with the rest of their bodies during snap-rolls. Lily could watch her students in a rear vision mirror, and if they froze when she rolled a Waco on its back and dove straight for the ground she tended to recommend they find a different way to serve their country.

There were those students who simply could not get the hang of reversed controls during inverted maneuvers and "dished out" when they attempted a simple roll. Lily lost track of the number of students who would have killed themselves if she hadn't taken over at the last possible moment.

With the tensions built up during such advanced flying the students were inclined to be taut and on the defensive. Most of them wanted to fly in the Air Corps and they knew that if they failed at this stage they could well be drafted into the ground forces. A few students, convinced they were much better than they actually were, attempted maneuvers beyond their own or the airplanes' ability, and Lily had to warn them they were pushing the "next-of-kin" button.

Lily's worst hurdle seemed to be her sex. As a woman she offered a handy target for students hoping to escape blame for their own failure to excel . . .

Maxwell Stark, a twenty-one-year old student at the University of Missouri had been having a bad day aloft with Lily. His loops were egg-shaped, his rolls inexact, and he had not once been able to finish off a spin on a predetermined point. When he came into land he bounced four times before Lily decided enough was enough, took the controls and eased the Waco down gently.

Stark was from Wyoming, born and raised on a ranch, a lean hard-muscled young man with a neck of outsize length and a small head that caused him to look not unlike a crane poised to strike. His little eyes were dark and honest, although he seemed to have difficulty focusing on anything but distance. He rarely addressed Lily head on, turning his head to avoid her eyes throughout their post-flight discussions.

This day Stark waited for Lily to slip out of her parachute and climb down from the front cockpit, then he pulled off his helmet and goggles and tossed them in the air. Lily tried hard to keep her voice even when she asked him what he thought he was doing.

Stark took his time emerging from the rear cockpit. When he reached the ground he picked up his helmet and stood looking at the horizon with his fists jammed down hard in his pockets. "I'm damned mad, that's what I am," he said through tight lips. Lily saw that for once his eyes were burning with expression. "Let's get somethin' straight right now, ma'am or whatever we're supposed to call you. I joined up to fly and fight . . . not to be mothered. How in tarnation are you supposed to teach anybody to fly when you ought to be worried about what's on the stove for supper tonight? If the maned ol' Air Corps wants me why do they hang me with some female instructor? Hell, a man'd be better off goin' into the infantry . . ."

Although Lily had long before prepared herself for some chauvinism she hadn't expected such a direct confrontation. She devoutly hoped it would stop with Stark.

She decided a collision was inevitable and she might as well settle it now. "Stark . . . if you're always going to fly the way you did today then there's no question you'll live longer in the marching army. You're far enough into the program now to avoid making so many dumbbell mistakes—"

"It just seems like you have the ol' whammy on us with you sitting up front there and watching us in your mirror. If you don't seem natural. Hell, you're a *woman* . . ."

"I'll take that last as a compliment. But what's my gender got to do with flying?"

Stark seemed to keep his eyes fixed on something miles in the distance, a way of many farm-bred people to advise another person that their conversation would best not be dragged out with extraneous chit-chat. "Like I say, ma'am," Stark went on, "like I say, it's plum hard on the nerves. I can't concentrate. And all the guys feel the same way. Hell, you never cuss us out, that's one thing . . . and then you never take over the controls before we hang ourselves. That's what all the guys say—"

"If I take over how are you going to learn?"

"Well, it just seems plum dangerous. Criminee, I don't want to kill myself, or you either."

Lily managed to smile. "That's nice of you. If it comes anywhere near your landing performance a few minutes ago you can be sure I'll take over."

She watched Stark as he shook his small head unhappily and continued to examine the end of the field. "Stark," she said, "if you're thinking about requesting a transfer to one of the male instructors, you go right ahead. But I'm willing to bet that if you fly for them the way you have for me you'll be washed out in ten minutes. You're not exactly a natural-born aviator, but I'm still hopeful that if this very husky airplane can tolerate just a little more of your ham-handedness, and if my patience holds out, maybe, just maybe I could solo you without covering my eyes and praying."

"Ma'am," Stark said, swiveling his head slowly to look straight down at her, "I jus' never was much of one for music, and a harp has never been my favorite instrument, so I'll just mosey along down and find me another instructor."

Lily was still trying to shake off the feeling that she had somehow failed with Stark and might be responsible for his future demise in a trench when she found him waiting at the flight line on the following afternoon. He stood in his crane pose, holding a small bouquet of flowers in one hand and his flight jacket in the other. He waited while Lily told another student about his tendency to hold his nose too high in side-slips. When they had parted Stark approached her, held out the bouquet. "I guess you deserve more'n these."

There went his eyes again, she thought, off to the most distant horizon.

"I goofed and I should have kept my mouth shut and not made myself mouthpiece for all the other guys. The ones who've flown with you don't think you're so bad . . . including me."

Lily accepted the bouquet. "If this is a peace offering, I accept. Thank you."

"Well, sometimes if you don't saddle a mustang jus' right he can be awful obstinate . . ." Stark's eyes returned from the horizon and focused on her directly. "Couple hours ago I went up with Porky Kiem and he wrung me out pretty good. When we landed he said he hoped I could ride a horse because he was recommending me for the cavalry. He said he never had seen a student who could inflict so much abuse on a flying machine in his whole career and that he'd been flying a long long time."

"He washed you out?"

"Yes, ma'am. I begged him not to be so drastic and he finally changed his mind, said he didn't want my blood on his hands either if I was on a horse or in an airplane. But he didn't close the barn door all the way. He said that if you would take me back you could make the final decision and he would forget he ever saw me."

That was big of Porky, she thought. Porky Kiem was a tough exbarnstormer and crop duster who considered abuse of flying students a part of his standard curriculum. He snarled his colorful profanity through a Gosport tube and was possessed of a unique ability to make a student wish he could find a place to hide in the airplane or crawl on his hands and knees once they were on the ground. "Airplanes," he would announce at the beginning of every lesson, "can think of more ways to kill you than any other thing man has invented. The worst thing I can do is solo you before you're ready and if you displease me or say nasty things about me, I'll do it. That's how I get rid of people I don't like, so pay attention."

"It was my impression," Lily said to Stark, "that you weren't learning anything from a woman." Let him squirm a little, Lily thought. Until she had a sudden, disturbing vision of Stark standing in a trench too shallow to accommodate his long neck and his head swiveling around between bullets.

"Please take me back, ma'am. You'd never guess it, but I do love this flying. Honest to God I do. Give me a chance and I'll show you . . ."

For once Stark's eyes failed to rove the horizon—his whole

attention was on her now and she suspected that his use of the word "love" had not come easily to him. . . .

Two months later Maxwell Stark graduated from the program and went on to the Naval Air Station in Pensacola. The last Lily heard from him was a V-mail note from the Pacific, where he was flying off the carrier *Lexington*. They'd both done pretty well, she decided.

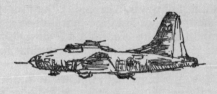

B-17 Bomber

By the spring of 1943 Lily had been instructing for more than a year and began to realize that much of her keenness for the job had disappeared in the slip-stream of countless landings, take-offs and aerial maneuvers performed by others. She knew the accumulated strain and tensions were beginning to tell on her; there were always the decisions that often had to be made instantaneously . . . should she allow a student to go just a little bit further before he found himself in trouble or stop him before he had a chance to acquire an unforgettable fright? The penalty for a wrong decision could too easily lead to tragedy. Before the demands of war, instructors led a relatively sedate life with long periods of ground time waiting on the next customer. Those prospective aviators who could afford the cost of learning to fly were few and far between and most pilots viewed instructing as only another way to avoid near-poverty. Now with the government paying the bills and an apparently unlimited supply of hopefuls, the tensions and pressures never let up. Instructors began to feel "burned out," some became careless and others found their sensitivities to the approach of a dangerous situation hazards in themselves and lost much of their value as instructors.

This time Lily did discuss her new intention with her husband because she knew she might be away from home for a week or more at a time. She wanted to follow her friend Betty Gillies' example and join the Women's Auxiliary Ferry

Squadron started by another aviatrix, Nancy Love—already established as an elite organization for ferrying military aircraft.

Since both Gillies and Love were two of the most attractive, feminine women Toby had ever met, he found it impossible to fall back on conventional arguments . . . even if he'd wanted to.

"You told me yourself they were doing a valuable service," Lily reminded him.

"This is a hell of a war," he said. "The man stays home and tends the hearth while mother goes off to battle. But I guess Flip and I and Mrs. Anderson will survive."

Of course that was a considerable exaggeration. Lily was not going off to battle but to New Castle Air Base in Delaware, and while Toby's headquarters remained in Kansas City the airplanes and crews he was responsible for were flying missions to every war zone for the Air Transport Command, and Toby's job was to troubleshoot, whether the problem was in Labrador or Cairo.

As in most wars, the most hard-pressed participants were frequently frustrated by the apparent slow pace of events. Yet now at last the combined efforts of the Allied nations began to crowd the skies with aircraft. Considering that it was an island besieged, England produced a remarkable number and variety of fighting aircraft. In addition to the familiar Spitfires, Lancasters, Hurricanes, Halifaxes, Mosquitos, and Lysanders, they improved the ugly duckling American B-24 and dubbed it the "Liberator." The British would name all aircraft rather than duplicate the American style and identify them by mere number. The Yankee air crews who now flocked to England like migrating wild fowl often needled the British about their name-calling, and because so many of their designs had the eye-appeal of Portuguese galleons tossed by storm in to the sky they labeled them all "Sidestrander Chuffingtons."

The absolute necessity of commanding the air was now apparent even to the most hidebound staff officers of every combatant. The airplane had flown the full circle of its history and progressed from a questionable plaything employed by warriors seeking the bird's-eye-view of their enemies to the most powerful system of destruction and potential for victory ever known. The political might in even the passive use of aircraft was growing with such speed it was obvious that it would soon replace the traditional role of a fleet.

The number and variety of aircraft launched from the American arsenal was astounding. The lumbering Consolidated B-24 made life and death miserable for Rommel's Africa Corps, and B-17s were changing the face of Germany. Coming hard behind them were the much larger B-29s destined to rule the skies of Asia.

There were the smaller twin-engined bombers; the formidable Douglas A-20G, North American's very versatile BO25, and Glenn Martin's B-26.

Among American fighter aircraft the P-51 easily was the match of the German Messerschmitts, the P-47s, or "Jugs," so-called because of their fat profiles, and the P-38s, a twin-engined fighter built by Lockheed. There were the Bell P-39s, one of the few American aircraft that proved a disappointment, the Grumman F4F and F6F, the "Black Widow" night fighter built by Northorp and the marvelous F4-U gull-winged Corsair fighting so well for the navy.

Even while the Germans were at their throats, the Russians managed to produce the rugged Yak, which was designed to operate directly with their ground forces and so was a sort of flying artillery. Unlike too many Allied aircraft they could be maintained in the field by relatively unskilled personnel using simple tools.

The Japanese, usually so innovative, were strangely lagging in the development of new designs. Their bombers, the Nakajima-43, the Val, the Dinah, and the Mitsubishi were relatively small and antiquated. They continued to rely on their lively little "Zeros" as fighters and had failed to make enough improvements in them to outfight their enemies.

The French and Italians, both in hostage to the Germans, produced only a few Junkers 52 transports for their masters.

The Germans, always air-conscious, scrambled about desperately for new aerial weaponry, and thanks to a national treasury of aeronautical talent sent aloft among many others the Focke-Wulf 190 fighter, the Messerschmitt 109, the Arade, the various Heinkels, Junkers and Dorniers. They also developed a highly experimental rocket-powered aircraft known as the ME—163. It could climb to 30,000 feet in 90 seconds and was at least a token forecast of aerial things to come. In secret, still fumbling, both the Germans and the British were exploring the feasibility of using pure jet engines.

It was because of the gigantic demands for manpower and

materiel to service the Allied armies sprawled over such distant territories that the United States found itself in a geographical position not shared by any other belligerent. The country was at war on two fronts, and the frontiers joined on the opposite side of the world.

From this central depository there flowed staggering amounts of materiel, food, medicines and transport, home-style amenities, shelters, fuels, natural resources and the raw ore of human beings. Most of the shipments were by sea, but the priority claims of emergency after emergency called for a constant increase in long range aerial transport. It became imperative then to develop techniques and auxiliary equipment to assure their dependable arrivals at worldwide destinations. The Air Transport Command, charged with the execution of these projects, proceeded with admirable daring to solve problems previously thought to be the private province of the now hopelessly inadequate Pan American Airways.

The beginnings of the Transport Command were humble, in contrast to the big Pan American flying boats. Both Air Corps and civilian crews flew the military version of the reliable twin-engined DC-3s to all areas of the war but they could only offer a puny assist until more and larger transport aircraft became available. Corsair began a trans-Pacific service with conversions of the BO24 bomber and Curtiss was launching a new very large twin-engined transport known as a Commando. The Douglas Company, under the watchful eye of Benny Howard, was turning out the DC-4 Skymaster, a promising four-engined transport.

All of these aircraft were soon bringing home the wreckage of the war in the form of young bodies, sick and mutilated beyond the average American's comprehension. They also provided a quick return for the carcasses of those who would never again occupy them and for handfuls of war heroes so disbelieving of their survival and imminent arrival on American soil they sat in glum contemplation of their feet or engaged without heart in the card and dice games held in the cabins. Many air corps passengers tried to remember what they had been like when they had flown off to war, but it was difficult to find any similarity to their present selves and they soon abandoned the thought.

*   *   *

By the summer of 1944 it became obvious that the Japanese were in trouble and the Germans headed for defeat. The leaders of both these Axis powers had failed to maintain air superiority, and having lost it now found it impossible to regain. While the losses of Allied air crews were painful and sometimes difficult to justify, the total number of aircraft engaged was stunning and the percentage of casualties much lower than had been anticipated.

Similar lopsided statistics became routine to the Transport Command because of the preponderance of outgoing passengers and cargo. Toby Bryant was only one of many pilot-executives involved in such a huge operation, and like his counterparts seized on every excuse to escape his desk and command a flight himself.

Boeing 314 Pan American Clipper

Soon after the liberation of Paris from four years of German occupation Toby was asked to supervise TWA's share of Air Transport Command flights out of the resurrected Orly field. Although the airport was still pocked with bomb craters the new Douglas C-54s were such fine performers that operations in and out of the field were already well-established. Toby had to pretend he was distressed and seriously inconvenienced when he was advised that the regular line captain scheduled to take the next flight back to Washington had eaten something in Morocco the preceding night and was absolutely incapable of commanding his bowels, much less a trans-Atlantic flight.

After visiting the ailing captain, sympathizing with his misery and making sure he knew where to find medical attention if he needed it, Toby reported to the hastily built operations shack at Orly and signed himself in as captain of the flight. The rest of the crew understood why he was smiling and looked forward to flying with a pilot of Toby's near-legendary reputation. . . .

It was seven o'clock in the evening when a sergeant-clerk pushed a sheaf of papers across the operations counter for Toby to sign. It was the weight and balance form for the flight and the cargo manifest which specified various pieces of a captured German V-2 rocket bomb. There was also a thousand pounds of mail, and for a nostalgic moment Toby wondered what he would have thought if in his helmet-and-goggles days someone would have foretold that a flight like this could happen.

The sergeant was saying " . . . and we have a dandy bunch of passengers for you, captain. Real V.I.P.s plus two lucky M.P.s going along as armed guards. Get a load of the ranks."

Toby glanced at the passenger list and saw that the names were all German—General Felix Baumgart, Colonel Henrich Falk, Colonel Otto von Worbach . . . Major Sebastian Muller, Captain Kurt Ritter . . . in all there were some twenty names, none below the rank of captain.

The sergeant said, "As I understand it these types are all from the German 7th Army who got themselves captured in the Falaise Gap. You'll be met with a guard in Washington."

In the last of the twilight Toby saw his passengers being herded toward the rear door of the C-54. He was not prepared for their appearance, and for a moment he wondered if he was watching a bad movie afflicted with the worst of ham actors. For if the Germans had been in a war, and certainly they must have known at least four long years of it, they had somehow managed to conceal the wear and tear. Their uniforms appeared to be immaculate right down to their gray suede gloves. Their boots were polished. "Staff Officers," he told his crew. Yet it was not so much their uniforms that made Toby wonder about the Teutonic military cult. It was their arrogant bearing in the face of defeat. They stood straight as posts and ignored the squad of guards surrounding them. They mounted the steps to the high rear door where they were checked off one by one, their progress all the way being more of conquerors rather than captives.

Toby flipped through the passenger list again. Generaloberst Helmut Brundschien . . . Generaloberst Victor Buchmann . . Generaloberst Peter von Loes . . . Oberst Ernst Mulhausen . .

Oberst Otto Schiller . . . If they would talk, which seemed doubtful at the moment, they should provide a gold mine of information back in Washintgon.

Twenty minutes later Toby eased the C-54 off the runway and climbed into the night. As he made a gentle left turn he saw a few red hazard lights on the Eiffel Tower, then the aircraft became enveloped in a cloud. If the forecast held true they would remain in cloud for approximately two hours, when the weather should become scattered to broken clouds. By the time they landed at Lagens in the Azores to refuel the night should be clear.

Except for his co-pilot Loggen, who Toby had actually hired a few years back, and Yanick the flight engineer, the old time TWA mechanic, the other crew members were relative strangers. Perry the navigator, he remembered having seen in Kansas City. He was a short, plump, serious man with a childlike face and a voice so high it sometimes sounded falsetto. He'd asked permission to turn on the light over his little table and was already engrossed in his charts. Since Toby could see no further than the instrument panel anyway, he had decided there was no reason to deny his request.

Soon Perry came forward and taped a small note just below the magnetic compass. It was the initial course for the Azores—"230."

Blum, the radio operator, sat directly behind Toby. He was a curly haired New Yorker, so myopic his glasses reflected the faint array of lights like crystal bowls . . . maybe it was his poor vision that led him to believe the world ended at Hoboken. Like nearly all radio operators he seemed to live in a world of his own and had already retreated into it via the staccato ticking of his "bug."

When Toby leveled the C-54 off at eight thousand feet Yanick pulled the four throttles and propellers back to cruising power and adjusted the mixtures. And once more it struck Toby as odd that he could still be flying after starting in Blériot days. The difference now was that it took a crew of five. He was already sleepy. Age coming on? Or was it just his sense of contrast with the rest of the crew, whose schedules allowed them a pre-flight nap?

Yanick said he hadn't been able to sleep. The huge fuel trucks of the "Red Ball Express" passed right by the crew quarters as they speeded to support Patton's tanks. The roar

of their engines and eighteen wheels pounding the cobble-
stone road never let up.

Yanick was small, taut and apparently incapable of speech
without a generous seasoning of profanity. Toby knew him
only by reputation as an excellent mechanic now graduated to
the flight deck.

If all went as planned they should arrive in Washington
about fifteen hours, Toby calculated—counting an hour's
layover in the Azores for fuel and a meal. Somewhere during
that time he would curl up in one of the two bunks in the
crew compartment behind the flight deck and try for a few
hours sleep. After the Azores the weather forecast was to be
benign all the way to Washington. Even the prevailing westerly winds were laying down a bit . . . proving that the
elements had some consideration for aging aviators? For sure,
there was no satisfaction for a man like leaving earthbound
duties behind and flying a fine airplane.

Somehow when aloft it was possible to become a mini-
god, at least temporarily. And there was a wide perspective
that was impossible to command under any other circumstances.
As now it was easy to visualize the far different night to the
east where other airmen were making Germany a nocturnal
hell, and to envision Patton's tanks closing with the desperate
Wermacht. England, still awake, would be taking a few buzz
bombs and maybe V-2s, but otherwise the skies over the
U.K. would belong to the RAF and to Americans like Kiffin
Draper . . .

Now the French coastline in the vicinity of St. Nazaire
should be below, and the Bay of Biacay off to the left.
Further south would be North Africa, at last controlled by the
Allies with fine air bases at Casa Blanca and Marrakesh.

Westward the Azores, those volcanic peaks extending from
the Atlantic floor, were like a tranquil haven from all the
world's stresses, and the lights of Lagens should come into
view just after midnight. Beyond, then far beyond, lay Ber-
muda still in daylight, and still further to the west—home.

Toby glanced at his watch, which was on Paris time. He
went through the ritual arithmetic trying to subtract from
Greenwich time which was displayed on the instrument panel
clock and calculate what time it would be in Kansas City. He
ran into his usual confusion on what should be a simple
matter. Seven hours difference? That would make it two

o'clock in the afternoon. What would Lily be doing this afternoon if she was in Kansas City? She could also be away flying. And Flip? At least he was in place. Doing what? Eating, most likely. The kid had an appetite to keep Mrs. Anderson jumping. Well, some things were right in the world.

And how about the rest of the world as seen from this special perch, where the horizon was less than three feet away and yet to the mind's eye, unlimited. There would be countless other airplanes over this ocean just now, one of them flown by friend Bob Buck also of TWA. He would be on his fascinating if not too enviable assignment to fly through the worst weather he could find anywhere over the Atlantic. Now after over a year at that job he had accumulated invaluable data . . .

It occurred to Toby that with all the problems involved in dispatching three aircraft to North Africa, two to Egypt, four to the U.K. with parts for P-47 fighters that had been missent to Paris, and two "litter ships" full of wounded for Mitchell Field, Long Island, he had not had a chance to eat since noon. Maybe he had passed on his appetite to Flip . . .

"Anything to eat on this airplane?" he asked the instrument panel, as if it could provide the information along with course, speed, and altitude. One of the peculiar perks of being a captain was the certainty that any comment he might make would be listened to with automatic respect and any request he might make would spark at least some kind of response from the crew.

Yanick said, "There should be some Spam sandwiches back in a box on the lower bunk. You want me to look?"

"No thanks. I'll look myself and take a leg stretch."

Toby nodded at Loggen as a gesture that he was now in charge. He twisted out of his seat and moved back to stand in the darkness between Blum and Perry. Both men were vaguely illuminated by little pools of light from the fixtures on their stations.

Toby watched Blum's extended thumb and forefinger dancing back and forth with incredible speed against the handle of his key. It was a sight that always intrigued him. When Blum moved a headphone away from one ear and looked up smiling, Toby asked, "Who're you talking to?"

"Kansas City. I gave them our departure time, fuel aboard load, all that stuff."

"How are they coming in?"

"Good . . . considering there's a lot of static. But we can usually get through with CW."

"I've always wished I could bang a key like that."

"I've always wished I could fly an airplane." Blum adjusted his heavy glasses. "But I probably couldn't find the controls."

They laughed and Toby turned to Perry on the opposite side of the flight deck, sitting in his own dim pool of light, copying numbers.

"Good. I like guys who think ahead."

Toby started to turn away when Perry suddenly got to his feet. The top of his prematurely balding head barely came to Toby's shoulder.

"Skipper? Could I ask you a question?"

"Sure."

"The scuttlebutt is that you flew in World War One. Is that a fact?"

Toby hesitated and hoped it was too dark for Perry to see the expression on his face. "I'm afraid it's true."

"You don't look it. Hey . . . wait till I tell my wife I flew with a guy who was in the air that *long* ago."

"I'll tell you something, *son* . . . maybe I don't look it but I'm beginning to feel it. Thanks anyway. I think."

Toby brushed aside the black curtain separating the flight deck from the crew compartment and let it fall into place behind him. It was a small room the length of the two six foot upper and lower bunks that could not quite accommodate a man of his size. He switched on the light and caught the image of himself in the mirror over the washbowl. Don't look it? There was a face that looked like a long traveled flight bag—rumpled and sagging, everywhere.

He drew a cup of coffee from the electric pot fixed to the bulkhead and sat down on the edge of the lower bunk. He opened a white cardboard box, found a sandwich wrapped in oil paper and bit into it without confirming its contents. Sometimes it was best not to be too inquisitive about flight food. This time the bread was not quite stale.

As he munched away he chided himself for even questioning the quality of a Spam sandwich. There was some argument as to the actual identity of Spam—mince of aged turtle—grind of buzzard claws—mix of walrus liver and testicle of coyote, with some bison thrown in. But it was a lot better than the scraps people in eastern Europe were scrambling for and the "C" rations that kept the fighting troops in business.

Here indeed was a luxurious war. There was a proper lavatory and hot water for shaving in the morning. There was the steady reassuring rumble of the four big Pratt and Whitney engines that flanked each side of the compartment. And best of all, no one was shooting at him.

He picked up a copy of *Stars and Stripes,* which someone had left on the bunk beside the sandwich box. Good cartoon by Bill Mauldin. The guy was a genius at drawing his sadsack GIs. As he began to read about a show Marlene Dietrich had given to the troops in North Africa he found himself squinting and rubbing his eyes. "Well . . . well . . . who's beginning to need glasses? Old Toby Bryant . . . old eagle beak, you have postponed the inevitable about as long as you can."

When he had finished his coffee he opened the after bulkhead door and let himself into the brilliantly illuminated fuel compartment. Here, supplementing the fuel stored in the wings of the C-54, were four round tanks holding two hundred gallons each. It was a noisy place with no insulation against the roar of the engines just outside. Air led into the compartment to assure ventilation combined with the slipstream against the fuselage and made a constant hissing noise.

Although he had never detected any odor of fuel he always sniffed suspiciously when he passed through the compartment. Nor had he ever talked to any crew member who had. Never mind. Still, he'd never been really comfortable with so much explosive material just waiting to spring a leak. It was an uneasiness dating, he figured, from the earliest days of the C-54s when the main fuel tanks leaked so badly it was dangerous to stand beneath the wings.

He opened a second bulkhead door and passed into the quiet of the cabin. The overhead lights provided an eerie twilight punctuated by a series of light pools along the length of the cabin. The passengers sat in metal bucket seats along both sides of the cabin, their faces and bodies in shadow. One of the Germans was reading a small book that looked like a Bible. He had to lean forward in his seat to see the print. The rest sat motionless, like so many wax dummies, Toby thought.

As he passed between them he saw that several were dozing although they remained erect. Those who were fully awake followed his passing with their eyes, but did not turn their heads. Literally and figuratively, stiff necks.

Now Toby was close enough to see that they were not quite as smartly turned out as he had first believed. Their boots were shined, but they were weary looking and the pants of those who were not wearing boots were wrinkled and stained with mud. Almost all of them needed a shave and there was a certain leathery toughness about them that was apparent even in the shadows.

The two M.P.s sat near the rear door where they could command a view of the entire cabin. Somehow they looked inadequate for the job . . . both were very young—barely twenty. One was black, a young fellow whose biceps threatened to burst his shirt sleeves. The other was lanky and hawk-nosed, his complexion pitted and weather-worn. Both wore their sidearms. They were sitting on two ammunition boxes playing acey-deucy. Their holsters were pipe-stoned white according to military police custom, and short lengths of braided white cord hung from the gun butts. Their collar ornaments glistened even in the dim light.

Toby found himself wishing there were just more of them. "Hi," he said.

"Hi . . ." They paused in their playing. "How we doin' up front?"

"Fine. We should be in the Azores in about another two and a half hours . . . maybe a little longer."

"Oh boy. When do we get to God's country?"

"Tomorrow morning. With luck, very early."

"Yea, man," both M.P.s sighed.

Toby turned to look forward at the Germans. Still stiff, trying to look unbeaten. Lean, hard faces, not an ounce of fat anywhere. Toby wished it was daylight so he could point out a convoy going their way. Maybe the sight of a few hundred heavily loaded ships would shake some of the arrogance out of them. Did they really believe Hitler's claim that their U-boats had everything under control on the high seas?

He turned back to the M.P.s. "How come there are only two of you guys for twenty prisoners?"

"Top sergeant says he can't spare any more. Nearly all the

est of our company's in Germany. Things are sure moving ast.''

''It's going to be a long night for you guys. Five hours onger than usual because we're flying with the sun.'' He lanced at the Germans. ''What happens when you get sleepy?''

The black M.P. laughed easily and said he didn't need any leep—he was too excited about a chance to put his ass right lown in the good old United States. The other said he felt the ame way, but if they had to sleep they would spell each ther. ''And besides,'' he added with a nod at the Germans, ''those Krauts won't make no trouble. They seen all the shootin' hey care about.''

''Well, just don't start shooting in their direction. There's ight hundred gallons of fuel beyond the door, and the tanks re only aluminum.''

''Don't you fret,'' hawk-nose said. ''We both babysat lots vorse than them.''

Toby stood for a moment balancing his body against the light swaying of the tail, a movement imperceptible to the iverage passenger. It was quiet and pleasant here in the cabin. He walked slowly back toward the fuel compartment, passed through it and then into the crew compartment. He pulled aside the black curtain and let himself into the darkness of the flight deck. He saw that Loggen had moved over o the left seat, and he told him to stay where he was. He sat lown in the right seat and waited for his eyes to adjust to the darkness.

He spent some time trying to make the automatic direction finder pick up the transmitter in the Azores, and when he finally succeeded he told Loggen he would relieve him. Loggen said that if it was all right with Toby he would like to leave the flight deck and take a leak and a fast nap, in that order.

''Sure, go ahead, it'll be my turn out of the Azores.''

Toby settled down to monitoring the automatic pilot. On course. Good speed. Engines drumming smoothly.

Some thirty minutes passed. Toby had turned the panel lights down until he could barely read the instruments. He leaned far forward, looking up. Yes, the cloud cover was beginning to break. A few stars, unknown to him because there was still not enough clear sky to fix them in a constellation, were glistening like small wet beads.

He remained in his forward position, forearms supporte
on the panel cowling, his chin on the back of his hand, th
only light a feeble amber glow from the magnetic compass. I
was his favorite position in C-54s . . . here, with his nos
almost against the forward windscreen, he knew the sensatio
of having all the world to look on during the day and hi
private planetarium at night. Here, cut off from the confine
ment of a very small room inhabited for many hours by fiv
individuals, he knew a sense of belonging to the elements h
could never quite explain. It was something like the old ope
cockpit days, and he wished his present job gave more oppor
tunities to enjoy it . . .

He heard a movement behind him. Perry the navigato
must also have become aware that there were a few stars t
be had. He would be climbing up on his four-foot aluminun
stool, octant in hand. When he'd mounted it he would straighte
cautiously and his head would be in the astrodome. He woul
hang his octant on a hook in the center of the Plexiglas
bubble, and when the stars he wanted appeared he woul
sight on each one for two minutes. When the octant moto
clicked to a stop he would be able to read the average of the
star angle on the vernier, then would record the angle anc
time, wind up the octant, choose the next star and repeat the
whole drill until he had three sights. After that he'd plot them
on his chart as a triangle. If Perry was a good celestial man
the triangle would be very small; if he was careless it could
cover fifty miles of ocean and unless he cheated he'd be
subject to certain ridicule from his crewmates and sometimes
a biting remark from his captain. No matter. Whatever position he came up with would be ancient history anyway. It
would only suggest that they had been in a certain air space
over a great ocean at a certain time. Useful . . . if not an
immediate fix.

He listened for a moment to the steady beat of the engines.
Kiffin crossed his thoughts. It had been almost six months
since he'd seen him, a full Flight Leftenant now, very dashing in his RAF uniform, of course incorrigible as ever. They
had arranged to meet in a London pub and had enjoyed a
wonderful two hours together until the arrival of his latest
experiment—an English WREN from the island of Malta who
was attractive if a little chubby. She was also a nonstop talker
and the get-together had gradually dissolved into a succession

f her bawdy monologues. Toby shook his head. When Kiffin vas a hundred years old he would still be looking for his deal woman and falling in love with the wrong ones. God elp him . . .

He was about to turn around and ask Perry if he'd any luck vith his sights and kid him about taking so long with his igures when he felt something hard against the back of his eck.

He started to smile. Apparently someone in this crew failed o share the common awe the others seemed to hold for the old goat who had flown so long ago and who was actually heir boss. Someone was having a joke, and being damn ough about it. He didn't much appreciate it—

"Change your course. Turn around. Go to Spain."

Toby turned his head very slowly. He saw a gloved hand ehind his right ear, knew the hard object was a gun.

He turned further to catch a glimpse of a German officer's ead and cap. The same voice said with hardly a trace of accent, "I am Oberst Schiller. I have killed a good many men so I suggest you do as you are told. We also understand navigation so there is no point in trying any tricks."

Toby remained motionless. "I'd like to turn up the lights."

"Why?"

"To set up a new course." He was surprised at how calm he sounded.

"Yes."

"I can't do anything with that gun against my head."

"Move as you need. If you move wrong . . ."

Toby eased back from the panel cowling and turned up the lights. The pilots' seats in the C-54 were elevated slightly above the flight deck, and when Toby turned to look at the German their eyes met at almost the same level. He recognized him as one of the younger officers. There seemed little question he meant what he said. An *oberst* . . . lieutenant colonel. He was heavy-featured although rather slight, and clearly determined.

Toby looked beyond him and saw Perry sprawled beside his chart table. Another German officer had a hammerlock on his head. A third officer had pinned Blum's head hard against his little table, he was gasping for air.

"Where's the rest of my crew?" Toby asked. Loggen had never returned from his trip to the lavatory, but Yanick, he

remembered, had been standing between the seats when he'
leaned forward for a look at the sky conditions.

"They are being sensible, captain. You be the same."

Sensible? He glanced over his shoulder at the curtain sepa
rating the crew compartment, its shape marked by a thin lin
of bright light. It did not extend down quite enough to mee
the deck, and now below it he saw three pairs of black boots

"Spain . . . now," Schiller said, and gave him a hard proc
with the gun.

Toby nodded toward Perry. "I need him."

"Why?"

"To confirm the new course. And calculate fuel. I doubt i
we have enough to make Spain." Which was a lie; there wa
enough fuel aboard to make Spain easily and much further
enough to make the eastern Mediterranean or Scandinavia.

"Captain, we have done all the calculating and timing. I
you have enough to reach the United States you have plenty
for Spain."

"We are not going to the United States—"

"We know better." Schiller jabbed him in the ribs anc
Toby tried to organize his shattered thinking. Franco's Spair
was supposed to be a neutral country, which was far from the
truth. The Fascist-dominated government had done every
thing short of engaging in actual combat to repay the Axis
powers—Germany and Italy—for their help during the Civil
War. They had surreptitiously provisioned German submarines
offered haven for spies and saboteurs and jammed radic
signals vital to the navigation of Allied aircraft and shipping.
Any German officer who landed there was certain to find a
least a lukewarm welcome and stood a good chance of being
returned to the Fatherland in a matter of days.

"I need him too," Toby said, nodding at the helpless
Blum.

"Why?"

"If he doesn't send the proper signals when we approach
the coast we might be shot down." Another lie.

Schiller smiled. "Who is going to shoot at us, captain?
The Portuguese? You think we are stupid?" The German
seized Toby's right ear in his gloved hand and twisted it until
he slumped far down in his seat and grunted in pain.

After a moment Schiller released him. "Now," he said,

"you think better. You have a family? You think about them and you think about Spain. You think about *nothing* else."

Toby felt his pulsating ear. It was not easy to keep his hands from trembling when he took the C-54 off the automatic pilot and started a turn toward the east. He heard Schiller say, "That is better, captain." He pointed at the magnetic compass and moved into the right seat, keeping his gun pointed at Toby. "I will be watching."

Even in the dim light Toby could see that the gun was an American automatic. It had obviously belonged to one of the M.P.s . . . the white cord was still hanging from the butt. He hadn't been wrong—the numbers were . . . two young G.I.'s were not enough for twenty German veterans who had spent the last four years surviving. Next time . . .

Perry called out from behind, "I don't have any charts for Spain, Skipper."

"Then just give me a general course." A *general* course? What a request. From their present position any course to the east was bound to pass through some part of Spain and that should satisfy the German, but it was important to make Perry appear needed. At least he was now sitting up straight and some of the terror had left his face.

Perry scribbled a course number on a slip of paper and started to take it forward in his usual fashion. He was slammed back down on his stool by the same German who had held his head in a hammerlock, who now snatched up the note and handed it to Toby, who solemnly pasted it below the compass. Zero-nine-zero degrees. When he had settled the C-54 on the new course he engaged the automatic pilot, sat back and waited for the trembling to leave his hands.

CHAPTER
26

Less than an hour later the C-54 was back in heavy cloud and increasingly rough air. Toby told Blum to hand him the flight folder, which had been prepared a few hours before their take-off from Paris. It contained the flight plan and a mimeographed chart of the North Atlantic and western European weather . . . it might be useful. Somehow he had to let the Germans know that the ball game was far from over.

The German who had held Blum down grabbed the folder out of his hand and gave it to Toby.

Toby told Schiller he had better tell his people not to smoke in the fuel compartment.

"They've already been told. I suggest you stop thinking we are stupid."

"Do you understand a weather map?"

"Of course."

Toby handed him the folder. "Then you'll understand we have some problems."

Schiller laid the gun carefully on the flat surface of the instrument panel cowling. Toby was pleased to see the magnetic compass swing twenty degrees toward the gun, and realized that if Schiller wasn't aware of the metal's effect on a magnetic compass . . . If he could follow the present 070 degree heading on the compass they'd soon be back over France. Maybe . . . just maybe Schiller wasn't as smart as he claimed to be.

Oberst Schiller examined the weather map carefully. He had put his gun just out of Toby's reach while keeping it handy to his own. "Where is the problem?" Schiller asked. "I see there is a low pressure system over Portugal and Spain. They cannot have sunshine always."

"We have no reports from Spain. And we have no charts.

It's a big country with a lot of mountains. If I start descending without knowing exactly where we are . . .''

Schiller smiled. ''You are a good pilot or you would not be here. You want to live, so you will find a way to get us down.'' Schiller tossed the map across the cockpit. It landed on Blum's little table. He reached for the gun and held it in his lap. He watched the compass swing back to its original 090 degree heading. ''Yes . . . I know about compasses. You had better stay on course.''

As the C-54 continued through the night the air became rougher and there were periods of heavy rain. Toby figured they were probably passing through the center of the low pressure area, and if that was so they should start picking up a southerly wind that would drive them toward the Pyreenes . . . He might as well be back in his dead reckoning days. Perry had a Loran navigational device on his chart table, but there were no reliable stations covering this area. And the cloud cover canceled any hope of using celestial navigation. Toby hardly needed Schiller to make this night a filthy one.

He turned around to Perry, who was hunched over his table supporting his head with the palm of his hands. Was he praying? ''How far off shore were we when we turned around?''

Perry raised his head and turned his face toward Toby. He looked like he'd been crying, not praying. ''I don't know, sir.''

''Take a guess.''

''Two-fifty . . . maybe three hundred miles.''

Toby tried to recapitulate the numbers. They had been airborne now for three hours, and eastbound for about one hour. In approximately one hour they should be over Portugal and in another thirty minutes, Spain. A reasonable but inexact estimate. Oberst Schiller shouldn't be so damned relaxed . . . they were bound into the unknown and would need some very fancy luck if they were going to survive the night.

As Toby bent his head and rubbed at the back of his neck to relieve the tension his eyes focused on the Automatic Direction Finder . . . abruptly a plan formed—a very chancy plan of action that *might* work . . .

He tried to remember a number, a simple three-digit number damnit, but it wouldn't come to him. All of the numbers he knew clicked off easily for him—office, home, street address. All stored in the brain so handy. But this all impor-

tant number? Where was it? Lost in the jungle of an aging
brain . . . unless he could remember it might not age much
more . . .

He tried thinking of unrelated numbers, still failed to resurrect the one he needed. Numerals . . . numerals three . . .
come to me, come to me, damn it . . .

He tried thinking of the gallons in their fuel supply that
determined the hours of flight still available to them. Two
hundred fifty-seven? Three hundred fifty-five? . . . Two hundred fifty-five? Something close.

And then it surfaced . . . two hundred seventy-five . . .
kilocycles. He cranked it into the automatic direction finder
and watched the arrow swing around until it halted twelve
degrees to the right of their present course. Now he would
have some help for his dead reckoning.

He tapped his finger on the glass covering the azimuth
circle. "There you go, colonel. Valencia. Coming in strong."

Schiller leaned forward slightly to study the needle. If he
were as rash as Kiffin, who he could certainly use right now,
Toby thought, he might just reach out, grab Schiller by the
back of his neck and smash his face against the direction
finder. The gun would be his . . . and then what? Dumb idea.
Not only would he lose an invaluable direction finder, but
someone in the back must have the other M.P.'s gun and
Toby Bryant, who had never been able to hit the broadside of
a barn with a pistol, would be lucky if he didn't do more
damage to the airplane than the Germans.

" . . . Valencia? How do you know?" Schiller asked.

"I know the frequency."

"Why would you know the frequency of a Spanish station?"

He would have to gamble some now, play it out. He might
even risk a bit of flippancy to show confidence. "Colonel,
you're the most suspicious man I ever knew. If you're so
convinced I can get you down in one piece you must believe I
know what I'm doing."

Schiller showed no evidence of a smile. "I want to be
assured you're doing what I want. The Spanish are not your
friends. So why should you know a Spanish station?"

"Sometimes on long flights we like to listen to their music.
Helps keep us awake. That's the truth."

Toby waited for Schiller to ask for some sort of identifying signal, but he seemed uninterested. Instead he said, "We do not want to go to Valencia. It will be better to go to Madrid."

It was time to take the long gamble. The firmer the stand he took now the more convincing he would seem when things got hairiest sometime within the next hour. Exactly when? Just for the sake of having some target to anticipate—say, within forty minutes . . .

"You're not going to Madrid as long as I'm flying this airplane, colonel. It's high, at least a thousand meters, which would put it in the cloud tonight. And there are mountains all around it. No thanks. Valencia is on the sea. When we pass over the station the arrow will swing around and point back. I'll wait a few minutes and hold course until I'm sure we're over the Mediterranean. I'll descend then until we see something . . . some lights maybe because there's no blackout in Spain. I'll turn around and follow the arrow back to Valencia, find the airport and land . . ."

For the first time Toby sensed that he was more or less back in command, not forgetting Schiller's gun. Still, Schiller needed him . . . if there was an aviator in his crowd he would certainly have been on the flight deck by now. "Take it or leave it, colonel," he said firmly as he could, "that's the deal. If you've hurt my men or are even thinking about it I'm just going to sit here until this airplane runs out of fuel. I'll cooperate and get you safely on the ground if you show me my men are okay. It's up to you . . . you've got a gun, I've got an airplane. If you shoot me you commit suicide."

Schiller rubbed at his eyes and shook his head violently, obviously a man trying to fight off exhaustion. After a moment he called out in German. The curtain to the crew compartment was drawn aside. Looking back, Toby saw Loggen and Yanick perched on the side of the lower bunk. Their arms were bound behind them. Their pants had been removed and had been used to tie their legs together just below their knees. One German officer was sitting beside them, smoking a cigarette. Two others were leaning against the after bulkhead, and the back of another blocked the rest of his view.

"What about the M.P.s?" Toby asked.

Schiller called back again. One of the officers went through the door to the crew compartment, disappeared for a moment, then came back with the M.P.s. He halted them in the brightly lit fuel compartment, and Toby saw they were standing in their bare feet, hands tied behind them. Probably with their boot laces. They looked grim. Beyond them in the dimmer light of the cabin, Toby noticed another German with an automatic in his hand.

"Okay, colonel," Toby said. "We got a deal."

He turned forward, pretending to concentrate on the flight instruments, an irrelevant action, since as the air became rougher the automatic pilot was doing a better job than any man could. He needed a moment to think . . . for all his show of bravado there were some very real problems ahead.

Toby put on his headphones, turned up the volume on the direction finder. He had to be certain the arrow was pointing at the station he wanted and not at the one the colonel wanted.

Schiller became interested in his movements. "What are you listening to?"

"Mostly static. Try for yourself." He pointed at the co-pilot's set of headphones. While Schiller was fitting the headphones to his ears Toby reached down in the darkness and turned off the "squelch" knob. Instantly there was nothing to be heard but heavy static.

Schiller frowned and pushed the headphones away from his ears.

"Bad reception tonight," Toby said. "Must be the weather." The first truth he had spoken in some time. The weather was of the sort that created ear-splitting static in the old days. Now the annoyance was almost eliminated by the new squelch controls that preserved the necessary low frequency signals and at the same time dissolved the static. Unless the colonel was very well acquainted with American electronics he wasn't likely to know about the little knob controlling the squelch device.

As Schiller removed the headphones Toby turned the squelch back on again, heard a voice speaking a few words in English.

The station was Gibraltar, just off the Spanish coast and, to the great benefit of Allied ships and aircraft, still in British hands.

Twenty minutes later the arrow on the direction finder took

n a lively quiver, a sure indication that the station it was
oming on was not far ahead.

Toby said, "It looks like we'll pass over Valencia soon. I
eed my co-pilot to watch for lights or the sea, to put the gear
own and a lot of other things."

Schiller spoke in German to the officer behind Blum. Soon
fterward Loggen appeared, rubbing at his wrists. Schiller
lipped out of his seat and stood behind it. "I will be right
ere watching."

One thing was for sure . . . if the weather below was as
ad as he guessed it might be, Schiller's nerves were in for a
ew kind of strain. His too . . .

After Loggen had taken his seat Toby couldn't resist a final
b at Schiller. "Can you read an altimeter, colonel?"

"Yes. Of course. We are now at five thousand meters.
ery high."

"No, colonel. We are at five thousand *feet*. Not so high.
here are some unavoidable inaccuracies in our indicated
eight because we can't communicate with the Spanish. Our
ltimeters read only our height above the sea level, not the
round. We won't know what the local barometric pressure
, so we'll be letting down into a black hole and we won't
now how deep it is. There's just one thing we can depend
n. An increase in the pucker factor. When those two needles
eet at zero we'll be damned sure we're too low."

"What is this pucker factor?"

"You'll find out, colonel . . . here we go . . ."

When Toby saw the arrow of the direction finder swing
round he pulled the four throttles back to an easy descent
ower and held his course. He had considered making a spiral
escent, decided against it. It was going to be hard to judge
is height above the sea at night, and if the C-54 was in a
ank he might catch a wing tip in the water—and that would
e that.

Gibraltar was very small. They would be leaving it behind
ow. The Mediterranean fringed the Rock to the east, but just
make sure it was where it was supposed to be he would
old course straight on for another four minutes, then do a
ne hundred and eighty degree turn back for the Rock. If they
assed through a thousand feet and still had no forward
isibility he would repeat the procedure in smaller time incre-

ments until he saw the sea or a Spanish light. Because o
submarines and trigger-happy surface ships he was reasonably
certain no one on the sea itself would be displaying a light.

One final determination. At all altitudes below one thou
sand feet he would check his time very carefully and neve
descend when he was bound west in the direction of th
Rock. He had passed over it once in '43 during a flight t
North Africa, and that view even from on high convinced him
that it wasn't easily punctured.

At three thousand feet they were still in heavy rain.

Toby let down another thousand feet, then turned abou
and held the C-54 level. He flew for three minutes toward th
head of the arrow, then reversed course and let down anothe
thousand.

He glanced at Schiller. The man's jaw was set, eyes riv
eted on the altimeter. Good. Let him sweat. He heard him say
something in a quiet, not so arrogant voice to one of th
officers behind him.

Toby made another course reversal. One thousand. Nothing.

The volume of rain hissing against the windshield in
creased rapidly, then abruptly stopped. Toby knew they had
passed through a squall. With the sudden quiet on the fligh
deck Toby figured the sound of his voice might be som
relief to his crew. "Do all of you understand what we'r
doing?"

Blum said he did. Perry's voice was weak, but it sounde
like a "yes." They must be trying to shore up their confidence
Toby thought, since from their present position in the rear o
the flight deck they couldn't possibly see anything except th
instrument panel.

The Germans, even Schiller, kept silent.

Loggen, who had extended himself as far forward as th
cowling around the instrument panel would allow, said h
thought he had seen a light a moment earlier but that it had
disappeared. He thought it might have been a reflection in th
windscreen glass from a flight deck light. It had not reappeared.

Toby turned back east away from the Rock. He let dow
another three hundred feet. Very gingerly. Rate of descen
barely one hundred feet a minute. Would a C-54 bounce if i
hit the sea while in nearly level flight? Or just come apart?

He heard Schiller say something to the other Germans

who now stood in darkness. His voice had become thin and nervous as he mentioned feet and meters, and Toby found a perverse pleasure in realizing he was at last very afraid.

"How are your bowels, colonel?"

It took a moment for Schiller to relate the question to the moment.

"Now," Toby said, "you know about the pucker factor."

Rain had started hissing along the windshield when Loggen shouted, "I see a whole bunch of lights ahead, they're all over the place . . ."

One of the design peculiarities in a C-54 was a small hinged window directly in front of each pilot. It could be opened at any speed and because of the inherent aerodynamics of the nose, the slip-stream bypassed the window and what little air movement occurred was outward rather than inward. The feature was invaluable in rain; the pilot was greeted with no more than a fine spray in his face, and had a clear view ahead.

Toby jerked the handle and opened this forward window. He watched Schiller jump at the explosion of sound. Even now, at a mere one hundred and sixty miles an hour, the sudden roar of engines and slip-stream was terrifying when heard for the first time.

Using the lights as a rough measuring device Toby judged their height to be about five hundred feet. The lights were now obviously fishing boats trying to protect their long gillnets from the continuous wartime traffic. They had to be Spanish boats, or possibly French, who knew they would be reasonably safe from attack by either side.

Now, Toby thought. Right *now* when it would be difficult to understand him over the roar he must take his next to last chance. He turned back to Blum. "Switch to five hundred!"

"What are you saying to him?" Schiller asked immediately.

"I told him we're at five hundred feet."

Pray to God Blum would understand he wanted the radio frequency switched to distress—five hundred kilocycles.

He picked up his microphone and spoke quickly and softly. He could not hear his own voice above the roaring. "Mayday, mayday. Hello Gib. American C-54 here. Several miles east. Twenty German prisoners aboard. Landing soon. No clearance. Please send large armed escort to aircraft. Appreciate your help. Don't reply."

Schiller asked, "Who are you talking to?"

"Valencia. We're practically on the ground."

As Schiller translated what he had said to the officers behind them Toby thought that if the German could tell one part of the Spanish coast from another on a night like this he deserved to win the war.

He slipped the microphone back in its receptacle and made a turn over the fishing boats until the direction finder needle pointed straight ahead. He waited, breathing in the dank night air, his intestines cramped.

The eastern face of the Rock became visible, a darker loom against the black sky. From this side it didn't look at all like the life insurance company's advertisements.

The rain stopped abruptly, and Toby thought the Rock now stood out too clearly. He closed the forward window and turned up the instrument lights. The less the colonel saw of the shoreline the better.

Toby's knowledge of Gibraltar was thin. He didn't, he realized, even know how high the summit of the Rock stood, but he figured the airport had to be on the western side.

He decided to circle around the south end of the Rock a few miles offshore and stay low. Once the arrow was pointing ninety degrees to his right he would turn north and follow it directly to the field. Where had he heard that there were apes on Gibraltar? Some enterprising soldier had brought them to the Rock generations ago, and it was said that when they left, the British empire would be no more . . .

They passed through several rain squalls before Toby sighted the field. The British must have heard him because he saw runway flares were burning. He could only hope those flares were not set for the arrival of some other airplane, in which case he might be mistaken for an unidentified aircraft and start shooting.

Toby circled over the flare path and saw several personnel carriers moving about. The rest of the field was blacked out.

He called for the landing gear. Loggen pushed down the control handle. A heavy rumbling followed and a final thump as the wheels locked in place. "I have three green lights," Loggen announced as routinely as if he were landing at Kansas City.

Good man, he's under control . . . "Give me fifteen degrees of flaps."

"Fifteen degrees . . . coming."

Toby jerked open his forward window and started the windshield wipers. He held one hundred and thirty miles an hour down to three hundred feet, then called for thirty degrees of flaps. Just before crossing the runway threshold he pulled off all power, and the C-54 touched down very gently.

"Nice landing, Skipper," Loggen said.

"I agree," Schiller said. He bounced the automatic in his gloved hand, and when it came to rest pointed the muzzle at Toby.

"I always make that kind of landing when I have nothing else on my mind." Toby was grateful for the rain. Try as he might there was little Schiller could see outside except the flickering flare pots.

When Toby had stopped the aircraft a jeep appeared beyond the nose, and he saw a dark figure beckoning with a flashlight. He followed the jeep off the runway, told Loggen to cut the engines. It was raining very hard now. Toby wiped the sweat from his face, looked at Schiller. "Here you are, colonel. For a non-revenue passenger you've had quite a ride. *Auf Wiedersehen.*"

Schiller looked at him for a moment, as though about to say something, then turned away without changing his expression and marched back toward the cabin.

Douglas DC-4 (C-54)

It was Yanick the engineer who went back through the cabin with the Germans and opened the rear door. A boarding platform had been pushed up to the door, and the Germans departed with great gusto. They were congratulating each other and chatting happily until their eyes became accustomed to the darkness outside and they realized they were surrounded by a platoon of British soldiers. A very British officer, complete with swagger stick, stepped out of the night. "I regret to inform you there has been a slight navigational error. Welcome to Gibraltar."

CHAPTER
27

The celebrations that came with the victory of the Allies in Europe were in dramatic contrast to the terrible six years that had now come to an end. Fifty-four million people had died, mostly civilians, and with them died many illusions about the limits of man's capacity to inflict death on his fellow man.

The bombs dropped on Japan soon after the German capitulation brought instantaneous death to many thousands at Hiroshima and Nagasaki and subsequent deaths and disfigurements to thousands more. Such statistics were to inspire more somber rallies, but just now the prevailing tone and mood were to be found in the shouts of triumph heard throughout the victorious nations. Of course new alignments were already forming . . . Russia was emerging as the post-war threat for the United States, Britain and France, taking the place of Nazi Germany in the minds of many leaders of these nations as the great threat to the face of the world . . . Some might say, with the French, *La plus ça change, la plus le même chose,* the more things change, the more they are the same thing . . .

Such thinking hardly applied to the airplane and its impact. The airplane ignored frontiers. The airplane erased the sense of protection offered by geographical distances. Now every nation knew that any other nation or combination of nations could be over their borders in a matter of hours. Sometimes minutes. Because of the airplane nationalistic islands artifically established so long ago became, whether they liked it or not, one. No matter how sophisticated or elaborate the defenses against territorial intruders might be they were discreetly recognized as imperfect, and as a consequence the major powers understood, for a while at least, that it was best to keep a relatively civil tongue in their heads. Even the worst of bullyboys risen since the celebrations of VE Day and VJ Day tended to measure their actions and military responses;

those improvident shin-kickers who convinced their few people they had nothing to lose continued to do battle in various lands, but they were skirmishes compared to what more informed leaders knew could now happen should they succumb to similar temptations. There was, of course, the A-bomb, though at the moment only the U.S. had it.

When at last the air age arrived fullblown it transformed the human race from the status of distant relatives to a family, and the characteristic squabbles were both diminished *and* augmented by the reality of the airplane.

The modern airplane was very much a product of the Second World War. All of the techniques from manufacture to operation were hugely influenced and accelerated by the exigencies of the war, and men like Toby Bryant would not presume to predict what former fantasies would become fact within the next few years.

Toby had found himself one of a small group of privileged pilots engaged in the swift transport of the history-makers. He flew several of President Roosevelt's contingent to meet with Stalin and Churchill at Yalta, and after the unconditional surrender of the Germans he joined with other carefully selected pilots to participate in a curiously Roman triumphal pageant—the flights of Generals Eisenhower, Patton, Bradley, and Clark, each from Paris to one of four cities in the United States. And as if to match the extravagance of those salute-thundering, ticker-tape convocations Toby was invited by Howard Hughes to be aboard the maiden test of his great flying boat—the largest airplane in the world. He was not in the least surprised when against all warnings and regulations Hughes decided actually to lift it off the water.

Glenn Martin, now in his early sixties, was also planning enormous flying boats to accommodate the anticipated civilian traffic across the oceans. He was also working on a more sinister project, the creation of a guided missile dubbed "the Matador."

Soon after VE Day Kiffin Draper was mustered out of the RAF and was immediately invited to become a member of a British team evaluating the German jet-powered fighter, which had seen only slight use before the Luftwaffe's final demise. Afterward Kiffin stayed in England and worked briefly for Rolls-Royce in a non-flying job. His "niece" the WREN, as he always introduced her, underwent a remarkable transformation once she was out of uniform, becoming almost over-night a Midlands barmaid with a voracious appetite and a sharp tongue. Early in 1946 she disappeared into the smoke of Manchester, and Kiffin was grateful that there seemed to be no need to pursue her.

But Kiffin took his time returning to the United States. He had received a modest inheritance on the death of his parents, who died within a month of each other, and when he decided that he'd had enough of England's postwar privations, he departed for Spain, where he spent a week trying to retrace his civil-war movements but found the country so changed he hardly recognized anything. Or was it he who had changed?

Trying to rediscover himself in the past, with the vague thought of thereby better planning his future, he even made a trip to the airfield on the plateau where Estrella had been killed. Only the nearby mountains were the same . . . a new crop of rocks had sprouted all over the field. Now all that he thought he remembered was gone, and there was no hint that the field had ever been anything but fallow.

Altogether he found the experience so melancholy he cut short his tour, went directly to Madrid and booked himself on the next available flight to the United States. That flight was in a Constellation operated by TWA, and the moment he stepped on board he felt at home. His sense of belonging was somewhat diminished, though, when he found that not one of the flight or cabin crew had ever met Toby Bryant or Howard Hughes. Here, he thought, was Rip van Draper, returning "home" once again.

Long before the hostilities came to an end the WASPs, started and led by the renowned aviatrix Jackie Cochrane, and the WAFs, led by Nancy Love, were told their services were no longer needed. There was an overabundance of male pilots; many were newly returned from combat and the official policy was to keep them flying.

Lily Bryant was among those who had flown so gallantly, and she tried not to be bitter about the general lack of recognition for what the women had accomplished.

Besides, she was ready for other challenges. Flip was now eighteen, a phenomenon that left her quite as astonished as when she first noticed his voice had changed. Where oh where had all the years gone?

Now she was determined that he learn the basics of flying.

"You can't keep your charter membership in a family like
ours without knowing how to fly," she told him. Flip was
more than willing, although he could not resist a series of
mock complaints about being the only flight student in the
world with a mother-instructor.

Toby settled down to the operational routine of keeping his
part of TWA as efficient as he could make it, but the problems were unending; more so, he sometimes mused, than
when there had been a tangible enemy over the horizon. It was
as if the world now suffered from a gigantic hangover; the
struggle for power continued as if the war had never happened,
especially with the emergence of a new and insidious
troublemaker.

Even with Toby's strong dedication to the air and his belief
in its future he had to wonder if what airplanes were doing to
the world he had known was all that beneficial . . . time and
distance were shrinking, but the clamor of the troublemakers
was also louder. There were fewer and fewer refuges in the
world, thanks in large part to the airplane.

American commercial aircraft were in tremendous demand
everywhere, and although they were far better machines than
the few new designs thus far produced by England and France
there were still many problems. Toby's own airline lost two
Constellations within ten months, a sorry record considering
they were flown by expert crews . . . Toby once said to Lily,
"I'm not sure if this business is keeping me young or making
me an old man in a hurry. Sometimes I think we're growing
too fast for our britches. It's open-season all year around on
airline executives, so don't be surprised if I show up unemployed one of these days." Lily said she was only after his
money. "Besides, the twenty-nine years we've been married
proves it's only a temporary affair." She added that sometimes he could be a terribly somber idiot, and, oh yes, she
loved him. . . .

The entire world now made hurried and often disastrous
attempts to take to the air. New nations created out of the
trade-offs from the war often chartered a flag airline before
elections had been held. England resumed air services to what
was left of the Empire in spite of her economic distress, and
there were rumors of a radically new British transport design
to be called the "Comet" and to be powered by four pure jet
engines.

France reentered the air with less imagination and flew only American-built aircraft, while Germany, in spite of defeat and partition, began service to New York and any other city where Lufthansa could obtain a landing permit.

Even the Japanese and the Filipinos, both exhausted from the ravages of war, employed American crews flying American aircraft to launch the name and reality of their flag airlines. As it once was in the great days of sail when England ruled the waves, now the United States dominated the skies.

Domestically there was a new threat to the established airline system that had been designed by the American government and assured by the financial subsidies of the Post Office Department. Everywhere new airlines proliferated, some with only one war surplus airplane, others with two or three and a few with several. The majority were speculative, even casual enterprises and many went bankrupt or had tragic crashes that put them belly-up out of business. A few, like the airlines started by the Santa Fe Railroad and the Matson Steamship Company, were well-financed and performed as well or better than the long established carriers, but within a year they were shot out of the sky by a ruling of the Civil Aeronautics Board that prohibited any surface carrier from taking to the air.

That sweeping verdict was vital to the survival of Toby's airline, which was suffering from the growing pains of establishing an international service, the grounding of all Constellations until certain modifications had been made, and a pilots' strike. The heavy demands for capital to buy the expensive new aircraft even made Howard Hughes uneasy, and as the top positions in the airline executive offices were changed almost monthly Toby deliberately lost himself in the technological flight problems of the airline.

As if the madcap atmosphere in the financial suites were not enough, the controlling force of TWA became increasingly difficult to find. Like Toby, Howard Hughes seemed eager to be a part of the flying, but preferred to avoid the political and investment infighting. He personally flew the new L-749 Constellations as well as the tests for a new radar unit that informed a pilot of his actual height above the terrain and warned him if he was too low. Toby thought how precious he would have considered such a device if he had it aboard during his descent into Gibraltar only three years earlier . . . .

Toby and Kiffin met frequently in California, which had become an aeronautical beehive, and in spite of the fact that they'd both spent nearly a lifetime in their profession, they were in awe of the developments surrounding them . . . "Hell, we lose more money in twenty-four hours than it would have taken to buy every airplane in the country when we were barnstorming," Toby said. Kiffin laughed and said that at least then he might have been able to find Howard Hughes.

By now Kiffin had, as he said himself, "gone full circle," and was back working as a freelance test pilot for Lockheed, Douglas, Northrop and North American. In recognition of his long flying career he had recently been made a Fellow of the Society of Experimental Test Pilots. He lived well, most of the time in a tiny house on one of the hills overlooking Burbank and in an apartment he kept near Edwards Air Force Base when he was working on a military project. "It's only a question of a few years now and we'll go all jets," he told Toby. "You're going to be burning instead of turning your engines no matter what kind of an airplane it is."

Toby was very much aware that the British were already flying the Vickers Viscount, a turbo-prop airliner that employed both burning engines and turning propellers and was worried that the English might take the lead in aeronautical progress. He was reassured when Kiffin told him Lockheed was already in the initial stages of testing a turboprop and both Douglas and Boeing were developing pure jets. Glenn Martin, once the most forward of thinkers, had become hardly more than a figurehead in his giant company, which had been failing since the war. His critics put the blame on Martin's continued obeisance to his mother, who, testy as ever, still advised him during their daily lunches together.

Kiffin was now fifty-two years old and was quick to point out that on his birthday the world's largest airport was dedicated by President Truman at Idlewild, Long Island.

He had mellowed and now drank sparingly. He had even bought a new violin and fiddled whenever he had a free evening alone, of which there were many. His taste in women had, he said, broadened some—no pun intended—and he now spent an occasional evening with one Martha Twill, an attractive *and* brainy bookstore proprietor who managed to lead him into some of life's loftier pleasures, including subjects other than airplanes, believe it or not. Martha Twill, in fact, became almost the total of Kiffin's social life except for his monthly attendance at Quiet Birdmen gatherings and the annual test pilot symposia in Los Angeles.

One occasion, however, commanded Kiffin's full involvement, and that was Flip Bryant's twentieth birthday. He insisted that "the family" gather in San Francisco at his expense and arranged with his good friend Johnnie Kan for an elaborate feast at his restaurant in Chinatown.

It was a round table in the best Chinese tradition, set in the corner of Kan's aromatic second-story establishment. The corner of Grant Avenue and Sacramento Street was visible through the bamboo screens over the windows. As the host Kiffin sat facing the door, the better to summon the waiters who knew him well and were in constant attendance whether he needed them or not. Lily sat on his right, and all agreed that she was the most smashing looking woman in the restaurant. "And probably," Toby said, "the most stunning looking woman of forty-nine in the world."

"Amen . . ." Flip said from his seat facing the windows. He had become what seemed almost a replica of Toby in physique, although somewhat less mooselike, but in spirit and temperament he was more a mix of his mother and Kiffin. He had Toby's built-in air of quiet strength . . . and a touch of Kiffin's wildness. Kiffin had invited him to bring a friend and he had brought a spectacular Norwegian exchange student named Paula Thorsen who thought Kiffin the perfect host. She blinked her cobalt eyes at him and after the first cocktail began calling him "Uncle Jolly." He said he accepted the title under protest because it identified him as being too old for the possibility of a romance between them. Nonetheless he raised his glass and thanked Flip for bringing such an enchanting creature to their midst. They all agreed that he could now begin singing "September Song."

While it was true that Kiffin appeared nearly as dashing as he had been in his younger days, Lily saw something else . . . She saw that the Norwegian girl's attraction to Kiffin was not insincere; if she preferred the look of older men she certainly had a corker in Kiffin with his unruly thatch of gray hair and cavalier manner. It was remarkable, she thought, that in spite of the grand total of his alcohol consumption he had managed to retain his wit and his perpetual small-boy excitement in nearly everything. Yet there was something about Kiffin's eyes . . . a distant look, a way of going away for moments at a time even while he seemed to be listening. Was it just Lily's imagination that he seemed so preoccupied, or was he suffering from an unacknowledged pain—his leg? She couldn't resist momentarily slipping on her glasses for a better look at him. And she thought, no, Kiffin was simply aging like the rest of humanity, and because, in spite of himself, he was so well preserved, any deterioration became more noticeable.

Lily quickly put her glasses away. Here, she thought, was the luckiest woman in the world, surrounded by three of the most exciting men she had ever known. "Be content," she told herself, "don't meddle . . ."

Toby had come straight to San Francisco from Germany, where he had been part of the Berlin airlift. He yawned occasionally from timelag and said that now he had been witness to the ultimate absurdity. "First we bomb the Germans so efficiently we damn near obliterate their principal city. Next we feed, clothe, and bring them coal to keep them warm. And then we lend them money to buy our airplanes so that they can compete with us around the world. The Russians don't like it. Naturally the Germans do. It seems our enemies have become our friends and our former friends our enemies. Sorry to sound off this way. Guess I'm still a sobersides . . ."

"Yes," Lily said, and kissed him, "but we all forgive you. Especially me."

Flip lifted his glass. "Here's to old dad . . . long may he be sober."

And Kiffin, despite being heavily engaged with Paula Thorsen, somehow overheard enough to remark, "Don't believe he's always been that way, kid. Behind that mighty chunk of bone and gristle there beats the soul of a poet. Just be thankful he can't rhyme!"

Between the wonton soup and what Kan, who had graduated from Stanford and spoke impeccable English, smilingly described as "baked chickee and flied lice," they talked of the new British "Comet" and its enormous superiority over the current American DC-6s, DC-7s and Constellations as passenger-carrying aircraft. "They've really made an end run on us," Toby said. "Who in their right mind is going to bounce around in the overcast with us when they can fly above most of the weather? And speed? They're twice as fast."

Kiffin said that the projects he had been testing during the past year had been almost all in jet development and there were still a lot of problems to be solved. "There's too much we don't know yet. When you get into those high altitudes and speeds you find yourself standing in the middle of a whole new basket of snakes. Grandma Douglas and Mother Boeing are sure slow, but I just hope the English aren't being too hasty, which I suppose doesn't sound much like me. Still . . ."

Lily asked Paula if she hadn't heard more than enough about flying for one evening. "They really can talk about other things, though I have trouble remembering just what. About six months ago I think they talked about a movie they'd seen . . . *The Third Man* with Orson Welles? They liked it so much they talked about it for at least two minutes, then hurried back to flying."

Paula said she'd been in love with Bernt Balchen ever since she was a little girl and had always been attracted to flyers.

Lily caught herself being a mother for a moment when she noticed how Paula had reached out and touched Flip's hand as if to emphasize her feelings. Talk about comets . . . The more they tried to ignore each other the more obvious their attachment.

When the fortune cookies arrived they interrupted their talk of flying long enough to read aloud from the strips of paper. Kiffin was the first. "How risk tears the wormwood from man, fills him with gusto and afterward in victory loads him with satisfaction."

Kiffin said it didn't sound very Oriental to him.

Lily read hers. "He who is really brave is never afraid."

Toby said, "Baloney to that," then opened his cookie, removed the strip of paper and found he was trying to read it upside down. Turning it around he said, "Damn, I need glasses . . . listen to this. 'Rejoice at your life, for the time is

more advanced than you would think.' Right on-target for
me . . .''

Paula's said, "One joy dispells a hundred cares."

Then Flip opened his cookie and Lily saw the mischief in
his eyes. "Talk about on-target, listen to this. 'You will
follow your desire and have a brilliant career as a lawyer.'''

A long silence followed. Lily saw that her son's audience
was stunned. He was still grinning when Toby found his
voice.

"You did say . . . lawyer?"

"My God . . ." from Kiffin.

"What's the matter with everyone? All of a sudden you're
down on me because I want to be a lawyer?"

Toby tried to sound calm. "They aren't all bad, I suppose."

And Kiffin tried to play the understanding "uncle." "Of
course you should be what you want. It's only natural we
thought you'd want the air force, or the navy flying . . . or
God forbid, the Marines, but what the hell . . . it's your life,
kid."

Lily had been watching her son carefully. The grin was
gone, but she was suspicious . . . she knew her son . . . She
reached out and snatched the paper from his hand. She glanced
at it, smiled. "You devil!" And she read aloud: " 'If a little
knowledge is dangerous, who has so much to be out of
danger?' Not a word here about being a lawyer!"

When the laughter of relief had subsided Flip said, "Maybe
I should've said I wanted to be a banker. You'd all *really*
have flipped."

Toby closed his eyes. Lily saw him shake his head
vigorously. He reached across the table and held out his big
hand and she saw Flip take it.

"Happy birthday, son."

CHAPTER
28

Here at Edwards Air Force Base in the Mojave Desert it was high noon and baking hot. Here almost all that was new in aviation, whether for military or civil use, came for testing.

The long runways simmered in the sun and stretched to the vanishing point. Since it was the normal lunchtime for ground and air crews, the students at the test pilot school, the staff and the higher brass, an abnormal quiet hung over the base and it appeared to be almost deserted.

An air force corporal who sat at the reception desk told Toby how to find Kiffin, although his directions had been superfluous. Toby had already heard the whine of a violin coming from halfway down the linoleum-floored hallway.

When Toby pushed open the door he saw Kiffin sitting in a chair precariously tilted back against the wall. He had removed his artificial leg, which stood independently beside him. He was braced against the edge of the desk with his good leg extended, plucking experimentally at the strings of his violin. His eyes were closed.

He opened his eyes now and swung wildly at a fly with his violin bow. The effort required him to turn, and he saw Toby standing in the doorway. "What the hell are you doing here? You could at least knock. Why aren't you back in Kansas City babysitting your prima donna aviators?"

Toby moved into the room and sat on the edge of the desk. "Thanks for the warm welcomes. Meet Mrs. Draper's little boy the porcupine."

"I feel like one."

"You look lousy. What's the matter with you that a better disposition can't fix?"

"I've been working with Tony Le Vier on the U-2. Very hush-hush. I've really got the hots to fly that bird. It's going to fly so high it'll be halfway to Mars. And I've just bee canceled out of the project.''

"Why?''

"Flunked the physical.''

Toby shifted his weight on the desk and squinted at th blinding sunlight outside the window. In the silence Kiffi put his violin and bow on the desk and lit a cigarette.

"What's wrong with you?'' Toby asked gently. Every pilo he knew lived in dread of failing their semiannual physical including, he thought, himself.

"I made the mistake of telling the examiner my gut hurts.'

"Everybody's gut hurts. You've always been a billy-goat You been eating tin cans again?''

"Maybe this goddamned desert is getting to me. How' Lily?''

"As ever, and she sends her love. She's about to fly in th Powder Puff Derby. Remember when Amelia started tha race?''

"That was a long time ago. Tell Lily not to come hom unless she wins . . .''

Toby did not like the way Kiffin's voice drifted way, bu he knew his friend too well to pry. Kiffin was a man who ha spent his entire life on the defensive. Change the subject . . "I've been down at Douglas looking at that new airplan they're trying to peddle. Twenty million dollars? For *on* airplane. I figure we'll have to sell more than a hundred seat every flight to break even, so I hitched a ride up here to cr on your shoulder and see if you thought I've been in th flying business too long.''

"Maybe we both have.''

"Give yourself a month's rest, then retake your physical You'll pass for sure . . .''

A distant rumble rapidly became a roar, and they bot instinctively looked out the window. A jet-powered bombe flashed past, its fuselage glittering in the sun.

Kiffin said, "Sometimes I wonder where this flying busi ness would be if guys like us hadn't been in it so long . . .' He took a long drag on his cigarette, blew smoke at th window. "Screw my physical. It's time I took up a nev career. Maybe I'll go back to Paris . . . learn to paint . . chase mademoiselles again . . . become a dirty old boulevar dier . . .''

"Cut it out. We promised to die with our boots on, remember?"

There was another even longer silence and this time it was Kiffin who made an abrupt change of subject. "What's new with Flip? I'm bad, I haven't even answered his last letter."

"He's tops in his class at Colgate and graduates May thirtieth. You've got to be there because the Navy's already accepted him for flight training at Pensacola and it may be a long time before you'll see him again."

"I'll be there if I have to arrive horizontally."

Toby had trouble making Kiffin look him directly in the eye. When he finally succeeded he asked, "Old friend . . . are you telling me everything?"

"Sure."

"Why don't we find out what really ails you? You know as well as I do that a government flight physical doesn't really get to the bottom of things. Maybe you should see a specialist about your gut. I'll call Hughes. He's a master hypochondriac, knows the name, rank and serial number of every quack in the country."

"Why don't you go back to Kansas City and cut some salaries?"

Toby moved off the desk and picked up Kiffin's artificial leg. He handed it to him. "I'm starving. Put your damned leg on and let's go get some lunch. Afterward, we'll do some telephoning. *No argument.*"

CHAPTER
29

. . . As he drove quietly away from the hospital Kiffin picked up speed. It was a new ambulance and cruised easily through the very heart of the city at sixty miles an hour. He thumbed his nose at red lights while weaving around buses and trucks. Sometimes when the pain momentarily subsided he smiled and waved at the curious noon-hour strollers who waited for him to pass through an intersection. Farewell, *auf Wiedersehen, adieu, dosdvedanya, adios, sayonara* . . . no one could ever say Kiffin Draper hadn't been around. First lesson for world citizen . . . learn the language if it's only Hello, I love you, and Good-by . . .

When he had left the environs of the city behind and approached the open country there was no longer need for the siren but he pressed the button anyway. He couldn't remember when he'd had so much fun breaking so many laws in so short a time. He turned off the highway and took a narrow graveled road that climbed upward toward the coastal hills. Now he took his finger off the siren button . . . an ambulance in the countryside would attract unwanted attention.

He followed the road until it passed along the perimeter of a grubby little airport, a melancholy hangover from the helmet-and-goggle days. The strip was dirt and short and aimed at an angle to the single dilapidated hangar. The area around the hangar was littered with rusting pieces of aircraft and beer cans.

He brought the ambulance to a stop. Habit made him glance at the wind sock now lifting lazily atop the hangar. A sea breeze. Good, as it should be . . .

For a moment he sat listening to the wind sighing through the fangs of the hangar's broken windows, then took the violin case and with the bottle tucked safely under his arm limped across the grass toward a row of small T-hangars. The shelters were open to the elements on all sides and offered only the most basic protection for a dozen airplanes, all ancient little putt-putts that had long since seen their day. This was a poor man's flying field where real people nursed their flying dreams. They flew for pleasure, not for blood or money, and they nickeled-and-dimed their passion into all kinds of schemes to keep themselves aloft. They would sacrifice almost anything for the privilege of flight, and no one could ever say that Kiffin Draper, who after all had led such an *exciting* life, did not wish them the same.

There was a Piper Cub looking too good for the project at hand, and beside a bedraggled Porterfield that didn't look good enough. Between them squatted a little Aeroneca with the side-by-side seating he wanted. A man had to have some place for his booze and violin. And even with his waning strength he should be able to spin the stubby propeller.

He approached the Aeroneca. The owner was apparently a casual sort, an iron-beam navigator who followed railroad tracks if he ventured beyond the horizon. There was no compass. A wrinkled Standard Oil roadmap was tucked underneath the single broad seat. The fuel gauge indicated one quarter full, which should be plenty. Nothing else really mattered. It really was not a long way to Tipperary.

And it just might be a fine place. For sure the journey there would be a damn sight better than lying passively while a gang of doctors educated themselves on the only thing that had always been your private property. They pumped stuff into it and they sucked stuff out. They frazzled your brain with goof-balls and countermanded the result by twiddling your nerves with boosters. They showed a morbid fascination with all of your wounds while speculating upon the invisible suppuration of this region and the stubborn blockade of that region. Where came this bubo and this disseminated membrane? Distemper of the lymphoid? Fistula of the withers? Someone even had the gall to suggest a Wasserman. What grand and, of course, properly licensed bullshit. Which was another reason to keep your boots on.

Your gut is full of fire but you cannot die. It is against the house rules. Until they are ready. Suffer on with your scorching spleen? Incinerate your entrails? Become the hulk of a one-time man? Who were they kidding when they hinted in their bedside voices that just maybe everything will turn out dandy? Although, of course, maybe not.

He took the checkbook out of his trenchcoat and wrote: "To the Owner of Aircraft N478 . . . two thousand dollars." As the 1950 market went for 1940s airplanes, that would be more than twice what it was worth, which was the way this transaction should be. Who knew? No matter how the owner felt about his little flying machine he would consider it a priceless heirloom once he discovered it was gone.

Kiffin now placed the violin case on the right-hand side of the seat along with the bottle of Glenfiddich. He closed the door and noted its flimsiness . . . some people would fly anything—or maybe they were just tired of living . . .

He decided that despite the Aeroneca's trifling weight he still lacked the strength to pull it toward the open. He grunted as he bent down to place the check under a rock, and it was some time before he could summon enough energy to address the Aeroneca's propeller. He stood looking at it for a moment, aware that the breeze was whipping his hospital gown around and about his bare legs, which constituted a hazard. A hazard to his health, ho-ho. If the engine started and by chance the propeller caught his gown or coat, well, maybe he'd be arrested for indecent exposure, or the little bird might lunge straight out of the shelter leaving behind a hamburger named Kiffin Draper. It was important to set the throttle just right, enough for the engine to start, but not so much forward that he would lose control of the situation. Bad form.

He had guessed correctly on the throttle setting. The engine fired at first cycle. He limped around to the door as fast as he could make it, somehow managed to squeeze himself through the door. Once seated, he shoved the throttle full forward. The little Aeroneca responded with a shiver, and leaped forward.

After he had gotten his frustrations with the hospital authorities under some control Toby went down to see Dr. Vernon Taylor, who had originally taken Kiffin's case.

Taylor listened sympathetically while Toby expressed his opinion of a hospital that allowed patients to go and come as they pleased and assured him that everything possible would be done to hasten Kiffin's return. Then he added, "You and our friend Kiffin Draper have been through a lot together. He tells me it's been close to fifty years. Is he older than you are?''

"By a year. But he's tough. He'll outlive us all . . .''

Dr. Taylor took a gold pencil out of his white smock and began to study the end of it. "The reason I called and asked you to come here is that I have to tell you that he won't. He's rotten inside. All malignant. I can't understand how he lasted this long. Someone should notify his family and relatives. I thought you might prefer to do it.''

Toby stared at the polished mahogany conference table. There had to be some mistake. God . . . life without Kiffin Draper? Impossible. Unthinkable.

" . . . Kiffin left home at a very early age. For the last thirty years we've been his family . . . my wife and son and myself. He has no close living relatives . . . Does he know what you just told me?''

"Not officially. But he's an intelligent man—''

"How long does he have?'' What a stupid question, Toby thought. Time was only measurable when you had enough of it. At Flip's graduation ceremonies at Colgate, Kiffin had talked a lot about time . . .

"Not much. Maybe ten days . . . maybe two or three weeks. Cancer builds slowly, then strikes suddenly.''

"There's no hope?''

Dr. Taylor shook his head.

Once outside the hospital Toby ran to his rental car. He knew where Kiffin would go as surely as if he had left a map. That wonderful, crazy, selfish, ungrateful, undependable king of sonsabitches was not about to expire with only a whimper.

For the first half mile or so Toby drove at high speed, then gradually slowed to the legal limit. No point in speeding, Kiffin wasn't about to wait for anyone. He never did. Damn him, why couldn't he die like other people? Have a nice regular funeral. They might even gather a bunch of Q.B.s and fly a missing-man formation over the ceremonies. People firing salutes. People bawling. Pastors throwing dirt around and saying sweet words about what a hell of a fine guy Kiffin Draper was. After the services guys could go on and on telling lies about how he had been kind to dumb animals, virgins, and drunks. Kiffin Draper would become a temporary saint, a man who had never strayed from the paths of righteousness. Kiffin . . . oh God, Kiffin . . .

             *   *   *

The loom of land was now far behind. And the little Continental engine was still humming out its sixty-five horsepower. Not so, Kiffin thought. His brain must be turning fuzzy or he would realize that at this altitude it would be doing its best to serve up fifty horsepower. Or less.

The air was smooth, although along the far horizon there stood a solid line of towering cumulus dragging their skirts of rain across the surface of the ocean. There would be no surmounting them in the Aeroneca.

He smiled as he watched the fuel gauge. The needle had crept down until it was touching the "E" for empty. He must be a hundred miles off shore by now. If the fire in his belly would go away this might even be a very challenging flight . . .

Kiffin looked down at the dark sea, reached for the Glenfiddich bottle and took another swig. He made a face, sighed, then the knowing half-smile returned to his face.

If the engine of the Aeroneca hadn't been so damn noisy his singing of "Oh you take the high road and I'll take the low road" might have sounded more on key. Or less. Now he seemed to be only mouthing the words, but when the engine finally backfired and quit he could at least hear himself giving forth full blast, the way he wanted. As the Aeroneca started into a gentle descent and the slip-stream sighed through the flying wires he threw up his arms and roared out the song with all the strength left in his voice.

The little Aeroneca slipped into an enormous cloud, escaped just long enough to glisten momentarily in the sun, then plunged into a lower jowl of the cloud.

The cloud extended all the way to the sea.

Toby had once landed at the little airport he hoped was still in existence. As he recalled it was on a natural shelf east of the shoreline. He passed a withered wooden arrow nailed to a post with the word "Airport" scrawled across it. The arrow sagged and pointed at the ground. Maybe the airport was now a housing development, the fate of nearly all the old flying fields he'd known. He came to a hangar of corrugated metal, and when he saw an ambulance beside it he knew he was in the right place.

He found a mechanic sitting on a fifty gallon fuel barrel sucking noisily at a mug of coffee. His coveralls were frayed and greasy and the words "Pacific Air Transport" embroidered over his breast pocket told Toby that the mechanic must be an old-timer.

They exchanged the briefest of greetings before Toby nodded toward the side of the hanger. "That ambulance. Where's the driver?"

"I dunno, I just noticed it a while ago. The driver is flyin'."

"What did he look like?"

"You some kind of a cop or something? Or are you from the looney bin?"

"Why do you ask?"

"Because it ain't every day a man comes here in a white gown and goes away flyin'. No engine run-up or nothin'. The guy must be tired o' livin'."

"Did you talk to him?"

"Nope. I don't talk to nuts."

"Why didn't you try to stop him?"

"It ain't my airport and it ain't my airplane."

And, Toby thought, he ain't your friend.

He asked if there was a phone he could use in the hangar.

"Nope. Pay phone on the other side, though. Won't work with Canadian coins."

The phone booth, littered with cigarette butts and grafitti, provided a sweeping view of the plateau and a patch of the distant sea. Toby placed a call to Kansas City and found he had great difficulty speaking. "Hi . . ." he said when he heard Lily's voice. "I . . . I'm here at an airport . . . Darling—"

He had to stop a moment, clear his throat. He looked out at but didn't see the sea and the sky and the sun. "Well . . . he's gone . . . did it up in his own style . . . what else . . .?"

He had to pause again. "He was one of a kind . . . last of a breed . . ."

And heard Lily say, "No, my love . . . you are."

He hung up and started walking along the side of the hangar. Suddenly he halted and turned to face the rusting metal, and closing his eyes, beat a fist slowly against it. He tried to keep his shoulders from trembling, but some time passed before he succeeded.

1963
RENO AIR RACES

The event offered the crowds more than a series of races. The navy's "Blue Angels" were about to give one of their superb displays.

The pilots had been told they were the best in the world so often they believed it. And everywhere they had flown the experts and the crowds agreed.

Bands played as they marched out to their aircraft and mounted their chargers in unison. Their faces seemed totally calm, although they each knew the other was keyed close to the point of explosion.

At each performance they stood on the threshold of a tyrannical routine that demanded they fly better than even they thought possible. If they erred at the wrong instant by a mini-second they could kill their friend or be killed by a friend. Their expressionless faces deliberately concealed the intensity of their concentration.

Their stage was fifty miles square.

The pilot flying number-three airplane finished strapping his safety harness and reached for the knob holding the sun shade of his helmet in place. He would lower it simultaneously with his comrades. Printed across the glistening back surface of the helmet were the letters "FLIP," and before he lowered the shade he looked directly at a tall man and a slight woman standing in the crowd.

He nodded twice, and from their joyous waving he knew how much they shared his sense of pride. And he knew that in spirit they would be flying with him, for this moment was their realization of long ago dreams and daring. They were among the few survivors of a gallant era that would never be seen again.